PRAISE FOR *INNATE MAGIC*

"Fay expertly crafts a delightfully adventurous tale, animated by Paul's chance encounters and audacious antics. This promising series starter announces Fay as a writer to watch."

—*Publishers Weekly*

"Great fun on its own and a series to watch for."

—*Kirkus Reviews*

"An enchanting tale . . . This first book in the Marrowbone Spells series leaves the ending open for what's sure to be an adventurous series; Fay is an author to watch."

—*Booklist*

"An absorbing debut fantasy novel . . . This great first fantasy outing from Fay will be well received by adults and young adults who like V. E. Schwab and Leigh Bardugo."

—*Library Journal*

"*Innate Magic* romps about a magic-infused mid-twentieth-century London with a plot packed with both charm and grit. What a fun kickoff to a new series!"

—Beth Cato, author of *Breath of Earth*

"Shannon Fay's debut is a delight . . . Just like its quick-witted cast of characters, underneath all the glamour *Innate Magic* has a big beating heart and serious guts."

—Rich Larson, author of *Annex* and *Tomorrow Factory*

"A fog-drenched fashion thriller full of romance, mystery, legacy, and panache. *Innate Magic* is a cracking romp through the postwar British class system with more twists and turns than the river Thames."

—Jennifer Giesbrecht, author of *The Monster of Elendhaven*

EXTERNAL FORCES

ALSO BY SHANNON FAY

The Marrowbone Spells

Innate Magic (book 1)

EXTERNAL FORCES

SHANNON FAY

47NORTH

This is a work of fiction. Names, characters, organizations, places, events, and incidents are either products of the author's imagination or are used fictitiously. Any resemblance to actual persons, living or dead, or actual events is purely coincidental.

Published by 47North, Seattle

www.apub.com

Amazon, the Amazon logo, and 47North are trademarks of Amazon.com, Inc., or its affiliates.

ISBN-13: 9781542032575 (paperback)
ISBN-13: 9781542032568 (digital)

Cover design by Faceout Studio, Jeff Miller

Cover image: © Accent / Shutterstock; Viktora / Shutterstock; © Ursa Major / Shutterstock; © caesart / Shutterstock; © Anton Watman / Shutterstock; © Archjoe / Shutterstock; © Agnieszka Karpinska / Shutterstock; © Devita ayu silvianingtyas / Shutterstock; © Ma ry / Shutterstock

Printed in the United States of America

For Chris

PROLOGUE

Peaceful living had not dampened Thomas's awareness of his surroundings. If anything, it had deepened it. Running a bar brought with it a kind of simple satisfaction. It was all about pleasure in the little things: cleaning cups, pulling off the perfect pour. Living on this island, a speck in the Adriatic Sea, carrying out these routine actions, he felt connected to something deeper. Like he could feel every ripple on the water.

Most nights, after he'd shooed the last patrons out, this feeling was a calming one. But tonight something was off. On the dark sea was the sound of a boat approaching, its motor cutting through the quiet.

"What's wrong?" Samira asked. Thomas stayed where he was by the window, looking out at the beach and moonless night.

"A boat's coming this way."

"Well, last call has come and gone," Samira said lightly. Samira sat by the cash register, counting the take for the night, their wavy brown hair falling forwards as they sorted coins from five different countries—daily the bar served not just locals but fishermen and pilots from every nation that bordered the Adriatic. Samira looked up from their work. "Unless you think they're not coming for a drink."

"My gut says they're here for either you or me." He hated voicing the suspicion aloud—it made him sound like a superstitious paranoid.

But in the years he'd spent working for Lady Fife, he'd learned that it was better to trust his intuition even when it went against what his rational mind told him.

Samira nodded and stood, money no longer a concern. They hurried upstairs and came back with a gun, a small pistol that they tucked into the back of their trousers. Thomas knew that Samira would also have a knife on their person, just like he had one strapped to his ankle. Neither generally needed to pull a blade when dealing with customers, but old habits died hard.

After clearing out the local kingpin, Samira and Thomas had declared the island a neutral zone, a place free from piracy, raiding, smuggling, or looting. Pirates, raiders, smugglers, and looters were still welcome to come for a drink, but no business could be conducted on the island, no fighting between rival gangs. And after a few weeks of Thomas and Samira enforcing this rule, the local criminal element had accepted it. It actually seemed to be in everyone's best interest to have a place where all could drink in peace.

Which was why this strange boat made Thomas uneasy—he didn't recognize the sound of the motor. What if it was some new tough looking to cause trouble?

Or worse, what if it was some old enemy, looking to settle a score?

"If it's for you or me, it doesn't matter," Samira said, coming to stand by Thomas. "We'll deal with it together."

Thomas smiled and reached out to take their hand. They'd been partners almost a year now yet still so much felt new. Well, not so much on the business side of things—that had settled into a predictable rhythm. But being so entwined with another person, that was new.

It was different from how it had been with Paul—sure, Paul and he had lived side by side and worked together, but they'd been brothers. Getting close to Samira had meant opening up in a different way, sharing things about himself and his life that Paul either had already known, could never know, or had blithely taken for granted.

The boat's motor cut out as it approached the dock.

Before becoming publicans, Thomas and Samira had often worked against each other, pawns being moved around by their respective masters. It had taken so much for them to leave that all behind, to join forces and own up to what they felt for each other. But even now, they both knew that someday the past might come knocking.

That night it was Thomas's past that knocked on the door.

Samira had their gun drawn as Thomas went to see who it was.

Lady Fife stood outside. She was wearing white pleated pants and sandals, a navy-blue cardigan to protect against the evening chill.

"Can I trouble you for a drink?" she asked.

Thomas sighed but let her in.

"Samira, it's all right," he said, resigned to whatever bad news Lady Fife had to share.

Samira did not lower their gun.

"All right? Your old spymaster shows up in the small hours of the morning, and you just assume it's 'all right'?"

"She wouldn't have come here herself if she did mean us harm," Thomas said, turning his back on Lady Fife to go behind the bar to start mixing a drink—a French 75, Lady Fife's drink of choice, and then a martini for himself. "If she had wanted to hurt us she would have sent someone like . . . well, us."

Samira did not look happy but lowered their gun. Lady Fife stepped inside.

"Thank you. I'm sorry to show up in the dead of night, but I was curious to see this place. 'Rogue's Roost,' hmm? It has quite the reputation on the mainland."

"I'm sure you didn't come all this way to sightsee, Lady Fife," Thomas said, taking a sip of his martini.

"You're right." Lady Fife strode forwards and tossed several photographs down onto the bar. Samira looked at them with a frown, moving them around on the bar top to get a better look. As they did so, Thomas's blood froze. He recognized the three men in the pictures. One was the current deputy prime minister of Great Britain. Another was the country's current Court Magician.

The third was a man who Thomas had killed years ago.

"Did you know about this?" Lady Fife asked. Her face was still a polite mask but her voice came out a hiss. "All these years, did you know he was alive?"

"No," Thomas said, voice cracking like thin ice. "No. I knew he'd come back to life, but I dealt with him. I never mentioned it to you because it was done with."

"All this time, *this* was the reason I lost my power of sight," Lady Fife said. "I can't see his actions because he is a man with no soul, this unconnected humanoid thing just moving through the world. And since everything is connected, the ripple effect means that I can't see *anything* as long as he is the one pulling the strings."

"What are you talking about?" Samira asked, holding up one of the photos to the light.

Lady Fife looked to Thomas. "Do you wish to explain it to them, Mr Dawes?"

No. Samira knew about some of the things he'd done in service to Lady Fife, but they didn't know about the things he'd done in England. How he'd failed to kill the man who'd threatened his best friend and how his best friend had then brought a man back from the dead. And not just any man but a would-be dictator, a hard-line warmonger. Thomas had set things to rights by killing the modern-day Lazarus, rendering him dead once more. It had all been tidied up.

But now Thomas was looking at a recent photo of him, walking and talking with his mates, looking right as rain. Was this why the country had seemingly backslid these last few years?

"Samira, I'll take Lady Fife back to her boat," Thomas said evenly. "You can close up here and head on to bed."

Samira shot him a look of such deep betrayal. Lady Fife cleared her throat.

"I'll wait outside, Mr Dawes. Come when you are ready."

She stepped out of the pub and closed the door behind her.

Samira held his gaze. "You'd go with her? After everything we've built here?"

Thomas sighed. "This isn't about her. This is about me. Years ago I failed to stop something big from happening. I thought I had it handled, but I was wrong. Now I need to go back to England and do it right this time."

"Then I'll go too," Samira said, a defiant jut to their chin. "We'll deal with it together and then come back here."

"No," Thomas said. "This is something I need to do on my own." Already Thomas had a suspicion about what it might take to pay for his failings. If Samira was there, he wouldn't be able to go through with it. He'd cling to life, unable to commit. He took a deep breath—might as well start now. "I won't be coming back."

Samira looked away. "We'd left that world behind, didn't we? We agreed we'd live for ourselves, for each other. Then you see one photograph and you're gone?"

"I'm sorry," Thomas said, and he hated himself for it. What did feeling sorry ever do for anyone? "I can't explain it; you wouldn't believe me. Just know that—"

"No," Samira said. "I don't want to hear it. I don't want to hear anything that will just make me miss you more. Just go."

Thomas did. He went upstairs to their bedroom to grab his bag, the one he always kept packed in case he had to beat a speedy retreat. Samira didn't say anything to him as he walked out of the pub. Once the door closed behind him, he heard a large crash, as if Samira had kicked over the table with the money on it, scattering coins all over the floor.

Lady Fife was waiting for him on the dock. In the darkness he imagined that she might have looked at him with pity, maybe even seemed slightly contrite about taking him away from all this. Wordlessly he walked past her to jump in the boat. For all her machinations, Thomas couldn't lay this at the feet of Lady Fife. This one was all on him.

CHAPTER 1

To get from the gardener's cottage to the main house meant walking through a copse of trees and through a faltering garden, the autumnal blooms fighting it out with the weeds. The sight always made me feel a bit guilty: I had no green thumb to speak of, but since I was currently living in the gardener's home the flowers always received me with an expectant air, like they knew I'd be the one to help them in their war against the shepherd's purse and thistles.

I thought of knocking on the back door of the house to get Mrs Spratt's attention, but that seemed much too informal. Laura Spratt, the lady of Hillcrest, seemed to put a great stress on the boundaries between the cottage and main house, tenant and landlady. Better to knock at the front door. I wasn't a mate coming round for a cuppa but an acquaintance asking for a favour.

A guard jumped out from the bushes, blocking my path. She was no more than three feet tall, a broken branch in hand and leaves in her hair, her fine corduroy dress and wellies splattered with mud. Beatrix Spratt, four years old, as fierce and spiky as the brambles stuck to her tights. If Laura Spratt's domain was the house, then the surrounding land belonged to her daughter. Too young for school and with no nanny or governess to keep her in line, Beatrix ran wild, a solitary figure whooping through the trees and tall grass.

When I was her age, I'd also spent time in the woods, friendless and forced to make my own fun. I remembered what it was like to be a lonely child.

"Who goes there?" she asked in a deepened voice.

"It's me, Trix. Mr Gallagher, who lives in the gardener's cottage." Beatrix knew me quite well: she was often hiding around the cottage making *oooooo* noises in an attempt to convince me the place was haunted, or telling me that there was someone on the phone for me in the main house when there wasn't, or leaving twigs and leaves on the ground in strange patterns. I didn't mind her pranks; if anything, I thought they were pretty good for a laugh. "Say, how is your mum today?" I felt guilty for asking since I knew Beatrix would tell me the truth: *The lawyers visited and Mummy cried afterwards. Mummy is angry today because she talked on the phone to Daddy. Mummy talked to her mummy, and then she went into her room and shut the door and won't come out.*

But today Beatrix just shrugged, which I took as a good sign.

"Okay, well, I'm going to go talk to her, all right? I'll play a game of tag with you later." I took a step forwards and Beatrix waved her stick in my face.

"You can't pass unless you pay a toll!" she declared, dry tree leaves rattling as she shook the branch.

I dug into my pocket for something that would buy my passage.

"Here." I held up a small wooden shank button. It was navy blue with the design of a bird carved into it. I'd bought the set to make a coat for Princess Katherine, but this had been left over. "Will this do?"

I placed the button in her hand. She looked at it, ambivalence tugging at her face.

"It's pretty, isn't it?" I asked. Beatrix started to nod but stopped herself.

"Can you show me how to sew it on?" she asked shyly.

Immediately a vision came to me of a teddy bear with mismatched button eyes, its body made from a mix of corduroy and a floral-patterned fabric. I could make it from scraps I had around my studio—then Beatrix would at least have a teddy bear to share in her adventures.

"Sure thing, Trix! I'll show you how to sew on a button, and lots more." Yes, that would be a fun afternoon—Beatrix could sew on the bear's eyes and help with the stuffing, and I'd do the rest. "We could make a teddy bear and use that button for one of its eyes. I mean, if it's all right with your mother."

Beatrix did not say yes or no but she looked down at the button in her hand with a pleased smile, then slipped it into her dress pocket. She rushed past me, running down the slope without a look back or goodbye in my direction.

With my way clear I finally made it to the front of the house and knocked on the door.

Laura Spratt was about a year younger than me, twenty-six to my twenty-seven. I considered myself very much a man of the world, but whenever I talked to Mrs Spratt she gave off the aura of being older or maybe just stodgy—when I'd first moved into the cottage I'd told her she could call me Paul, but she'd persisted in calling me Mr Gallagher. She'd already done so many things I hadn't: gotten married, had a child. And now she was attempting to get a divorce.

Mrs Spratt answered after a minute or so. She looked at me evenly, seeming neither delighted nor put out at the sight of me. In my younger years, I would have fallen hard for Mrs Spratt: she was an attractive woman with a square-shaped face and round cheeks. Straw-blonde hair fell just past her shoulders. She usually wore loose, simple clothing, such as today's ensemble: a long white cotton dress with a tawny-brown corset belt. Sensible but attractive.

But I wasn't a foolhardy romantic anymore. I prided myself that I'd grown past all that. I was too mature to be falling for every woman and bloke who crossed my path, even ones who caught my eye, like Mrs

Spratt. In the month since I'd moved into the cottage on her property, I'd kept my distance as much as I could.

"Good afternoon, Mrs Spratt," I said. "I hope you are well."

"I am quite well, thank you." The poshness in Mrs Spratt's voice nearly obliterated any regional accent she might have: when it's that clear you come from money, it doesn't matter where else you come from. "And how are you, Mr Gallagher? Is there something wrong with the cottage?"

There were many things wrong. The bathroom ceiling leaked, the bedroom / kitchen / dining room (all one room) was drafty, and the one bulb that lit up the place flickered more than it shone. But I wasn't there about all that: I had no desire to add to Mrs Spratt's troubles.

"Everything's fine, thanks. But I do have a favour to ask of you. Yesterday I met with my old professor, and he asked if I'd be willing to take on some cloth magic students, give them some tutoring in the craft. We were thinking sessions twice a week. They are paying me a good wage for it, and they seem like nice kids from what my prof said . . ."

Mrs Spratt nodded in understanding. She'd learned recently what it was like to have to scrimp and save and could appreciate an easy payday.

"That sounds like a fruitful endeavour, Mr Gallagher. Is there some way I could assist you?"

"Yes!" I said, glad she had brought it up. "I was hoping, if it's not too big of an ask, that I could use your living room for the tutoring sessions."

She cocked her head to the side. "You wish, twice a week, to commandeer my living room in order to teach magic?" She had a way of speaking that had just a hint of incredulousness, making her hard to read.

"Er, yes. Which, now that I say it aloud, it is a big imposition, yeah? Sorry, it's just one of the kids, it's Prince Naveed, and the cottage—oh, don't get me wrong, the cottage is great, but—"

"Of course you may," Mrs Spratt said. "I think it would be rather cruel of me as your landlady to impede your ability to earn a living. Perhaps I can even provide some refreshments for you all."

"Oh, well, thanks, but you don't have to do anything special."

"Nonsense." An actual smile came to her face, as well as a little colour in her cheeks. "It will be nice to have company after so long without."

If I'd been a weaker man, I'd have for sure fallen for her then. But I was too smart, too self-aware, too cautious, to just tumble head over heels like I would have as a younger lad.

"When will you have need of my living room?" Mrs Spratt asked.

"In about an hour," I said.

This took her aback.

"Ah, soon. Well then, please give me twenty minutes to tidy up the place," she said, before shutting the door. I went to play the game of tag I'd promised Beatrix.

An hour later, I was sitting in the living room at Hillcrest, anxiously waiting for the students to arrive. Mrs Spratt was off in the kitchen, preparing some refreshments. I was a little worried about what she might produce—Mrs Spratt was used to having cooks and maids and butlers to do that kind of busywork. Now it was just her and Beatrix, alone in this empty house.

The doorbell rang and I shot up to answer it.

Standing on the doorstep were a young man and woman, both in their late teens. He was tall and lean but in a graceful rather than gangly way. He wore a tan suit, a brown-and-gold striped vest, and a black tie with a tigereye brooch pinned to it, the gem matching his bright amber eyes. His skin was light brown, his hair black and slicked back. He had an excited smile on his face, like he'd just thought of a joke and was eager to share it.

"Prince Naveed Parkeesh?" I said.

"Yes, I am the man, Mr Gallagher! What a pleasure to meet you!" He shook my hand with gusto. I felt the same bloom of magic I always felt when I met someone new, the innate magic that gave people a good first impression of me. But with Naveed it felt superfluous: he was already excited and predisposed to like me. "And this is my friend and fellow student, Rosemary Panyi."

The young lady stepped forwards. She wore a dress with a wide skirt made of pink satin and black lace. Her white skin was pale save for her cheeks, which were round and red. There was a slight sunken quality to her eyes that suggested that, while things might be good now, to get to this point she had lived through hard times. Her eyes were the green brown of a calm pond, but as we shook hands there was a slight ripple. I wondered if she sensed my magic. She looked at me with new interest, an intrigued smile spreading on her previously apathetic face.

"Ms Panyi, a pleasure to meet you." It was amazing how much things could change in just a few years: Back when I'd graduated, Gabs had been the only girl in our whole class. Now most of the students studying cloth magic were women.

I had not even let go of Rosemary's hand when Naveed pushed past me, his focus shifting to the house. "So *this* is Hillcrest, eh? Well, if one were to make oneself a prisoner of conscience, you could pick worse gaols, I suppose."

"There's a prisoner here?" Rosemary asked, following him. Her voice had a hint of a Hungarian accent. I was left to hurry to catch up.

"Yes. Mrs Spratt," Naveed said. "I heard Mother and Grandmama talking about her plight. Quite the scandal, wanting a divorce just for the sake of it."

"I'm sure Mrs Spratt has her reasons," I said, wishing I could somehow change the subject. Naveed spoke before I could.

"Oh, I'm sure she does! But we all know it isn't as easy as that. Word is that Mrs Spratt isn't claiming her husband abused her in any way, so if she wants to legally cut ties with him, she has to prove that he neglected her. So she's kicked him out of the house! While he lives with his mummy and daddy, she and her child are trying to make a go of it without taking a penny from her husband. If she can last a few years without his help, she'll be able to say in court that he's left her on her lonesome."

"And does Mr Spratt also wish for divorce?" Rosemary asked. She had picked up a large china vase and was examining it, her voice distracted as she looked it over.

"God, no!" Naveed said. "Mother says that he's spitting mad about it all. But he's decided to call his wife's bluff. He thinks that Mrs Spratt will not last very long without him, that it's only a matter of months before she comes back to him, and once she folds the matter will be settled for good. It's a domestic game of chicken."

It occurred to me that I had let two slippery eels into Mrs Spratt's home, both of them eyeing up the items in the living room like butchers looking over a piece of meat, Naveed with a wide smile, Rosemary with a keen eye. Maybe I should usher them out and herd them down to the gardener's cottage. But there was also a part of me that was curious about Mrs Spratt and her estranged husband, and that part of me let Naveed go on talking.

"Even the bookies are in on it," Naveed said with relish. "They are taking bets on how long Mrs Spratt will be able to hold out."

"How fascinating," Mrs Spratt said from the doorway. She was holding a tray with a pitcher of limeade and a plate of cucumber sandwiches. Her voice was as chilly as the ice in the lime drink. "I had no idea. Thank you so much for telling me, Prince Naveed. Perhaps I should go down to Ladbrokes and bet against myself. That way, when I lose my reputation, freedom, and home, at least I'll be able to collect a couple of shillings."

Rosemary had silently put down the vase and stepped over to stand next to me, looking at Naveed with a disapproving frown. Naveed's eyes were wide, like a prison escapee suddenly caught in a searchlight.

It only took him a second to recover.

"Mrs Spratt, it's a pleasure to meet you. From everything I've heard, you are a singular lady, a woman ahead of her time," he said. "And just for the record, if I were a gambling man, I would place my bet on you."

Mrs Spratt seemed more or less mollified. She set the tray down on the table in the middle of the room.

"Well, I shall leave you to your magic, then."

She'd almost left the room when Naveed spoke up.

"Speaking of magic, how is Gabriella von Melsungen?" he asked. "Old Professor Lamb said she was one of the best students he ever had."

That question was double barbed—like most British aristocrats, Naveed had heard about me and Gabs and was obviously needling me for more info. What really got to me was the idea that Lamb had been lauding Gabs as his best student—I mean, it was true, but I liked to think Lamb had been a bit more biased towards *me*, with us being old lovers and all.

Back in the early summer I had taken a trip to Germany to visit Gabriella and her husband, Kristoff. Ever since the incident with Hector Hollister, I'd wondered about the power I had, why I could do the horrible miracles I could do, like bring a man back to life. As far as I knew, not even the Court Magician could do that. For the past four years, I'd been trying my best to research what exactly I was, but it was slow going since I didn't want to reveal that I had innate magic—the current government had come to power by being tough on crime, and I didn't want to get locked up or worse. When I felt like there was nothing left for me to learn in England, I reached out to Gabs.

Gabs had made quite a name for herself as a powerful cloth mage, and her husband was also a mage, though nonpractising. They had amassed quite the canon of magical texts, and I wanted the chance to look at them. The von Melsungens happily invited me in. Gabs helped me go through the texts and Kristoff translated the tricky bits. What I found didn't reveal anything new so much as confirm a theory—when I was a child, a mysterious mage had broken my finger and put a spell upon me that made me charming. But I had long suspected she had done more than that. She had created two breaks in my finger, one for the spell that gave me the ability to win over people, and another break that changed me, gave me unknown power.

"Gabs is fine," I said, my smile somewhat tight. Mrs Spratt was still at the entrance of the living room, a worried look on her face, as if wondering if she should step in or not. Mrs Spratt had no doubt heard the rumours about me, but she'd taken me on as a tenant anyway, and I was grateful to her for that.

A few months after I'd returned to London, Gabs had called me up in tears. She was being blackmailed—she'd been having an affair and her love letters had fallen into her blackmailer's hands. For Gabs, it wasn't the affair coming to light that scared her so much as it being revealed who she was having the affair with—Kristoff's brother.

"Please, dear heart, you're the only one who can save me," she'd cried over the telephone.

I'd had no reason to get drawn into Gabs's over-the-top penny drama, but I could never say no to her. Even when it meant that my own long-term partner, Tonya, had finally dumped me and that I'd been branded a louche lothario. With Tonya gone, I couldn't afford the rent on our flat in Islington, which had led to me moving out here into the countryside.

"You ever think of making a go of it, the two of you?" Naveed asked idly, like he was just chitchatting rather than asking a pretty personal question. "You and Gabriella would make a dashing couple."

Mrs Spratt looked at me curiously, clearly lingering to hear my answer. I wanted to say no, that Gabs and I were just friends, but if I didn't act the part of the heartbroken suitor, our whole facade might fall apart, and then the lies would have been for nothing.

"Her husband took her back," I said with a tight-lipped smile, as if it were no thing at all for me to account for my love life to near strangers. "There's nothing between us now."

Mrs Spratt finally looked away. "I should call Beatrix in for teatime," she said. "Please, take as long as you need here."

"Thank you again, Mrs Spratt," I said, watching her go, wishing we could step into another reality so I could talk to her privately and explain that I wasn't the rake all the rumours said I was.

Once Mrs Spratt left Naveed cleared his throat. "Mr Gallagher—you know, it feels off calling you Mr Gallagher if you're going to be teaching us. I think you need a grander title, hmm?" His eyes lit up. "Like Professor!"

"Hardly. That makes me sound like an old man."

"Well . . ." Rosemary stopped and traded a look with Naveed and I realized that, in their teenage eyes, I *was* an old man.

"I think Professor Gallagher has a dashing ring to it," Naveed said. "Say, Professor, I have a question for you."

"Ask away." I had thought teaching would be fun. I had thought it would be an easy way to make some extra cash while also bettering my own craft. Now I felt wrung out and I'd been on the clock for all of fifteen minutes.

"When it comes to romance, who do you prefer, men or women?"

I'd never thought of myself as shy or a prude, but these kids were making me want to join the priesthood.

"Well, that's a rather broad question," I said.

"Let's make it more specific," Rosemary said. "Who do you find more attractive, me or Naveed?"

They both sat up straight and shot me sharp grins. God, had I been this annoying when I'd been nineteen? Probably. This was perhaps payback for all the times I'd thrown myself at an older partner. About a decade ago I'd been in their spot, making eyes at my own professor.

The difference between him and me was I knew better than to make a move on my students.

Before I could fob them off with a nonanswer the doorbell rang.

"Oh, I must answer that!" I walked so quickly to the front door I nearly bowled over Mrs Spratt. Even then I didn't slow down, just continued onwards until I flung open the door.

Standing on the step was a young woman the same age as Naveed and Rosemary. She had wavy brown hair and was wearing an olive-green shirtdress under her black coat. Something about her was strangely familiar. Behind her a car pulled away back onto the road to the motorway.

"M-Mr Gallagher," the girl stammered. "I'm sorry to just show up like this, but I'm a classmate of Prince Naveed and Rosemary Panyi. I heard they had hired you to act as a tutor, and I was hoping I could also participate."

This girl, in her somewhat frumpy stockings and unkempt hair, was clearly an angel in disguise. She'd been sent by God to save me. It was clear she was a different type from the troublemakers currently sitting in Mrs Spratt's living room. She would never cast come-hither stares my way or ask about my sex life. She barely had the nerve to look me in the eye.

"Of course, of course! The more the merrier!" I said. I took her hand in mine. "It's a pleasure to meet you, Miss . . . ?"

"Um, H-Hollister," she said, finally raising her head. "Harriet Hollister."

The smile froze on my face. Harriet Hollister. The daughter of Hector Hollister, the man that I'd murdered. The resemblance was faint but there: similar jaw and eye shape, pink skin so fair it almost seemed like it was underlit by the blood rushing through the body's veins. She had a few sparse freckles across her nose. I tried to remember if Hector had had freckles in the same place—at least, if he'd had them before I'd skinned him alive.

That was four years ago. I was an idiot back then, too quick to trust, even quicker to brag about myself.

In that moment Harriet and I were just two people staring at each other as we failed to maintain passable poker faces. I was scared that my past sins had caught up with me—I always knew I'd have to account for myself after death, but I'd started to fool myself into believing that, as far as earthly matters went, I'd gotten away with it. For Harriet's part, she didn't seem angry or like she was about to pull out a gun and shoot me. She just seemed nervous.

"Oh, Harriet, welcome," I said, my voice somewhat high and strangled. We shook hands mechanically. I still felt the magic work on her, but a spell like that had its limits; could it really make her think well of her father's killer? Did she know? "Come on into the living room."

We walked together stiffly, like windup toys. Naveed and Rosemary had been conspiring while I was gone, leaning in close together and speaking low through mischievous grins. But when they saw Harriet their smiles dropped: Naveed frowned while Rosemary just looked confused.

"Miss Hollister here is one of your classmates, I hear," I said. "She asked to join in on our tutoring sessions, and I see no reason why not."

Naveed huffed but didn't make any objection except to cross his arms. Rosemary smiled at Harriet and patted the space beside her on the settee, and Harriet seemed relieved to have a space to go to. Once she sat down the three of them looked at me expectantly. After the flurry of activity that had happened in the past hour I'd all but forgotten what we were there for. Then I remembered and started the cloth magic lecture I'd written up the night before.

CHAPTER 2

We went for about two hours, stopping only when Beatrix tromped into the room and demanded to be introduced to everyone. The three students were all very gracious and gave Beatrix their full attention, even following her out into the backyard to play a game of tag with her in the long grass.

I stayed back, standing at the glass doors that separated the dining room from the stone patio behind the house. Mrs Spratt came to join me, and we watched as the children—three of them practically adults, one still very much a child—romped around the grounds.

"I'm sorry about Prince Naveed," I said. "I'd never even met the bloke; I only took him on because my old prof asked me to. I didn't know he'd act like such a prat."

"It is all right," Mrs Spratt said. "He's young and doesn't know better. And he's right. I know how people talk about me."

She said it flatly, her words as natural as water flowing over a round rock.

"I do think he's right about one thing," I said. "Anyone who's banking on you buckling is in for a surprise. You're stronger than they think."

It felt mighty bold to say that when I'd known Mrs Spratt for only a short time, but I believed it.

Mrs Spratt didn't seem flattered or assuaged by my words—if anything, a grey cloud passed over her face.

"Naveed is right that my husband never abused me," Mrs Spratt said carefully. "But there were days where I wished he would, because then I could leave."

"Right, because then you'd have grounds for divorce."

For just a split second Mrs Spratt looked at me like I was the dumbest motherfucker on the planet. Then she shook her head. "No, no, it had nothing to do with that. It had to do with the promises and standards I'd set for myself. He never did hit me. But he would say such cruel things to me. Eventually we were able to have Beatrix, and I told myself that things would get better, or when they didn't, that it was better to stay with him for Beatrix's sake." She stopped to swallow. "But then, when Beatrix was three, she started talking. And she'd say to me the same things her father had said, a toddler's mimicry of adult cruelty. And that's when I knew I had to leave."

"Mrs Spratt, you don't have to explain yourself to me—"

"But I do. See, even after I knew how being around that man was warping my daughter, *it still took me a year to leave*," Mrs Spratt said. "If I were truly strong, Mr Gallagher, I wouldn't have waited. And now for the rest of my life I will worry that I didn't get out soon enough." She said the last bit looking out at Beatrix, who had just tackled Naveed and brought them both to the ground, the two of them laughing as they tumbled down the hill.

I tried to think of some comforting words to say to Mrs Spratt, but after the look she'd given me earlier, I was terrified of once more showing my ass. I reached out and let the tips of my fingers graze her shoulder, too nervous of crossing a line to give her a comforting pat.

"Say, Mrs Spratt, you and I should go to the pub by the petrol station and grab a pint sometime. My treat. You can go on about your horrible husband until the sun comes up then."

Mrs Spratt's lips twitched, perhaps at the idea of getting a beer in a pub—she seemed like a woman who'd never even set foot in one before. "Thank you for the offer, Mr Gallagher, but the locals would talk if they saw us stepping out together, and such gossip could really hurt me right now."

"Oh, sure. I see."

"There's a chance that Jack backs down and agrees to a divorce," Mrs Spratt said. "But in that case he might sue for full custody of Beatrix. I have to keep my reputation as pristine as possible to guard against that."

"Ah. Of course." A clock chimed on the wall—how was it already five o'clock? I had an appointment at Buckingham Palace. "Well, I am a cloth mage, Mrs Spratt. If you do want to go out on the town sometime without prying eyes all over you, I could make us a couple of magical disguises."

Her blue eyes brightened. "Truly? Why, that sounds delightful. Could you really . . . ?"

"Oh yes, that's child's play." I hadn't expected her to actually take me up on it, but I found I kind of liked the way she was looking at me with happy surprise. It was a new side to her. "Let's make it a date. Saturday night?"

"I'll have to find a sitter for Beatrix," she said thoughtfully. "But I will look into it."

"Aces." I was glad I'd been able to flip Mrs Spratt's mood from glum to excited. As I left I thought I even heard her humming a tune.

~

It was a "small" party at Buckingham Palace, which meant around twenty guests, twice as much staff, and me, standing against a wall with a glass of champagne in hand, like someone trying to avoid sharks by staying in the shallows. Perhaps it was a mistake for me to come, but an unavoidable one. When your patron, especially one as sweet as Princess Katherine, asks you to accompany her to a social event, it makes sense from both a chivalrous and a mercenary point of view to say yes.

But even though I had come here on Kitty's arm, I was still very much alone, marked. As the figure of gossip, the polite thing would have been to stay home so everyone here could talk about me. Yet here I was, looking good, smiling, trying to ignore the raised eyebrows and snide remarks about my affair with Gabs. Usually at an event like this I'd have two buffers—one, my good friend and faithful-to-a-fault mate Andrew. But Andrew was up in Scotland, visiting his mother. The other, my now ex-girlfriend, Verity Turnboldt to the world, Tonya to me . . . well, she was back in New York now and wanted nothing to do with me.

I only allowed myself to miss Thomas once a day. I'd been saving up today's loneliness, knowing that this party would be a trial. I'd made a point of not thinking about him earlier so that I could now let out a sigh and wish he were there.

But he wasn't. He'd taken off after I'd killed Hector Hollister, telling me he was done cleaning up my messes.

That left only one bulwark to me, Princess Katherine. Kitty was sitting on a couch in the middle of the room, gloved hands twisting oh so slightly in her lap as her brother and his friends laughed.

She was such a sweet kid, especially for a royal. She was nineteen years old and still had baby fat on her round face. Curly orange hair framed her face, the lightness of her hair bringing an extra glint to her eyes. She had been born with a slight facial deformity, some nerve on the right side of her face badly damaged during birth. It meant that her right eye never opened as fully as the left, and the right side of her mouth never lifted as far up when she smiled. But what a smile! Even at her most exuberant, her grin had an edge of shyness to it that made it all the more endearing.

Was she having a good time? Was her stupid lout of a brother spouting unkindness again? Should I step in and give her an out from the conversation? Perhaps we could devise a system of signals so that in the future, Kitty could let me know when I needed to intervene.

I thought of the first time we had ever spoken, two years ago now. It had been the spring of 1956. Ralph—one of my old mates from college—had the big idea to create a cloth magicians guild. The plan was to make learning magic more accessible to the working class of the city. We'd collect dues from members and part of the funds would go towards paying tuition for young lads and gals from working-class families who wished to become mages. I was all for it—in order to pay for my own schooling I had gone deep into debt, beholden to dangerous underworld types. I would have died had Thomas not been there to match those thugs blow for blow. So of course, if there was a way to make things easier for kids coming up after me, I wanted to do it.

There was also the fact that it seemed like the kind of cause that Thomas would champion. I'd been a bit all over the place after Thomas had taken off to God knows where. I wasn't alone—at the time I still had Tonya. We had decided to do away with social norms and live together, unmarried though we were. Andrew stepped up to fill the role of best mate. But Ralph, always a perceptive bloke, I think he knew I needed a purpose. I'd come so close to possibly becoming the country's next Court Magician but had given up on the dream when I'd gotten a glimpse of just exactly how my country had tried to weaponize magic. I didn't want to be a part of that, but I still wanted respect, some way upwards. I wanted to be someone.

Ralph could see that I was at loose ends, hence him asking me to join him on the board of the newly formed guild. We were planning to have a meeting with the other London guilds when word came to us that a member of the royal family was interested in our project: the young Princess Katherine wished to come to the meeting and say a few words. Having a member of royalty there wowed the other guild leaders, even if the girl's shaky speech had been barely audible—the meeting had been held in a school classroom and her voice didn't even reach the back desk. But her presence alone legitimized us, and the other guilds promised to lend their support.

Afterwards Ralph and I were putting the desks back in place when a royal aide came and said the princess would like to speak with me. I looked at Ralph. I think in that moment we both knew my time and commitment to the Cloth Magic Guild were over and done with. Even if I returned from my chat, something was about to change. But really, my two choices were stacking chairs with Ralph and chatting with a young royal. Anyone would have made the same choice.

Princess Katherine was sitting in the teachers' lounge. Her dress created a hazy, shimmering air around her—a magic effect that I used quite a bit myself, though this dress overdid it in my opinion. It obscured her so much it was like looking at someone through a fogged window. But despite her facial features being somewhat concealed, her body language was that of someone deep in thought and despair, shoulders rolled forwards, head tilted down, hands clasped as if she were trying to contain an ocean of feelings.

"Mr Gallagher is here, miss," the aide said.

"Ah, Mr Gallagher." The princess stood up, correcting her posture. "Thank you for speaking with me. Please, sit down."

The aide withdrew to give us some privacy. We chatted for a little bit about the guild and the weather but I could sense there was something else she wished to speak of.

"Mr Gallagher," she said eventually. "A friend of mine is in a bit of a quandary and she has no one to turn to. It involves matters of the heart and courtship. I am far from knowledgeable when it comes to these matters, so I fear I don't know what to tell my friend. May I ask your advice so that I can in turn advise her?"

Had this girl, a princess and second in line to the throne, really come all the way to this dingy little schoolroom in Dalston in order to ask *my* advice on matters of the heart? For her "friend"?

"Of course, Princess Katherine," I said. "I shall listen and give my best insight into the matter."

"Well, you see, there's this man," she stammered out. "A much older man, from a well-established family. He has been acting . . . very familiar around my friend, and she has heard rumours that he wishes to marry her."

"I see," I said. "And she doesn't return his feelings?"

"No!" Katherine replied bluntly. "I don't wish to be unkind, but he is more than twice her age, always has an odd odour to him, and . . . please do not misunderstand me, he can be very nice and kind, but in a leering way, if that makes any sense."

It made perfect sense. I myself had met many men like that, even had a few of them hit on me. But obviously my situation was very different from young Princess Katherine's.

"May I ask who this man is?"

The princess looked out the window. "A politician. Deputy Prime Minister Fairweather."

I knew him. He was a gangly, overbred bit of landed gentry who deigned to live in the city. He had the unsure gait of a greyhound that had never learned how to go up stairs. Rumour was that he liked young women—well, not women. Girls. He liked teenagers. And Princess Katherine was both young and a fantastic match for any well-bred bachelor. No wonder he was buzzing about her.

I *also* knew that the royal family would never let the match happen. Fairweather was simply too old; he was forty-eight to Kitty's seventeen, for Christ's sake. The optics of that were too distasteful, even for the aristocracy. It was 1956, not 1300, and while the princess might not have a lot of say in who she married or didn't, they wouldn't foist her off on that old goober.

But I felt like telling all that to Princess Katherine wouldn't lighten her anxiety. And in that moment, there was something I was curious about.

"Princess, I'll assist you however I can, but why have you come to me about this?"

Through the haze of the magic surrounding her I could see a blush come to her cheeks. "A mutual acquaintance said that you were a good person to turn to when it came to matters of the heart, that you would go to the ends of the earth to help a lady in trouble."

"Well, then I suppose I better live up to that reputation."

She smiled at me. "So, Mr Gallagher, what can my friend do to ward off this man's attentions?"

"The thing is, with a man like that, there's probably little *you* can do," I said, forgetting to keep up the pretence that it was her friend we were talking about. "If these men cared about the feelings of the women they bothered, they wouldn't bother them in the first place. No, what you need is some guy to tell him off. Maybe you could tell your father and ask him . . ." As I spoke an idea started to form in my mind. Katherine's position as second in line to the throne meant that she would be expected to marry, and marry a man with considerable social standing. Her wishes would be taken into account somewhat, but only if her chosen beau was acceptable to the royal family. If she could find a man she liked who fit the needed qualifications, then horseflies like the deputy prime minister would have to buzz off.

"If you had a beau, Princess," I said, "some tolerable man on your arm, Fairweather would keep his distance."

Katherine twisted her hands in her lap. "Oh, but Mr Gallagher, there's no one I can think of that could possibly . . ."

"Perhaps, Princess," I cut in, "I could introduce you to a friend of mine."

The friend in question was Andrew, a.k.a. Lord Fife. A young man who was kind, considerate, and easily one of the prettiest faces in London. He had met the princess before briefly at social functions, but it was only when I started playing matchmaker between the two that they really got to know each other. They were a good match, both softhearted people who could never hurt a fly. They didn't love each other—even I wasn't delusional enough to think that. But their families approved and they were at least comfortable in each other's company. They had duties I never had to worry about. Unlike them I could marry for love.

Could I? I wondered what Tonya was doing right now. Maybe she was writing late into the evening. In London she had managed to make a pretty penny doing ghostwriting work for celebrities and the like. Maybe she'd picked up work like that back in America. By immersing herself in another person's life, she could ignore the mess I'd made of ours. Or maybe she was finally doing some writing of her own; she'd always spoken of writing the great American novel. Or maybe she was doing late-night copyediting for some New York fish rag, getting the words on the page in order to pay the bills.

Thinking of Tonya made a new wave of loneliness wash over me. But I tried to push it down—I was at a party, and already the other guests were looking me over for weakness. I wasn't like them, born in manor houses or colonial chalets, the sons and daughters of admirals and duchesses, princes and princesses of this land and ones farther afield. Everyone knew I was the son of a shop clerk, and because of that no one believed I belonged there amongst them. If I didn't keep my wits about me, if I got too swept up in morosely feeling sorry for myself, this lot would have me out the door.

I'd done well for a Liverpool lad. Sure, I wasn't the Court Magician, but being employed by the princess was still a good gig, making magic dresses for her and keeping her confidences. I'd already lost so much—Thomas, Tonya, any shot at heaven—but I'd worked hard to get what I had now, and I wasn't going to lose it.

CHAPTER 3

Of course, it wasn't fair to say that everyone in the room had it out for me—Princess Katherine, or Kitty, had been nothing but sweet to me.

As though she could hear my thoughts she turned and smiled at me, giving a slight nod as if to say that everything was fine. I sighed in relief, partly for her, partly for me. It had been a mistake to come here. Usually I lived for parties, the chance to meet new and interesting people and win them over. But ever since the news had broken about me and Gabs, well, suddenly people were a little *too* interested in me.

I smiled back at Kitty. Court Magician Peter Van Holt appeared next to me, arising like a bad smell.

"Do you know what I like about you, Gallagher?" he asked. "You really do find every woman beautiful."

Van Holt was wearing an odd bit of frippery, a tuxedo-cut suit where the collars and cuffs had an almost mossy appearance to them. My outfit for the evening was rather plain: grey pants with a grey jacket with a green paisley lining. There was magic to it, but just a little bit of glamour to make me look good. A bit bland, but for once I hadn't felt like calling attention to myself.

There were two types of magic in the world. First there was external, everyday-type magic that people interacted with when they wore magic clothes or used their Books. Then there was the internal kind, innate magic, which became a part of you when a mage maker broke your bones. In England, only the Court Magician could practise innate magic on others. It always made me a little nervous being near Van Holt, the current Court Magician. When we'd first met three years ago, shortly after he'd become the Court Magician, I'd been terrified he'd see the breaks in my finger and sense the illegal magic coursing through me.

"What makes you say that?" I asked Van Holt, trying to keep my tone light.

"Well, my suit allows me to read minds," he said. "And also I saw you looking at the princess as if she were a world-renowned beauty and not an awkward little piglet."

He always spoke in a pleasant tone, his Afrikaans accent further softening his words. He was just a bit taller than me, in his midthirties. He was a white man, the son of an aristocratic British mother and Dutch father. His parents' union had brought them to South Africa, where little Peter Van Holt had been born. He had long dark-brown hair, a goatee, and brown eyes that were always watching everything with quiet interest.

"A psychic suit, eh?" I tested it out by imagining Van Holt being chomped into pieces by a horde of hungry alligators. He didn't flinch, which confirmed a theory I had: maybe his suit did let him catch stray thoughts or vague feelings, but it was hardly all-encompassing.

"Perhaps now that you are single again, you're looking for your next conquest," Van Holt said, gesturing with his eyes towards Princess Katherine.

In my mind's eye an alligator snapped off Van Holt's head.

"Hardly. I don't have that kind of designs on the princess. Besides, she's engaged." Since I was the one who'd set that whole business up, I was quite proud of the match.

"Yes, but you've shown you don't have much regard for common decency," Van Holt said. "Cheating on poor Verity Turnboldt, and with a married woman at that . . . well, who knows how low you'd stoop?

As the Court Magician, it is my duty to protect the royal family. I'm keeping an eye on you, Gallagher."

I was getting a little fed up with Van Holt's low-key intimidation.

"Look, Van Holt, if you personally have a problem with me—"

"Mr Gallagher, Court Magician Van Holt." It was Princess Sabina, the birthday girl herself and guest of honour, the crown prince at his usual spot by her side. Van Holt and I fell silent and bowed to them both. Sabina's status as a royal was more in name than anything. Her grandmother had been an African princess from Dahomey, sent to live in England as Queen Victoria's ward. Her descendants still had royal titles but no land to go back to, as their home had been carved up by the British and the French and claimed by neighbouring empires. But Sabina still carried herself with royal airs, and because of that she had caught the eye of Crown Prince Arthur. Hence the intimate but still extravagant party here in the palace.

Sabina fixed her gaze on me. For a split second I admired the curve of the brow over her dark eyes that were looking so judgementally at me. There was just something about the lines of her face that would make both mathematicians and poets fall in love with her. Then I remembered Van Holt's comment about how I found every woman beautiful and wondered if I was perhaps going overboard. Well, fuck him—I wasn't going to start doubting my senses now.

"Mr Gallagher." Sabina spoke with an accent that was the poshest of posh—I could imagine her as a toddler in a nursery, a governess rapping her knuckles as little Princess Sabina burbled in baby talk, tsking her and instructing her to say *mummy* rather than *mama*. "It's been a while since we've seen either you or Ms Turnboldt. Is she not well?"

Just because I thought Sabina beautiful didn't mean I was blind to her faults—her question might have sounded innocuous or even caring to a neutral, uninformed third party, but everyone present knew better. She *knew* Tonya and I had split up.

Plus, if Tonya had been there, Sabina would have been nothing but cruel to her, making some remark on how Tonya was dressed or saying something about Tonya's "crude American manners." It drove me out of my skull since Tonya was Sabina's own flesh and blood. They were cousins: Tonya's mother, Abigail, had been Sabina's mother's little sister. If Dr Myers had kept Tonya for his own rather than swapping her for a male child, Tonya and Sabina would have grown up together.

"I don't understand what that woman has against you," I'd said to Tonya one evening before our rift. "She'd swallow her own teeth in shock if she ever learned you're cousins!"

Tonya had given me a pitying look. "Oh, Paul. She *knows*."

That had given me pause. "Really? She does?"

Tonya shrugged. "Well, I don't know if she knows a hundred percent, but she suspects. Back in the day, when I reached out to some family members for help, it already seemed to be family lore that Dr Myers had switched his kid with someone else in order to get his father-in-law's money. I wouldn't be surprised if some of that whispering trickled down into Sabina's ear."

"Then why is she so cruel to you?"

"When Dr Myers got his hands on Reginald's money, he used part of the windfall to pay my other relatives off," Tonya explained. "When Sabina sees me, it's a reminder of that. Her father was able to go into business thanks to the money he got from *my* dad. And now she's got the crown prince on a string. She's also worried that I'm going to open my big mouth and ruin everything for her."

Tonya had spoken plainly, like she actually understood and even felt sorry for her cousin.

Maybe Tonya could make peace with it, but Sabina's cruelty revealed a flaw in her character that I couldn't stand—and maybe that was hypocritical of me since I'd hurt Tonya far worse than Sabina ever had, but I'd never claimed to be consistent. However, there wasn't much

I could do or say against her, since at the end of the day she was still Prince Arthur's flame.

"Verity and I are no longer an item," I said. "She's gone back to New York. But I'm sure she sends you her best birthday wishes from across the ocean, Princess."

Sabina gave a half smile at that, the well-bred woman's equivalent of snorting and rolling her eyes.

"Well, bad luck, Gallagher!" Prince Arthur said, a surprisingly booming voice from a skinny frame. "I'm sure you'll bounce back quick enough! Maybe I could set you up with someone, like you set up my sister with your mate Andrew."

"Well, I think the first order of business is finding a match for *you*, Prince Arthur." It was a low blow and I didn't feel good about it, but between the lot of them I was on my last nerve. Arthur already had a partner in Sabina, but because of the fact that she was Black the queen and king had not allowed them to go public with their relationship. The king had even asked me, the one time we'd ever talked, if I could produce another miracle by fixing his son up with someone "suitable."

Both Arthur and Sabina looked at me, shocked. Van Holt hid a smile, ducking his head down to sip from his cocktail glass. I decided I should make a quick getaway.

"Ah, I think Kitty needs me. Please excuse me." I quickly made my way to her side.

Kitty was still sitting on the couch. She wore a beautiful yellow dress I had created for her, and she was quietly using its magical ability: one after another she'd reach out and snap off a flower bud from the bouquet in front of her and then make the flower bloom. I had designed it so she'd have a party trick, something she could show people if the conversation flagged. But instead she sat there alone, buried in flower petals.

"Princess Katherine," I said to her, "may I sit down?"

"Oh, of course, Gally!" she said, brushing the petals onto the floor. That was the way of things: she could call me Gally in public but I knew to call her Kitty only in private. I didn't even like the nickname—Gally was what Andrew called me, and Kitty had picked up the habit from him.

We sat in silence for a moment.

"It's too bad Andrew is missing this party," I said lamely. Kitty nodded vigorously.

"Oh yes, but of course as a lord he must tend to his domain." She smiled. "He actually asked me to go up north with him, but I told him no. I didn't think it would be proper for us to travel together, as if we were already man and wife. And besides, just because we're engaged, that doesn't mean we need to spend *all* our time together."

"For sure." As far as I could tell, however, Andrew and Kitty hardly spent any time together at all. I knew theirs wasn't a conventional match, but it still seemed odd. Whenever they did spend time together they both insisted I join them on their garden promenades and concert visits, like they were desperate for a chaperone.

"Gally, I think I'd like to retire for the evening. Could you walk me to my room?" Kitty said. I felt a flood of relief. Kitty smiled and it occurred to me that perhaps she wanted to leave for my sake just as much as her own.

"Of course, Princess." I stood and she took my arm.

We went over to where Prince Arthur stood with Princess Sabina.

"Brother, I am retiring for the evening," Kitty said, speaking with the stiffness and fragility of a house made of sugar. She nodded at Sabina. "Many happy returns on your birthday, Princess Sabina."

"Oh, don't go! The party's just getting started," Arthur said, more to me than to Kitty. "You didn't even bring a gift for the birthday girl, Gally. Stick around and tell us about what Gabriella von Melsungen is like in bed. I bet she's a wildcat."

Kitty gripped my arm tightly. Neither of us was a stranger to Arthur's casual crassness. Arthur wasn't an imposing figure on sight: he was of average height, with wavy blond hair perpetually slicked back, the slightest hint of an overbite, a face that was neither ugly nor enticing. But a lifetime of privilege had cultivated a dangerous air about him. Maybe he hardly had any muscle to his frame, but he had the knowledge that he could do just about whatever he wanted and not suffer for it.

"Mr Gallagher and I are going to look over some sketches before I go to bed," Kitty said, her voice a defiant squeak.

Arthur cocked an eyebrow.

"You really give this Scouser too much liberty, Kitty Cat," he said. "Now, Mr Gallagher, I hope you don't have designs on my little sister. If that was the case, I'd have you chopped up and dumped in the Mersey."

I decided to ignore the prince's graphic threat, instead placing a protective hand on Kitty's. "Kitty is engaged to my best friend. I'd never betray his trust."

I had left a pretty big opening there, and as soon as the words were out of my mouth I figured the prince would attack, citing the fact that I'd betrayed Tonya's trust.

"Ah yes. I suppose you wouldn't betray Andrew by sleeping with his girl, would you? Not even a cad like you would sink that low. Well, like I said before, Gally, don't get any ideas about my sister or we will see if you sink."

Not for the first time since meeting the prince did I marvel at the idea of the monarchy, that supposedly God himself ordained the figurehead of our nation.

"Arthur, you're drunk," Sabina said.

"No, no, I'm just happy. Just having a good time. We're all having a good time here. Right, Kitty? Right, Gally?"

"Let's go, Gally," Kitty whispered to me and pulled me out of the room.

We walked in silence down the hall and up the stairs to the royal family's living quarters. Kitty's room had a receiving area with couches and a view of the grounds. One of her maids was waiting, but Kitty waved her off ("I'm not ready to turn in just yet, Mary; I'll call for you in fifteen minutes or so to help me undress").

We sat on the couches. I knew this room well—the moulding of the ceiling and intricate rose-gold wallpaper. Kitty and I had spent many hours in this room just chatting and laughing.

"Shall I call for some refreshments, Gally?" Kitty asked, bringing me back to myself. I shook my head.

"I'm all right, Princess. But thank you."

She nodded and looked down at her hands, which were in her lap. The slope of her shoulders brought me back to the day we had first met, when the weight of the world had been bearing down on her.

I shifted forwards on my chair, elbows resting on my knees.

"Princess, may I tell you something?"

Kitty blinked and looked my way.

"Of course, Gally. And please, call me Kitty when we're alone."

"Thank you. Well, you've probably heard all the talk about how I cheated on Verity Turnboldt with Gabriella von Melsungen, yeah?"

"Oh!" Kitty's eyes widened. "Well, um, yes, I have heard such things, but Gally, I—"

"It's not true," I said. "I never cheated on Verity. I never slept with Gabriella." The last part wasn't totally true—Gabs and I had briefly been an item back during our school days, when we'd both been studying cloth magic at the UCL. But that was such old news I didn't feel the need to bring it up now.

"Truly?" Kitty cocked her head to the side. "Then why don't you say so? Everyone has been saying such nasty things about you, Gally. I really can't stand it. And Ms Turnboldt . . . she left you over this. Went all the way back to America."

"Yeah. That's right."

"So why not tell people that the rumours are false, then?"

"Well, you see, Gabs and me, we go way back," I said. "About a month ago she gets in touch. Someone has proof that she cheated on her husband. It's only a matter of time before it comes out that she's being unfaithful, but it would be really bad if her husband finds out who she's been unfaithful with." Kristoff worshipped the ground Gabs strode upon, but even he would struggle to forgive a woman who had slept with his brother. "So to head things off, she asked if I would play the fall guy. See, I'm just such a charming lad; no one would blame Gabs for cheating on her husband with me."

It was a joke but Kitty took it seriously. "I suppose so. But you haven't told Verity about your deception?" Kitty asked, guileless eyes on me. "Oh, Gally! If you truly love her, you must let her in on this. The pain and heartache she's suffering right now, because of you, for the sake of another woman . . . well, it's almost tantamount to cheating in a way, isn't it?"

"Is it?" I said, uneasily.

"Well, either way, you should tell Verity the truth of the matter."

"At this point, she'd think I was lying," I said. "That I was just telling her a yarn so she'd forgive me."

"Well, perhaps so, but still . . ." Kitty fell silent.

"I'm sorry for bringing it up," I said. "It's just been such a weight upon me."

Kitty smiled. "I understand. And I can also understand why you'd agree to such a plea for help. You know, it was Gabriella von Melsungen who first recommended you to me."

"Really?" I said, sitting up straight.

"Oh, yes. It was back during the Fairweather incident. Gabriella and her husband were visiting court and she was just so . . . well, words can hardly do her justice, can they, Gally? I'd call her impressive, but even that is far too vague and underwhelming."

"I know what you mean," I said. "Gabs's one of the best mages alive."

"Ah yes, you would know how amazing she is," Kitty said. "But when I first met her, I was just bowled over. I figured if anyone knew how to deal with bothersome men, it was her, so I told her how Deputy Prime Minister Fairweather had designs upon me. That's when she told me to seek you out." Kitty finished her story with a broad smile. Mentally, I gave thanks to Gabs for setting me up with the princess—Kitty had me on the payroll as her own personal cloth mage, which meant a salary as well as money for materials. It was a sweet gig. I was making amazing clothes for a young woman of unlimited means who attended nearly every fashionable event. I was only twenty-seven and yet I had it made.

Best of all, the job was a rather apolitical one. Unlike Court Magician Van Holt, who had to weigh in on affairs of the land and keep knobs like Prince Arthur placated, I was free to just create. I'd seen what it cost to be Court Magician—it meant taking part in experiments to push the bounds of magic, doing horrible things in the name of king and country. I'd dreamt of taking on the role at one point, but no longer.

So yes, I owed Gabs quite a bit. But now, as my personal life circled the drain, I felt like perhaps we were even.

"If you and Verity are meant to be," Kitty said carefully, "then you should talk to her and find a way out of this together."

I felt shamed then, that this young, sheltered teenage girl could speak so clearly on what needed to be done. I knew she was right, but the thought of following her advice made my gut twist. I hadn't told her my secret expecting such a thoughtful response; it had been more of a ploy to get her to open up in turn. She'd been especially withdrawn all night, beyond her usual shrinking violet self. Something was clearly bothering her, and all I wanted was to help her smile again.

"You have a point, Kitty. I'll pray on it." I smiled weakly. "But for now, I feel better just for having shared my secret with you. Thank you."

"Of course, Gally."

"Perhaps I can help you in return?" I said. "You seem troubled by something. Please, tell me. Maybe I can help."

"Oh, Mr Gallagher, it's nothing," Kitty stammered. "Well, nothing in particular, I suppose. It's just . . . even here in the palace I hear about people suffering in this country. We had to reinstate rationing, and our prisons are filling up with degenerates and delinquents . . . I suppose where I struggle is that I can't truly believe that our nation is full of so many rotten people that would justify our prison population rising by fifteen percent in the last five years," Kitty said, her brows knitted in serious concentration.

"Oh?" I was starting to worry that perhaps this was a bigger problem than I—or even Kitty—could tackle.

"So I'd like to go out amongst the populace and see for myself. See if the masses truly have lost all moral discretion." She fixed me with an intense look. "I should like to go out amongst the people in disguise."

"Oh!" Now, this *was* in fact in my wheelhouse. Heck, the princess and I had gone on plenty of adventures in the past year—ice-skating at Ally-Pally, gawking at the dinosaur bones at the science museum. For each outing I had created outfits that would magically disguise the princess's identity. "Oh yes, Kitty! Let's go out on the town! Where would you like to go? A radio show? A village fair? A dance hall?"

"I should like to go to a gay bar," Kitty said.

That stopped me in my tracks. "Excuse me?"

"Many of the people in prison or awaiting court dates are people who have been charged with civic disorder," Kitty said. "It's a blanket law that is used to harass everyone from gay men to prostitutes. I have lived too far removed from the common folk to know if such a law is warranted. I would like to go out into the world myself so I can better judge its purpose and effectiveness."

Ever since the new government had gained power after the last election, paranoia was the constant mood. Everyone lived in fear of a third world war, of spies and traitors in our midst. Gay folk were easy targets.

I was impressed that Kitty had heard how tough it was out there for the common folk, but it wasn't totally out of character for her. For one of our more daring outings, she had requested that I make us disguises that made us look like rough sleepers so that we could spend a night on the city streets. She had wished to know what it was like, even if just for one night, how it felt to be homeless. We'd pulled it off, but that seemed like a walk in the park compared to what she was asking of me now.

"I . . . see." So many questions were swirling in my head but I felt it unwise to voice them.

Kitty blushed. "I don't wish to sound cheeky, Gally, but I have heard that you frequent such establishments."

Frequent was a strong word—ever since Tonya had chucked me over I'd gone a few times. I would go with my assistant, Cobalt, and knock back a few pints. I preferred the gay bars to the more blokey pubs; they just had a better atmosphere. And I also liked that it made me seem rakish and dangerous to the aristocrats who I'd been hanging out with more and more often. And all right, I also liked to flirt a little bit with whatever lad happened to sit at our table on a busy night and sometimes even go home with him. Sure, I was worried about raids or being arrested, but the one time I'd been stopped by the cops I was able to pay them off with some American dollars on me. And as for blackmail, well, my promiscuity with both sexes was already an open secret.

"I do know a place or two," I said, tongue tumbling over itself. "But Princess, these aren't places for a nice girl like yourself."

"And yet it is where I wish to go," Kitty said, some steel coming into her voice, the cross voice of someone not used to being told no by the help. For a second she looked a lot like her brother before she softened.

"Please, won't you do this thing for me, Gally? I promise to be discreet and do as you say, but I must do this."

I couldn't say no. At the end of the day, she was not only a princess but my boss. Besides, I had started to think about it as a challenge and how it might actually be fun. A bit of mischief, a night we'd laugh about decades from now when we were both old.

And Kitty was right. Years ago there had been a big push to do away with the various "decency laws" that in particular targeted gay men, but after the Virtuis Party had risen to power all talk of dropping them had stopped cold. If anything, the laws had grown even harsher. I wasn't sure if Kitty could in fact do anything to make things better for the common folk, but it was worth a shot.

"All right, Kitty," I said, standing. "But give me a couple of days. I need to come up with an outfit for you, one with a specific effect."

"Oh yes, Mr Gallagher?!" Kitty said, standing and clapping her hands together. "What effect, exactly?"

"I need to turn you into a boy."

CHAPTER 4

The next day I met my assistant, Cobalt, at my studio on Gray's Inn Road, a long stretch of a street that served as one of the city's major arteries, buses and cars zooming along like red blood cells. My studio was on the fourth floor, which meant a long hike up the stairs every day, but I liked being able to look down at the tops of buses as they went by.

"Say, Paul, are you going to stare out the window all day or would you deign to look at some of my designs?" Cobalt asked crossly from where he was sitting at the drafting table.

My sketchbook was open in my lap, a partial design of the teddy bear I wanted to make Beatrix on the page. It had started out as a simple project, but as I'd worked on the pattern concerns had crept into my head. Was this too much? Was I overstepping? I wasn't trying to take the place of her real father, but it broke my heart to see Beatrix all by her lonesome. From the way Laura had spoken of her estranged husband he didn't sound like a nice guy, but Beatrix still clearly needed more attention than her harried mum could give her. Was I really willing to step up and be there for this child?

I clapped my sketchbook shut. I'd have to sort through that some other time—Cobalt was tapping the top of the drafting table impatiently with a pencil, waiting for my response.

"Sorry. My mind's a million miles away. Late night last night." I'd ended up staying over at Andrew's place rather than driving back out to the countryside. Good mate that he was, he'd given me a spare key and told me I could crash there whenever I wished. The servants were used to seeing me coming and going often enough that it was no surprise when I showed up. It still felt odd sleeping under Lady Fife's roof, even though she mainly lived in Scotland nowadays. Even from miles away I could feel her chilly gaze, cutting through me like an icicle knife. I'd try and reassure myself that, supposedly, Lady Fife no longer had her fearsome psychic powers, but I still couldn't shake the uneasy feeling that I had once more earned Lady Fife's disapproval.

Cobalt shook his head, his bobbed black hair swinging to and fro. "Right. A party at Buckingham Palace, hmm? How taxing. Well, next time, I can go and spare you the torture. It's the least I can do as your assistant."

Cobalt had been working for me for about four months now. He'd graduated from my old school, the University College London, just last spring and was hungry to make his mark on the world. I'd never been someone's boss before, and I still wasn't sure if I was doing it right—on day one I'd told him to call me Paul rather than Mr Gallagher, wanting us to be mates, but Cobalt had curled his lip like I'd offered him corked wine. He still called me Paul, though, perhaps because he saw it as a directive rather than an invitation to be friends.

Cobalt had come to me recommended by my old cloth magic teacher, Professor Lamb. "Cobalt is a delight," Lamb said. "Very hardworking, highly ambitious. Creative but practical. He's like if you and Thomas had a child."

Bringing Thomas into it had been an obvious emotional ploy, but it had worked. I could see aspects of Thomas in Cobalt: Cobalt was quick witted and never held back with a retort to some bit of nonsense. It was fun to wind him up. He had dark hair in a pageboy cut and often wore kohl around his eyes, making me think of a face from a playing card.

He wore some of the most elaborate clothes, such as today, when he was wearing a jerkin with puff sleeves and tight pants that flared out at the ankles, like what navy men wear.

"You joke, but that place is a viper's nest," I said. "God help this country when Arthur is king."

"The country is in bad enough shape already," Cobalt said. A troubled look came over his face, one that made him look far younger than twenty-three. "Ever since we lost Lady Fife . . ."

"Jesus Christ, she didn't die," I said. "She's just retired from public life and fucked off to Scotland."

"Yeah, but people say it's because she saw something really bad coming and decided to get out while she still could."

"Is that what you heard? Because I heard that she couldn't predict the future anymore, and because of that all her friends took off like birds in a field," I said with a touch of satisfaction. It was petty, I knew, to take joy in Lady Fife's fall from power, but she and I had always had a bit of a tense relationship. I was happy that I no longer had to deal with Andrew's mother judging me and finding me wanting.

However, Cobalt was right that something bad had fallen upon the country. With Lady Fife no longer pulling the strings from behind the scenes, other Machiavellian types had rushed in to fill the void. The Virtuis Party had risen to power. They'd sprung into existence about four years ago as a new right-wing party and managed to steal away MPs from both the Conservative and Labour Parties. In the last election back in 1956 they'd gotten enough votes to form a minority government. Their big selling point had been a combination of being tough on crime and national defence, with their leader, George Hywell, proposing a way to make each feed into the other: use the prisoners to protect the nation.

"Say, Cobalt, if you weren't working for me, what would you be doing right now?" I asked, still sitting by the window. It was nice to feel the cold of the windowpane and the heat from the radiator, to sense the slight rattle as a bus passed by.

Cobalt took my idle question seriously, head shooting up from his work. I cringed and realized too late that my words could have been taken as some kind of passive threat.

"What I'm asking," I clarified, "is, if you weren't here, would you be making clothes for prisoners?"

Not only were prisons across Great Britain packed to the gills, but the prisoners were forced to wear magic clothes in twelve-hour shifts. This magical uniform, when worn by a concentrated number of people in close quarters, created a barrier that protected the country from both nuclear and magical attack. But to pull the effect off, you needed a lot of people, and so the police and courts had been working overtime to throw more bodies in the clink. All so that the "good" people of the country could live in peace.

This meant, for the first time in my life, cloth mages were in high demand. Each prisoner's uniform had to be made to fit and by hand, which required skilled mages. This new penal system was the brainchild of the prime minister and Court Magician Van Holt, a cloth mage himself, the first one to ever become Court Magician.

Cobalt shook his head.

"No, no," he said, vehemently. "Every other one of my classmates were hired right out of school for that work, but I would *never*."

"Right!" It made me sick, honestly, to see cloth magic being used in such a way. Lamb had recently done a spell in prison—I'd only been able to get him out after crying to Kitty and having her pull every favour she could. When I'd seen him after he'd gotten out, he'd seemed so . . . diminished. Cloth magic was supposed to help people, to make their lives better. It wasn't about using people as tools, a way to relegate people to little more than a stone crushed under a mill.

"I'd never work in such filthy conditions," Cobalt said with a shudder. "Or work with criminals? No thank you."

I was taken aback, not expecting his reasoning.

"But Cobalt, we're . . ."

He looked at me expectantly as the words died in my throat. I wanted to tell him that he should have more compassion for the people locked up, that people like him and me could just as easily be in their shoes one day. But even though I was pretty sure Cobalt was gay, he was awfully tight lipped about such things—he went with me to bars but never went home with anyone as far as I could tell. I didn't quite get how someone who dressed as flamboyantly as a harlequin could be so bashful about such things.

I cleared my throat and, in an effort to change the subject, came over to where Cobalt was sketching various designs, all of them different masculine uniforms.

"We're going to Soho, not the opera," I said, tapping a design of top hat and tails. Cobalt puffed out his cheeks in frustration.

"But that's the point—it's so over the top that the magic will practically be already baked in!" he said. "It's like the male impersonators from the vaudeville days."

"This isn't vaudeville; it's real life." I picked up another drawing, one that was just a simple design of brown pants, white shirt, and suspenders with a jaunty little cap on the figure's head. "Now this is more like it. Cute and youthful, just like Kitty."

"Yes, but a shirt and suspenders? I don't wish to speak crudely of the princess, but she has certain measurements to account for." He made a vertical wavy gesture in the air and then blushed.

"Do you mean boobs, Cobalt?" I asked. Cobalt blushed harder. For all his bravado he came undone by the simplest things. I didn't really know much about Cobalt's past. Heck, the lad only went by one name, and I doubted his ma and pa had christened him "Cobalt." Lamb had always been coy, implying that he knew all about Cobalt's history but was sworn to secrecy. The hints he dropped implied that Cobalt was the illegitimate son of some rich man, a doted-upon bastard. I was curious about if this was true or not, but Cobalt clearly wanted to keep his identity under wraps, and I felt it was only right to accept that.

"You're right; the princess does have an hourglass figure." I loved making high-waisted, full gowns for her because of it, but it presented a challenge when it came to disguising her as a lad. "Well, lucky we're mages, eh? Plus, we'll add a jacket."

"And just how are we going to create this effect?" Cobalt asked, critical but also curious. I prided myself on my ability to imbue cloth with the desired magical attributes, and even Cobalt seemed to respect my skill in that area.

"What if we played up what is already there?" I said. "Once we tuck her hair up under the cap, she'll look far more boyish. What if we just played up her youth?"

"All right," Cobalt said. "We could use yellow for the shirt—"

"No, I want the shirt to be white."

"But yellow is the colour of youth and vitality, associated with the Manipura chakra!" Cobalt put a lot of water in the colour-theory school of magic, that certain colours lent themselves to different effects. Colour selection certainly played a part, of course, but I felt that the real power came at the imbuing stage of making a magic outfit.

"Maybe you could make a bow tie out of yellow, then? That may be cute. And can you make those pants to Kitty's measurements? Oh, a jacket of something heavy, to disguise her figure. Tweed? That should do it."

"And while I'm doing all that, what are you going to do?"

"Well, magic, of course."

~

I took some white linen, hopped on a bus up north, and got off near St Michael's Orphanage. The orphanage was on the Harringay Ladder, a part of town where Thomas and I used to live. I was feeling a bit nostalgic, and I indulged in my once-a-day fantasy that Thomas was there. If Thomas were beside me, he'd never go along with the idea of cloth magic prisons or shudder at the thought of working with criminals.

There were young boys playing in the schoolyard and I joined them for a bit, kicking around a football. Once I had my fill of that I took the bolt of fabric and went into the school. Eventually I managed to talk my way down to the bowels of the orphanage, where staff were washing clothes and sheets in an industrial washing machine. I transferred a pound into someone's Book and in return they put my fabric through the wash alongside the boys' dirty shirts and grass-stained trousers. I hoped that by being in close proximity to these things, my fabric would likewise contain a kind of youthful exuberance.

Once that was done I rolled the linen back onto the bolt and headed out, not entirely satisfied. I felt I could do more to ensure the fabric had indeed become magic—it gave off a faint aura, but I knew I could elicit something stronger. As I left the building I saw two lads sitting by the wall. They would have been five or six at most. One had brown hair, the other black. They were sharing a piece of bread between the two of them, a heel ripped in half. How many times had Thomas and I been in a similar state? We were a lot better off than these two—my mum and dad had done their best to make sure we never starved—but during the war we'd still sometimes gone to bed hungry.

I walked over to where they were but froze. I had been going over to give them some coins to buy some sweets, but as of this year cash money was illegal in the UK. All transactions, even lending a bob to a friend, had to be recorded in a Book. Children, especially orphans like these two, would not have a Book of their own.

"Hey there," I said, crouching down. "Where'd you scrounge that up, eh?"

They looked at me suspiciously. The black-haired boy tightened his grip on his food, as if I might grab it and swallow it whole.

"I'm Paul," I said. "I'm a mage! I need your help." I pointed to a large oak. "For my spell to work, I need a boy to climb the tree and wave this fabric in the wind. If you do that, I promise to buy you each a hot pie from the stall at the tube station. What do you say?"

The boys had a hushed conference and then nodded in sync.

It was tricky to climb while holding the bolt of fabric so the boys had to work together, each holding one end or taking turns holding on to it while the other climbed up.

"Boys! Boys!" A middle-aged woman ran out of the orphanage. "You know climbing that tree is forbidden. You'll get the strap for this!"

"Ma'am, please," I said, stepping in front of her. "I'm a cloth mage in employ to the royal family. These boys are helping me with an assignment."

She looked right sceptical at that, and I had to admit that a grown man just wandering around an orphanage was suspect.

"My name is Paul Gallagher," I said, holding out my hand. The woman, still giving me the evil eye, shook it. As she did I felt the innate magic in me unfurl, from my left hand and through my right. The woman's gaze softened.

"A cloth mage, eh?" she said, giving me a second look. "Well, that would explain your getup."

I wasn't wearing anything that outrageous, just a green pin-striped suit and red tie, brown shoes, and white shirt. The clothes weren't even magical—wearing magic clothes used up a lot of energy, and even cloth mages liked to conserve their power.

But the woman was right. I did stand out. In the city I'd noticed clothing becoming more and more drab, browns and blacks becoming the norm.

"So please, spare the boys the strap. They were only trying to help me," I said.

The woman huffed but nodded in agreement. The boys were near the top of the tree now. As they stood on the top branches, they unrolled the fabric.

"That's right, lads! Wave it in the air like a banner!" I called up. The tykes did so, and as they did they started hooting and hollering. The wind picked up and the fabric began to snap in the wind, causing the boys to shout even louder. Other children gathered round and it was only the stern words of the matron that kept them from climbing up the tree to join their friends. Instead they started to shout up to the boys in the tree, which caused the lads with the cloth to jump up and down.

The brown-haired boy holding the bolt slipped. He fell through the branches, ripping the other end of the fabric out of his friend's hand. Cheers turned to screams. Both the matron and I tried to rush forwards to grab the child but we were stymied by the crowd of children before us. Even through the cacophony we could hear the young boy hitting each branch on the way down, picking up speed. And then he was free of the branches, nothing but air between him and the ground. The fabric flowed behind him like the tail of a kite, and my heart lurched as I readied myself to hear the horrible sound of the boy hitting the earth—

But what came instead was a loud rip. The fabric had caught on a branch, slowing the boy's descent. He dropped the final height with little more than an "oof!"

The crowd rushed forwards. The matron roughly shoved the children out of the way to reach the brown-haired boy.

"Peter! You rotten bugger!" she growled. "You've ruined this man's fabric!"

"Is the boy okay?" Who cared about the fabric? I was a mage—I could always get more and magic it anew. I was more shaken by the thought that I had almost killed a child.

"I'm all right, guv," the kid said, getting to his feet. He patted himself off and grinned at me, his wide smile making all his freckles seemingly bunch together. His friend was cautiously climbing down, stopping to lift the fabric from where it had been caught on the branch.

"Let go of it; I'll catch it," I said. The boy did and the cloth fluttered down, the gash in it obvious as the wind made it billow. I grabbed the fabric and held it out, looking at the long diagonal slash.

"Oh, Mr Gallagher, I'm so sorry!" the matron said. "We'll find some way to pay you back the cost of the cloth—"

"No," I said. "No, this is perfect." I could feel a new energy in the cloth, a brimming enthusiasm and devil-may-care-ness. I could work with that cut, using it in the design of the shirt. I carefully rolled up the fabric onto the bolt and nodded to the two boys. "Thank you, lads. I couldn't have done this without you."

Their mates crowded around them and I started walking towards the orphanage gates.

And bumped right into Ralph Gunnerson.

"Hullo, Paul," Ralph said. Behind him were five young people peering shyly at me. They were armed with their own bolts of fabric and sewing kits. I knew just by looking at them that they were first-year cloth magic students, teens who were trying valiantly to look grown up. There were three girls and two boys, a mix of white, Black, and Asian. One of the girls looked pretty posh, but the rest seemed to be middle class. Once again I was struck by how much the demographics had changed since I was in school. Not only were women now graduating on the regular, but more nonwhite folks were as well. But it was the change in class that surprised me the most. In my time, the cloth magic programme had been the refuge of upper-class men who wanted to spend time at college but not necessarily spend time studying, who wanted to be able to call themselves mages without ever really practising magic in any real way. But now, for the first time in my lifetime, there was a demand for cloth mages: all those prisoners across the country weren't going to clothe themselves after all.

I should have been happy to see these young people getting the chance to study magic, but knowing how they'd put their skills to use, I wasn't sure if it was worth it.

"Hello, Ralph," I replied. "What are you doing here?"

"Through the guild, I run a volunteer programme with the UCL. We go to schools and orphanages and teach basic sewing skills to the tykes," Ralph explained. "Figure it will help them later in life. Maybe even some of them might go on to be cloth mages."

"Future gaolers, you mean."

Ralph frowned at me, an almost fatherly reprimand on his face, an unspoken admonishment not to ruin this for the kids, orphans and students alike.

"It sounds like a great programme," I said, trying to shore things up. I smiled at the young people. "Aren't you going to introduce me to your companions?"

The posh girl stepped forwards but Ralph held out an arm. "No. We're on a tight schedule and need to get to it."

He nodded towards the orphanage. I stepped in Ralph's path.

"C'mon, Ralph. Don't give me the cold shoulder—I haven't seen you in ages. How are Janine and the kids?"

Ralph sighed. "They're fine." His mouth was a tight line. Ralph had always been a bit world weary, but I'd never seen him so grim. Things had been a bit tense between us since I'd quit the board of the Cloth Magic Guild—it had been forever since we'd even grabbed a beer together, let alone talked one on one like this.

"Well, that's good," I said carefully.

"Janine's mum might get sent back to Trinidad," he said bitterly. "The new freedom-of-movement bill is just fucking us over."

The freedom-of-movement bill was one of those ironically named laws that actually did the opposite of what it sounded like. Prior to the bill, a Commonwealth citizen from Trinidad, like Ralph's mum-in-law, could come and live and work in England, for example. But the new law restricted such privileges to Canada and Australia.

"Wow. That's awful, mate," I said and felt slightly relieved that Ralph's bad mood wasn't because of me.

"Her mum can't go it alone, not since the heart attack, and if her mum is sent back, Janine might go with her. The kids too."

"And you? Would you go?"

Ralph shrugged. "I don't know. I really don't. I've already put my hat in to run for Labour in the next election, but . . ." He looked away.

"I'm . . . I'm sorry. That sounds really tough," I said.

"It is what it is." Ralph squared his shoulders. "Anyway, I need to focus on what I can do here and now." He eyed my bolt of fabric. "You want to stay here and sew with us? The kids would love it—both the students and the tykes."

I wetted my lips in anticipation of saying yes. I'd hardly seen Ralph in months, and it would be fun to talk with the current crop of cloth magic students. I even liked kids. But I remembered I had an assignment to work on, that Cobalt was slaving away back in my studio. I really should go back there and get to work.

"Sorry, mate. I have work to do. A job from Princess Katherine herself."

Ralph sucked in some air. "I visited Lamb the other day. He said you've fallen in with a bad crowd."

"A bad crowd? I've been hanging out with the top flakes of the upper crust."

"Exactly," Ralph said. "You don't have to read the blind gossip columns to know that Prince Arthur is a bad egg. Be careful, Paul. Before you do anything too dire to get ahead, make sure it's worth it."

My hackles rose at that, partly because I did in fact feel guilty for leaving Ralph and his good works behind so I could party with dukes and dames. "You make it sound like I'd do anything to get ahead. That's not true. I haven't and I won't." Ralph didn't know about the power I had, the deep magic that I had uncovered four years ago. I already knew the lesson Ralph was trying to teach me. I knew that it wasn't worth selling your soul to gain the whole world. "I'll be fine," I said firmly.

"Yeah. You've always been good at looking out for yourself," Ralph said with uncharacteristic meanness. Immediately he looked contrite. "Please give me a ring, sometime, yeah? The kids would love to see you." Ralph had been clearly trying to end this awkward encounter on a happy note, but after he spoke a sad look came over his face, and without another word he turned and walked into the orphanage.

I stood there for a moment, before taking off double time to the bus stop, muttering the whole way about self-righteous busybodies who liked to look down on a man merely for surviving in this crap sack of a world.

Once at the main thoroughfare I remembered the deal I had made with the two lads: I owed them two hot pies. I muttered a curse—I did not want to juggle my fabric and two pies and head back to the orphanage, where I might run into Ralph again. But I owed those tykes. They were skinny little things, as slim as the bread crust they'd been nibbling.

I was right by the tube station, and next to the entrance was a man with a cart full of hot pies. I took out my Book.

"How much for the lot?" I asked the pie slinger. The man blinked at me but eventually quoted me a price that I knew for a fact was inflated. No matter. The princess would reimburse me. I had the man pack up the dozen pies he had left, then hired a cabbie to take them all to the orphanage.

CHAPTER 5

"Oh, Gally! It is simply stupendous!" Kitty twirled around in her new outfit, pirouetting shakily on one foot. The brown pants were a perfect fit and the shirt looked quite fetching as well. She was wearing a type of corset that Cobalt had produced, a device that flattened her chest so the shirt lay flatter on her. The shirt looked like an ordinary white button-up, except for the large rip going up diagonally through the front half. I had repaired it with black thread so that it stood out. The magic gave her a boyish energy—anyone looking at her would see a lad in his mid- to late teens.

"Try on the jacket and cap," I said, holding out the items. Kitty, Cobalt, and I were in the princess's rooms at Buckingham Palace. Now that we knew the clothes fit her, we needed to move on to the next part of the plan: getting her out of the palace.

Kitty put on the jacket as daintily as if she were tugging on a lace shawl. Cobalt and I shared a look. Sure, the magic would make people perceive her as a boy, but her feminine mannerisms might give them pause. Part of me wanted to put off this outing for another night so that Kitty could practise being a little more manly, but when I had put that idea forth Kitty had said that she didn't want to wait, that she wished to go to Soho *tonight*.

"Cobalt, I think it's about time you got ready."

Cobalt gathered up his disguise and went over to the princess's bedroom. When it came to dressing and undressing, Cobalt was a very shy creature, a somewhat odd trait in a cloth mage. During school you usually saw all your classmates naked at one point or another since we often volunteered to be models for each other's projects. But Cobalt always changed in private.

A few minutes later he emerged, an unhappy frown on his face. He was wearing the Princess Katherine disguise we had created. It was a mirror image of one of the princess's dresses, magicked so that Cobalt's voice and general appearance would imitate Kitty's. It wasn't flawless—Cobalt was about an inch shorter than Kitty and the disguise didn't give him any extra height. But from a distance, one would think they were looking at Princess Katherine.

"Oh, Cobalt, you make for a prettier princess than I do," Kitty said. Neither Kitty nor Cobalt looked happy about this fact.

"Here you are, Princess," Cobalt said, holding out his clothes. Kitty took them and skipped off to her bedroom to change, leaving us.

"I still think this is a bad idea," Cobalt said. No matter how many times we did this, it was always odd to hear Cobalt speak with Kitty's voice. He'd covered for the princess in the past when we'd gone on trips around the city—once, when we'd been late getting back, he'd had to sit through dinner with the king, queen, and prince while pretending to be Princess Katherine. He'd just stayed completely silent the whole time. I found it a little bit heartbreaking that her family had hardly noticed the difference.

"You're just jealous that you can't come," I said. "Don't worry. We'll go, have a few drinks, sleep at Andrew's place; then we'll be back here in the morning so you two can swap back. Easy."

The princess emerged from the bedroom wearing Cobalt's clothes. In anticipation for this night, Cobalt had arrived in something that the princess could easily put on: a puffy white shirt, khaki pants, and loafers under a large peacoat. Once we set the pageboy wig on her head and she put on a pair of oversize sunglasses, she looked passably like Cobalt. It was just old-fashioned trickery, no magic. We hadn't gotten around to making a magic outfit that would disguise her the way Cobalt was disguised. As it was, having Kitty wear a wig and Cobalt's clothes worked well enough. Part of me wanted to test out Katherine's new magical outfit, but then I'd have to come up with an explanation of where this strange boy had come from.

"Okay. Ready?" I asked Kitty.

She picked up an overnight bag she had packed. "Yes, Gally."

Cobalt stepped forwards. "Princess, please be safe out there. Don't leave Mr Gallagher's side."

She nodded and smiled, both the wig and glasses threatening to slide off her head.

We went out the door, where a maid was waiting.

"Good evening, sirs," she said.

"Mary, I have no need for your help tonight," Cobalt called from inside the room, his voice identical to Kitty's. "I have already gotten myself ready for bed."

"Yes, miss." The maid looked at us suspiciously. Kitty shrank behind me—a very un-Cobalt-like gesture, but I could understand why she did it. Then the sunglasses fell off her face. Mary stepped forwards to pick them up, her face too close to Kitty's.

I reached out and took Mary's hand, taking the sunglasses from her as I did so.

"Mary, is that an engagement ring on your finger?"

Mary blushed. "It is. My fiancé is a valet here at the palace."

"Well, congratulations to both of you. I suppose I'll have to dream about someone else tonight."

Mary giggled and I was able to usher Kitty down the hallway.

Andrew's home wasn't as ornate as Buckingham Palace but it still had the stately displays of wealth: wooden floors so shiny they could be mirrors, classical statues standing in alcoves. The staff had already gone to bed, and with the master out of town they were a bit relaxed. They knew that I came and went at odd hours and did at least a good surface-level job of staying out of my business.

"C'mon, Cobalt," I said to the princess, in case any of the help was in fact standing around a corner and listening in. We went up to the guest bedroom, which looked out on the street. I made a point of looking out the window while Kitty got changed, staying in the room just in case she needed help.

"Gally, do you ever do anything like this?" Kitty asked me.

"Like what?"

"Dress as a woman, I mean," Kitty said.

"Oh, sure. Not often, but now and then for fun." A handful of times Tonya and I had gone out on the town, her as the man and me as a woman. That seemed like ages ago, when we were still discovering each other. Still enjoyed each other's presence. Were still in love.

Out of the corner of my eye I saw that Kitty was struggling with the buttons on the shirt cuffs. I came over to help her.

"You enjoy dressing like this, like the opposite gender?" Kitty said in surprise. "It seems quite an odd sensation to me. I still feel like myself, but I know the way people are looking at me and . . . it feels wrong."

"I feel a bit similarly when I wear a magic dress," I said. "I know in my heart I'm a man, but no one else is acting that way. It is disconcerting. But that's the great thing about clothes, be they magic or not. If you feel one way in your heart but the world tells you otherwise, you can use clothes to present your true self to the world. There are lots of people out there who know they are a man but the world treats them like they're a woman, or vice versa, or they are something else entirely. Clothes allow them to be seen for who they are."

Kitty nodded.

"You know, there is one thing I really enjoy when I dress up as a woman," I said. "When I'm dressed like one, it's the only time in my life that I'm considered tall."

Kitty laughed. "I see. Well, I fear I am a short boy."

"Short boys are perfectly cute." Perhaps I should have gotten some lifts for her, added an inch to her height. Too late now.

We left the house quietly. Kitty went over to my car but I shook my head.

"We're walking, Princess." The word was out of my mouth before I could check myself. "Oh dear, we're going to need a new name for you, aren't we? I can't exactly call you Princess or Kitty when you're dressed like this."

"Ooh, a boy's name?" Kitty said. "Why not Englebert? I think that is a most distinguished name."

"Perhaps too distinguished," I said. "Let's go with Bert." We started walking through Kensington to Soho, chatting as we went. Kitty began to grow quieter as the posh town houses became brick storefronts, the dim streetlamps giving way to harsh traffic lights. There was a noticeable grimness to this part of town, as if the cloud of petrol exhaust from Piccadilly Circus were just blowing through the crooked streets and back alleys, trapped by the cobbled twists and turns and left to cling to the damp brick walls.

"We can always go back, Princess," I said, forgetting myself. "Sorry, I mean, we can always go back, Bert."

Kitty shook her head. "No, Gally. Let's press on."

Soho was such a clustered rabbit warren of a neighbourhood: the streets were barely wide enough for a Roman chariot, let alone an automobile. We passed several men and each time Kitty would clutch my arm.

"Bert," I said, gently lifting her arm off me. "You can't hold my arm like that. People will get the wrong idea."

"Oh, yes. Of course, Gally." Kitty held her hands in front of her and rocked on her heels.

"And Bert, square your shoulders. Keep your upper arms back, hands at your sides."

Finally we reached my usual haunt, a small pub called Barnaby's. A young lad named Connor was the bouncer. He looked like a James Dean knockoff, with enough Brylcreem in his hair to grease a whale.

"Oy there, Connor," I said. "Room for two?"

Connor was about to let us in when he caught sight of who was with me.

"Nope, nope. No way," he said, pointing at Kitty. I felt Kitty stiffen up, as if Medusa had just looked at her. "I can't let a kid like that in here. He's too young."

Both Kitty and I relaxed.

"Hardly. He's nineteen."

Connor snorted. "Nineteen my arse."

"It's true, swear to Jesus."

"Okay. Let me see his Book."

Kitty and I traded helpless glances. The princess had a Book, but for one as pampered as her it was more of a formality as anything—it wasn't like she ever handled money or used public transportation, the two things that the common folk mostly used their Books for. Her Book was sitting in a safe in Buckingham Palace. Even if we had it, showing it to Connor would reveal her true identity.

I stepped closer to Connor.

"Look, mate, he's a cousin's son, visiting from the country. I'm just trying to show him what life's like in London. It's quite isolating for him, living out in a little spit of a village with no one else . . . well, no one else like him." For good measure I cast a pitying glance at Kitty, who shot us a smile brighter than a sunbeam. I could see Connor was weakening. Under all his Hollywood swagger he was a country boy, and I figured such a story would hit home.

"All right, fine. But keep him close, yeah?" Connor waved Kitty over to the door.

Barnaby's was dark, as it always was. It was a Thursday night and there was a moderate crowd. A large bar took up the middle of the room while smaller booths lined the edges of the space. Kitty was taking it all in, a wide-eyed tourist. I saw two empty barstools at a high table that seated two.

"All right, Bert, you keep our table and I'll go get us some pints."

Kitty carefully climbed up onto the stool, moving as if she had never sat on such a contraption before. I went to the bar and had to wait for the crowd to thin out before I could get to the counter. By the time I returned to the table with two pints of ale, there was a man sitting in my seat. He had his elbows on the table, leaning forwards to leer at Kitty. Kitty meanwhile looked like a cornered cat, her shoulders up around her ears.

"Nice to vada a pretty eek like yours in a place like this. You ever gone cottaging, chicken?"

"I'm sorry, sir, but I don't understand your meaning," Kitty replied primly. I stepped up to the table and set the beer down loudly.

"You're in my seat," I said.

The man looked as though he was about to argue. He had a large frame, ropy arms—perhaps he was an East End dockworker. He took in my well-cut suit and gave Kitty another look. Even though her attire was humble, there was an air to her that suggested she was upper class, a certain removed quality that even her disguise couldn't mask.

"Out on the town with your boy toy, my lord?" he said, getting out of his chair.

"Just having a drink with my friend," I replied. He snorted and moved on.

I took my seat on the stool and watched as Kitty relaxed.

"Are you all right?" I asked.

"Yes," she said. "It was just so strange. I could guess that he was saying something lewd, but for the life of me I could only understand every other word he said. Was he speaking Welsh?"

I laughed. "No. He was speaking Polari. It's a dialect used by gay men to keep their dealings secret. Especially circumspect when the law is out to get you."

"Oh my," Kitty said. "I didn't know the situation was that dire, that it warranted a whole secret language." She sipped her beer, frowned, and put the glass down like it was a letter delivering bad news. "Well. I suppose I've learned one new thing already. I've also confirmed something: I don't appreciate men soliciting me, regardless of whether they think I am male or female."

"Well, here's to learning new things and confirming long-held suspicions." I lifted my glass and we clanked them together. We chatted for a while, me drinking my beer while Kitty sipped hers. No one else came to hit on her (or me, for that matter), and I was starting to think that maybe this wasn't such a bad idea after all.

Then Connor came in. He strode towards us, while at the same time giving a signal to the bartender. The bartender quickly started taking money out of the till and hiding it under the floorboards behind the bar, stashing the illegal cache of coins and bills out of sight.

"Connor? What's going on, mate?" I asked.

Connor jutted his chin over towards the gents'. "Toilets, now, both of you."

Kitty looked at me questioningly, but I trusted Connor and heard the urgency in his words. I slid off my seat and Kitty followed my lead.

Connor led us to the toilets. Once we were inside he locked the door.

"The law is cracking down on Soho tonight," Connor said. "They're on their way here now, will be breaking the door down in minutes. It will be bad for all of us if this kid is caught here, so you two need to get gone." He opened a small rectangular window up near the ceiling at the back of the room.

"Shit," I muttered.

"I'm sorry, what exactly is happening?" Kitty asked.

"The police are raiding the gay bars," I said.

"C'mon. There's a skip on the other side; it's not a far drop." Connor squatted down and held his hands out, waiting to give us a leg up out the window. Kitty didn't move.

"What will happen to all the men back in there?" she asked.

"They'll probably be arrested on some trumped-up charges," I said, too agitated to try and sugarcoat it. Kitty tensed even further.

"Then I should put a stop to it," she said. "I'll just tell them who I am and order them to stand down."

Connor looked at her in puzzlement, probably wondering why this kid thought he could order the London Metropolitan Police around.

"Bert's a wee bit touched in the head. Doesn't know what he's saying half the time," I said by way of explanation. I turned to "Bert." "We really need to go." If Kitty revealed herself, both she and I would be in a world of hurt.

Before we could argue further there was a loud bang as the front door of Barnaby's was kicked open. Yells and screams, both authoritative commands and ones of surprise, followed. The sound of fighting erupted, pint glasses shattering against the wall, batons landing on limbs.

"C'mon!" Connor hissed.

"Kitty, you go first."

Kitty had gone horribly pale. She stood frozen in place, and I could see in her eyes that she was still weighing whether she should go confront the cops. That's when a copper kicked in the bathroom door, the flimsy sliding lock breaking free of the doorframe.

"Kitty!" I cried, rushing forwards. The cop grabbed her arm and she cried out, trying to pull away. With his other hand the cop brought his club down on her side. She screamed and then she was in my arms as the cop let go of her. The cop raised the club for another blow and I braced for it to come down on my head. But Connor was faster. He launched his fist into the cop's face, sending him staggering back, waving his club in the air like a weather vane.

"C'mon!" Connor said, grabbing both me and Kitty. He dragged us to the back wall. Kitty was whimpering and holding her side, but this time when Connor held out his hands to hoist her up she stepped into them. With surprising ease he lifted her so she could climb out the window.

"Once you're in the alley head left," Connor said to me. "First door you see on the right, knock three times. They'll let you through."

Then it was my turn to be lifted up by Connor. It was like moving between worlds, the brightly lit bathroom of Barnaby's into the smoky, neon-washed alleyway. I landed on the lid of the skip. Kitty was there, shivering as she held her side. I took her hand. We hit the ground running, heading left. Even from there we could still hear the sound of Connor being beaten in the bathroom.

CHAPTER 6

At the end of the alley I could see some cops milling about. Luckily they didn't see us and we reached the door Connor had spoken of. I rapped on it three times. It swiftly opened and we were ushered into the kitchen of a Chinese restaurant. The chef, an older Asian man with a stern face, gestured towards the restaurant's dining room. I took Kitty's hand and exited the kitchen, walking past confused diners wondering why two white dandies had just left the kitchen of a Chinese restaurant.

Once we were on the street I let out a sigh of relief. It was a busy main road, and there were lots of people just walking along without a care in the world. You'd never know that just a block away a police raid was being carried out.

"Oh, Mr Gallagher." Kitty always sounded so much younger when she called me by my last name. She grabbed hold of my arm and started crying, hunched over as if trying to curl into a foetal position while still standing up.

"Kitty, it's all right. We're all right." A few cars chugged by, the scent of petrol making my eyes sting. "We're safe now."

She nodded but I saw how her other hand went to her ribs, the same side the copper had whaled on.

"Are you hurt?" I said, panic creeping into my voice.

"It does smart quite a bit," Kitty said, trying to put on a brave smile through her tears.

"I'll flag us a cab." I held my free arm out. A black cab pulled over and I gave Andrew's address. Kitty stayed grimly silent the whole ride, eyes fixed on the back of the driver's seat. When we arrived I used my Book to pay, only afterwards wondering if I had made a blunder in doing so. All taxi drivers logged their rides in their Books—would it come back to haunt me that I, Paul Gallagher, had taken a cab from Soho to Andrew's house?

I helped Kitty up the stairs into the guest bedroom. The princess whimpered with every step, and my heart clenched each time. Eventually we reached a plush, high-backed chair in the bedroom for her to sit in.

"Where does it hurt, Princess?" I asked.

"M-my side."

"I'm going to take off your clothes now, all right?"

Kitty smiled. "I was warned you'd make a move on me sooner or later."

Quickly but carefully I unbuckled her suspenders and unbuttoned her shirt. On her right ribs, just below the strange corset she was wearing, I could see some discolouration, the forewarning of a massive bruise to come.

"The binding on my chest . . . it hurts," Kitty said. "Please help me take it off."

It was an awkward dance but we managed it, and I looked away to help preserve the princess's dignity. Once it was down she sat on the bed and buttoned up the top buttons on the shirt to protect her modesty.

"It still hurts so much," she said. I knelt down at her side.

"I need to put my hands upon you, all right? I'll roll up the shirt just so I can see your side." Once she nodded I did so, feeling the bone. She yelled out and I wondered if it would rouse Andrew's housekeeper—then again, even if it did, the servants in this house would probably err on the side of discretion. I closed my eyes and listened to Kitty's pained breathing. When I'd researched innate magic, one text had outlined a technique of matching another person's breathing. Once you did it long enough, you'd be able to sense if any bones were broken by becoming attuned to how their energy flowed through them. I could see it clearly, like a light in the darkness: the flow of magical energy through the princess was the same as always. Everything was connected, the circuit intact.

"All right, the good news is your ribs aren't broken," I said. "Maybe a slight crack, but as long as you don't jostle them, it won't get worse."

I sat down next to her, the slight dip of the mattress making her wince. I resolved to be more careful.

"I must apologize, Gally, for putting you in danger," Kitty said.

"No, no, Princess, it was my carelessness that—"

"I just—I desire so greatly to go out in the world," Kitty said. "In particular, I thought that by going to such an establishment, I might meet other women."

I tried not to laugh at that. "Princess, you thought you could meet women at a gay bar?"

Kitty could sense my unspoken laughter. She pouted. "Well, I thought there might be *some*. Some like me."

"Like you . . . ?"

She wouldn't meet my eyes. Suddenly I thought of all the times she had shied away from men, how fortunate I felt that the princess seemingly was okay with me being close to her. I had written off her aversion to men as teenage skittishness, a shyness that came from her sheltered upbringing. But now I saw there was more to it than that.

"Princess Katherine," I said. "Have you ever felt attracted to men at all?"

She shook her head, cheeks turning bright red. I thought of Andrew, the friend I had set her up with.

"Does Lord Fife know?"

"We've never talked of it plainly, but I think he has figured it out for himself," Kitty said. "He's very much a gentleman, and I know as far as men go he is considered quite good looking, or so I'm told." Her gaze shot up to me. "Oh! But I am grateful to you, Gally, for setting the two of us up. I always knew I'd have to marry *someone*, and Andrew will be a great partner, I know. He is very kind and considerate and not overbearing. And I think it is a smart match, seeing as we are both inverts."

"What?" I was doubly thrown, both by the rather clinical term *inverts* to refer to gay people and by her implication that Andrew was one. "Andrew's gay?"

Kitty looked at me, head cocked. "Didn't you know, Gally? Haven't you two been close friends for years?"

Well, yes, that was true, but I still had trouble conceiving of Andrew as a sexual being. He always changed the subject when talk of dating came up and had never had any serious relationships before becoming engaged to Kitty. The only time I had known him to step out with someone was during our first year of cloth magic, when he and Gabs had been together. That had only lasted a couple of months though.

"Oh dear. Maybe he didn't want you to know," Kitty said anxiously. "Please don't let on that I mentioned it to you, Gally. Oh, I am just the worst at keeping secrets. Please don't say anything! I'd hate for him to think I betrayed his confidence."

"Of course, I won't breathe a word," I said, still somewhat distracted. The princess shifted in her seat and gave a little whimper, bringing me back to the present. I got off the edge of the bed to kneel on the floor next to her, covering her hands with my own.

"I'm so sorry, Kitty. I know it hurts. Years ago I had my ribs busted up. It's a real motherfu—it's quite a painful experience."

"Yes," Kitty agreed. Tears started to well in her eyes. "But I suppose we got off easy. What became of the men in the bar? Do you think Connor is all right?"

I thought of Connor cornered in the bathroom as the cops piled in. I doubt he would have let them arrest him without a fight—he'd be lucky if he only ended up with a couple of broken ribs. "I'm sure he's fine. Probably cooling his heels in a gaol cell right now."

"Will they charge them all?" Kitty asked. "Will they all end up in prison? I should have done something . . ."

"No, you would have just gotten even more banged up, maybe even murdered. It's a dangerous world, Princess. I shouldn't have brought you out into it." What if Kitty had taken a blow to the head and been killed? How would I ever explain to her parents—*the king and queen of this country*—that my actions had led to her death? And if something happened to Kitty, what would become of me? She was my patron, one of the few bridges I hadn't burned. And how would I live with myself, knowing that I hadn't been able to keep this sweet kid from harm?

Kitty was crying once more.

"Oh, Gally, I feel so *ashamed.* Back in the gentlemen's toilets, I made myself sound so grand, spoke of how I'd march out and order the police to stop."

"Kitty—"

"And in the moment, I meant it. I was so sure of myself, so secure in the knowledge that I could save us all if I just stood out in the open and asserted myself. But then, as soon as that baton hit—no, even before that, as soon as the bathroom door was kicked open—all my bravado fled. I no longer thought of anyone but myself, thought only of my own survival. And I ran, leaving all those people behind."

I let Kitty cry for a bit, a comforting hand on her knee as the tears rolled down her cheeks.

"Kitty, you're very important to me, and to this nation," I said, still holding her hands. "You don't have to apologize for anything. I'm the one at fault here. You could have died tonight because of me. I'd never be able to live with myself if anything happened to you."

"Oh, Gally. I'm all right. It's like you said: it's just a crack—"

"Tonight, yes, but what if something else were to happen?" It was a fear I could empathize with—ever since innate magic had been practised upon me as a child, I'd been at the mercy of others, unable to fight back thanks to the conditions of the spell. I knew what it was like to live afraid and powerless. I didn't want that for Kitty. "Princess, let me protect you."

Kitty looked at me with curiosity. I'd always been a good friend, but I'd never really been much of a bodyguard in the physical sense. "Protect me how?"

"I have knowledge of a type of magic that is illegal in this country," I explained. "Innate magic. It's a type of magic that means breaking bones to redirect the magical energy within you. I can break a bone of yours and make it so that no man on God's earth will be able to hurt you ever again."

Kitty looked at me wide eyed.

"You could do that?" she said. "Could you protect me from anyone? Even my own brother?"

"Hell, even the king himself," I said. "But you must want it, Princess, for the magic to work. And since it's illegal, you could never speak of it to anyone."

Kitty took a deep breath and then winced, holding her side. I saw her mentally debating it.

"If we do this, you'll be nigh on invincible," I said. "And so next time you're in a bad spot, where you know you could help people, you won't be scared."

That seemed to resolve the debate. She nodded, face resolute.

"Yes," she said. "Yes, I wish to have it done."

"All right," I said, relieved. Once she had innate magic cast upon her, Kitty would be safe, even if I wasn't there to look after her. "Luckily for us, your rib is already cracked. So it won't take much to break it all the way."

Kitty did not seem happy about this bit of good news, but even as her face paled she did not back down.

I started carefully feeling her ribs, sensing the flow of magical energy like feeling for currents in the stream. "Don't worry. This is a delicate operation, but I know what I'm doing." She didn't need to know that I was largely self-taught. "I know this isn't comfortable, but can you put your hands behind your head, elbows wide?"

She hesitated for a second, then did so.

"Good. Now, I need you to picture something that for you is a symbol of strength. You don't have to tell me, but please keep it foremost in your mind, all right?"

She nodded. Her breathing skipped a beat as I pressed her side.

"Tell me where the pain is worst."

"There!" she gasped out.

"Just keep breathing," I instructed, then drew my hand back and delivered a palm blow to her side. Both Kitty and I were startled when I made contact—her because of the pain, me because I still wasn't used to being able to physically hurt people. It was a strange loophole in the spell upon me, that I could still harm people if it was while performing a spell. The only time I could hurt someone was while doing innate magic.

The hit wasn't as hard a blow as the wallop the copper had landed on her earlier, but Kitty still cried out. She lurched forwards to her knees and I managed to catch her. She was shaking, no longer yelling, but a low keening came out of her mouth.

"I feel . . . strange," she managed, then vomited on the carpet. She sat there for a moment, one arm around my neck, the other on the ground to steady herself, still huffing, her shoulders shaking.

"Come now, Kitty. Lie down. I'll take Andrew's bed."

She said nothing as I helped her under the covers.

"I feel strange," she said again.

"It's an odd feeling, for sure. But if you just rest, you'll feel better in the morning," I said. "If you wake up early, we can grab some breakfast here before going back to the palace."

That at least got a half smile from her. "Oh, Gally. Always thinking about food." She turned onto her uninjured side, hand cautiously feeling where the break in the rib was. "Can I take something for this? Or does that ruin the magic?"

"Oh, no. I'll go get you something." I grabbed some pain meds from the bathroom and returned with them and a glass of water. Kitty thanked me and bade me good night.

I hoped the pills would help and let Kitty catch some rest. As for myself, I was way too keyed up to sleep. In the living room Andrew had a piano. I wished I could play some tunes to help me relax, but as it was the middle of the night that seemed like a bad idea. I grabbed a book off the shelf at random and tried to read it, trying not to think about Connor's yells as we'd left him.

CHAPTER 7

I was nodding off when there was a heavy knock on the door. I got up to answer it before surprise could give way to worry. It was 1:00 a.m.

Standing at the entrance was Van Holt, along with a couple of palace guards.

"Good evening, Mr Gallagher," Van Holt said, in his usual just-above-a-whisper voice. "I'm here to collect the princess."

"I . . . I don't know what you mean," I said, using my sleepiness to make my confusion seem genuine. Van Holt gave me a patronizing look.

"We want to do this quietly," he said. "Which means, ma'am, no prattling about this to the neighbours. Or the papers, for that matter." The last part wasn't directed at me but at Susan, Andrew's housekeeper, who had finally been raised from her bed by all the commotion and had come to stand next to me.

"Of course, sir," Susan replied. "I would always keep mum about what goes on in my mistress's house."

Interesting that Susan specified that her allegiance was to Lady Fife rather than her son. Even though the woman's power had waned in the past few years, it seemed her servants still stayed loyal.

Van Holt nodded. "Good. Mr Gallagher, please bring us to the princess."

There didn't seem to be much point in protesting, so even as I wondered how they'd known where to find us (or even that the princess was missing), I led the way up the stairs, Van Holt and Susan following behind me. When I opened the door Susan gasped at the sight of vomit on the rug. Van Holt strode over to Kitty's side.

"Princess?" he said softly.

She groaned in response but did not open her eyes. He looked over sharply at me.

"What happened to her?"

I was at a loss for what to say, so I kept quiet. Van Holt straightened back up and tapped the edge of his goatee thoughtfully.

"I heard the raid on Soho got a bit heated," he said. "Was the princess caught in the cross fire?"

"The raid?" How did Van Holt know about that?

"Yes. When we learned that the princess was deep in a den of degenerates, of course we had to send the police in to retrieve her," Van Holt said.

"You sent the police into that bar?!" I said. "What did you think would happen?!"

"I could ask you the same thing." Van Holt seemed to be enjoying himself. "Bringing the young princess to a place like that—really, Mr Gallagher, your bad judgement knows no bounds."

"She has a fever," Susan said, a hand softly on the princess's forehead.

"I think her rib was broken by a police baton," I offered, trying to lay the groundwork to cover my tracks.

"We need to get her to the palace, quietly," Van Holt said. "Princess Katherine, can you please wake up?"

She opened her eyes with difficulty, as if there were some kind of sap keeping her eyelids shut.

"Court Magician Van Holt," she muttered. "Did you know that the human body has as much salt as the ocean? Proportionally, I mean. Mr Gallagher told me that."

"I did not know that," Van Holt replied, with the air of one used to humouring royals. "Can you walk? We're taking you home."

She was able to swing her legs over the side of the bed. Susan left and returned with a wet cloth, which she used to wipe Kitty's face. Kitty wobbled as she got to her feet, and I rushed forward to support her. The two of us then lumbered down the stairs, Susan following closely behind, Van Holt at the rear.

There was a driver waiting with the car. Susan and I helped Kitty into the back seat.

"You should probably sit next to her, Mr Gallagher," Van Holt said. I stared at him.

"You want *me* to come with you?"

"Oh yes. The king wishes to speak with you." His tone was neutral but his smile held a hint of glee.

Once again, no point in arguing. I got into the back seat and then found to my displeasure Van Holt sliding in next to me. The palace guards got into the driver and passenger seats and we were off, Susan watching us go with a worried expression.

Kitty was soon snoring on my shoulder, which I supposed was better than being awake and in pain. Van Holt sat next to me, looking out the window.

"I think your nine lives may be up, Gallagher," he said.

"What exactly is your problem, Van Holt?" I said angrily but in a hushed voice so I didn't wake the princess. "You're the fucking Court Magician! You've got it made, so why do you always have it out for me?"

"I wonder," Van Holt said, as if it were a puzzle to him as well. "On some level, I'm actually quite impressed with how well you've managed to do for yourself. You even got on the list of candidates for Court Magician. Number fourteen, wasn't it? You were ahead of me! I was lucky to get in at number twenty-five."

To become the next Court Magician of this country meant undergoing a ritual at the hands of the current Court Magician, who would break certain bones in order to change one from a regular old mage into someone who could do innate magic. But the ritual was a dangerous one, and most of the young men who took part died horribly. Back in 1954, twenty-four young men had died before the magic had taken with Van Holt. If I'd stayed on the list, I would have just been one more corpse paving the path. Or maybe the magic would have taken with me. I'd never know.

Before Van Holt, the previous Court Magician had been a man named Redfield. Redfield had been the Court Magician all my life, but in 1956, just two years after making Van Holt his successor, Redfield had died unexpectedly from a brain aneurysm, God rest his soul. Van Holt's ascendancy to current Court Magician had been somewhat controversial—usually one spent at least a decade learning under the country's current mage maker before taking on the mantle. Plus, a lot of folks took issue with a so-called foreigner having such a top role—never mind that he was a British citizen thanks to his mother, that he'd lived in this country since he was thirteen, or that lots of Brits started out life far from the British Isles. Because he couldn't shake his accent, in certain circles he'd always be the "Boer mage."

"Do you ever think about what life would be like if you hadn't given up your spot on the list?" said Van Holt, thoughtful inflection suggesting *he* had given it some thought.

"Well, sure. I'd either be dead or I'd be doing your job right now," I said.

"*You* sent the police into the bar?"

Both Van Holt and I looked over at the princess. Her eyes were open, and with a wince she sat up straight, looking past me to Van Holt.

"Yes, Princess. I did it to get you out of that lawless place," Van Holt said. "Who knows what harm might have befallen you if we hadn't stepped in?"

"And yet, you caused lots of harm tonight, not only to me but to the dozens of men in that bar."

"It is indeed regrettable that you were injured, Princess," Van Holt said. "But I did what needed to be done. For your sake."

"So those men were beaten and their lives possibly ruined for *my* sake?"

"Princess Katherine," I said, not wanting to help Van Holt but not wanting Kitty to blame herself either. "That bar is no stranger to raids. If Van Holt here hadn't called one in, it may have happened anyway."

Kitty's hands clenched into fists. "That's the problem, isn't it?"

We arrived at Buckingham Palace. Some more guards came over to assist Kitty, though she was able to take shambling steps under her own power.

"Mr Gallagher, please come with me," one of the guards said. Van Holt gave a small wave as we walked away.

The guard deposited me in an office. It was well furnished but relatively small for a royal palace. One wall was floor-to-ceiling books. There was a large wooden desk with a plush chair behind it, several small chairs on the other side. One window gave a view of the palace grounds, the city skyline a mere suggestion in the darkness. We were about three storeys up. Idly I wondered if I would survive the fall.

The door opened. I saw King Harold.

"Please, sit," he said. I did so, taking my seat before my legs gave out. King Harold was in his early fifties, a round face, thin white hair, clean shaven. In many ways he was the type of older man I fell for, an emotionally distant authority figure. But my more superficial preferences kept me from forming a crush on him: I liked my guys taller.

The king took his seat behind the desk. He did not look like a man who'd been roused from bed. Maybe he'd just been up all night, or maybe he was so used to getting dressed and trotted out for all manner of things that he was just well practised at being unruffled.

"Would you like some scotch?" he said. I nodded. He opened a cupboard near the bottom of the bookshelf and poured us each a couple of fingers. Knocking it back did help steady my nerves somewhat, but I couldn't meet King Harold's eyes. I wasn't a father, but I'd like to have kids someday. If some man had taken my daughter out and brought her home with a broken bone, I wasn't sure what I would do. And I was just a man—what if I had the power of a *king*?

"You know, I'm not one to court controversy," King Harold said, swishing the drink around in his glass. "I was warned about you. That it was only a matter of time before you did something that would drag the royal family through the mud. But when Kitty asked if she could hire you to be her own dress mage . . . well, Kitty has never been one to ask much of myself or her mother. She's a good child. She has had a hard go of it. I know that may sound preposterous to one of a low birth such as yourself, Mr Gallagher. I know you have worked hard to gain the social capital that you do have, and it is hard to imagine a royal struggling in any way at all. But the princess has had a hard road. She was born marred into a family that by its very nature is public facing. She was never very good at making friends with the other girls, nor ever deft at handling boys. As she went through her teen years, I feared I would never truly see her smile again. And then you befriended her. And somehow you managed to make her happy, even found a fiancé that was a good match. So when she asked to hire you on . . . I am still a father, you understand, weak when his daughter smiles so hopefully at him." He finally sipped his scotch. "A gay bar, Mr Gallagher? Really?"

"It—" It felt wrong to say it was Kitty's idea. I'd already endangered the girl enough tonight.

"Going skating or to the museums is one thing," King Harold mused. That made me sit up straight. "Oh yes, both myself and the queen knew about that. We figured it was fine. I was somewhat happy to see some pep in the girl. But going to a place full of moral degenerates . . . that's a bridge too far, sir."

I stared down at my empty glass. I'd always been attracted to men and women, and it had only felt like an anomaly to me when others acted like it was. I never felt like there was something wrong with me.

"You'll understand that we want to keep this quiet," King Harold said. "Which is why I expect your silence as part of the severance pay you will receive."

"Severance pay?" I said.

"Yes. You can't very well keep working for the royal family after such a fiasco," King Harold replied. "And do not think about going to the papers with this story, or to your gossipmonger ex. You might earn a payday for your betrayal, but I think you'll find that such indiscretion will cost you very dearly."

The king sighed and got to his feet.

"Can I see Kitty one more time?" I wanted to make sure she was okay, that the innate magic had in fact taken.

"No. A guard will escort you home." The king rapped on the door and a guard opened it. As I got up and moved towards the door I felt like all my limbs were asleep, like I barely had control over them. I was miles away. My association with the princess was my one last claim to respectability, not to mention a steady pay cheque. Without her, I was nothing, just another useless cloth mage. I'd be unable to pay the rent on Mrs Spratt's cottage. What could I do? The old refrain sounded in my head: *Return to Liverpool in disgrace*. The only things there for me were my brothers, who I didn't even get on with, and my dad, nearly comatose after his second stroke. Maybe I could move in with him, look after him in his old age as penance for the mess I'd made of my own life. I could make clothes for the well-to-do of Liverpool, the descendants of slave traders who had laundered their money in the public coffers by building schools and galleries. Maybe I'd meet someone new, someone who didn't know about my past or who did but didn't mind the fact that I was a bit of a clipped coin.

As I dwelled on these thoughts it occurred to me that the young guard and I had been walking for a while. We went down some stairs and into a courtyard.

"This isn't the way to the garage." I had assumed the guard or some valet was going to drive me home. Instead we were heading to the royal stables. The guard led me to an old carriage house nearby.

My shoulders went up around my ears. It was about 3:00 a.m. and the only light came from a few palace windows. What if the palace guards were looking to rough me up in retaliation for getting the princess injured?

I took a step back but the guard grabbed my arm, pulling me into the carriage house. He hastily shut the door. There was a string of electric lights overhead, illuminating the collection of horse-drawn carriages.

Nearby was an open black buggy. Sitting in it was Prince Arthur.

CHAPTER 8

"Ah, Gally," he said jauntily. He was wearing a long coat over his pyjamas, slippers on his feet. But despite his sleepwear he seemed alert and awake, his hair brushed. He smiled at me. "You look like death warmed over."

I peered around, as if I'd see some clue or hint as to why the prince had brought me there. I saw nothing but rows of carriages.

"You're supposed to say, *Yes, Your Highness, I do look like death warmed over,*" Arthur said. "Never mind. Matt"—this was directed to the palace guard who had brought me there—"go guard the door. Don't let a soul in or out." Matt did so. Once the door closed quietly behind him Arthur patted the carriage seat. "Don't just stand there, Gally. Come sit with me."

Curious, I climbed up into the carriage and sat next to the prince.

"I heard you were just sacked," Arthur said.

"Word travels fast."

"Well, I've been up all night worried about my dear little sister," Arthur said dryly. "So I'd been eagerly waiting for updates when I heard you'd gotten the boot. My sympathies. I'm sure that's a bloody rotten experience. Not that I would know. I've never been sacked."

"You've never had a job either," I said.

Arthur looked at me. "Pretty brassy, talking to me like that."

"I figure I can say what I like at this point." The adrenaline was once more wearing off. I wanted to be out of the city, asleep in my bed in my little cottage.

"A man with nothing to lose, hmm? Again, not an experience I can directly identify with," Arthur said. "I've always had so much weighing upon my shoulders. Preparing to ascend to the throne once my father passes, representing the country in the meantime, looking after my young sister. Now I have one more worry." A hint of hesitation cropped up before he spoke again. "Sabina's gone missing."

"Princess Sabina?" I said.

Arthur nodded. "After her birthday party, we had an argument. She left and hasn't been seen since."

Sabina's birthday had been a week ago. Though I didn't much like her, that was still worrying. She didn't seem like the type to lie low. "What did you two argue about?"

"None of your fucking business," Arthur snarled in my face and for a moment I worried he was about to push me out of the carriage. He took a deep breath and drew back.

"It was something we'd argued about in the past," he said cagily. "But this time Sabina decided to disappear in order to make her point. I wish for you to find her."

"Me?" It sounded like a thankless job: find a woman who didn't wish to be found, for a man who had been practically bred to be an ungrateful shit. "Prince Arthur, surely there are others better suited for this task."

"Oh yes. I had some of the palace guards try and track her down, but as soon as they leave the castle grounds, they're useless. No street smarts." Prince Arthur nudged me in the ribs a little too hard. "But I know that's not the case with you. And you are quite the ladies' man, Mr Gallagher. I'm sure you can get on that confounding female wavelength and figure out where Sabina has squirreled herself away."

"What about Court Magician Van Holt? Shouldn't he be the one doing this?"

Arthur winced. "I went to him, and that was a big blunder on my part. Now my father knows all about my business. It's a catastrophe, truly. Plus . . . Van Holt is in deep with that Virtuis lot."

"What?" I said in surprise. "You sure about that?" One of the big tenets of the Virtuis Party was severely limiting immigration, and Van Holt was an immigrant. Plus, the position of Court Magician was supposed to be apolitical, the Court Magician's chief concern being the royal family, not politics.

Arthur shrugged. "I don't know how he justifies it, but he is. He is hand in glove with those racist fuckers." It was odd agreeing with Arthur on something, but it was also reassuring to know that even he had standards. "And no one in the Virtuis Party likes the idea of me and Sabina together." Arthur perked up. "So I need the aid of one like you, Mr Gallagher. Someone no one will suspect of helping me. It's well known that there's no love lost between us."

"Is that so?"

"Oh, yes," the prince replied cheerfully. "Everyone knows that I hate your extravagant suits, how your stupid Scouser accent makes your speech sound like a cow trying to talk around its own cud, how you fawn over my stupid git of a sister—"

"And they also know, then, that I think you're a puffed-up blowfish?" I replied.

"Yes, exactly," Prince Arthur said. "So no one will suspect that you are in my employ. Sabina won't be on the watch for you. You'll be able to get close to her without tipping her off that I am on her trail."

"Prince Arthur, why should I help you? And don't say it's my duty to follow a royal directive because I don't really care, especially if the royal in question is you."

"Help me because I can make it worth your while," Arthur said, then winced. "*Ugh*, listen to me, bartering like a Covent Garden hawker."

"Make it worth my while *how*?"

"Well, with money, of course!" Arthur said. "I have a sizeable allowance that I can use to pay you for your services. And if you do this thing for me, I could even see about keeping you on a retainer. A monthly payment for just an odd job here or there."

I suddenly recalled a night nearly four years ago when Welcome Wheelock, a notorious East End thug, had tried to buy Thomas and me. His pitch had been similar—steady money for just the occasional distasteful act. Back then I had stayed strong and refused to take him up on the offer. But now I didn't feel so sure.

"Look, what else do you want?" Arthur asked, exasperated. "Do you have any other friends in prison you want out? Is that it?"

"I'll take the money," I said slowly. "Just a onetime payment will do. Let's say two hundred pounds."

"Yes, yes, all right," he said quickly.

"And we can talk about long-term employment later," I said. "But there is something I want from you, as part of my payment."

"Well, get on with it, man!"

"I want you to be nicer to Kitty," I said. "Stop saying cruel crap to her. Leave her alone if you can't do better, but don't hassle her anymore."

Arthur looked indignant, like he wanted to argue against it, but he shut his gob and nodded.

"Fine. Break a bone, make a promise, I will be pleasant to Kitty from here on out," he said. "And I'll pay you once you find Sabina. Deal?"

"Deal." We shook on it. Arthur quickly withdrew his hand and jumped down to the ground. I followed after him, taking my time to climb down since I wasn't as practised at getting in and out of carriages.

"Oh yes, one more thing," Arthur said. "Hopefully no one saw us meet in here, but, well, the walls have ears, they say, and that's doubly true in palaces. So if anyone asks, we met here so I could teach you a lesson about endangering my sister."

He punched me in the eye. It wasn't a hard blow but it was quick and I backed into the side of the carriage from the force.

"There. That's done," Arthur said before leaving the carriage house.

CHAPTER 9

A member of the palace guard drove me back to Andrew's house. I didn't feel like going in, so instead I hopped in my car and drove out to Hillcrest, traffic crawling into the city as the sun came up and the day began.

I collapsed in bed and slept for a couple of hours. When I woke I felt so confused—I'd had a dream that Kitty and I had gone to Soho and gotten swept up in a raid, and then the prince had asked for my help finding his missing lady friend. As I woke up horror swept over me when I realized it wasn't a dream at all.

I had no leads regarding Sabina, but Arthur's words about friends in prison came drifting back to me.

If I had to list all my friends and then put them in order of moral rectitude, I would have placed Christopher Lamb quite low on the list. He was a gifted cloth mage and under his guidance a decade's worth of mages had graduated from the UCL. But it was also a well-known fact that he slept with a different male student each year. I'd felt so special when he'd grown interested in *me*—I'd known his reputation, but I had thought it was different with us. I winced whenever I thought about what an idiot I'd been, for falling so hard and getting so hurt. Now, as an adult, I knew better than to strive for Lamb's attention and approval.

Last year a government official from the Department of Magic Regulation had told Lamb to focus on teaching protective magic. They'd wanted him to prime his students to work in the prisons across the country, to learn that one skill to the exclusion of all others. Lamb had refused, which had led to him getting fired from the college and then arrested. He'd spent three months in prison before I'd been able to get him out. I wasn't sure if he was still the best source for gossip in the city, but he was the best lead I had.

"Paul," Lamb said when he answered the door to his flat in Harrow. He was bundled up like a babushka, a handkerchief covering his hair and tied under his chin.

"I know, I know, I'm dressed like an old washerwoman," Lamb said as he shambled back to the couch. "Lately I find I can never feel warm. A scarf on my head helps, and feels better than a hat."

This was a common ailment amongst people who'd spent time in a cloth magic prison—wearing magical cloth for so long seemed to sap something essential out of them, like the ability to retain heat. Despite it being the early afternoon, flames roared in the fireplace. Sketches and notes were burning up in the flames. Piles of papers sat in stacks around the room, making the place look like a model city.

I started to tell Lamb that I could make him a magic coat that would keep him warm, but I stopped. It would be easy to do, but the toll it would take on Lamb's energy levels would make the whole thing pointless. After being forced to wear magic cloth for such a stretch, he'd only be hurt by the stuff now.

"I bumped into Alberto on the stairs." Alberto was Lamb's live-in partner, someone age appropriate for once. He was the same age as Lamb, a tailor rather than a cloth mage. I gathered the two of them went way back and had reconnected after Lamb's arrest. "He said you're moving?" The flat was small, with a kitchen alcove next to the living room, a bedroom, and a toilet. Alberto's and Lamb's belongings were everywhere, making it seem even more cluttered than usual.

"Yes. To Italy," Lamb said.

"What?!" I'd been expecting to hear that they were moving to some other borough of London, or maybe to somewhere by the seaside like Brighton. "Italy? *Why?*"

Lamb chuckled. "You really have to ask? I won't survive if I have to do another stint in prison."

"But . . . but I fixed things. I got you out of there." I had a whole mess of feelings about Lamb—he'd been my first great love, a man who'd broken my heart and taught me many things about adulthood, both good and bad. He was someone I still grudgingly went to for help and advice, today being the case in point. Every interaction between Lamb and me was a fraught give-and-take, but I wasn't sure what I'd do without him. "Are you seriously moving to Italy? Not just for a holiday?"

"Yes, not just for a holiday," Lamb said. "This country hasn't been safe for me since my arrest. I'm tired. I just want to rest my old bones somewhere sunny."

"You're not that old," I said. "You're only forty-two."

Lamb smiled. "How kind of you to keep track."

"Were you really going to leave without saying goodbye?"

"I don't know. I figured it might be better for everyone that way, both emotionally and, well, legally. But you came here for a specific purpose, didn't you, Paul, hmm? What can I do for you?"

I felt like a heel asking for Lamb's help while he was going through so much. Being in prison had aged him, made him seem shrunken and weak. He still had that same blasé, nonchalant air, humming quietly as he waited for me to speak, looking through the pile of dress shirts and holding them up to the light like each one was the Turin Shroud, deciding which ones to keep and which to toss. But his easygoing affect didn't quite seem as effortless as it had prior to his arrest.

"It's about Princess Sabina," I said.

"Ah. The prince's secret lady friend."

"Have you heard anything on the wind about her? Aside from her not-so-secret relationship with the prince, I mean," I said.

Lamb leaned back into the couch and closed his eyes. "Only that she's gone missing for about a week now."

"Have you heard any rumours of where she may have gone?"

"No. I don't have many friends in common with Princess Sabina, and no one's told me anything. I'm sorry, Paul," Lamb said.

"'S all right." I was sitting half-perched on the arm of the couch, but mentally I was pacing, tearing at my hair. If Lamb, gossipmonger extraordinaire, didn't know anything, where else could I turn?

"I hope you do find Sabina and that she and the prince patch things up," Lamb said. "I think she'd make a good queen."

"Are you kidding? She's snooty, snobby, haughty, cold."

"Exactly," Lamb said. "The royal family should be removed from us common folk."

"I don't agree with that." I thought of Kitty and her eagerness to know what daily life was like for her subjects. My heart twinged—I missed her already. Usually right now I'd be at the palace, going over sketches with her or just chatting.

"How is Princess Katherine, by the way?" Lamb asked, reading my mind.

"You haven't heard?" I said.

"I've been away from social circles quite a bit, so I'm behind the times."

I ended up telling Lamb how Kitty and I had been going on adventures around town, about our trip to Soho and how I'd been sacked, and how I'd come to work for the prince.

Lamb let out a hiss. "Well, that is a troublesome situation. And I feel somewhat responsible for your predicament. After all, you took on Cobalt only because I recommended him—"

"Wait, what does Cobalt have to do with all of this?"

Lamb blinked at me. "Who do you think ratted you out?"

It took a few seconds for me to process his words, and once I did I shot to my feet.

"Fuck." Last night at Buckingham Palace I hadn't mentioned Cobalt to the king because I hadn't wanted to get him in trouble, but it had never occurred to me that maybe he was the reason we'd been found out. King Harold had known so much, which made sense: he had an inside man.

"Well, I did warn you about him," Lamb said.

"No, you did not!"

"I told you he was ambitious. I figured you'd read between the lines," Lamb replied, pulling his coat closer around him. He sighed. "I do worry what will become of you, what will become of all my students. But there's nothing more I can do for you all." He looked to me. "I'm glad you dropped by, Paul. I'm glad we got a chance to say goodbye."

"Don't act like you're dying. You're just going to Italy," I replied.

"I never was able to repay you for getting me out of prison," he went on. "If, in my travels, I see Thomas—"

"Christopher, don't."

"I'll tell him to come home. Come home and help you."

"I don't need any help," I said.

I would have said more but Alberto returned from doing the shopping and he and Lamb started discussing the logistics of their trip. I slipped away, figuring that the less I knew the better.

CHAPTER 10

Not sure where to go, I went back to my studio on Gray's Inn Road. I was hoping that once there I'd be struck by inspiration.

What I found instead was Cobalt. He was moving quickly around the studio, deeply immersed to the point that he didn't even notice me. For about a minute I stood silently in the doorway, watching him. He looked through the sketches, leaving some and putting others in his portfolio. He went to the workstation and sorted through the tools, putting his into a bag. He crawled under a desk to retrieve an old handkerchief of his that had been languishing down there.

"You little rat," I said. "You little Judas Iscariot."

Cobalt bumped his head on the underside of the desk at my voice.

"Paul," he said, rubbing the back of his skull. He was wearing a billowy lace shirt and pleated grey trousers with pointed black boots. "I didn't expect you to be in."

"And I didn't expect you to sell me out," I said. "How long did you wait before you ran and tattled on us to the king and queen? Five minutes? Ten?"

Cobalt looked away. "I told you it was a stupid, dangerous thing to do. I couldn't let anything happen to the princess."

"Well, because you told, something *did* happen, not just to her but every man at Barnaby's," I said. "Jesus Christ, man, you'd sell out a whole room of strangers to further your own career?" I thought of

King Harold's comment about museums and ice-skating. "And it wasn't just last night. You've been grassing on us ever since you came to work for me. I took you in, paid far better than any other mage pays their assistants, treated you like an equal—"

"You're right. I've been looking out for myself," Cobalt said. "I've always had to. But you're the same as me, so don't act all high and mighty."

He grabbed his bag and portfolio and pushed past me out the door. I stood there for a moment, at a loss for what to do with myself. There were a few half-finished outfits around the studio, dresses for future events that the princess would attend. I supposed she wouldn't be wearing them now. At least the material was all bought and paid for. A silver lining.

I tried to think of a magical outfit that would help me find Sabina, but none came to mind. My head was still too muddled, processing my dismissal from the princess's service and my under-the-table recruitment into the prince's employ.

This funk followed me over the next couple of days, affecting me even when I was doing my tutoring sessions. We had settled on a schedule of twice a week, on Tuesday evenings and Sunday afternoons. My three students had just started their second year of cloth magic school, which meant that they weren't actually mages: their bones had yet to be broken by the Court Magician and they were still learning the basics of sewing. With Lamb no longer teaching at the UCL, the new cloth magic professor was some government lackey who hardly knew one end of a needle from the other (which was why Naveed had sought me out for extra tutoring).

"Professor, you seem rather distraught," Rosemary said. It was Sunday afternoon and to have them practise their stitches I was showing them how to darn stockings. (The stockings belonged to Mrs Spratt. She hadn't been so sure about letting the students work on her clothes at first, but she'd warmed to the idea when she'd realized that it would save her from buying new ones.) Beatrix was there too, relatively calm as she oversaw our work.

"What's wrong, Professor?" Harriet chimed in.

"He got sacked," Naveed said before I could answer. "Sorry, Professor. It's just, my nan is good friends with the queen and all, and so we heard about it from her."

"Sacked? So you no longer work for the princess?" Harriet asked. "What will you do for work now?"

I still hadn't figured out what Harriet's angle was. Her presence at the tutoring sessions helped keep Naveed and Rosemary in check somewhat—Naveed didn't seem to like her much but when she was in the room he was more subdued rather than his usual chaotic self. Rosemary seemed to have a rosier view of Harriet. Sometimes she'd sit close to the girl, leaning in and chatting like they were old chums. To my eye, it seemed like Rosemary mainly did this to make Naveed jealous and to make Harriet blush.

So far, Harriet hadn't tried to kill me or do anything but studiously follow my lessons. Still, I never turned my back on her, just in case her mousy exterior hid an assassin in waiting.

"I'll get by," I said. "I've got lots of other projects lined up." That was a lie but one that every cloth mage told themselves at one point or another.

"You could always come work for my family," Naveed said excitedly. "I have two sisters, a mother, and a grandmother, and they always need something flash for parties and whatnot."

"You could also work for prisons," Rosemary said, watching to see my expression. I winced, partly because I had accidentally pricked my finger on a needle.

"I'll be fine, but thanks for your concern," I said.

Harriet looked like she wanted to ask more questions, but instead she dropped her head and focused on her work. She was the best seamstress of the three. Even now she was already on her third pair of stockings while Naveed mangled his first.

"Bloody hell, Harriet! When it comes to sewing, you are PDQ!" Naveed said.

"PDQ?" Harriet asked gingerly, clearly afraid she was being set up.

"Pretty damn quick," Naveed said. Harriet smiled in pleasant surprise. Beatrix giggled at the curse word and I hoped she wouldn't repeat it in front of her mother.

"Did you learn how to sew in the insane asylum?" Naveed asked, tone still pleasant but a malicious glint in his eyes. Harriet's quick hands stilled.

"No," she said after a beat. "Don't be silly. They never would have given us sharp objects in there."

Rosemary laughed at that and went over to sit by Harriet. Naveed didn't have anything more to say, so he just scowled as he looked to his own sewing and tried to fix his mess.

The rest of the session flew by. Soon a car had come to pick up Harriet. I saw her to the door, waving as the Rolls-Royce pulled away.

"Pretty flash car, eh?" Naveed said from behind me. Rosemary was off in the backyard, playing with Beatrix. It occurred to me that it was the first time I'd ever actually been alone with Naveed.

"It's her fiancé's," Naveed said. His voice wasn't the usual giddy tone he had when he was sharing gossip. "Surely you've noticed the ring on her finger, eh, Professor?"

I had—a simple gold band with a tiny diamond. It had seemed out of place, a flagrant signifier of adulthood on one still so young.

"Her beau's an older man," Naveed went on. "Deputy Prime Minister Fairweather."

Fairweather! The same old prick who'd gone after Princess Katherine was now engaged to Harriet Hollister? How did the guy keep finding vulnerable teenage girls?

"So be careful around her," Naveed said. "I know she seems like a sweet, empty-headed thing, but she's in deep with the powers that be, and those powers don't like people like us."

I'd never known Naveed could be so serious—I hadn't known he could be serious at all.

"Thank you, Prince Naveed," I said, "but don't worry. I know to keep Harriet Hollister at arm's length."

Naveed nodded. "Yeah, I noticed. Oh, and don't call me Prince! Just Naveed will do."

"Only if you stop calling me Professor."

"Fat chance of that," Naveed said with a laugh.

"Mind if I ask you something?" I said. "How did you and Rosemary become friends?"

Naveed grinned at that. "We are an odd pair, aren't we? She's a strange one, all right, but I love her for it. She was born in Hungary but spent most of her life in a displaced-persons camp. Girl came here just a few years ago with not a single shilling to her name. Rumour is that she blackmailed Dean Abernail into giving her a scholarship so she could study cloth magic at the UCL."

"Blackmail Dean Abernail?" I said sceptically. "Man's lived a blameless life."

Naveed snapped his fingers, nodding. "Exactly! And he wants everyone to *keep* thinking that, right? Anyway, first day of class, I walk in, expecting to see lots of young men like me—well, not like me, I knew I'd probably be the only brown person there—but lads of a similar class. But no! It's all upper-class and middle-class *girls*. And honestly, I was a bit disappointed, because, well, I'd dreamt for years about studying magic alongside a bevy of handsome young men. I was crushed, and then I noticed one girl no one would go near."

"Rosemary?"

"Bingo. She'd been singled out by the other girls, marked on day one. Maybe it was because she was foreign. Maybe because she came from nothing, so the posh girls felt the need to shit on her and the middle-class gals did so they weren't lumped in with her. Anyway, I sat with her, and we started chatting. My God, Professor, that girl, she's *lived*. She's seen some things," Naveed said, eyes growing wide before he remembered himself. "Anyway, those aren't my stories to tell, but she's a force to be reckoned with."

"Who is?" Rosemary asked, slightly breathless after playing with Beatrix. She came to stand with us, cheeks even redder than usual, hair slightly loose from the braid that circled her head.

"Oh, I was just telling the professor about Harriet Hollister's fiancé," Naveed said.

"She's only eighteen, right?" I said.

"Yes, but she looks younger, doesn't she?" Rosemary often spoke like her words were pebbles she was tossing into a pond, statements lobbed forth in order to see what effect they might have on the other person. She watched me eagerly.

I'd helped Kitty shake off Fairweather's attention, and he had moved on to Harriet Hollister. Was I indirectly responsible for the two of them getting together? Maybe Harriet actually loved him, but that seemed like a stretch. If her father had been alive, would he have allowed a marriage between his teen daughter and a man in his fifties?

"Yes," I finally said in response to Rosemary's question. "She does seem younger."

CHAPTER 11

That Tuesday I made good on my promise to take Mrs Spratt out to the pub. We wore magical outfits that changed our appearance just enough that no one recognized us—for Mrs Spratt I had it so her hair curled into ringlets and a band of freckles went across the bridge of her nose. My suit basically made my eyebrows bushier, my brow more pronounced, and my hair black rather than brown.

The pub was only about ten minutes up the motorway. I drove us. It was an awkward ride over, neither of us sure what to say, but once we were at the pub that awkwardness melted away. I taught Mrs Spratt how to play darts, hand on her hand as I showed her how to aim. It felt exhilarating but a bit nerve-racking being so close to her. It was like having a wild bird perch on my hand, and I didn't want to make the wrong move. Mrs Spratt didn't seem too bothered though. She revealed quite the competitive side to herself and soon we were both laughing as we scored points on the dartboard.

We didn't drink much or stay late since Mrs Spratt had left Beatrix with a sitter and didn't want to keep the poor girl up too late.

As we were driving back Mrs Spratt became thoughtful once more.

"Thank you for tonight, Mr Gallagher," she said.

"No need for that. I had a good time! Hopefully you did as well, Mrs Spratt."

"Yes." Mrs Spratt looked at her hands. "You know, I'd never really gone on a 'date' before. For girls of my class, it just wasn't done. I'd hardly spent any time alone with my husband before we were married. So tonight was . . . nice."

I saw her smile out of the corner of my eye. It was just a faint one, nearly obscured by the curls falling around her face. I tried to imagine what she'd look like if she smiled widely, how it would feel to have that smile directed at *me*. Our so-called date had just been a friendly night out, but I couldn't deny it anymore—I was starting to carry a small torch for Laura Spratt.

Then her smile dropped and she shifted in her seat.

"The other day, when you were with your students . . . I didn't mean to eavesdrop, but I happened to overhear you say you were no longer in the princess's employ."

My hands tightened on the wheel. Of course Mrs Spratt would be concerned—her sole tenant had just lost his job. As far as I knew, collecting rent from me was Mrs Spratt's only source of income.

"I want you to know," Mrs Spratt said, "that if things become dire for you financially, we can work something out. A promissory note or something of the like. I won't toss you out on the street."

I glanced at her, amazed that *I* was the one she was concerned about.

"Thank you, Mrs Spratt, but I should be fine for this month." Next month was an open question, but she didn't need to know that. Hopefully I could find Sabina soon and collect a large payday from the prince. Not that I'd gotten any further in my search for the missing princess.

"Is it hard? Driving, I mean," Mrs Spratt asked, perhaps wanting to take the conversation off money. "I've always been curious, but growing up I was told that there was no need for me to learn. I'd always have chauffeurs or my husband to drive me places, they said."

"Who's 'they'?" I asked.

"My parents."

There was a resigned sadness in her words, like she was speaking of people long gone. It astounded me that Mrs Spratt's family didn't help her out more during this trying time, but word was that they also didn't approve of their daughter's attempts at getting a divorce.

"I learned when I was a teen," I said, trying to keep my voice light. "My father had a music shop, and he also did piano repair. When I was sixteen, he sunk a ton of dosh into buying this big lorry. The idea was that we could use it to deliver pianos and the like to places. So he taught me and my best mate Thomas how to drive it. It was terrifying. Sitting in the cab of it made you feel like you were a whole storey off the ground."

"Oh my, I could never," Mrs Spratt said.

"Yeah, it was scary, but after that trial by fire, I felt like I could drive anything, so that's something at least."

"You are a man of many talents," Mrs Spratt said.

I laughed. "Well, thank you. I comfort myself with the fact that, if this whole cloth magic thing doesn't work out, I can always become a lorry driver."

"Oh, I hope it doesn't come to that," Mrs Spratt said. I wasn't quite sure what to make of that, so instead I told her the story of taking the lorry out for a joyride with Thomas. She was in a better mood by the time we got home, laughing as I talked about Thomas taking the wheel while I'd been below in the footwell, using my hands to press down on the brakes. I parked outside her house to drop her off. For a moment we sat there, still in our magical disguises.

"Won't you come in for a cup of tea?" Mrs Spratt said. It seemed neither of us really wanted the night to end, so I agreed. As we got out of the car and shut the doors, I saw the babysitter Mrs Spratt had hired standing in the doorway of the house, watching us.

It was Harriet Hollister.

"Coming, Mr Gallagher?" Mrs Spratt asked. It would look quite odd if I backtracked now, so I swallowed down my nervousness and nodded.

"Mrs Spratt?" Harriet asked, unsure as we approached the front door.

"Yes, Harriet, it is me. Your professor made magical disguises so we could go to the pub incognito."

Harriet nodded, looking at me with wide eyes as she realized who I was. "You . . . you're back earlier than I expected."

"I'm not used to leaving Beatrix, so I didn't want to be out too late," Mrs Spratt explained. "Mr Gallagher is coming in for a cup of tea. Won't you join us, Harriet?"

Harriet glanced at me, a look of unease on her face that probably mirrored my own.

"Yes, sure," she croaked.

If Mrs Spratt noticed how odd we were acting, she pretended not to. We followed her to the kitchen where she faltered for a second, then seemed to remember that there were no housekeepers or servants to call upon. She set to making a pot of tea herself.

"Thank you so much again for looking after Beatrix tonight," Mrs Spratt said.

"Oh, it's no trouble at all, ma'am," Harriet replied.

"Does your fiancé mind you staying out so late?" I asked. Harriet looked at me, her eyes wide. Then she looked down at her engagement ring as if she'd forgotten it was there.

"Oh. Yes, well, no, he doesn't mind," she said. "I don't live with him—that would hardly be proper—I live with an old spinster aunt of his, and I told her I was helping out a friend tonight."

"You're engaged?" Mrs Spratt asked, curious.

"Yes." Harriet took a mug of tea from Mrs Spratt. "I'm engaged to Peter Fairweather, the deputy prime minister."

Mrs Spratt's mouth made a surprised little O, but she was too well bred to say anything more.

"I know we seem an unlikely pair," Harriet said, a rueful smile on her face as she looked down into her mug. "But he's a very kind man. He's done so much for me, and we have such great plans for the future."

"Oh yeah?" I asked. My aggressive tone made Mrs Spratt give me the side-eye. "Like what?"

Harriet slowly walked over to the table I was sitting at and took a seat. Mrs Spratt came to join her, handing me my own mug of tea.

"People are so quick to judge me being with Peter, but oftentimes those people don't know my situation," Harriet said, speaking deliberately. "When I was young, my father left us. He walked out on my family and just disappeared without a trace."

That was a punch to the gut—Hollister hadn't left his family. No, he'd been swept up in his own grand schemes, a plan to bring back to life his best mate, Jim Godfrey, a plot that had required his own death. I had killed him. I'd killed him slowly and painfully and it had all been at Hollister's own demand. I'd left his bloody body in the basement of The Nail, and later that day the pub had burned down, further disfiguring the corpses inside beyond recognition.

"Shortly after that, my mother—she passed away," Harriet said, her voice still level, her gaze fixed at a point on the table, but there was a slight bob in her throat as she took a deep breath. "We—my brother and I—we were sent to live with some distant relatives. Troy was only ten; I was fourteen. The people we lived with, as far as everyone else was concerned, they were pillars of the community, but . . . but behind closed doors they were monsters. No one would believe us, or . . . or a few times, someone *did*, and they told us that our lot could be so much worse, to just endure . . ."

Mrs Spratt didn't say anything but her eyes were deep wells of compassion. Her hands twitched around her mug as if she wished to reach out to Harriet.

"Troy and I, we decided to run away. We didn't get very far, and when we were caught the police didn't call it a runaway attempt. They said that I'd lured Troy out there, that I was hysterical, like my mother had been." Harriet's voice was shaking now. "They said that I was taking Troy to the river to drown him and drown myself." She looked up at me, the quick motion making tears spill over her cheeks. "Professor, I know many untrue things have been said about me, and I can't defend myself against all of them, but please, I beg you, don't believe that one. I'd never hurt Troy."

I nodded. That seemed to console her somewhat. She wiped her nose on her sleeve before continuing.

"I was sent away to a mental asylum for young women," she said, her voice somewhat steady. "It was horrible. Better than being in *that* house with *those* people, but still horrible. I figured I'd be in there for the rest of my life." She sat up straight and a slight smile graced her face. "But then Peter heard about my predicament. He came to see me, visited often. And eventually he championed for my release, said I could live under the care of his aunt. He saved me, you see. But not just that. He is paying for my studies at the UCL and has always been very supportive of me becoming a mage, so he's quite progressive." She looked to Mrs Spratt and me eagerly, as if waiting for us to clap and lavish praise on Fairweather. When that didn't happen she took another deep breath. "A few months ago Peter proposed. He made a very good case for himself, and part of it was that, once we are married in the spring, we can adopt my brother. Troy's fourteen now, and all these years I've felt so powerless, unable to help him, to get him out of that house."

Mrs Spratt made a sympathetic *hrmm* noise at that. Harriet nodded as if she'd just given an eloquent soliloquy.

"Yes, exactly. I'll be the wife of the deputy prime minister. I'll finally have the power I need."

"But . . . do you love him?" I asked. "Fairweather, I mean?"

Harriet blinked at me, then smoothed out her skirt. "I don't think love has a great deal to do with it," she said. "But he's been good to me. A perfect gentleman, in fact."

"Thank you for telling us all this," Mrs Spratt said, taking one hand off the tea mug to press it flat on the table. "You've been through so much and are a remarkable, strong woman. But I fear you may be setting yourself up for future heartache by marrying so young."

Harriet was quiet for almost a full minute.

"Mrs Spratt," she said. "I greatly respect you and admire you in turn. You are trying to divorce your husband because you think it's what's best for your child. I honestly don't see where you are coming from and think it's a rather foolhardy way to go about things, but in the end it is your choice to make. Even if you don't agree with my choice of action, it's mine."

I looked to Mrs Spratt, half expecting her to lecture Harriet on how little she knew, both about Mrs Spratt's situation and about the adult world. But instead Mrs Spratt just gave a low nod.

"Fair enough." She stood. "It's getting late. Harriet, I made up the guest bedroom for you. Please let me know if there's anything else you may need. Thank you again for the night out, Mr Gallagher. Good night."

~

That night I couldn't sleep. At one point I got up to use the lavatory—it was an outhouse near the gardener's cottage, a small wooden shack surrounded by lavender bushes. The cold only woke me up further, so after I'd done my business, instead of going back inside I went through the trees to look up at the main house.

The lights were off. I'd never been upstairs, but I could guess which windows belonged to the master bedroom, which ones were Beatrix's windows, and which belonged to the guest bedroom where Harriet was currently sleeping.

After Hollister had died I had never checked on his family, never gone to Mrs Hollister and told her what had happened. I'd been too ashamed of my part in it and wanted only to put as much distance between myself and that night as possible. But by not owning up to what I'd done, I'd caused even more pain for the Hollister family. Would Harriet and her brother have gone through so much if I'd been there to provide answers? Would their lives have been better if I'd been there to watch over them?

I didn't know. And I didn't know what exactly Harriet knew either. As candid as she'd been that night, there was still so much we were keeping from each other.

CHAPTER 12

The next morning Beatrix ran around the outside of my cottage, banging on every window before pounding on my door.

"Yes? What is it, Beatrix?" I said, cinching the belt on my housecoat. I had already been up for a few hours, being an early riser even when I hadn't slept well the night before.

"There's a man on the telephone for you," she said while trying to balance on one foot. Close to her side she clutched the teddy bear we'd made together, its button eyes already a bit loose. Ever since we'd made it the thing had hardly left Trix's side.

"Now, Beatrix," I said, "is that the truth, or are you telling porkies again?"

"What you mean, 'porkies'?"

"Lies, child. Is there really a man on the phone for me or is this another prank of yours?"

"There is a man!" she said, stomping her foot down. "A man who sounds just like Prince Arthur."

That got my attention.

"All right, I'll be right there." I did take a few steps outside, then stopped. I couldn't go into the main house in my housecoat and pyjamas, not when Mrs Spratt and Harriet would be around. I hurried back in. "Beatrix, just keep him on the phone, all right? I'll be up in two minutes."

Beatrix nodded eagerly. "Let's go, Paul," she whispered, which confused me until I realized she was speaking to the teddy. Bear in hand, she zoomed off towards the main house and was out of sight before I got my socks on.

I put on the nearest pair of trousers and shirt, laced up my shoes, and double-timed it up to the main house. The phone was in the main hall on a little table, just outside the living room. Beatrix leaned against the wall, phone pressed to her ear.

"No, that's not the answer either. You're not very good at riddles, are you?"

"Beatrix, give me the phone," I said, taking it from her. She hopped away but stayed nearby to listen.

"What the bloody hell is going on, Gallagher?!" Prince Arthur said, so mad I feared spittle might fly from the receiver. "I do the honour of calling you directly, and you leave me on the line with a child who tortures me with riddles like some kind of sphinx in short pants!"

"Sorry, Your Highness. That's my new secretary. She's still getting the hang of the job." I smiled at Beatrix—anyone who could get the prince's dander up had earned a gold star in my book. I reached down and pretended to pluck her nose from her face, then tossed it out the door. She let out a cackle and ran outside to retrieve it.

"Har har har," Prince Arthur said. "It's fine that you can tell jokes in a time like this. Have you found Sabina yet?"

"No, but I'm still following up on some leads—"

"It's been a week, Gallagher! She could be anywhere in the world right now." His anger turned to worry as he spoke, then circled back round to anger. "You better have results for me by Monday or else I will make sure you get Lamb's old cell."

Arthur's threats chilled me, partially because of how casually he made them.

"There's no need for talk like that," I said. "I'll find her."

"You better," he said, then hung up.

I likewise put down the receiver, heaving a great sigh as I did so. I was so lost in thought that I almost missed the sound of a creak behind me.

I whirled around to see Harriet above me on the stairs. Her face had a panicked, guilty cast to it.

"Professor," she said, voice high. "I was just coming down for breakfast." She started walking down the stairs as if I had interrupted her midstride. "Are you going to join us?"

"No," I said flatly. "I'm going into town." I turned and left, in a bad mood that was growing worse by the minute.

~

I decided to go to my studio—I'd brainstorm what to do while sewing. I was thinking that maybe I could sell some of the dresses I'd been working on for Kitty to a new buyer—that might cover my rent for next month.

As I pulled up to my regular spot next to the kerb I saw two figures waiting outside the building. I got out of my car and walked over to them. It was the two Peters—Peter Fairweather and Peter Van Holt, standing outside my place of business like a mismatched pair of cups, Fairweather tall and jittery, Van Holt calm and controlled. A crane and a crow.

"Deputy Prime Minister Fairweather, Court Magician Van Holt," I said. "Funny to see you two together. I didn't know you were friends."

Fairweather and Van Holt replied quickly and simultaneously:

"Well, we are!"

"We're more like work acquaintances."

Fairweather shot a betrayed look at Van Holt, who refused to meet the other man's eyes. Fairweather smoothed down the lapels on his all-black suit. He looked as though he was on his way to another day in Parliament.

"We know the prince has recruited you to track down Sabina," Fairweather said.

"Oh? Did your fiancée report that to you?" I asked.

Fairweather started to feebly protest that no, no, he had no idea what I was talking about, when Van Holt cut in.

"The prince made a call through the switchboard to Hillcrest, an estate where you are renting some property," Van Holt said. "It doesn't take a genius to figure out who he was calling and what about."

"Yeah, I suppose so since I don't see any geniuses here," I said. Van Holt chuckled at that while Fairweather just looked confused.

"Well, we wanted to know how things were going in the hunt for Princess Sabina," Fairweather said, trying to regain some control of the conversation.

"The hunt, eh? Pretty strong choice of words there," I said. "I don't see why I should tell you two."

Fairweather leaned forwards. "I know we haven't always seen eye to eye, Gallagher. I know I've often been uncharitable towards you," he said. "Though to be fair, you *did* ruin my life."

"Ruin your life?" The man was a lord, an old aristocrat with more money than sense. "How could *I* ruin your life?"

"You got between me and Princess Katherine," Fairweather said. "We would have been very happy together, I'll have you know. And it would have been so much better for the country than her marrying that clotheshorse you set her up with."

"Look, mate, you were never going to marry Katherine. The king was never going to sign off on having a son-in-law five years younger than him."

Fairweather's cheeks turned red at that. "Really, what business do you have interceding in the affairs of your betters? Katherine and I would have produced fine British children, the pride of the nation." He took a deep breath. "But I'm truly willing to move past that. Let us join forces and find Sabina together."

"And then what? What exactly are you going to do when—*if*—you find her?"

Fairweather blinked. "Well, I suppose then we can make an offer of cash payment to help her resettle somewhere else in the world. That way we can get on with finding the crown prince a more suitable life partner."

"Right. So the two of them can produce fine British children."

"Exactly! And Gallagher, we all know how good you are at matchmaking. I'm sure you'll be able to find the prince some lady that will help him get over this minor heartbreak."

"And what if Sabina says no? What if she turns down your bribe?"

Fairweather shrugs his shoulders. "It doesn't really matter. As you so bluntly pointed out, the king must approve of his children's marriages. He will never allow Arthur and Sabina to marry. Better for her to realize that and take what she can get out of the situation. And if she doesn't, she'll end up with nothing at all."

"If it's such a nonissue, why search so hard for her?" I said.

"Because it's not good to leave loose ends," Van Holt said. He always spoke softly and flatly in an effort to hide his accent. "You really should throw your lot in with us now, while it's still an offer. We have been very solicitous up until now. We won't be, going forwards."

For a moment his manner reminded me of Thomas's, even though the two were drastically different—Van Holt had cold eyes while Thomas always looked like he was holding back a fire inside of him. But Thomas, even when shaking, would also deliver similar measured threats, saying them carefully in a way that let the other bloke know he'd follow through.

"The prince is not an easy master; believe me, I know. When you fail him, we can protect you from his wrath."

"Right. Thanks for the warning," I said and stepped past them into my studio.

~

It was a bit unnerving to have the two Peters come to me directly like that, but it also gave me a sliver of hope; if they were turning to me, they were probably even more lost than I was. I had found myself quietly rooting for Sabina—here in London we'd all suffer, but if she could escape from this mess, good on her.

I was happily working away, deciding to just forget about the whole thing, when my reverie was broken by the phone ringing. I picked it up warily, afraid I was about to get yelled at again. But the voice on the line was friendly, jolly even.

"Oy, Gallagher!" It took me a second to place the booming North London accent—it was Adam Shipwright, Van Holt's English cousin. He worked as a dogsbody for the Court Magician, carrying out errands, digging up information, doing all kinds of unsavoury things so that Van Holt could keep his hands clean. I'd known him for about as long as I'd known Van Holt and I vastly preferred Shipwright's company. We'd even grabbed drinks a couple of times, something I could never imagine doing with the Court Magician.

"Let me guess why you're calling," I said. "Your cousin asked you to butter me up and see if you could get anything out of me regarding Princess Sabina."

"Can't slip one past you, eh, Gallagher?" Shipwright said, good cheer not diminished in the least. "Yeah, it's true he asked me to see what you knew, but I don't see why this can't be an exchange of information."

I sat down, intrigued. "An exchange?"

"Yes. One, I'll feed you. Come join me and my family for dinner tonight. A real home-cooked meal. My woman, she'll make three different kinds of dumplings if I tell her a guest is coming."

I was actually quite hungry—I looked at the clock and realized I'd worked right through lunch and it was almost five o'clock.

"Also," Shipwright said, perhaps mistaking my silence for reticence, "I'll show you the cloak my cousin made. The one he put together to track Sabina down."

If I hadn't been sold already, I was then. Van Holt was a cloth mage like me, but as cloth magic wasn't as respected as Book magic he downplayed it. Prior to him, all the Court Magicians of the land had been Book Binders, and Van Holt being primarily a cloth mage was just one more mark against him in the eyes of British society. I'd be very curious to see just what exactly he'd come up with in an attempt to find Sabina—at the very least, it would save me from going down the same dead end.

"All right," I said. "When's supper?"

~

I picked up a bottle of red wine so I wouldn't arrive empty handed and then headed up to Shipwright's home in St John's Wood. The Shipwrights lived in a skinny town house near the tube station. Shipwright greeted me with his usual good cheer. He and Van Holt shared a lot of similarities: the same cheekbones and chin and the shape of their eyes. But Shipwright had a larger frame and blond hair, and instead of a manicured goatee he had messy stubble. His wife, Olena, was a quiet woman ("She's shy about her English," Shipwright explained) but his daughter Gayle was a delight, a chatty girl with plaited hair. She talked excitedly about her day and school, and after dinner she hugged both her mother and father and waved goodbye to me before skipping upstairs.

Olena gathered up our plates, smiling when I complimented the meal. She disappeared into the kitchen.

"You have a lovely family," I told Shipwright.

He smiled. "Thanks. I don't mean to get too sentimental, but Olena and I tied the knot five years ago and they've been the best years of my life."

"Five years ago?" I said in surprise. Gayle looked to be about seven years old or even older, so the math didn't add up.

"Olena and her first husband came over here from Ukraine shortly after Gayle was born," Shipwright explained. "But when Gayle was a wee tyke, her father died in an accident down at the docks. Tragic stuff. I met Olena while doing some work for my cousin, and things just fell into place."

I was somewhat surprised that Gayle wasn't Shipwright's biological child, simply because they seemed so at ease with each other. I thought of Beatrix, a child who'd been more or less left on her lonesome. I didn't blame Mrs Spratt for this: I knew she had a lot to deal with. But Beatrix was still only a kid and it wasn't right for her to be by herself so often. More and more I'd been spending time with the girl, but the whole time I wondered if I was doing something wrong, trying to fill shoes that weren't mine to fill. I'd always wanted to be a father—having kids someday was one of the many things that Tonya and I had disagreed on. So when I was with Beatrix, I felt aligned with myself. Like I was being the version of myself that I was meant to be. But it felt almost selfish, like I was using Beatrix to feel fulfilled. What if, someday, when I moved out of that ramshackle gardener's cottage, I made her feel lost and lonely all over again? And even though I'd come to have feelings for Mrs Spratt, it seemed like Laura needed a friend more than a lover. If I lived elsewhere, could I still be a part of their lives? Would that be odd? Would either of them want that? Would the bond Beatrix and I had be strong enough to overcome the fact we weren't related by blood?

"Was it ever difficult?" I asked. "Fathering a child who wasn't yours by birth?"

Shipwright tilted his head to the side. "You asking rhetorically or looking for practical advice?"

"Well, it's just, it seems like a lot to live up to," I said. "I know a lady who is in the same position that your wife was in—well, not the same. Her husband's still alive, but he's not really present in her life or her child's. And I just want to figure out what I can do for them."

"Gallagher!" Shipwright slapped the table, a grin on his face. "Are you stepping out with a married woman?"

I sat up straight, waving my hands in panic. "No, no! God, no. It's not like that! I'm trying to be a good neighbour, that's all!"

Shipwright grinned conspiratorially and I remembered what made him so dangerous; beneath his "just one of the lads" persona, he had a sharp cunning that disarmed you. Whenever I talked to him, I always felt like I ended up giving away more than I was comfortable with.

"Look, I won't say it was always easy," Shipwright said. "Plenty of times I felt like I was being compared to not just a dead man but a saint. And with Olena and me, that might always be a sticking point. But Gayle? Gayle hardly remembers her da. You heard her natter away during dinner—she's got the same accent as me. And when she grows up, she'll marry a nice British lad, take on his last name, and no one will ever guess that she wasn't born here." He raised his wineglass up as if to clink it up against mine but I just stared at him. I remembered now that this was often what cut our evenings out short: Shipwright always ended up saying something creepily xenophobic.

"You said you'd show me your cousin's cloak," I said coolly.

"Right! Step this way!" Shipwright downed the last of his wine and stood. I followed him outside to a little shed in the corner of their postage-stamp-size backyard. The coat hung on the wall. Shipwright held up an oil lamp so I could take a look at it. It was a red, felted coat with a brown collar that—

"Is that human hair?" I asked, drawing my hand back. It had been braided all around the high collar of the coat.

"That's right," Shipwright said cheerfully. "Van Holt used some of the prince's, the king's, and then even had some hair of the old king's on hand, amazingly enough."

"But why . . . ?" I didn't see what exactly Van Holt was going for—how would a coat like this help find Sabina? "May I try it on?"

"Be my guest."

I shrugged the thing on—Van Holt and I were close enough in size that it fit me fine. With magic clothes, if the fit is off, it can affect the magic. But with this I could feel it work right away, my soul giving form and function to the cloth, my life energy powering it. I felt drawn to face northwest.

"I guess it was able to give him a general direction," Shipwright said, "but no more than that. Northwest doesn't really narrow it down, does it? She could be in Liverpool, Cardiff, Chester . . ."

"But why the human hair?" I wondered aloud, gingerly touching the collar. "Why would that help find Sabina?"

Shipwright stayed silent, just watching me with eager eyes, like Beatrix when she'd posed a riddle or Rosemary when she'd said something needlingly.

I looked at the bloodred of the coat. Blood and hair. Hair from three generations of royal men. A bloodline.

"Holy shit," I said. Shipwright nodded.

"You see it now?"

I did. Van Holt's cloak wasn't designed to find Sabina at all. It'd been designed to find the baby growing in her belly, the next link in the royal line.

CHAPTER 13

Learning that Sabina was pregnant explained why both the prince and her enemies were so eager to find her, but it didn't help me any. Prince Arthur had called me once more while I was out and left a message with Beatrix: "Your friend called. He said if you don't find her soon, you're fucked."

With things getting dire, I felt like my only option was to turn to the one person who might tell me where Sabina was: her uncle, the minister of health, Dr David Myers.

I called him up at home, and to my surprise, he agreed to meet with me, telling me to come to his office but to wear a disguise.

Myers was an odd duck, having given up medicine and gone into politics around four years ago as one of the founding members of the Virtuis Party. Even as he'd moved up in the world, he had never given up the idea of reconciling with Tonya. Once or twice a year he'd send us invitations to dinner or some charity ball. Tonya would set to work putting kindling in the fireplace, fixing up a little pyre before balling up the invite and tossing it into the flames.

"I hope he feels that," she'd say, the orange firelight reflecting off her dark skin. I know it always ate her up that we hadn't been able to expose him for the crimes he'd committed, the children he'd killed as part of a government experiment. I know she hated that Dr Myers was her biological father. I wondered if perhaps the old gremlin was so eager to reconnect with Tonya since his other child, Oberon, had not been heard from in four years.

As I approached the Parliament building Thomas's voice berated me: *Why would you want to meet with a man who tried to kill you?* It was a valid question, but at least on a practical level I wasn't worried. If I met him at his office, it wasn't like he'd be able to do anything to me, surrounded as we were by fellow ministers and security guards. Now, on a moral level? Sure. Going to ask for help from a man who had seemingly been willing to kill me, a man who had murdered children and used it to further propel himself to power, who had abandoned his own daughter for riches—seeking assistance from a man like that clearly spoke badly of me. But what else was I to do? If I were to find Sabina, he was my best chance. Maybe as her uncle he knew something.

At my studio I got my snakeskin dress out of the closet. I say *snakeskin* but it wasn't made of snake or any reptile at all, but rather it had hundreds of little glass beads sewn on it, their diamond shape giving it a reptilian look. I had made it while studying with Gabs, had even gotten her help with it—I constructed a dome out of plywood and hung the beads around her so they would be imbued with some of her feminine beauty. I then had a lizard sit amongst the beads—specifically an Australian bearded lizard, a creature whose sex can change based on the surrounding conditions. The fabric took on the qualities of both Gabs's bewitching beauty and the lizard's adaptability. When I wore it people always gave me a second look, and I'd gotten my share of compliments from both friends and strangers.

I managed to zip myself into the dress. It was more of a cocktail dress than something you'd wear to go to see a government minister, but once I'd thrown on a woman's peacoat over it, it seemed a little less flash. I applied kohl around my eyes the way Cobalt had taught me, then put my brownish-red hair under a hairnet and covered that with a ginger wig. Satisfied that no one would recognize me, I headed down to Parliament.

I knew well enough not to go in through the main door: that was for school groups and tourists. Instead, I strode deeper into the grounds. One gentleman stopped to ask me if I was lost, but I assured him I knew where I was going. At least three more men stopped me, some brusquely in an accusatory manner, some with a kind of sleazy chivalry. I had come here in disguise, but I had forgotten just how much notice this disguise gathered. When I presented as a woman, I couldn't walk through the halls of power without everyone I passed looking at me sideways, wondering what I was doing here.

Eventually I reached the small security booth that guarded where the ministers and members of Parliament worked. I told the guards that I was there to meet with Minister Myers. They looked dubious for a moment and asked me to take a seat while they phoned to tell him that a Jane Holden was here to see him. Myers arrived five minutes later. When he saw me he did a double take before schooling his features into a neutral expression.

"Ah yes. Jane. Let's go to my office."

The office wing of Parliament was far sparser than the ceremonial main structure. It had the look of a grey bureaucratic building, with speckled white plaster walls lined with identical wooden doors, only artificial light to see by. Eventually, after going up a few flights of stairs, Myers led me to his office. It was surprisingly stately, with a secretary behind a wooden desk and another door leading to the next room where Myers actually worked. He opened the door for me, a gallant smile on his face. Finally the dim lights gave way to sunlight: Myer's office was a corner one with windows looking out onto the street and Westminster Bridge. I could see the statue of Boudicca. Years ago, Tonya and I had sat next to it as she'd explained how she had come to this country in order to bring her father to justice. Now here I was, seeking his help.

"Quite the disguise," Myers said, tilting his head up to meet my eyes—my heels actually made me taller than him. He had a half smile on his face as he went to sit behind his desk. "Good thing you warned me ahead of time that you were coming, or else I might have turned you away. Please, take a seat. Can I get you anything? I could send my secretary out for coffee."

"Actually, yeah, that would be great," I said as I flopped down into a chair. I *was* in fact hungry. Even though I had the means to eat three meals a day, years of living with nothing had made me used to hunger. I'd forget that I had the means to alleviate it, that most people didn't just put up with it. As if triggered by my thoughts, my stomach growled.

Myers picked up his phone and pressed a button.

"Darlene, dear, could you pop down to the canteen and pick up two black coffees and a couple of muffins? That's a good girl."

He hung up and smiled widely at me. Always so solicitous. Even after his son had nearly beaten me to death, he had painstakingly bandaged my wounds. While he'd been doing so he'd probably been thinking about whether it would be better to just kill me. That memory was a good reminder not to trust his smile.

"I'm glad you came to me," he said. "How is Tatianna?"

"She's fine. I heard from mutual friends that she's doing well in New York."

"Oh, good. I've been so worried. What a tough time for her. I wish I could support her directly, but I understand our relationship isn't there yet. You've really put my poor daughter through the wringer, Paul."

"*I've* put her through the wringer?!" Pretty rich from a man who had traded his own child away in order to get his hands on a pile of cash.

"Now, now. Let's not resort to recriminations. We've all done things we're not proud of—one can't really call himself a man until he has. So how about we let bygones be bygones, hmm?"

He looked to me, waiting for me to agree.

"I have a question about a niece of yours," I said. "I don't know if you've heard, but Sabina's gone missing."

"Oh yes, I've heard. You're not the first one to come asking, Paul." He leaned back in his chair. "And luckily, I know nothing."

"Luckily?"

"Yes. I can see you sitting there, judging me. You have weighed every decision I've made to get here and it disgusts you," Dr Myers said. "And it's true. I have done awful things. But I came from nothing, Paul. You understand that, don't you? What it takes to rise up in this country?"

"Just because I can relate in general doesn't mean I'd do the same things you've done," I said. "I wouldn't sell out little children."

Dr Myers tilted his head. "That's good. I've delivered several children, you know. Oberon. Tatianna. Several nieces and one nephew. It's an amazing experience. I like to think that since I helped bring children into the world, it somewhat evens out the evil I've done."

"You're probably the only doctor in the world who thinks like that," I said. "Most of them don't go around keeping a tally. *Oh, I did a successful heart surgery today; guess I can treat myself to a free murder tomorrow.*"

Dr Myers laughed hard at that. "True. Very true. You're right. I suppose what I'm trying to say is that you might see me as this ruthless figure, but I do have some priorities higher than my own ambition. I value family greatly. Sabina and I may not be related by blood, but we've always been close. A little over a week ago she came to me and asked for some money. Said she needed it in order to get out of the city. I gave it to her but told her not to tell me where she was going. So I can't help you, Paul. Sorry."

At that moment the door swung open. I turned, expecting to see Myers's secretary, coffee in hand. Instead I saw the gangly form of Deputy Prime Minister Fairweather.

"Hullo, hullo! Sorry for bursting in, Myers, but your girl was gone."

"Quite all right," Myers said, his usually jovial tone clipped.

"Ooooooh, and who is this?" Fairweather said, turning his attention to me. He swooped in and sat his bony arse down on the arm of my chair. "My, aren't you a pretty little thing. I see now why you sent your secretary away, Myers." He gave a wink in Myers's direction. Myers's face was as stony as an Easter Island statue.

I was glad my disguise had hidden my true identity from Fairweather. I *didn't* like that my disguise was so good that it meant he was now leering at me, peering down like a cat staring into a fishbowl.

"This is Jane Holden," Myers said. "She's a junior reporter at the *London Times*. A fellow believer in the empire. I was thinking of inducting her into our ranks. That's why I had her come here to meet with me privately."

He said all this with the smoothness that came from a lifetime of lying. Fairweather looked at me as if seeing me in a new light.

"My goodness, really?" he said. "Pardon my surprise, Ms Holden, but most of our compatriots are not so young as you. Or so beautiful. We could use a little more feminine charm in our ranks."

"I'm sure," I said, smiling.

"Has Myers given you the whole pitch yet?" Fairweather asked eagerly. "No? Then allow me." He leaned in closer, enough that I could smell a rotten odour rolling up through the back of his throat and over his molars, assaulting my nostrils. Even worse, he put his arm around me.

"Now, I won't be so boorish as to ask your age, but you are clearly from a younger generation, Ms Holden, one that never really knew Britain at its prime. Oh, I don't mean to disparage our brave boys in the war or all the effort on the home front. Make no mistake, that was a shining hour. But I came of age in a time when our glory wasn't counted in hours or minutes. It was a never-ending event. The sun never set on the British Empire. But now we have multiple colonies rising up and shaking us off. Even though we had gone out into the world, sent our best minds to the colonies to improve life there. In return they not only cast us out; they send the worst amongst *them* to our shores! We've lost our footing in the world by piecemeal. When war breaks out between America and Russia—that's hardly a scoop, everyone knows it's coming—Britain will be the one to emerge victorious!"

I'd always thought of Fairweather as a pretty comical creature, a snob with a long heraldic line but not an iota of wits. But now I saw that he was a fanatic as well.

"How?" I said. "I don't doubt your intent, but how can you be so sure of such a thing?"

"Well, the Virtuis Party has a certain ace up its sleeve, my dear," Fairweather said, gripping my shoulder tight. "A unifying vision. You've seen the opposition, clucking around like chickens with their heads cut off. There's no need for such corralling on *our* side. We all are moving in lockstep, guided by a vision that will last until the end of time."

I looked to Myers.

"I think that's enough for now, Fairweather," Myers said. Fairweather sprang up from his perch on my armrest.

"Oh, don't worry, Minister Myers, I wasn't going to overstay my welcome," Fairweather said. "I was just popping by to see if you wanted to grab a gin and tonic once you clock out for the night."

"I'm sorry, but I'm already engaged this evening," Myers said.

Fairweather looked from him to me.

"Oh. I see. So it *is* like that." He winked once more. "Well, I'll leave you two to it, then."

He left the office. Once the outer door closed both Myers and I sighed in relief. Neither of us spoke for a minute, and in that time Myers's secretary did in fact bustle in with the coffee and a couple of slightly stale croissants.

"Sorry, ma'am. These were all that were left at the canteen," she said to me. She was young but her hairstyle was old-fashioned "victory rolls."

I put my hand on hers. "Thank you so much for these. You're an angel."

She blushed and went back to her desk, closing the door behind her. I hadn't meant to flirt with the girl, just thank her for bringing me food. I shuddered, still feeling where Fairweather's hand had gripped my shoulder and his arm had laid across my back. I hoped that I never came on as strong as that sex pest and that if I did God would strike me down.

"You shouldn't flirt with women while in that getup." Myers's voice was still that stoic tone he'd used with Fairweather. His usual smile had also yet to return from the war. "There are laws on the books against lewd behaviour."

"And just who put those laws there, eh?" I said. "The health ministry has signed off on plenty of ghoulish stuff." I stood. "It was a waste of my time coming here."

"I don't know where Sabina is," Myers said. "But I know who does."

That made me stop.

"Why would you tell me?" I said. Myers swivelled his chair so he was no longer facing me, but I could still see his face reflected in his office window.

"Everyone you know and love is in danger," he said. "It's true for you *and* for me. I'm glad you cheated on Tatianna, even if it hurt her. At least it finally got her away from you."

"Aww, and here I thought that you'd always liked me."

"I do. But as long as Tatianna was close to you, she was in danger. The leader of the Virtuis Party, he has his eye on you, Paul Gallagher. He said you can do miracles. Very dangerous miracles."

My blood ran cold. Suddenly I wasn't in Westminster but in a basement of a pub in Dalston, blood running over my hands. But no one knew about that. The only other men who'd been there were all dead. Except Thomas.

"The prime minister said that?" It seemed beyond belief—Prime Minister Hywell seemed to be the only member of his party dumber than Fairweather.

"No. Not Hywell. The *true* leader of the Virtuis Party. I can't say too much; he's always so close by. He's close right now, hiding in plain sight, as consistent and present as Big Ben's chimes." A glassy look came over Dr Myers's eyes. It spooked me greatly, but then the man snapped out of it.

"Talk to General Brennan," Myers said. "His father was Captain Brennan. The same Captain Brennan who first brought Sabina's grandmother from Africa. Those two families have been intertwined over the generations. If there's anyone she'd trust with her life, it's him."

"Again, why tell me this?" I said.

"Sabina is my family. By marriage, granted, not blood, but still. I've known her since she was a little girl. My colleagues in the party, they'd rather see her dead than risk seeing her—or her descendants—on the throne. As a minister in the government, my options are limited. If I help her I will lose my position and perhaps end up getting her killed. But you're still a free agent, Paul. Find her and help her escape from this country."

"I got on this track because Prince Arthur asked me to look for her," I said. "He's the crown prince. Surely he can protect her?"

Myers shook his head. "It's not enough. This is bigger than him. Bigger than the royal family." Myers turned his chair just enough to look me in the eye. "If you do find Sabina, don't tell me where she is. And don't tell Arthur, unless you have a damn good plan in place to protect them."

CHAPTER 14

Between dealing with Fairweather and talking to Myers, I felt drained. Stomach grumbling, I drove out of the city to Hillcrest, idly thinking about how nice it would be to eat a meal with Mrs Spratt and Beatrix. Since our visit to the pub, it felt like some of the walls had come down between us. Mrs Spratt regularly asked me to join them for lunch or invited me to stay for dinner after my tutoring sessions were over. Neither Mrs Spratt nor I was a good cook, so mainly we ate soup and sandwiches, but the company made it worthwhile.

I pulled into the driveway by the gardener's cottage, already looking forwards to some cheddar on rye or whatever else Mrs Spratt had in the larder, when I heard a voice crying out through the woods.

"Beatrix! Beatrix!"

The voice belonged to Harriet Hollister.

"Shhh."

I looked up to see Beatrix nestled in the fork of a tree branch, just a few feet above my head. She had a finger to her lips, a mischievous smile on her small, vulpine face.

Harriet came around the side of the cottage and froze when she saw me.

"O-oh, Professor," she stammered. Her long honey-brown hair was pulled back and she was wearing a simple rust-red dress, mud on her tights. "S-sorry. Beatrix and I were playing hide-and-seek, but for the life of me I can't find her."

"What are you doing here?" I said. It was Friday—our next tutoring session wasn't until Sunday.

Harriet paled, then looked down at her shoes.

"I'm staying with Mrs Spratt for the time being."

"You're *what*?"

Her head snapped up at the force of my words. "Y-yes. It's something we've worked out between us." She swallowed. "I . . . I had a disagreement with Peter and called off our engagement." She held up her left hand to show that it was bare, the engagement ring gone. "I can no longer stay with his aunt, and he's also stopped paying my tuition at the UCL. I have nothing, b-but Mrs Spratt has kindly taken me in."

For a moment I just stared at her, Beatrix silently watching over the two of us from her spot in the tree like the serpent in the Garden of Eden. I couldn't think of what to say, so instead I turned on my heel and marched up to the main house.

I knocked on the door and then, in a fit of impropriety, tried the handle—the door was unlocked.

"Mrs Spratt?" I could see her in the dining room, arranging a bouquet of autumn branches in a vase. She came to meet me in the front hall.

"Mr Gallagher?"

"I was just talking to Harriet and she says she's moved in here?!"

"Oh yes." A pleased smile spread across Mrs Spratt's face. "She's broken things off with that old lecher. Isn't that wonderful?"

"No!" I said. "Mrs Spratt, listen to me. Things are far more complicated than you understand. Harriet isn't here because she has nowhere else to go. She's here to spy on me. The whole of the Virtuis Party is against me, and Harriet is clearly working for them. By taking her in you're putting me, yourself, and Beatrix in danger."

Mrs Spratt folded her arms. "I'm not sure I follow. How could Harriet be a danger to anyone?"

"It's not so much her . . ." But of course it was—I still didn't know what exactly Harriet wanted from me, but I was sure she knew I had something to do with her father's disappearance. "It's more about her fiancé. He has it out for me, and I know for a fact that she's already spied on me once for him."

"But as I said, he's no longer her fiancé—"

"That's a load of bullshit!" I said, and Mrs Spratt narrowed her eyes at the expletive. "It's a cover story they concocted in order to get Harriet in here. And as long as she's here, none of our secrets are safe. Damn it, Mrs Spratt, I thought you were smarter than this."

Mrs Spratt's expression made it clear that she'd had enough of *my* bullshit.

"Maybe you should consider, Mr Gallagher, that things are more complicated than *you* understand. I'll kindly ask you to keep your opinions about what I do in my own home to yourself, thank you very much. Remember yourself: you are but a tenant."

I stared at her, aghast—I'd thought we'd gotten to the place where we could call each other friends. Mrs Spratt flinched at her own words, but then she drew herself up to her full height and fixed her face into a hard cast.

"That's right, I *am* a tenant," I said once I was over my surprise. "This might be your own home, but I live right next door! I pay rent! I can't feel safe here while Harriet Hollister is here!"

"She has nowhere else to go!"

"I don't care!"

"Well, I don't care if you don't care, but *I* care!" Mrs Spratt said, voice louder than I'd ever heard from her. "Good God, you men are all the same! Let you in even just a little bit, open your heart even just a smidge, and you think you can dictate a woman's whole life! And here

I'd dared to think you were different, Mr Gallagher. I suppose not. Well, I've heard you out, but not another word on the matter. Harriet stays."

I tried to protest but the words died on my tongue. Mrs Spratt clearly thought she was doing a good deed, extending a hand to a fellow woman in distress. No doubt she saw a lot of herself in Harriet. But I'd like to think that her overriding concern should not be for Harriet but Beatrix.

Locking eyes with her I could see that Mrs Spratt was not going to budge.

"Fine!" I said, throwing my hands in the air. "But don't blame me when this act of kindness bites you on the arse."

I turned and retraced my steps to my car. Harriet was still dithering about.

"Oh, Professor!" she said. "Please help me look for Beatrix! It's been hours and I still can't find her!"

"She's in the fucking tree," I said, before starting the car and driving back into London.

CHAPTER 15

The next morning I snapped awake, disoriented by the luxury around me. These sheets were too fine to be mine, the bed too big, the wallpaper too ornate. Then I remembered that I was in Andrew's house.

I had slept the night in Andrew's bed—he was still up in Scotland, and the guest bedroom reminded me too much of the night I'd almost gotten Kitty killed. Susan, the housekeeper, hadn't looked pleased to see me when I'd arrived late in the evening, but since her master had made it clear I was to have run of the place while he was gone, she kept her mouth shut.

I lay in bed, watching the light creep up over the city skyline. I couldn't go back home, not with Harriet, the Virtuis spy, living right next door. Would I have to move out of the gardener's cottage? Even though the place was a shack, it was still a good deal rentwise. It would be nearly impossible for me to afford anything in the city on my lonesome. I could sleep on a cot in my studio, but if the building superintendent ever caught me I'd be kicked out completely. And with my dwindling funds, how long was I going to be able to afford rent on the studio?

There was another factor that made me reluctant to move out of the gardener's cottage: Laura and Beatrix. I knew that Mrs Spratt was counting on my rent money to feed herself and her daughter. If I left, would she be able to find another tenant?

Thomas, ever the class warrior, would be disgusted with me for feeling sorry for my landlord.

But she was just like me in a way, someone in a bad spot and in dire need of money. It seemed to be a constant refrain: Dr Myers had said that when Sabina had come to him for help, she had asked him for money.

I sat up in bed, an idea germinating. Transactions nowadays were all done in Books—people were able to transfer funds from one Book to another, and skilled Book Binders could take a look at a single shilling in someone's possession and untangle its whole history, seeing each and every Book it had been in before coming to rest in yours. So odds were Dr Myers hadn't given Sabina money that way—it might look bad for him when it came out later that he'd funded her disappearance. Plus, thanks to Books, studious records were kept of many purchases related to travel: at the end of the day purchases made at individual ticket stalls at railways and airports were loaded into a massive Book, and cab drivers likewise had to load all their transactions at the end of a shift.

There was, though, an illegal alternative to using your Book to make purchases—you could use cash money. British money was no longer printed, so criminals had taken to using the American dollar. It wouldn't be impossible for a high-level politician like Myers to get his hands on a bunch of US currency and then give it to his niece so she could pay some unsavoury type to smuggle her out of the country.

No. I felt like she was still in the UK. That was what I had felt while wearing the bloodred coat Van Holt had made. She was somewhere to the west, but not over the ocean.

I didn't really consider myself a detective, but I did like listening to crime dramas on the wireless. One of the phrases that detectives often used was "follow the money." My bet was that Sabina had kept her flight off the books, but maybe there was some other way to track her.

My thoughts were broken by the sound of the front door downstairs opening and a fair amount of people tromping in. I got up, combed my hair, and put a housecoat on over my rumpled pyjamas. I went to the top of the stairs to see what was going on. Andrew stood in the front hall, servants carrying in luggage around him like ants going around a rock.

"Ah! Gally! You're home!" He clasped me close. My own arms came up to hug him back—it dawned on me that I was starved for human contact. He smelled like pine and petrol with just a hint of cologne. He drew back. "I'm sorry for not coming home sooner! I know you've had a rough go of it over the last few weeks! I wanted to come back as soon as I heard, but Mother—" He stopped, a look of concentration on his face, like someone trying to break themselves of a bad habit. "Well, I just had so many duties to attend to up north; I couldn't get away. But last night I hopped on a sleeper train to get back here as soon as I could! What exactly has happened here, Gally?"

Around us servants were taking various items to different parts of the house—chests of clothes upstairs, packages of fresh food to the kitchen, their own items to the servants' quarters in the basement. When it had just been me and Susan the housekeeper we had more or less stayed out of each other's way, two ghosts existing on different planes. Now that the house was coming alive again it drove home how out of place I was here, an intruder.

We went back to his bedroom. Andrew raised an eyebrow at the unmade bed.

"Oh dear, Gally. Is there something wrong with the guest bedroom? Is it drafty or the mattress lumpy or—"

"No, it's fine. I just . . . I just didn't think I could sleep in there." In broad strokes I told Andrew about the night Kitty and I had gone to Soho. He sat on the bed next to me, a serious expression on his face as I spoke. I left out the bit about me performing innate magic on the princess or her talking about her attraction to women.

"So then King Harold sacked me," I said.

I had expected Andrew to be indignant, but the force of his displeasure still took me by surprise. He huffed before speaking. "How ridiculous! You've done so much for Kitty, been her true friend and helped that poor girl come out of her shell. And you played matchmaker between her and me! Why, I only agreed to marry the girl because you convinced me that it would be a good match! If you're not hired back, I'll march right up to bloody King Harold and tell him that my engagement with Katherine is over—"

"Don't do that!" I said. "Kitty's had a rough enough go of it already. Please don't do that to her, not for my sake."

Andrew seemed to calm down. "Yes. Yes, you're right. I know how dearly you care for the princess, Gally. I swear I won't harm her."

It seemed so odd for Andrew to make that promise to *me*, seeing as he was the one engaged to her.

"Still, what a bloody mess," Andrew muttered. "Well, I will talk to King Harold about that matter nonetheless. Once some time has passed, I am sure you'll get hired back on."

"Andrew," I said, carefully, "do you want to marry Princess Katherine?"

He cocked his head to the side. "What do you mean?"

"I mean, you said you were only doing it because I convinced you . . ."

"Oh! Let me clarify, Gally. She's a grand girl. I certainly have nothing against her personally, and if I found her abhorrent, like, say"—he leaned in close—"her brother"—leaned back—"then no, I would not be marrying her. But she has a sweet disposition, and our social status makes us a good match. It's advantageous."

"I see." I was thinking about what Kitty had said, that Andrew was an "invert" like her. With many of my friends I was pretty open about things like sex and sexuality, but with Andrew, approaching the subject seemed like approaching a balloon with a pin, being scared of the pop.

Andrew gave me a pitying smile. "I know I sound rather heartless, don't I?"

"No, no."

"All my life, Mother has looked out for me," Andrew said. "Father died when I was just a wee lad, and when I was old enough to take his seat in the House of Lords, Mother was always in the background, telling me which way to vote. She managed the estate and the land back home while also being a social fixture here in London, while *also* using her power to run the country." He rubbed his temples. "When I was younger she used to talk about me becoming prime minister one day, but all my tutors told her that was a long shot. When I said I wished to study cloth magic, she didn't object, just arranged it so I could." He steepled his fingers. "Perhaps you've heard the rumours that she has lost her powers of precognition?"

"I have, yeah."

"It's true," Andrew said. "God knows how. She's . . . well, her power isn't the type that one loses." Andrew was being coy here, but I knew what he meant. Lady Fife was a Superconductor, a once-in-a-century miracle. The amount of magic flowing through her body made it so whatever she touched became magic. For her that meant that she saw signs and omens in everything. But in the past few years her predictions had been wrong, leading to her losing control of the country.

"She is still a brilliant woman," Andrew said, "but the loss of her second sight has been a blow. She worked so hard for me all my life. Now I have to make my own way in the world. And if that means marrying a woman as a union of convenience rather than love, well, there are far worse fates." Andrew smiled. "Plus, it keeps me close to you! You'll work for the royal family, and I'll *be* a member of the royal family."

"Yes, well, we'll see about that," I said, thinking about the idea I'd had that morning. "There is a way that I could work my way back into the royal family's good graces. Arthur's in a bit of a pickle—he and

Sabina had a fight, and it's been weeks now since anyone's seen her. He said that if I can find her, he'll make sure I have a job working for him once he becomes king."

"Ah, well, why didn't you say so, Gally?" Andrew said. "So you do have a plan after all!"

"Well, a bit of one," I said. But that was false modesty. The seed of an idea had grown into a tree, its branches unfurling. "Say, Andrew, think you could help me out and come with me on some errands today?"

"Why, I'd be delighted, Gally!"

My reasons for taking Andrew along were multifold—one, it *was* nice to see him again. After weeks in the countryside, he was thrilled to be back in London, and as if to repay his interest, the city was at its best, sunlight glinting off the white stone pillars and red buses. His enthusiasm was contagious, and I felt cheered just being next to him.

The other reason I wanted Andrew there was monetary—he paid for the material we bought at the fabric market. He paid for the lunch we had at a pub in Leicester Square. After a bit of dithering, he also paid a large amount to some East End lowlifes, buying about a hundred physical American dollars at an inflated price.

"I'm really sorry about this," I said, as we left the smoky snooker hall that doubled as an illegal currency exchange. "It might not be anytime soon, but I'll pay you back—"

"No," Andrew said firmly as we got into his car. "If it gets you a job with the royal family again it will all have been worth it."

We took our goods back to Andrew's house. The material we'd bought was a green tweed, the darkest green I'd ever seen. I'd been trying to get a material with the same shade of green used on American money, and if we'd gotten the money first I would have chosen something with a lighter hue to match the mint green of the American bills, but the tweed was so lovely that I couldn't be mad about it. The slightly coarse material felt pleasant under my fingers.

"Hand me the money, would ya, Andrew?" I asked. Andrew did so. I took the stack of ones and fives and put it in the middle of the swath of material, then folded it up, making sure my hands moved over the fabric as I did so. The contact with me, a mage, would help turn it from regular cloth to something magic. The surrounding elements would give that magic form. I folded the tweed over the stack of money, repeating the motion until it was a wrapped-up brick of cash.

"Is there a safe in this house?" I asked. There was. Andrew showed it to me in the study downstairs, somewhat nervously, like a child stealing a biscuit. Inside were some jewels and various wads of money from all around the world.

"Can you empty it?" I said, holding my cash/tweed bundle. Andrew hesitated for a beat, then put all the items in the safe in a drawer. The safe was small, about the size of a bread box, but I was able to fit my bundle in there. Andrew shut the door and turned the latch.

"So what exactly is the aim here again?" Andrew asked.

"I'll tell you if it works."

We had a delicious supper, Andrew's cook putting together a poached fish dish featuring some trout Andrew had caught himself up in Scotland. We talked—and drank—late into the night. After almost two weeks of being harried and frazzled, it felt nice to relax and spend time with an old friend. I felt like everything was going to work out—I'd use the magic cloth I was working on to find Sabina, I'd help her reconcile with the prince, and then my place in the world would be secure once more.

~

The next morning I had Andrew open the safe. When I removed the cloth, it felt changed—it now had a papery smell to it. But until I actually made clothing out of it, I wouldn't know if it had changed in the specific way I wanted it to.

Around lunch I realized with a start that it was Sunday. I called up Naveed and told him that today's afternoon tutoring session would take place in my studio rather than Hillcrest. He and Rosemary showed up, curious about the change in venue and also Harriet's absence. I fobbed them off by showing them how to construct a suit, using my tweed material. I felt very efficient: I was killing two birds with one stone, doing my tutoring duties while also making an outfit that might finally lead me to Sabina.

After Rosemary and Naveed left I set to work on the next part of constructing the outfit. I had made a three-piece suit to fit my own measurements: trousers, waistcoat, jacket. It looked pretty flash. My inspiration for the outfit had been the moneymen working in the financial district of London. If the theme of the outfit was "follow the money," it only made sense for the cut to mimic what bankers and other businessmen wore. But I worried I had put too much panache into it and in the process gotten away from the central theme.

Well, no matter. I'd have to hope the magic would still hold. Using a special paste I'd concocted after consulting a clerk at an art-supply store, I started painting individual dollar bills and plastering them to the inside of the vest. Just to be safe, I also added a layer to the back of the vest, one that would be visible when I wasn't wearing the jacket. I kind of loved the gaucheness of the concept—so many people wore clothes to show off their wealth, and this was just a more literal interpretation of it, the money blatantly on display.

I was eager to try it out, but I had to let the thing dry.

I took one of the dollar bills with me when I went out to buy a sandwich for supper. I sat in a café to eat, watching people walk by. On the street corner was a rough sleeper, his Book open on his lap. Occasionally someone might stop to give him an apple or a small bit of food. One kindhearted soul even stopped long enough to take out her Book and do a transfer spell to put some money in the beggar man's own Book. But most people passed him by.

Once my sandwich was done I figured the vest would still not be dry, so I decided to call it a day. Before I headed back to Andrew's I said good evening to the rough sleeper and gave him an American dollar.

~

The next day the vest was ready. I'd recruited Andrew to help me test it out—he was sitting in his house back in Kensington, the stack of the remaining money next to him. I was shaking slightly as I put on the trousers, more so when I put on the vest and jacket. I'd made easily hundreds of outfits, but few had so much riding on them.

The suit fit perfectly, of course. As I was wearing it I felt that tingling, almost light-headed sensation that came from wearing magic clothes. I clenched and unclenched my hands, trying to relax. Eventually, I did feel a kind of pull. I leaned into it, and soon the smells of my studio—the lingering scent of paste, the puff of petrol from a passing bus, the odour of coffee—were swept away by fresh air. I was outside, standing on the street corner next to the beggar I'd given money to the day before.

"Bloody hell!" he swore at my sudden appearance. "Where did you come from?"

"My studio." I laughed—the suit had worked, more or less. "Say, yesterday I gave you an American dollar bill. Do you still have it?"

He hunched over, as if afraid I'd attack him. "What? You want it back?"

"Oh, no! No, Pops, I just want to know if you still have it on you."

The man gave a grudging nod, still watching me warily. I tried to give him a reassuring smile.

"All right. Thanks!" I could feel another slight pull on me—I mentally leaned into it. The city smells of the London streetscape dropped away and were replaced by the scent of pine and freshly baked bread. I was in Andrew's living room.

Andrew was perched on the couch, a pile of money sitting next to him idly like a bored date. At my appearance he leaped to his feet.

"Gally! It worked!" he said.

"Yes, it did!" And in my excitement I kissed him.

I didn't mean much by it—I kiss a lot of my friends without it being anything more than a nonromantic sign of affection. But Andrew looked stunned, and I realized that maybe I'd gone too far.

"Sorry, mate. Just in the moment I—"

Andrew stepped in and now *he* was kissing *me*.

Then we both kind of stumbled away from each other.

"Sorry, Gally," Andrew stammered.

"N-no, don't be sorry," I said. The moment felt so odd—it was still midafternoon, the sunlight streaming in through the windows. Around the house servants were tending to their duties, out of sight but nearby—the cook making bread, maids polishing silverware or cleaning the upstairs bedroom. I could never get my head around how the upper class lived, seemingly unconcerned about the legion of human beings in their employ who knew every aspect of their private affairs. I couldn't make time with someone knowing that someone could walk in on us at any moment.

But that wasn't the only reason for my ill ease. I'd nursed lots of crushes on friends over the years, but I'd never looked at Andrew in that way. And until that moment, I'd never considered that he looked at me as anything but a pal.

Andrew glanced at the floor, his face flushed.

"I'm sorry," he said once more, voice controlled. "Not for kissing you just now. I'm sorry for not making my feelings clearer to you years ago. I feel like if I had, I could have saved you from much heartbreak. First, Thomas—"

"Wait, what?" I said. "Thomas left, but it's not like we were—I mean, we were just mates, it wasn't a breakup—"

"He left you," Andrew said. "And because you'd depended on him so dearly, it broke your heart. And then Verity left you—"

"Yeah, but she had good reason to," I said. "You know about me and Gabs."

Andrew shrugged. "I could have told you it wouldn't have worked out between the two of you. Verity was always so independent, but you—" He straightened his shoulders and took a deep, fortifying breath. He reached out and caressed my cheek lightly with the back of his hand.

"What you need, Gally, is someone to look after you."

Oh. Oh, damn.

"Show me," I said. He smiled, and for a split second he looked like his usual overwhelmed self, before he was able to relax. He took my hand and we went upstairs to his room.

~

About an hour later we were lying in bed, Andrew asleep and snoring softly while I was starting to get hungry—it was almost suppertime.

Next to me Andrew rolled over and threw his arm over me—who knew the man was so clingy? He was smiling in his sleep, curls plastered to his forehead. I looked at him and tried hard to see him as a lover, not as a friend. It should have been easy considering how we spent the last hour. But try as I might, those feelings weren't coming, at least not from my end.

I got up, took a shower, got dressed, and headed downstairs without waking Andrew.

Sitting in the living room was Lady Fife. Andrea McDougal, Andrew's mother, the widow of the previous duke of Fife, and while no longer the most powerful person in the United Kingdom, still the scariest witch in the country.

"Gyaah!" I said in surprised greeting, nearly stumbling down the stairs. Lady Fife took it calmly and I tried to mirror her.

"Lady Fife," I said smoothly, as if I hadn't just screamed at the sight of her. "I did not know you were home."

"I arrived about half an hour ago," Lady Fife replied. "I would have said hello to my son but I was told by the maid that he was otherwise engaged."

Once again, life with servants boggled my mind.

I came down the rest of the stairs to stand in the living room doorway. Lady Fife was looking rather prim, wearing a nonmagical skirt and suit jacket. It was a far cry from the magical gowns she used to wear. The years hung on her, like the worries of the world were just a blink or glance away.

Next to her was my stack of American dollars.

"Oh, that's mine," I said, hurriedly gathering it up.

Lady Fife made no move to help.

"I hear you have joined the search for Princess Sabina," Lady Fife said, not bothering to explain *how* she had heard about it. "Before you commit yourself fully to the task, you should think of the ways this may play out and ask yourself if you're willing to see this through."

I stepped away, holding the wad of cash awkwardly in my hands.

"And *you* can see how it will play out, Lady Fife? I didn't think that was in your wheelhouse anymore."

"I still have brains in my head," she snapped. "Once more you are rushing headlong into danger, and now you've entangled my son in your schemes as well."

I shrugged, which was admittedly a bit glib but I'd been caught off guard by the sight of Lady Fife and now was on the defensive. Her eyes narrowed.

"Please just remember how things played out the last time you ignored my advice."

Of course I remembered: I'd nearly gotten Thomas killed, actually skinned a man alive, and brought James Godfrey back to life only for Thomas to promptly kill him. I could still see Godfrey's face in my mind, naked save for a bloody shirt, eyes wide in frozen surprise and a bullet hole like a third eye in his forehead.

But I still didn't take kindly to being lectured by Lady Fife. It was petty, I know, but I think a part of me blamed her for the state of the country. If she had managed to keep a handle on things, maybe my friends wouldn't be fleeing the country left and right or unable to stay out of gaol.

"You know, Lady Fife, I think you're just jealous that your son loves me more than you."

I imagined my words in the form of a slammed serve, hitting hard into Lady Fife's side of the court while the crowd cheered.

But Lady Fife didn't look stricken or even mad. She merely fixed me with a pitying look.

"Oh, Mr Gallagher. I just wished that you loved him at all."

Lady Fife had countered my serve with a shot that was unreturnable. I went back upstairs and gathered my things.

~

"I think we all knew I'd end up here," I whispered that night as I laid my head down on my pillow. The "here" was a cot in my studio, the "we" more nebulous. I'd left the McDougal house claiming I had prior engagements, though Andrew had begged me to stay, saying I was free to use the spare room for as long as I liked. The whole time he was speaking Lady Fife stood impassively behind him, staring at me. It was still very much her house, the look said, and I was not welcome there.

The studio had large windows that stretched up to the ceiling and as I lay in bed I could see the moon in the sky, a night away from fullness but still so bright that it blotted out any stars. Or maybe that was just London's light pollution at work.

If I were out at Hillcrest, I'd have been able to see the stars. Maybe I'd even be looking up at them with Mrs Spratt. I hoped she was all right.

My stomach growled—I hadn't bothered to grab supper before coming back to the studio, deciding instead to work. I resolved to go to sleep before my stomach got emptier.

CHAPTER 16

"Mr Gallagher, nothing you have told us so far has been anything new," General Brennan said. "Surely you didn't come here today to waste both our time."

I was in the office of one General Brennan at the army's London offices near Westminster. Also in attendance was Private Janey, who Brennan had introduced as his nephew and aide-de-camp (I had to bite my tongue about nepotism being alive and well in the British Army). Young Janey was in his early twenties and nursing a bad case of acne. While Brennan and I talked Janey sat to the side and took notes, which had the effect of making him look like a student in school.

"I thought it was important to let you know that Sabina is in danger—"

"Again, something we bloody well know," Brennan said, agitated.

"Van Holt's been using magic to try and find her," I said. "He knows she's still in the country."

Brennan gave a little huff at that, his nostrils flaring and the exhale fluttering the bristles of his ornate moustache. He had clearly not wanted to meet with me, but Myers had called and put a good word in for me—more specifically, I imagined, he had told them I had news about the hunt for Sabina.

"Well, that's to be expected," Brennan said. "Van Holt is the Court Magician, and he serves the king."

"If you don't mind me asking, sir, don't you as well?" I said.

Brennan squared his shoulders and looked at me like I was a bug he was about to squash with his polished boot.

"Of course I do," Brennan said. "But I am upholding an oath that I undertook before I ever became a military man. Young Janey here too. Our whole family. My father, he was the one to bring Sabina's grandmother here to England. He always felt responsible for the girl and charged that his kin would look after hers. Now, I don't like Myers, but I more or less believe he's on the right side of things when it comes to Sabina's best interests. I'm not so sure about you, Mr Gallagher."

"I can help," I said. "I could do some cloth magic and—"

"Oh yes, I've heard about your escapades," the general said. "Nothing but trouble comes from dealing with cloth magicians!" He stood. "I have given you a chance to explain yourself, Mr Gallagher, and I'm not moved. Please, stop your pursuit of Sabina and leave her be. Janey, please see him out."

Janey did so. The lad was silent as we walked through the hall, a troubled frown on his face.

"My uncle comes from a line of military men who don't have much time for cloth magic," he said as we neared the entrance of the building. It was a wide lobby with pillars around the edge of the room. "Since it can't be mass produced, he doesn't see much use for it."

I nodded—it wasn't the first time I'd come across that line of thinking.

"I mean it about helping Sabina," I said. "I don't know what happened between her and Arthur, but I want to help her however I can." I took a few steps back so I was standing behind one of the many pillars in the room. Janey, almost on impulse, stepped forwards to stay next to me, and once he was out of sight of everyone else in the lobby I pushed the wad of American money into his hands. "Please, take this and give it to her. I imagine she's trying to live off the grid, yeah? Be a bad idea to have her transactions recorded in Books. So some cash would probably help, wherever she is, right? Oh, but I wouldn't tell your uncle about this—he'd probably reject it on principle or something like that."

Janey stared at the money like he'd never seen it before. Then he curled his fingers around it and stuffed it inside his jacket with a curt nod.

I did mean it about wanting to help Sabina. I knew looking for her was a risk, but there were some things I needed to tell her directly, and I didn't even trust a stalwart intermediary like Janey to relay the message.

I waited five days. Five days of dodging calls from the prince, five days of quickly getting Andrew off the phone when he called, five days of ignoring Rosemary's and Naveed's judgemental glances when they figured out that I was living in my studio, five days of turning down Shipwright's falsely friendly invites to dinner. Five days of silence from Laura.

Then I was done with waiting. I figured that, wherever in the country Sabina was, surely Janey had gotten the money to her.

I had reason to suspect he had. I'd been practising wearing the money suit. When I put it on and closed my eyes, it was like being plunged in a cold, dark universe with no up or down but two lights: one, I suspected, was the single American dollar I'd given to that rough sleeper, that note still making its way through the London underworld. But the other light was the wad of cash I'd given Janey, and in this dark universe it was a green, glowing sun. I had to hold myself back from going to it—if I teleported to it too early, I'd give the game away before Janey had a chance to hand the money over to Sabina.

But now the sun had exploded—there were a dozen little stars in the universe, little green pinpricks giving off their own small quantities of heat. Someone was spending the money.

I tried not to get too excited lest I lose my concentration. I kept breathing, focusing on the sense of warmth.

I picked the biggest source of light and focused on it. Time to see where my trail of bread crumbs led.

I felt a shift: I was still inside somewhere but there was suddenly a coolness and the slight scent of dirt in the air. Two women were chatting in Welsh. When I opened my eyes they were staring at me, mouths agape. I was in a greengrocer. Out the big main window I could see a village street with the usuals: a butcher's shop, a post office, a pub.

Sabina was in town here somewhere.

"Hello, ma'am," I said to the woman standing behind the counter. "Could you please tell me where we are?"

She just stared at me. I didn't blame her for being wary of this random, well-dressed Scouser who had appeared out of nowhere in the middle of her shop. I could introduce myself and sweet-talk her a little bit, but for a variety of reasons that seemed like a bad idea. So instead I closed my eyes and felt for the next point of heat. I smelled raw meat and heard the crinkling of packing paper. I had arrived in the butcher's shop—across the street I could see the greengrocer's I'd been in just a second ago.

"Hey! Who the bloody hell are you?!" the butcher yelled at me. There were two other people in the shop, an older woman and a young male shop clerk, both looking at me wide eyed. The butcher came out from behind the counter. He was unarmed but burly enough that a weapon seemed like an afterthought.

"You can't just suddenly appear in people's place of business like that! What game are you playing?" he shouted at me. Again, perhaps I could placate him by introducing myself, but I felt like perhaps I had made too big a mess of things for that to work.

"Sorry, wrong address," I said, ducking past him to get out of the shop. I walked down the street, trying to find any identifying markers. I heard people speaking English and Welsh, but the road signs were only in English, which meant I was probably in some tiny village on the England side of the English-Welsh border. I passed a few people on the street who gave me odd looks. I was underdressed for the weather. It was a lot colder here than it was in Central London and I rubbed my arms to keep them warm. As I passed I heard some people mutter "wizard," the term more commonly used to describe mages in Wales.

It was a hilly place, more than I was used to, having lived in the relative flatness of London for years. At one lookout I could see farmland laid out below, tiny homes scattered across the valley. Sabina could be in one of them but I had no way of knowing just by standing here.

I closed my eyes and I felt for the closest pinprick of heat. A musty smell hit me and there was a sudden dryness in the air.

"That must have been a—oh, Lord, he's here!"

I was in the post office. There was an old lady behind the counter, talking on the phone.

"Ma'am, I mean no harm. Truly," I said, holding up my hands. "Perhaps you could help me. I'm just looking for someone, to see if she's all right—"

The old lady grabbed a stapler and chucked it at me. "Go back to where you came from, wizard!"

My quick reflexes allowed me to bat the stapler out of the way.

"Hide, girl," the old postal clerk said, clutching the phone receiver tight. "He's looking for *you*."

Sabina was on the phone right there. If I could just talk to her, I could tell her that I didn't mean her any harm, but before I could shout something the old woman hung up the phone and started looking for more things to throw at me.

I backed out onto the street, where a crowd of about a dozen people had started to gather outside the butcher's shop.

"There he is!" someone shouted and the crowd turned towards me.

I ducked into an alley in an attempt to get away but I realized I was at a disadvantage. These people knew the ins and outs of the village. I didn't even know *where* I was. I could hear shouting in the street. I closed my eyes. There were still pinpricks spread out all around me, little sources of heat. Any one of them could be Sabina's location. I could just randomly teleport between them until I found her, but that seemed risky. The villagers were onto me, and if I teleported to the wrong spot it seemed likely that I might get beaten up or even killed.

Then I noticed that one of the pinpricks of heat was different from the others. It was decreasing in size and warmth, dwindling down by the second. That was odd.

There was only a little bit of that pinprick left. I closed my eyes and hoped it was enough to lead me to her.

The ground beneath my feet changed, going from stone to wooden floorboards. Warmth hit my face and when I opened my eyes I saw a crackling fire in front of me, American dollar bills curling in the heat as they turned from green to black.

Ah, clever. Sabina had figured out that the money was enchanted and was trying to destroy it before it could lead me to her. She just wasn't quite fast enough.

A floorboard creaked behind me and I had enough time to turn out of the way before Sabina swung a candlestick at my head.

"Whoa!" I hopped away out of strike range. We were in some kind of stone turret, up in a wooden loft. It was dark, the light from the fire the only illumination besides the grey sunlight coming through a smeared, high window. There was a bed up in the loft and a barrel with two boxes serving as chairs. It was a barren place, like a cell, littered with dirty cups and clothes.

"I'm not here to hurt you," I said to Sabina, who was readying for another swing.

"Just you being here could hurt us," Sabina spit out. "How did you find us?"

I noted the *us* rather than *me*. My eyes went down to Sabina's stomach. I supposed she was showing a little, but I didn't have much experience with these things. She wore a simple red cotton dress, long sleeved to guard against the cold, and a long white woollen vest.

"Magic," I said. "I made a magic coat that went where the money was. I gave it to Janey to give to you."

Sabina huffed. "That idiot. He really should have known better than to trust a shifty wizard like you."

"There's a lot going on back in London," I said. "I wanted to make sure you're all right."

"Who else knows you're here?" Sabina asked, eyes narrowed.

I paused. The smart answer would be to lie, to tell her that several people knew exactly where I was, that if I didn't return safe and sound they would all converge on this location and she'd be discovered. That would be the correct answer to keep me from ending up dead in a shallow grave, but it wasn't the answer that would win Sabina's trust.

"No one knows I'm here or where I am," I said, lowering my hands. "I came here on my own, just to talk with you, nothing more."

She gripped the candlestick tighter. My curse didn't allow me to hurt another person, even as an act of self-defence, so if Sabina wanted to clobber me to death there'd be nothing I could do about it. Sabina looked closely at my face and seemed to decide that I was telling the truth. Regret flitted across her face followed by a grim determination. She set the candlestick down on the makeshift table.

"Did Arthur sic you on me?" she asked.

"Yes, but . . . Princess Sabina, I know we haven't always been on the best terms, but I'd never betray the confidence of a woman in distress. Tell me what's going on here and let me help you."

Below us on the ground floor a door flew open.

"Sabina! Are you all right?!" a woman called up, gasping for breath. It sounded like she'd run here—wherever *here* was.

"Yes, Angie, I'm fine," Sabina said, eyes still on me. "This is Paul Gallagher. He came all the way from London to talk to me."

I waved down from the loft. Angie's eyes slid over to me, uncertainty clear in her wobbly gaze.

"The lads in the village figured that was the case," she said slowly. "Do you need any help?"

"No, no. He'll say his piece and then he'll go," Sabina said firmly.

"Well, we'll be outside if you need us," Angie said. Sabina said her thanks and Angie went back outside.

"It seems like the whole village is set on protecting you," I said.

"Kington is like that. They protect their own. Brennan's wife is from here; she asked them to look after me."

"Kington, eh? Never heard of it."

"Then how did you get here—oh, right, magic. Please, no, don't explain it to me. I hate when mages go on. What exactly have you come here for, Gallagher?" Sabina suddenly seemed tired. She took a seat on the edge of her bed, hand on her belly. I sat on the wooden box turned makeshift chair.

"All right, let me tell you what seems to be going on from my perspective," I said. "The Virtuis Party don't want you to marry Arthur and your kid to inherit the throne. You flounced off, and now the Virtuis thugs have been using that as an excuse to get rid of you—easy to make you disappear if you've already done half the work, right? Van Holt and Fairweather and God knows who else has been looking for you so they can convince you to leave the country, but more likely they are out to kill you."

"Mm. Sounds about right."

"Now, I don't think Arthur is part of this plot," I said. "He's not a member of the Virtuis Party but . . ."

"No, Arthur isn't part of that party," Sabina said. "He considered joining as a shadow member—as a royal he could never openly join any political party—but they made dropping me a prerequisite." She smiled proudly as she spoke, but her words turned into a scowl. "So no, I don't think Arthur is looking for me to kill me. But I still don't want him to know where I am."

"Because you don't think he can protect you?"

"Protect me? *Ha!*" Sabina said. "No, I'm hiding from him so he can't hurt me again."

My blood ran cold. "Hurt you?"

She hesitated. "It was just the once," she said, her tone suddenly apologetic on his behalf. "But still, that was the line." I thought of Mrs Spratt's words, about how her husband had never hit her, but "there were days where I wished he would, because then I could leave." How many women were living in situations like Mrs Spratt and Princess Sabina, just bracing for that first hit? And they were both well-off women with means and resources. If they struggled, what about the many women who were less fortunate?

"Didn't anyone stop him?" I pictured members of the palace guard standing nearby, maybe not in the same room but close enough to hear.

Sabina shrugged grimly. "He's a prince. Who'd stop him?"

I knew she was right. Kitty had told me as much, how when they were children he'd hold her down and slap her again and again, saying he just wanted to make the right side of her face match the left. Even when he was finally pulled off her, he suffered no repercussions. And this was a guy I'd actually considered working for. What had I been thinking?

"The night of my birthday party," Sabina said, "we had a big fight. As you might have heard, I am expectant with child." For a moment a fond smile passed her face, and then it was gone. "I wanted to go public, to make it known I was his wife—"

"Wait, what?"

"Oh, we're married. Didn't you know that?"

"Since when?!"

"Three years ago," she said. "Arthur had just had another fight with his father, so to spite the old man we'd gotten married in secret. Of course, it was merely a church wedding—we couldn't risk actually registering it. But we are married in the eyes of God, and what God has bound together the law of man can't undo. Correct, Mr Gallagher?"

"Sure, but the king might disagree." I rubbed my temples. "So what happened the night of your birthday?"

"I told him I was pregnant and that it was time for us to go public. He gave me the same line about it not being time yet. I pushed back. Eventually he had enough and punched me in the face." She spoke calmly.

"And now?" I said. "What do you want now, Sabina?"

She smoothed out her dress. "I want a promise from Arthur that he will never hurt me again. I want him to declare me his queen, for us to be married once more, this time in Westminster Abbey."

"Sabina, you've really picked an uphill battle here, you know that?"

"Why?" She tilted her chin upwards. "My family were part of the ruling class in Dahomey. My grandmother's country was weakened by the British—"

"Right, because Dahomey was selling slaves to America, and Britain was trying to end the slave trade—"

"Only after they used slavery to build an empire!" Sabina said. "If the bleeding hearts of Britain wanted to rectify their ancestors' wrongs, they'd give me an army to go back to Africa and retake my throne," she said. "But they won't, and all their meddling in West Africa means I have no home to go back to. If I can't rule over the nation of my grandmother, at least my child shall rule over Britain. I will challenge anyone who says my child does not have rights to that."

"No, that's not the uphill battle I was talking about," I said. "Expecting Arthur to change, that's the impossible part."

Sabina looked away. "Once he realizes that I am able to leave him if I wish, he'll change. He'll rein himself in if I can show him there are consequences."

I highly doubted that Arthur even knew what *consequences* meant.

"I hope you're right, Sabina," I said. "But still, I worry. I don't think you should stay here."

"What, in Kington?"

"No, not just Kington. I mean the whole country. You should go someplace where a lone Black woman won't attract much notice." When I'd been popping around the village, I'd seen only white faces.

"The people here would never snitch on me," Sabina said defiantly. "Like I said, they're a loyal sort."

"I'm sure," I said. "But if I could find you, it's only a matter of time before Van Holt does. He has this magic coat, one he made using hair and, I don't know, blood from Arthur and King Harold. It traces a family line from father to child, father to child. It can vaguely hone in on the child you're carrying, so as long as you're carrying it . . . well, you're in danger."

Sabina wrapped her arms around her belly. "I'm not ending my pregnancy, if that's what you're getting at."

"I'm just letting you know what your enemies are up to," I said wearily. "Look, I will relay your terms to Arthur—"

She turned to me. "You won't tell him where I am, will you?"

"No. No, I won't tell him where you are—"

"Promise me. Promise me you won't tell *anyone*."

"I promise," I said. "I'd never endanger a woman like that."

Sabina let out a sigh of relief. "Thank you. Someday, when I am in power, I shall remember this."

"Don't go doling out royal favours just yet," I said. "Not while you're living in some stone hovel."

"It's an old windmill, thank you very much," she sniffed.

We went outside. A couple of cars had pulled up alongside the house and some lads were milling about. I think I might have even recognized a few of them from my time teleporting about the village.

Sabina talked to them briefly before waving me over.

"Trevor here will give you his Book. Use it to take the bus to Chester, then to buy a ticket back to London. Don't use your own Book for anything until you are back in the city." Sabina stepped in closer.

"And be nice when they give you a ride to the bus stop, hmm? These people rightfully don't trust you. Try and put them at ease."

"Any news you want me to pass along to anyone back in London?" I said. "Besides what we discussed, I mean."

Sabina shook her head. "The less you say, the better."

"All right." I didn't know how to say goodbye to this woman. We still didn't particularly like each other, but now we were bound by my promise to keep her safe.

"I can see why she liked you so much," Sabina said.

"Who?"

"My cousin," Sabina replied casually.

"Ah, so you *did* know," I said.

"Of course. It had long been family lore that Uncle David had traded away his own daughter for a stranger's son. My parents might have done the same, if they had gotten the idea. And had easy access to infants." She shuddered and rested a hand on her stomach. "I know you think me power hungry, but I'm not my uncle. I'm not just using this child to advance my own lot. If in the end, I truly believe it is safer for us to just disappear from London society, I'll do so. I want them to sit on the throne, but even more than that I want them to live to a ripe old age."

"I understand." Once more Sabina reminded me of Mrs Spratt. She was also just trying to do right by her child. "Sabina, you really shouldn't stay here."

She nodded. "Yes. I have somewhere to go, though it's somewhere I really don't want to go."

"Oh, well, that's perfect then. No one will think to look for you there, wherever it is."

"Speaking of leaving . . ." Sabina looked over to the crowd of townsfolk. One of the men was coming over to us.

"Mr Gallagher, are you ready?" he asked.

"Ah, yes." But when I stepped forwards the man held up a hand.

"That coat stays here," he said gruffly.

I didn't protest, just slung it and the vest off my shoulders. I handed them over to Sabina.

"Give them to the kid when they're old enough."

CHAPTER 17

After a night on a sleeper train I arrived back in London. I dropped Trevor's Book in a postbox—lost Books were dangerous things in the wrong hands, but the postal service would return it to him free of charge. Worn out and not exactly sure of my next step, I hopped on a bus to my studio.

It was early morning, the sun barely over the city skyline. The sandwich shop on the corner was open and the owner was just frying up some sausages to make breakfast baps. I bought one, enjoying the warmth in my hand as I headed up the street to my studio. There was a crispness in the air, the streets relatively quiet before the big rush to work. I felt relieved to be back on my patch—the countryside was nice but it had all felt too remote. I guess what I liked was the nature and beauty of the countryside but the ability to enjoy the city easily too. A place like Hillcrest. I pushed the thought away and tried to focus on how good I'd feel when I finally tore into the sandwich I'd bought.

That happy thought died when I saw Fairweather and Van Holt standing outside the building door.

"Morning, Gallagher." Van Holt's gaze swept me up and down. I was wearing a heavy, patched tweed coat—a kind Kington local had given it to me after I had given up my vest and jacket.

"Nippy morning, hmm?" Fairweather said. "Perhaps we could step inside to talk."

"I have nothing to say to you two." I hadn't really formulated a game plan just yet. I had turned over the matter in my mind as the train had rattled through the countryside. I had no plans to give up Sabina—not to Prince Arthur or to the thugs of the Virtuis Party—but beyond that I hadn't figured out my next move.

"You don't have to talk, just listen," Van Holt said. "And believe me, you'll want to hear what we have to say. In private."

Van Holt and Fairweather had very different physiognomy, Fairweather with his gangly limbs, long face, and balding dome, Van Holt shorter and more compact but graceful, paired with a sharp, angular face. But they were both sporting malicious, identical smiles that made them seem like twins.

"Yeah, I still think I'll pass."

Van Holt looked over my shoulder and gave a little wave. I heard car doors open and slam shut. About four tough-looking lads had gotten out of two nearby parked cars and were standing by and waiting for further instructions.

"We could go somewhere else to talk, but as a courtesy I figured we'd come to you," Van Holt said. "Only Fairweather and I will come up. We don't mean to impose on you any more than we have to."

I took a deep breath of cool air and stepped forwards. Fairweather and Van Holt were blocking the entrance to the building, parting only slightly to let me unlock the door. In silence we took the stairs up to my studio. Once I opened the door to the space Fairweather looked around wide eyed.

"Wow, so this is what a cloth mage's studio looks like?" He picked up some shears.

"Don't touch anything," I said. I put the kettle on, partly so I'd have tea to go with my bap and also because I was making an effort to act as normal as possible. Van Holt watched me with piercing eyes, as if I might give away all my secrets in the slant of my shoulders or the way I poured hot water into a mug.

"I'll have a cup of tea too," Fairweather said brightly.

"We won't be here long enough for that," Van Holt cut in. "How about you take a seat, Gallagher?"

I shot an annoyed glare at him—this was still *my* studio, not his. I took my time, getting out the crystallized sugar and powdered milk from the cupboard, giving my tea a good stir before chucking the tea bag in the bin. Only then did I come over to where Van Holt and Fairweather were. Van Holt had pulled up a chair while Fairweather awkwardly sat on the edge of the sewing table. He eyed my mug and looked as though he wanted to ask where his was.

"Why are you dressed like a farmer, Gallagher?" Van Holt asked. I had just started to take off the coat I was wearing.

"The rustic look is going to be big this year," I said.

Van Holt gave me a condescending smile. "Oh, really?"

I started to unwrap my bap. Even in the presence of my enemies, I couldn't deny the hunger that was gnawing at me. I hadn't eaten anything for nearly a day at that point, and I wanted that bap in my mouth while it was still hot.

"Mr Gallagher, we're here—" Fairweather said, interrupted by me taking a big bite of my sandwich. "We—" Another big bite, followed by a slurp of tea.

Van Holt sighed and took out a small envelope from his coat's inside breast pocket. He removed several photographs and threw them down on the table. They landed picture side up. There were seven of them, capturing the same moment in quick succession: Andrew and I, standing in front of his bedroom window, midkiss. The lighting wasn't great—we were backlit by a bedside lamp in Andrew's room—but it was clearly us. The picture appeared to have been taken by someone outside, perhaps up in a tree.

I made the effort to swallow the bite of sausage I had in my mouth. "Resorting to Peeping Tom tactics, eh?" I said.

"Whatever tactics will win the war," Fairweather said. "You think you'd have learned your lesson after the scandal with Gabriella von Melsungen, but I suppose it's just your nature." He tsked. "It's one thing to want to sow your oats, but this is plain sexual deviancy."

"If this gets out, it will ruin three lives," Van Holt said softly. "Yours, of course, though with your already scandalous reputation you have the least to lose. That's not true of the others involved. The princess—poor girl hardly has a friend in the world. How will she feel when she finds out that her dear Gally slept with her fiancé? And speaking of said fiancé, he might be a duke, but even a duke can't socially survive this kind of public outing."

Van Holt spoke so softly that for a second I couldn't tell what were his words and what were my thoughts. I picked up one of the pictures.

"You can keep those," Fairweather said. "We have the negatives to make more."

"But we will hand over the negatives if you just cooperate with us," Van Holt said. "Tell us where Sabina is."

"Like I'd know," I said, but I was too distracted to sound overly defiant.

"You *do* know," Van Holt said, some steel coming into his voice. "Yesterday you came to this studio. At four fifteen you disappeared. You then resurfaced this morning at Marylebone station. You take a bus from there to here wearing some yokel's patched-up coat. I don't know where you've been, but I know you've found Sabina. Don't try to lie to me; this coat will tell me if you are."

Oh, right—he was wearing his usual outfit. I smiled at that. "Imagine. Going to all the trouble to become a cloth mage just so you can get a clue."

Van Holt twitched and I thought he might punch me. But instead he stood.

"I'm amazed you can still laugh at all this," Van Holt said. "You better get serious very quickly. Call me by three with Sabina's whereabouts, or else we will deliver these photos to the *London Times*. You and your lover will be tomorrow's big news."

Van Holt turned and stalked out the door. His sudden departure seemed to take Fairweather by surprise. Fairweather slid off his perch on the table, looked back and forth between me and the door, then hastily strode out after Van Holt.

He didn't bother to close the door behind him. Once their footsteps faded away and I heard the front door to the building close, I got up. I felt numb. It was bad enough when I'd just had my own and Sabina's fates weighing on me; now I had Andrew's and Kitty's as well.

No. Something was becoming clear to me—it was the fate of the nation, maybe the whole world. The Virtuis Party seemed determined to control the country, both the lives of its common citizens and the succession of the throne. Giving in to them would be giving them just a little bit more power to make everyone's life awful.

I could throw my lot in with the prince, tell him where Sabina was. But no, that would do no good. Sabina didn't feel safe with Arthur, and he might not be able to protect her from the far reach of Virtuis's thugs. Plus, Arthur wouldn't stick out his neck to save *me*. He wouldn't care if incriminating pictures were printed in the paper. Heck, he'd probably get a good laugh out of them.

Maybe I could fake out Van Holt and Fairweather. Give them a false location. Of course, once they investigated, they could still send the pictures to the paper. In fact, if I gave in now, for the rest of my life they could hold those photos over me, making me twist in the wind whenever they wanted something out of me.

Van Holt had only given me six hours to come to a decision. In a way, he was being generous. If he had really wanted to put the screws to me, he would have threatened to send the pictures to the paper by noon so that they could make the cutoff for the evening edition—

I suddenly felt wide awake. That was it. If not a solution, it was a way forwards—if I couldn't hold off my own fate, why not rush headlong into it?

I grabbed the pictures off the table and got ready to head down to the offices of the *London Times*.

~

A little after lunch I arrived at Andrew's house. The maid opened the door and let me in, taking me to the sitting room. Andrew joined me a second later. He had a worried look on his face and for a moment I thought that he had somehow already heard about what I'd done.

"Gally, did you hear about Minister Myers?"

"Dr Myers?" The man didn't deserve the title of doctor, but sometimes titles are a hard habit to break. "What about him?"

"They found his body down on the banks of the Thames," Andrew said, wringing his hands as we went to the living room. "Mother told me this morning. Some mud larkers found his body—not their usual find, I imagine. How horrible! I wish I knew where in the world Oberon was. Someone should tell him his father is dead."

For a moment I was struck by Andrew's compassion, that he was worried about our old schoolmate. Oberon Myers had been in our cloth magic class and, thanks to an act of baby swapping, Dr Myers's son. The two of them had a complicated relationship, especially once Oberon had discovered that David Myers wasn't his biological father. But he would probably still need to hear of his father's death. I just had other things to worry about in the moment.

"Did he drown?" I asked, morbidly curious.

"No. He shot himself. I suppose he thought the tides would take his body out to sea. A very tidy plan, that, if it had gone off."

"That is . . . that is something." Had Dr Myers actually killed himself, or had he been done in by his Virtuis colleagues? Maybe they'd been trying to get Sabina's location out of him, or maybe he had killed himself to keep that from happening. Either way, it drove home just what a dangerous world I was moving in. "Andrew, we need to talk."

"We certainly do, Gally! You haven't been returning my calls at all! I've been worried about you—"

"Andrew, listen to me," I said, speaking quickly. "In a couple hours the evening edition of the *London Times* will come out. They will include a story about you and me being lovers."

Andrew froze, smile still on his face. "What?"

"The other night . . . when we were kissing by the window, someone saw us and took a photo."

"What? They just happened to have a camera trained at my bedroom window?!"

"They were following me. Some people have been looking for a way to discredit me, and they tried to blackmail me with pictures of us together," I said.

Andrew blinked like I'd just blown sand in his face.

"Gally, if they wanted money, you could have come to me—"

"I didn't want this hanging over me," I cut in. "So I took the photos myself to the papers."

Andrew had somehow become even more incredulous.

"*You* gave the photos to the papers?" Andrew repeated. "You did? But . . . why?"

"Because I didn't want it hanging over my head—"

"Well, it's going to come down on all our heads now," Andrew said. "My God. Kitty will be heartbroken when she sees what you've done."

"What I've done?" I said. "You came on to *me*, Duke Fife."

"Yes, but . . . Gally, she doesn't love me the way she loves you."

"How did you think this would play out?" I said, getting a little angry that this was all being dumped on my shoulders.

Andrew's big blue eyes stared at me.

"I've loved you from the day we met," he said. "All I wanted was for you to look at me the way you looked at pretty much everyone else."

I didn't have a reply to that. I wanted to tell him that he didn't really love me, it was just that the innate magic upon me had made it so, but I knew that wasn't totally true—even if the magic had had some hand in making Andrew like me the day we'd met, it was his own feelings that had kept that torch aloft.

He'd been one of the few friends to stick by me all these years and I had taken advantage of that.

Andrew was taking quick, deep breaths and I worried he was hyperventilating. But after about thirty seconds he seemed to calm down.

"All right. All right. It's all right," he said. "When the paper comes out, it will be bad. I don't know if I can protect you—or myself, for that matter—from the fallout. But that's all right. My family has property in France. We'll just leave the country, go abroad—"

"Wait, what?"

"Well, we can't stay in the UK," Andrew said, equally bemused. "This is a scandal that needs to be weathered from afar. But it's all right, Gally. Honestly, I'm happy." He smiled and it looked genuine. "It's okay if the world turns against us. We'll be together, and—"

"What?" I said yet again. "Andrew, I'm not leaving the country."

"But Gally—"

"For fuck's sake, don't call me that!" I said, losing my temper. "I've always hated that nickname. I'm not one of your little Eton mates, all right?"

Andrew stared at me.

"Gally, if you stay here, you could end up in prison," he said. "Or worse. Please, just come with me."

He was so earnest, clutching my hand as if I were in danger of slipping under the waves otherwise. Andrew was so kind and loving, which was to his disadvantage when it came to winning me over: I preferred to be the one chasing after people, not the one being chased. Andrew was just too much of a nice guy for me to ever fall for him, and now I had drawn him into this web.

"I don't love you, Andrew," I said. "I slept with you because you were there. You could have been anyone. I've never spent more than a minute thinking of you."

Andrew's hands fell away from mine. Looking into his face was like looking at a cracked mirror.

"I think you should leave," Andrew said. "I plan to be out of the country by tonight, and I have much packing to do."

When I left him sitting there in his living room, like a slumped-over doll, I felt awful but also slightly relieved. With Andrew out of my orbit, that was one less person who was in danger.

CHAPTER 18

I went back to my studio. On the corner a newspaper seller was undoing the twine around stacks of the evening edition. It didn't look like I had made the top fold, which was some comfort—that space was reserved for the news of Minister Myers's death. I bought a copy. There it was on the society pages—Duke Fife's Affair with Mage. I supposed it made sense that Andrew was the headliner; he was more of a public figure than me. Ah, but there it was in the article: The other man, cloth mage Paul Gallagher, was recently let go from a position at Buckingham Palace as Princess Katherine's personal dresser. Great.

Part of me was surprised that the *Times* had run the story at all, considering that it involved not just a duke but the princess. Usually the press was a little more circumspect when it came to the royal family. But perhaps the Virtuis Party had infiltrated the *Times* and had primed them to run this story.

I tossed the paper into a bin next to the paper seller, who gave me a disgruntled look and fished it out as soon as I walked away. I felt bad for not giving Kitty a heads-up about all this. I'd go talk to her now. I'd heard that Cobalt had been given my old job. I'd get in touch with him and convince him to set up a meeting with the princess for me—

A black car cut across the street, crossing over into the wrong lane so it came over the kerb with a screech, its front bumper stopping a mere foot away from me. Two burly lads got out of the car while the driver sat behind the wheel. Before I could wrap my head around what was happening one of them had grabbed my arm while the other stared down the newspaper seller.

"Government business," the bloke said to the seller. "Don't bother calling the cops."

"What? Let go!" I tried to yank my arm out of the man's grasp but he continued to drag me over to the car. People on the street watched with startled expressions and frozen faces. "Help! Stop them!" I yelled at a couple walking their poodle. No response. I'd like to think that *I'd* spring into action if I saw a stranger being abducted, but these people just stood there. No, worse—they broke free of their petrification and walked on, clutching each other as the dog moved double time to keep up with them. Even the newspaper seller cast his gaze away and tried to look busy, straightening magazines.

The thug shoved me into the back seat. The other thug was already back there. He tugged a dark sack over my head and pulled a cord tight so it closed around my neck, not tight enough to choke me but tight enough to make me hyperventilate. He then used a thick twine to tie my wrists together. The other thug got in the car and slammed the door shut. We all jolted forwards as the driver backed off the kerb, horns around us blaring as he did a uey to get back on the right side of the road.

The sack around my head was black but not too thick. Every breath made the cotton damp and unpleasant. And I was breathing a lot, quick huffs in and out of my mouth as I tried not to panic. I was too startled to speak. If I had full possession of my mind I would have chatted to the two thugs sitting on either side of me, charmed them into telling me something, anything. Maybe I could even talk them into letting me go. That was a long shot but I'd talked myself out of worse spots.

Have you really? a voice inside my head murmured. It was true: this did seem pretty bad. Since I couldn't speak, I turned inwards. What would Thomas say in this situation? Thom always had a better handle on the criminal mindset than I did. He'd say that it was a good thing, actually, that they'd covered my head. It meant that there was a chance they would let me go later. If they wanted to kill me they wouldn't care if I saw where I was going. And I was still alive, so I must have some value to them.

Them. Was this Arthur's doing? No, it had to be the Virtuis Party behind this. Arthur was a brute, but he preferred to lean on his royal status as a show of power, not use thugs. The two lads even looked slightly familiar. Maybe they had been two of the bruisers standing outside my studio this morning.

It occurred to me that I should be paying attention to the turns the car was taking so I could figure out which part of the city we were in, but I soon gave up on that idea. I wasn't a cabbie; I didn't have "the knowledge." The turns and bumps just made me feel even more nauseous than I already was.

Twenty minutes later the car stopped and the driver turned the engine off. The door to my right opened and I was dragged out. With my wrists tied together it was even harder than before to try and tug my arms away. We went up a metal fire escape and I had the horrible sense that they were dragging me up to the roof so they could throw me off it. My legs gave out. The thug behind me accidently trampled on my calf. He grumbled and grabbed my other arm, and between the two of them they carried me up to the second floor. They opened the door and I felt such immense relief to be inside. We went from a hallway and turned, squeezing through another doorway. The thugs' footsteps echoed and I sensed we were in some kind of larger, sparse room.

And just like that they dropped me. I tried to break my fall but with my hands bound as they were all I ended up doing was taking the hit to my elbow, making me cry out.

"Ah, good. I was starting to worry that you'd died of fright," Van Holt said from somewhere on my left. "Odd for you to be so quiet."

Then came the pressure of someone straddling my chest and pulling the cloth sack from my head. Van Holt was sitting on my chest. The thugs stood back near the door and Fairweather was on my right, looking nervous like he'd wandered into the wrong meeting and didn't know how to gracefully extricate himself.

"You think you're so clever, don't you?" Van Holt said, his voice as soft as usual but with a growl to it. "Blow up your own life before we can? Maybe you should have just finished the job and jumped into the Thames, hmm?"

He actually had a good point there—if I had truly wanted to protect Sabina and Andrew and Kitty, I could have killed myself. That's what Dr Myers had done. But my will to live was just so strong, my sense of suicide as an unforgivable sin so deeply ingrained, it honestly hadn't crossed my mind.

We were in a large room, like some kind of storage space. There was a big rectangle of a window, so large it made me think of the window in a cathedral. It looked out on an industrial wasteland, a few blocks of grimy warehouses like the one I presumed we were in. A filmy orange light from the streetlamps outside filtered in, the only light in the room.

I smiled. "Maybe I just wanted to see your handsome face again."

Van Holt scowled and stood. I rolled onto my side in order to sit up.

"I'm going to give you one more chance to simply tell us Sabina's whereabouts," Van Holt said.

"And if I don't?" That wasn't a rhetorical question: I knew that Van Holt and Fairweather would employ some kind of torture, but I figured if I knew what was coming I could prepare myself for it. I started to think of the tales of saints I'd heard growing up. St Lucy, who had plucked her own eyes out. St Sebastian, who'd managed to strike a pose even while struck through with arrows. I prayed to them, hoping they could give me some of their strength.

Van Holt just gave me an annoyed look.

"Fairweather, unbind his hands," Van Holt said.

Fairweather frowned at the order. "You know, Van Holt, I'm the deputy prime minister of this country."

Now Van Holt looked doubly annoyed. "So?"

That was enough to chasten Fairweather. He came over and knelt beside me.

"Now, Gallagher, no funny stuff," Fairweather said, reaching out to undo the twine around my hands. I stayed still, eager to be free of the damn twine. When Fairweather was done he leaped back as though I might strike at him. I just rubbed my wrists. It was nice to have my hands free but I wasn't so naive to think that Van Holt had done this out of the goodness of his heart.

"I actually don't want to have to resort to violence, Gallagher," Van Holt said, with a soft sweetness. "So I've worked hard to make a magic coat to sidestep the necessity for that." From a dry cleaner's bag he pulled out a long coat. "I made this for you. I realized that my truth-sensing coat wasn't enough. It can vaguely tell if someone is lying or telling the truth, but it's unable to garner specifics. But *this* . . . this will make sure that every word you speak is the truth."

It was a beautiful coat made of alternating panels of leather and velvet.

"How'd you construct a coat like that?" I asked. Cloth mages loved to talk shop and Van Holt was no exception. He smiled and looked pleased with himself, like he was answering questions during a lecture at the UCL.

"I went to Liverpool and requisitioned the material used in the Liverpool Catholic church's confession box. That's what the velvet panels are made of."

"Wow, the Liverpool Catholic church, eh? That's where I used to go as a kid. I probably sat my arse down on that very fabric a hundred times."

"Exactly!" Van Holt said. "And now it will compel you to tell us the truth." He tossed the coat to me. I caught it and held it in my hands.

A magic coat can't do anything until someone puts it on—it needs the human soul to make it work, to act as the battery that powers the magical circuitry inside it. Van Holt was a good cloth mage, but this was a big ask. If mages could make coats that compelled people to tell the truth, law courts around the world would put them to use. But it was a hard effect to pull off. It seemed that there was no one coat that compelled people to speak honestly. Instead, like a lot of magic, it had to be tailored to the individual. Van Holt was wise to use something personal to me—my relationship with God, the fabric used in my childhood church—to create a truth-telling device.

"If you don't put it on yourself, I'll have Sam and Brett break your arms and pull your limbs through the sleeves," Van Holt said.

I realized with a start I was shaking. I'd had bones broken violently before—not just when I'd been made a mage, but when Oberon had nearly killed me with a pool cue. I couldn't bear the thought of going through something like that again, of coming that close to death or dying. I reached up and slowly started to undo the buttons on the coat I was wearing.

Pathetic. A second ago I had been fantasizing about plucking out my own eyes and presenting them to my enemies. Now, with merely the slightest threat, I was doing whatever they asked.

God, I thought as I pulled on the new coat, *please find some way to deliver me out of this. Help me stay true to my word and protect Sabina.*

The confessional coat was a perfect fit. Van Holt crouched down, a pleased smile on his face.

"All right, let's go over some baseline questions," he said. "What's your full name?"

"Paul James Gallagher," I said, the words rolling off my tongue even as my teeth started to clack together. Was it from the cold or the fear? I really couldn't tell.

Van Holt nodded. "How old were you when you lost your virginity?"

"Fourteen," I said. Van Holt raised his eyebrows.

"Wow. You really do start young in Liverpool, hmm? Fourteen. Was that before or after your mother died?"

"After."

"Hmm. Do you think you were just trying to replace one kind of love with another?"

"Most likely, yeah."

"Van Holt, old boy, is this really necessary?" Fairweather said.

"You want to ask him a question?" Van Holt gestured towards me. Fairweather straightened his shoulders.

"Well, I suppose to help test the coat," he said. "Has Princess Katherine ever spoken of me? What did she say?"

"She said that you're a horrid old man. That you take your tea black because your breath would curdle milk."

Van Holt snorted and even the two goons by the door ducked their heads to hide smiles.

"Van Holt, your coat doesn't work!" Fairweather said in an affronted tone. "There's no way a creature as sweet as Princess Katherine would say something so cruel!"

"No, it works," Van Holt said, still chuckling. "All right, enough fun and games. Gallagher, where is Sabina?"

I clamped my mouth shut, trying not to speak, but just like with the previous questions I could feel the answer bubbling up inside of me, as involuntary as a burp. Finally I opened my mouth.

"You can't make me tell you."

All three of us—Fairweather, Van Holt, and me—sat there in stunned silence. Fairweather recovered first.

"See?! I told you the coat was a misfire."

"No. No, no, no. I'm sure it works." Van Holt's voice was as soft as always but a little bit more of his accent was bleeding into his words—a sign of stress? He pointed a finger at me. "Did you ever sleep with Professor Lamb?"

"Yes, back when I was a student," I said. "Really, Van Holt, are you just going to make me talk about my sex life all night?"

Van Holt frowned. "This isn't right. The coat should compel him to tell the truth."

"Maybe it's flawed, like your mind-reading suit," Fairweather suggested, and Van Holt shot him a look that was pure murder. They both looked to me when I cackled.

"It does. It works. You're a genius, Van Holt." I felt a rush of giddy delirium, like the Holy Spirit had descended upon me, gifting me with understanding and the ability to explain things in this asshole's language. "While I'm wearing this coat, every word I speak is the truth. And the truth is that you can't make me tell you where Sabina is." I started laughing, an over-the-top reaction, sure, but the despair I'd felt early had broken into something just nonsensical. "In fact, maybe you've made a coat that's *too* powerful. You ever hear the theory of consensual reality? Surely they covered it while you were in school. The idea that because we all believe something, it becomes true? Let's test it out." I looked upwards at Fairweather. "Hey! Hey, Fairweather! Someday I'm going to watch as you die horribly!"

"Van Holt? He's wrong, right? This is just wild speculation, correct? Not an actual prophecy?" Fairweather asked with a waver in his voice.

Van Holt was very still. "We need to get him out of that coat."

Before I could speak more of horrible things befalling Fairweather and Van Holt and their ilk, they were on me, pulling the coat off me so quickly a button flew off.

"Can I keep it?" I asked, rubbing my arms. I was wearing a button-up shirt and V-neck jumper and it wasn't nearly warm enough for the early-November evening—the dingy room we were in was clearly unheated. "Since you made it especially for me and all?"

Van Holt looked angry. I could see it by a subtle shift in his features, the angling of his eyebrows and how he seemed to be sucking his cheeks into his skull when he breathed.

"I've given you many chances to join the right side of history, Paul," he said. "If I have to get the answer out of you under duress, so be it."

No one ever says *so be it* about happy things. Van Holt motioned to the thugs and they pulled a chair out from a far corner of the room.

"Jesus, I could have been sitting in a chair this whole time?" My arse was frozen from sitting on the concrete floor. But as the chair came into the orange light I fell silent. It was a heavy chair, made from thick blocks of wood. There was nothing sinister about it in itself except for how bulky it was.

Van Holt grabbed me and shoved me into the chair, which was unnecessarily rough; I would have taken a seat if he'd asked. But then one of the thugs was using rope to tie my hands to the arms of the chair. I remembered Van Holt's threats from earlier about breaking my arms and I felt my breath catch. I tried to think of saints who had suffered from broken bones: Catherine on the wheel was the only one who came to my panicked mind. I prayed to her.

Once they were done tying my wrists the thugs retreated to their posts by the door. From a bag Van Holt removed a small hammer and piece of wood. The bit of wood was tiny, even smaller than a book of matches.

"Hold down his right hand, Fairweather."

Fairweather gingerly pressed his hands down on top of mine, wincing as if touching a slug. Van Holt wedged the thin piece of wood under the nail of my right pointer finger.

"Van Holt, you don't have to do this. It's pointless," I said, my teeth already clenched in anticipation of pain. Van Holt looked at me, his eyes somewhat glassy.

"At this point, I'd do it even if you did tell me," he said, then swung the hammer. It connected with the wide edge of the wedge and the fingernail of my index finger popped clean off, revealing a little bed of red underneath. I screamed but it was like an infant's scream, one of pure sensation beyond words. It was such a tiny wound but it was like my whole self had been laid bare.

"Where is she?" Van Holt asked, positioning the wedge under the nail of my middle finger. Before I could say anything at all he brought the hammer round and drove the wood under my fingernail. This one didn't pop off so cleanly. It was still half-attached. I kicked at the floor as Van Holt used his hand to push the wood in deeper. The nail was straight upright now, barely attached but somehow freestanding. Van Holt finally pulled the piece of wood away and I screamed, then again when he reached out and pulled the nail off.

He flicked it at my face.

"Tell me where she is," he said.

I was whimpering and crying and I felt like every nerve in my body was exposed to the air but I still managed to shake my head no.

Van Holt positioned the wedge under my right ring fingernail.

"Van Holt, should we—"

Fairweather didn't get to finish his sentence. Van Holt brought the hammer round and I screamed, louder than before. He had hit the wedge so hard that beyond just taking off the nail it scraped deep into the skin of my finger. I jackknifed in the chair, body twisting in pain as much as my restraints would allow.

"Tell me where she is," Van Holt said flatly. I barely heard him over the noises I was making, but I stilled when he started to place the wedge under my pinkie fingernail.

"Van Holt, I told you, it's pointless," I said. "I'm never going to tell you."

And even in pain my words came out strong. They filled me with a sense of calm and certainty. Even if I did die here, I'd die before I went back on my promise.

Van Holt's face twisted but just before he could bring the hammer down Fairweather grabbed it.

"I say, Van Holt, this doesn't seem to be getting us anywhere," he said. Van Holt looked at him as if he were a lamp that had suddenly come to life and spoken. Van Holt stood and for a moment I thought he might just start swinging the hammer to clobber Fairweather to death.

Instead he let go of the hammer. I jumped in my seat as it clattered onto the floor.

"What would you suggest?" Van Holt said, sounding like his usual chilly self.

"Well, perhaps Mr Gallagher is of strong enough stuff to withstand physical assaults upon his person, but what of his loved ones?" Fairweather said. "He has family back in Liverpool, yes?" Fairweather looked at me. "You have a father who's dear to you, don't you?"

"His dad has been on death's doorstep for years," Van Holt said bitterly. "Even now he's in a coma, barely hanging on. Gallagher's not going to protect the old man if it means giving up a woman and her unborn child."

"Well then, what about your brothers?" Fairweather pressed on, still looking at me, like we were bartering over a used car. "You have two older brothers with typical Irish names, yes? Let's see, I'm trying to remember . . ."

"Patrick and Michael," Van Holt supplied. "He hates them, doesn't care for their wives, and hasn't ever even bothered to meet their sprogs. Even if we threatened the lot, he still wouldn't budge."

"Well, if not flesh-and-blood family . . . what of Verity Turnboldt?" Fairweather said. Van Holt actually looked over at me, curious. "Yes! If you don't tell us where Sabina is, poor Ms Turnboldt may suffer from a horrible accident and untimely death. You don't want that, do you? Whatever loyalty you feel to Princess Sabina, surely your personal loyalty to Verity is greater?"

I laughed, and even that seemed to send new waves of pain through me. "Just try going after Verity," I said. "She'll make mincemeat out of you."

"See? There's no reasoning with him," Van Holt said.

"Well, if not a loved one, how about a stranger?" Fairweather said. "You're digging your heels in because you hate the thought of a mother and child in danger, yes? Well, if you don't give up Sabina's location, some other young mother and babe will meet a grim end."

I was astounded by how casually Fairweather suggested this. There wasn't even any cunning to it; he was merely trying a different figure on a balance sheet to see if the numbers worked out.

"If I don't tell you where Sabina is, you'll kill some random family instead? What is this, a game show?" I asked.

"No, not random," Van Holt said, perking up. "A certain mother and child. Two people you've grown close to over the past few months."

Fairweather looked confused, but I caught on to Van Holt's meaning immediately. He was talking about Laura and Beatrix. And for the first time I felt my resolve truly crack. I'd made a promise to Sabina that I'd protect her, but the thought of anything bad happening to Laura or her child made me feel like I was falling into a dark hole with no bottom. Nausea rolled through me.

But under my fear was confusion. Something wasn't right. I'd only ever shared my thoughts about Laura and Beatrix with one person. Shipwright, Van Holt's cousin and henchman. Lamb had warned me once, told me that anything I told Shipwright Van Holt would also know, but he'd given that bit of advice with his usual smirk, the one that implied that he knew an even greater secret but wasn't going to share it. Maybe Shipwright had told Van Holt that I had a crush on my landlady. But it just seemed so oddly personal.

I thought of all the times I'd seen Shipwright over the years and how he always wore the same simple outfit. I thought about how, though they were cousins, I'd never seen Shipwright and Van Holt in the same room.

Maybe because they were the same person. One man living two lives: in one he was Peter Van Holt, the United Kingdom's Court

Magician, a South African married to an upper-class British woman. In another life he was Adam Shipwright, just "one of the lads," married to a woman he loved and adopted father to her daughter. It was crazy to imagine that Van Holt might have been carrying on like this the whole time, using magic cloth to transform himself into practically a stereotype of a British bloke. But it made a weird kind of sense.

I had nothing to lose by finding out for sure.

"Yes. A certain mother and child," I said. "Maybe a woman and her daughter. A widow, both of them immigrants here."

Van Holt went from looking pleased with himself to uncertain.

"The girl would be seven, with her blonde hair in plaits, the wife a good cook. Quiet, unsure of her English," I said. "What if something were to happen to them? Wouldn't that be awful."

"I say, Gallagher, that's an awfully specific random example," Fairweather said, then let out a squeak of surprise when Van Holt twisted a hand in my hair and pulled. Pain lanced through my scalp.

"Shut up," Van Holt said. "Don't you say another word, Gallagher." He looked over at Fairweather, who was blinking at this sudden display of violence with wide eyes. "We should just kill him," Van Holt said, trying to sound cool, but panic was clearly rising in him. "He's not going to say anything."

If I hadn't been sure before, I was now. Peter Van Holt was a married man. Shortly after becoming Court Magician he'd married Lady Albright. It had been something of an arranged marriage, with the Albrights looking to marry their daughter off to whatever bloke became the Court Magician and Van Holt looking for acceptance to upper-class British society. Supposedly there wasn't any love between Van Holt and his wife, but it was still a legal union. It would be a huge, life-destroying scandal if it came out that, while using an alias, Van Holt had married another woman.

"You're right," I said. "I won't say anything more if you drop this. We'll both never speak of them again, either woman or either child.

Two lives for two lives. I won't go near yours if you leave mine out of this. Deal?"

Van Holt stared down at me, anger clear in his eyes even as he calculated all the possible outcomes of my offer. I could hardly breathe, eyes locked on him. What if he didn't truly love Olena and Gayle and was willing to cut them loose? Or what if he loved them so much he decided it was better to just cut my throat?

"Van Holt, we can't kill him. He's our best bet at finding Sabina," Fairweather said. "You told me that. You said you'd given Gallagher clues specifically so that he'd sniff her out. And it worked! Now we just need to get the details out of him, all right? So stay your hand, old boy."

"I'm not saying anything until I have Van Holt's word that we will leave the women and children out of this," I said, still wincing at the hand pulling my hair.

"A gentlemen's agreement, then, Gallagher?" Van Holt said. "I'll consider your loved ones under a special protection if you will do the same for mine?"

"Yes," I said. Relief rushed through me as Van Holt let go, letting my head drop down to my chest. I wanted to rub my scalp and fix my hair back in place but the ropes held me down, digging into my skin.

"Good. But I still need to know where Sabina is." Van Holt took out a switchblade. Fairweather stepped forwards and gingerly put a hand on Van Holt's shoulder.

"Now, be calm about this, my friend. Insanity is doing the same thing over and over again, expecting different results. Yes, we could remove Mr Gallagher's remaining fingernails and move on to his toes, but if past evidence is any indication, it will get us nowhere. So maybe we need to have a little think about what to do differently."

Van Holt didn't say anything, just stood there, staring at me. Finally he turned and walked towards the door.

"I'm going to call our leader," he said, the usual flatness in his voice giving way to the slightest quiver, "and find out just exactly how far we can go here."

He left through the door that led to the hallway. One of the thugs went with him while another stayed near the back of the room.

Fairweather let out a long sigh and gave me a rueful smile.

"I'm impressed by your fortitude, Mr Gallagher. I myself am feeling quite squeamish, and I'm not even the one having his nails ripped out!"

"Ha ha. Ha ha ha," I said.

He squatted down in front of me.

"I'm sorry about what a nasty business this has become."

I could see what he was doing, playing the good copper to Van Holt's mean one. And even knowing that, I could feel it working. For the first time I felt like I could see Fairweather's good qualities: an easygoing nature paired with a highly adaptable sense of morality.

"Can I have some water?" If Fairweather was going to try and get on my good side, I'd milk it while I could.

"Of course, my good man. Brett, can you get us some water?"

Brett, the thug at the back of the room, looked like he wanted to object, but in the end he wordlessly left. I wondered how far he'd have to search—did the taps even work in this place?

It also occurred to me that this might be my best chance to escape, seeing as it was just me and Fairweather in the room. I could maybe slip my uninjured left hand out from under the ropes, but then what? Fairweather would be on me before I could untie my other hand, and the innate magic upon me meant that I couldn't fight him. So escape seemed out.

But then, what was I to do?

"How is the princess?" Fairweather asked.

"Better now that you're not creeping on her all the time," I said. He shook his head.

"I only sought to protect her. She's such a sweet, dear thing. I would have been good to her. But you had to come along and pour poison in her ear."

I laughed. "That's what you think? She came to *me* because she wanted you out of her hair."

Fairweather sighed. "And what a fine friend you turned out to be."

He had me there. The door opened and someone—not Brett but some new, burly thug—came in.

"Couldn't find water. Will this do?" he said, handing Fairweather a bottle of beer.

"Who are you?" Fairweather asked.

"Mike. I'm new. Brett had to go take a piss." This Mike character was a large man, tall and wide with a bushy black beard further adding to his size. He definitely had the build of a bruiser but his attire made him seem more like an intellectual: he wore little round glasses and a tailored, dark-maroon pin-striped suit. It looked to be magic—why would some Virtuis bone breaker be wearing a magic suit?

"Beer is fine with me," I said quickly. Mike used a pocket bottle opener and handed the bottle back to Fairweather, who obligingly held it up to my lips. It was a somewhat astringent pale ale, but the taste of it was a nice distraction from the pain still throbbing out from my hand and the top of my head.

Fairweather sniffed the bottle and winced before putting it on the ground gently. Mike drew back a few paces to stand in the shadows.

"I know things here have been rather . . . unpleasant," Fairweather said. "But really, Paul, there's nothing here that you can't recover from. Nails grow back. At this point, Van Holt hasn't done anything unforgiveable."

"I don't think you get to call that, mate," I said.

"Well, he's done nothing irrecoverable, then," Fairweather amended. "But honestly, I don't know how much longer I can make him listen to reason. When he comes back into this room and sees that you're still uncooperative, he won't be satisfied with taking your nails. He'll want a whole finger."

My hands instinctively clenched into fists, causing another wave of pain to go through me as my raw red nail beds came into contact with the skin of my palm.

"Please, relax. Such things are extremely preventable," Fairweather said. "Just tell us where Sabina is and you walk out of here a safe, whole man. You have a surprisingly strong will, but no man can last forever. Right now you can decide if you want to leave here with ten fingers or none."

I still had my fists balled up, too scared to unclench them. Fairweather's words were admittedly getting to me. If I didn't have my fingers, how would I sew clothes and do magic?

Perhaps, if Fairweather had been given a chance to coax it out of me, I might have told him everything. But before he could, Van Holt stormed back into the room, looking triumphant. The other thug trailed in behind him.

"He's coming here," Van Holt said.

"Who?" Fairweather asked.

"The leader," Van Holt said with a smug smile. Fairweather spun back around to face me. He clamped his large hands over my fists and squeezed, causing me to scream in pain. Fairweather didn't flinch though I was yelling in his face. Instead he just stared at me with terrified eyes.

"Tell us where she is now, Mr Gallagher," he pleaded. "Tell us and we'll let you go. We'll let you leave before the leader gets here. Don't hold out now. You won't survive this."

"It doesn't matter," Van Holt crowed. "Tell us now, tell us later—the leader still wants to see Gallagher." Van Holt's mouth stretched open into a wide grin. "Wants Gallagher to see *him*."

"What?" I croaked out, voice still cracked with pain. I didn't understand what they were saying, why their words were so weighted with meaning. Neither answered me.

Fairweather let go of my hands and sat his arse down on the cold concrete floor. He picked up the bottle of beer and took a deep, long swig.

"Should have done this from the start." I could tell that Van Holt was excited because not only was his voice growing louder but his accent was coming on thick, unchecked by his usual self-consciousness. "If you'd known the power and vision behind the Virtuis Party, maybe you would have joined us. But it's too late for that now. Now, you'll see it too late. See it and die."

"This leader of yours, whoever he is, he's just some guy," I said. "I'm drawing my strength from a higher power. What can some bloke do to change that?"

Van Holt shrugged coyly, still a smug smile on his face. Fairweather was still staring off into space, seemingly a million miles away. When he spoke it gave me a start.

"I remember when I first met the leader. It was four years ago," he said. "I've been a faithful C of E man all my life, but I don't think I ever truly believed in it, mm? Just went to services because, well, that's what one did. I thought the world was more or less as one saw it. Then I met the leader and realized how wrong I was."

Van Holt was still grinning wildly. He picked up the hammer.

"Hey, where's my little piece of wood?"

That snapped Fairweather out of his daze. "Why?"

"Because I want to take off a few more of Gallagher's nails."

"What? There's no need for that now."

"I know."

"Well, I'm not going to help you. I've had enough unpleasantness for one night," Fairweather said primly, still sitting on the floor, drinking beer. Van Holt rolled his eyes and spotted the little block of wood—it was next to my chair.

"Hey, come hold his hand in place," Van Holt said over his shoulder to the thug who had followed him in.

"I'd really rather not," the thug said.

Van Holt huffed in annoyance and looked to the other thug.

"Fine then. Brett—wait, you're not Brett. Who the fuck are you?"

"I'm Mike." His voice was familiar—deep tones, upper-middle-class London accent. It wasn't enough for me to place him but I was sure I'd heard his voice before. "I'm new."

"Oh? Well, welcome to the party. Come over here and hold his hand in place."

Mike made his way over. Even though he had a hundred pounds of muscle on me, he still seemed tentative as he came to my side and held my hand down. I stared up at his face, trying to make out his features under the glasses and beard. Who was he? How did I know him?

I was still mulling it over as Van Holt wedged the bit of wood under the nail of my pinkie. Mike looked down and his eyes were filled with remorse.

"I'm sorry," he said.

And then I knew. It was Oberon fucking Myers.

CHAPTER 19

Van Holt brought the hammer round and removed my pinkie nail.

"Gaaaah!" I yelled. I threw my head back to look up at "Mike," so hard that I bumped it on the wooden backing. "You motherfucker!"

Van Holt laughed as he poked at my now-nailless pinkie. "Ah, finally getting a proper reaction from you, Gallagher! Good!"

"Why?! Jesus Christ, why?!" I said, more screaming than speaking.

"Just because I could," Van Holt said.

But I wasn't talking to him. I was talking to Oberon.

He had stepped away, holding his hands in front of him like a child who'd just gotten caught pinching some sweets. It was his voice that had given him away, but now that I knew who he was I could see it in his face as well. The Oberon I had known years ago had always been tall with a broad frame, but in the years since then he had bulked up even more. Younger Oberon had been all about neat hair and stylish eyewear, whereas the man in front of me had the look of an improvised radical. What was he doing here, looking so changed, using a fake name and helping my enemies torture me?

He met my accusing glare and gave a little shake of his head.

"I wonder if the thumbnail is harder to remove?" Van Holt said, crouching down to look at my hand.

"Van Holt, my man, stop," Fairweather said listlessly from where he was sitting on the floor. "Your conduct is not becoming of the Court

Magician. This gloating and unnecessary cruelty . . . it's not how British gentlemen should behave."

That made Van Holt freeze. When the shock passed a new, cold anger was in his face. He glanced towards Fairweather and once again I got the sense that he was considering braining him with the hammer.

"Fine." He stood and walked away. "But when the leader gets here, Fairweather, you might just have to reconsider that."

Oberon looked as though he wanted to ask a question but stayed quiet. There were a few minutes of strained silence.

"So just who is this leader anyway? Who's got you so spooked?" I asked.

"You'll see soon enough," Van Holt replied as he lit a cigarette.

Ten tense minutes passed. There was the sound of footsteps coming down the hall. We all perked up, gazes collectively turning to the door.

A young man opened the door. He was in his early twenties, his face pockmarked and eyes hard. He glanced around the room, taking us all in. He didn't even flinch at the sight of me, hand bloody and bound to a chair. Then he ducked into the hall to let someone else step inside.

It was James Godfrey.

"What?! No!" I yelled.

He looked nearly the same as when I'd seen him four years ago. The same age, the same milquetoast smile. He hadn't aged a day—he still looked like a man in his late thirties. A pleasant enough face, with round, blameless features. When I'd last seen him he hadn't had a stitch on him besides a man's shirt. Now he was dressed in a black three-piece with a pale-grey shirt and nice shoes.

Oh yes, one more big difference: His forehead was totally clear. No sign of the bullet that Thomas had put into his brain.

Fairweather clumsily got to his feet, fumbling with the now-empty beer bottle before setting it down on the floor. Even Van Holt stood up straighter, casting a glance to my bloody fingernails, perhaps worried he had gone too far after all.

"Godfrey?" I said.

"Hello, Paul," Godfrey said, as casual as if we were simply meeting for tea. He was trying to contain a wider smile, but he failed. "I've been curious to see your reaction. You didn't disappoint." He looked to the young man standing in the hall. "Harry, I want you to go and wait by the car. You two can leave as well."

He said the last bit to Oberon and the nameless thug still hanging back in the shadows.

"Are you sure, boss?" Nameless Thug asked.

"Oh yes. I doubt Mr Gallagher will be giving us much trouble, and we have sensitive topics to discuss."

Nameless Thug ambled out of the room. Oberon gave me a helpless look before following him.

I considered calling out to him—I still didn't know exactly what Oberon's game was here, but he was perhaps the only person in the room who could help me. But if that was the case, I'd only be ruining things by blowing his cover. So I stayed quiet as the door closed behind him and I felt in my stomach like I had made a huge mistake.

"He won't tell us where Sabina is," Van Holt said, like a child tattling to Mummy.

"No worries," Godfrey said. "We'll get to that soon enough. But let's give Mr Gallagher a chance to ask some questions, since I'm sure he has plenty."

"How are you alive?" The shock I felt was so consuming it had actually pushed away the physical pain.

"Am I?" Godfrey said wonderingly. "Alive, I mean?" He flexed his hands and looked at them as if they were not his own. "I breathe and eat and shit but I rarely feel like I *need* to. When I'm cut, I bleed, but the wound just sews itself back up." He rubbed the middle of his forehead. "Even after your friend Dawes gave me one between the eyes, an hour later I was none the worse for it." He looked to me. "Getting shot so soon after being revived was a shock, but it was even scarier coming to and being all alone in that dingy pub. I wasn't quite sure what to do with myself, but I knew it'd be a bad business to announce my resurrection publicly—as a nation, Britain's never really been the type to believe in miracles. Too stodgily rational for that kind of fluff."

"You set the pub on fire." I had always thought it was Thomas who'd done it in order to cover our tracks. But even though it was thorough (like him), it was a risky move that had endangered innocent people (not like him). "But there were four bodies in the pub—"

"Yes, I found a rough sleeper and did him in, then left his body there as a stand-in for mine," Godfrey said. "I'm glad you noticed—you were one of two people who would have cared about the exact number of bodies. I'm glad my work paid off. After that I sought out old friends"—he nodded to Fairweather, who gave him a faltering smile—"and new ones." A nod to Van Holt. "And we set about getting this country back on track."

"By starting the Virtuis Party," I said.

"Correct. I couldn't very well be the public face of a political party, but I could be the unseen hand that guides it. Before I died I'd had many plans. Plans that, even over a decade later, could still save this great nation. I've never had the desire to become a mage, but I've always been interested in how magic could be used in service to king and country."

"Oh? Tell me more." I figured each second he kept talking was another second I kept breathing. I still didn't know how I was going to get out of this room alive.

Godfrey paused. "Well, no need to get into specifics *now*. I know you've had a rough time of it here tonight, but you can't blame Fairweather and Van Holt for being a little overzealous. The future of Great Britain is at stake, after all. And we're the only ones who can save it."

"What? By keeping a mixed-race child out of the line of succession?" I bit my tongue, angry at being goaded into talking back. If I wasn't careful I might let slip something that would tip them off as to where Sabina was hiding.

"Yes!" Godfrey said. "And don't look at me like that, like I'm some common racist. The monarchy has long been used to forge alliances with other nations. If Artie marries Sabina, the descendant of some deposed African princess, what does that get us? Nothing. And no one will want to marry their child either. It's true! If you think Britain's bad about issues of race and purity, the rest of Europe's even worse."

"It's hard to picture worse than you," I said.

Godfrey shook his head with a pitying smile. "I'm just looking out for the greater good. Our empire crumbled, but as a nation we can still be saved. When I was alive—" For a moment Godfrey looked as though he had lost his train of thought, and then he recovered. "Back before I died, I was involved with various studies and experiments to help Britain during the war."

"Oh, I know," I said. "You and Hollister and Myers cut up little children."

"For king and country, yes. But that went nowhere. Since we couldn't crack innate magic, I looked into cloth magic. And we discovered that cloth magic could do wondrous things, but only ever on a small scale, since it was always limited to what one person was capable of. But what if you were able to concentrate that power?"

"You get the magical shield generated by the prisons," I said tiredly.

"Yes, exactly! We tried to impose order on the world and it didn't take. The lands beyond our shores are too wild to be civilized. America and Russia will destroy each other: America will send A-bombs to Moscow; Russia will deploy suicide mages to the US. The rest of the world will be caught in the cross fire as collateral damage. But the UK will survive and emerge from the ashes to rule the world once more."

"Rule a pile of rubble, more like it," I said.

"Well, sometimes you need a blank slate," Godfrey said. "We have a plan. Not just a plan, a vision. And when the average Brit hears that, even if they don't agree with all our values, they feel comforted. We offer them a vision of the future they can imagine: one that looks exactly like the past, like two mirrors set up facing each other. And we will stick the course, because unlike other parties where the leader can be deposed at a whim, it is *my* hand at the helm. And I'm not going anywhere. Not for hundreds of years. Virtuis members, even if they don't live to see our success, know that it will happen because they know that *I* will be there. My vision and reach extend beyond that of mortal men, and I have you to thank for it."

There was a bluish tint to his face, but perhaps that was just my imagination. He moved and talked as easily as a living person, but just looking at him made something in my brain screech, setting off warning bells that had been silent in my life until now. Until I had come face-to-face with this ungodly horror.

"You should join us, Paul. You could save lots of lives," Fairweather said. I turned to him and it was a relief to look at a human face rather than Godfrey's.

"Save lives?"

"Yes. With our plan to protect the United Kingdom, we want to shield Ireland as well," Fairweather said. "You're of Irish extraction. If you joined our party, you could lead the charge to unify Ireland and have them rejoin the UK."

"Wow. I'm flattered that you think so highly of me that you'd ask me to untangle one of the thorniest knots of the twentieth century."

"We could use you for other reasons too, Mr Gallagher," Godfrey said. I had to force myself to look at him. "You are one of the country's most gifted magic users. I myself am proof of that. Beyond being a learned mage, you have the ability to produce actual miracles. Join us and put those wondrous abilities to good use."

Thomas's words echoed in my head: *Do you want to spend the rest of your days skinning people alive?* That was what Godfrey would have me do. Lord knows he had enough fanatics lined up, ready to let themselves be skinned as part of some kind of fascist death cult.

"Could I be Court Magician instead of Van Holt?" I asked, mainly to see Van Holt's reaction.

He flinched as if a bug had just flown into his eye.

"Sure," Godfrey said. He looked to Van Holt. "I'm sure Van Holt, in the name of unity, would bow to your superior skill if you were to come aboard."

Van Holt took a deep breath.

"If Gallagher needs the post to satisfy his own ego, of course I would give way," he ground out. "But I think he's just winding us up."

"Yes, I also think so," Godfrey said easily. He looked to me. "Well, Mr Gallagher? Is Van Holt right? Are you just having a laugh at us?"

I was tied to a chair, my hand still bleeding, and surrounded by my worst enemies. I certainly didn't feel like I was having a laugh. I was in very dire straits, and if I didn't find some way to talk myself out of that chair I'd never live to see sunup.

"No, not at all," I said. "I have to admit, what you say makes some sense."

"It really does," Godfrey agreed.

"I'd be curious to learn more about this plan you have to protect Britain," I said. "Especially if it involves cloth magic. I'm sure Van Holt's done a good job and all, but maybe I could help shore things up a bit."

"I'm sure you could," Godfrey said amiably.

"And now that I've met you, I can see it would be stupid to go against someone who is, for all intents and purposes, immortal," I said.

"It would be rather foolhardy."

"So if you could just undo these ropes, maybe we could start over?" I said.

"Gladly," Godfrey said. "But first, as a sign of good faith on your part, why don't you tell us where Sabina is?"

Well, damn. That *would* be a sign of good faith, wouldn't it? A line that once crossed I could never go back on. Not that I was planning to make that crossing, but it did make it difficult to convince Godfrey and his goons that I was on the level.

"They've gone to Europe," I said. "Sabina told me they were planning to escape to Spain, travel down to Morocco, and hide out there."

Godfrey looked to Van Holt. From a bag in the corner Van Holt took out a coat. It was the one for tracking down Sabina—or, to be specific, the child growing inside her.

Van Holt shrugged it on and closed his eyes.

"He's lying," he said, eyes still closed but a vein on his forehead twitching. "I can still feel them in the northwest, but it's much fainter." Van Holt quickly took off the coat and put it back in its bag.

"I guess they haven't left yet," I said, trying to cover up my fumble.

"Haven't left yet?" Godfrey said. "So you *do* know where they are?"

I could usually rely on my brain for a quick retort or joke or lie, but it was failing me. I was full of doubt, scared that anything I said might actually put Sabina in danger.

"They're in Manchester," I said.

"Where in Manchester?" Van Holt asked.

"Living in an apartment near the west market."

I was making stuff up. I didn't know Manchester at all, but luckily, from the confused looks around me, neither did the other men in the room.

"He's lying," Van Holt said. He'd changed into his regular coat, the one that supposedly helped him read people.

Godfrey shook his head. "I expected as much."

"I'm not!" I said. "You must have a man in Manchester. Call him up! At least check what I'm saying!"

"No need for that, Gallagher," Van Holt said. "My coat can tell me that you're lying."

"Too bad it can't make me tell you the truth, eh?" I said, scorn filling my voice. If I couldn't convince them with my lies, I'd go down telling them off. "For all your power, you can't do a damn thing if someone stands against you. Your kind thinks that you can get anything if you have enough power, but you can't change the mind and will of another person."

"That's all very good, Mr Gallagher," Godfrey said. "But where does holding out get you?"

Van Holt was taking out more items from a bag. Tools, such as a handsaw and garden shears. I supposed he really had been holding back earlier when he'd stuck to just taking my fingernails off.

Didn't look like he was going to be holding back much longer.

"If you aren't going to see the light, Mr Gallagher, I'm afraid you can't leave this room alive," Godfrey said, his tone cloyingly apologetic. "Surely you understand the position your existence puts me in? I can't have you bringing my enemies back to life or something even worse. Power like yours can't be allowed to fall into the wrong hands. I have a moral responsibility to kill you."

CHAPTER 20

He paused as if waiting for me to protest, to break down and give him what he wanted. But I was too chilled to speak.

"The problem with your amazing powers, Mr Gallagher, is that if they fell into the wrong hands the results could be catastrophic," Godfrey repeated, as if worried I hadn't heard him the first time.

"Oh, believe me, I know that," I said. "Last time I was forced into doing magic, I ended up bringing *you* back."

"Exactly. And since you've proven that you can't be trusted, it would be a massive mistake on our part to let you walk out of here. So I want you to know that it is a certainty that you will die in this room. But if you wish, you can still aid our cause and tell us where Sabina is hiding out."

I laughed but it had a thick layer of fear to it. "Why in Jesus's name would I help you? You just said you're going to kill me anyway!"

"Yes, that's true. But how much you have to suffer up until that point is up to you," Godfrey said.

I stopped laughing. Van Holt came over, holding the gardening shears. He wasn't wearing his lie detector coat anymore. I supposed he did not want to get my blood on it.

Fairweather started inching towards the door. "Hey, chaps, if I don't have to be here for this then—"

The door opened and Fairweather leaped a foot into the air—to be fair, I would have done likewise if I weren't tied to a chair. Oberon stood in the doorway, his massive frame blocking out any light from the hallway.

"Who are you?" Godfrey asked.

"I'm new here," Oberon said, stepping into the room.

"Oh, right. Mike or something, wasn't it?" Fairweather chimed in.

"No. Oberon Myers." Oberon drew a gun. Godfrey looked at him quizzically while Van Holt took a step back, closer to me. Fairweather threw his hands up in the air. "Van Holt, put down the shears or I will shoot everyone in this room."

"Well, Van Holt? Is he lying or telling the truth?" I asked, giddy now that rescue was at hand. Van Holt scowled at me but let the garden shears fall to the floor.

"Good. Step away from Gallagher," Oberon said. Once Van Holt complied, Oberon swung the gun around to point at Godfrey. "Now, let me ask you the same thing you asked me a second ago: Who *are* you?"

"Myself? Well, my name's James Godfrey."

Oberon blinked. His composure was steady but the name seemed to throw him. "James Godfrey? Are you the son of the man my father worked with during the war?"

"No. I am the same man."

Oberon tightened his grip on the gun. "You're a liar and a fraud. Everyone knows that Godfrey died when the Germans bombed St Paul's."

"Yes, it's true, I did," Godfrey said. "But here I am, back again. My nation needed me and so through a miracle I was resurrected."

"This is a sham," Oberon said. "You've just concocted some outlandish story in order to create your own little cult."

Godfrey gestured to me. "Ask Mr Gallagher."

Oberon looked at me.

"It's true," I said. "Watch him, Oberon. He's not a man like you or I."

Godfrey grinned like I'd just given him a compliment. "See? I am who I say I am, believe me. Your father recognized me the moment I walked into his office. That's why you're here, isn't it? You heard about your father's untimely death?"

"He would *never* kill himself!" Oberon said, control melting away. "He was a selfish, opportunistic, self-serving bastard who never met an angle he couldn't work. If his back was up against the wall, he'd find a crack and slip through it! I'd heard how he was in the cabinet, and a man like that never rises up except through shady back deals. You killed him because he knew too much!"

"Well, it's not so much that he knew too much; it's that he wasn't willing to share his intel," Godfrey said. "You wouldn't happen to know where Sabina is, by any chance?"

"My cousin?" Oberon said, his confusion clear. "What does she have to do with all of this?"

"As far as you're concerned, nothing," Godfrey said. Behind Oberon, Fairweather was starting to slowly make his way towards the still-open door.

"Obie, behind you!" I yelled. Oberon spun around, but instead of firing he just locked eyes with Fairweather. For seemingly no reason at all Fairweather cried out, clutching his face. Oberon grabbed his shoulder and tossed him into the centre of the room so he landed by Godfrey's feet.

"I can't see!" Fairweather cried out.

"Shut up," Oberon said.

"Cloth magic?" Van Holt said, eyeing Oberon's suit. His gaze flitted upwards and the moment he made eye contact with Oberon, Van Holt cried out, clutching his forehead. Oberon turned his head towards Godfrey. I could see from Godfrey's back that his posture was relaxed, hands gripped loosely behind him, shoulders open. Whatever had befallen Van Holt and Fairweather seemed to not affect him. Oberon stared into Godfrey's eyes, gun shaking in his hand.

"What?" Oberon asked. "Why isn't it working?"

"You're right; your father was a coward," Godfrey said, voice level. "He knew that if he didn't tell us where his niece was, we'd get it out of him by hook or by crook. It really shouldn't have come to that—he was a high-level party member, after all. A cabinet minister. One of us. A true believer. But he always placed his own personal pride above the good of the nation. He saw his family as an extension of himself, so when it came down to protecting his family or helping the nation, he made the selfish choice."

"What are you talking about?" Oberon seemed to be losing his grip on the situation, fear creeping into his voice. The fact that Godfrey was seemingly impervious to cloth magic had clearly unnerved him.

"Or maybe he killed himself for purely selfish reasons," Godfrey mused. "He knew that it would be all the worse for him if he ran. Once we found him, well, he knew what was in store." Godfrey made the smallest gesture back towards me, strapped to the chair and bleeding. "He knew that our victory was inevitable, and so he chose a quick death over a slow one. Maybe you should follow your father's lead, young Myers. If you truly knew who we were and what you had pitted yourself against, you'd put a bullet in your skull now rather than wait and see."

I noticed that Fairweather was blinking rapidly and no longer in pain—was his vision coming back?

"Why doesn't cloth magic work on you?" Oberon asked. Godfrey said nothing in reply, just tilted his head to the side.

"He has no soul!" I shouted. "Oberon, stop talking to him and just shoot him!"

Oberon seemed relieved to have a clear directive. He fired and the bullet went straight through Godfrey's head—I swear I heard it cut through the air a foot above me.

Fairweather yelled and jumped away as Godfrey's body hit the floor. Van Holt stood locked in place. Honestly, I wasn't sure if shooting Godfrey would actually "kill" him; I'd seen Thomas shoot him dead once before, after all. But it did seem to incapacitate him at least.

Fairweather's vision had returned. He was looking at Godfrey's body and making strangled, keening screams.

"Shut up," Van Holt said through gritted teeth. "It's fine. He'll be fine."

"How soon will he be fine?" I asked. How much time did we have before Godfrey was up and walking and talking again? Van Holt did not answer.

"Fairweather," Oberon said, "undo Paul's ropes or the next bullet's for you."

Fairweather stopped his keening and looked between Oberon and Van Holt.

"Don't move, Fairweather," Van Holt said harshly. The man's vision had seemingly returned since he was fixing Fairweather with a stern glare. "Just wait this out."

"*I'm* not going to wait," Oberon said.

Fairweather, staying low to the ground, crabwalked over to me and started undoing the ropes.

"Fairweather!" Van Holt shouted.

"No. No. Don't want to get shot. No," Fairweather said, eyes fixed away from Van Holt's glare, his focus on undoing the knots. He got my right hand free and my left hand shortly after. The ropes had been tight and I hissed at the sensation of blood rushing into my hands, making my nail beds throb anew. I rubbed my wrists where the rope had dug into my skin.

"C'mon, Paul," Oberon said. He had swung the gun away from Fairweather to Van Holt. Van Holt stared back at him, leaning forwards as if he was desperate to lunge at Oberon.

I shakily got to my feet. The edge of the seat had been cutting into the backs of my knees and my left leg had fallen asleep. I nearly stumbled to the ground as I stood.

"Paul," he said, "take the rope and tie Van Holt's hands to the pipe on the back wall."

"Oh, just try," Van Holt hissed.

"Go along with it, Van Holt, or I will shoot you," Oberon said.

"For Christ's sake, man, do it," Fairweather said.

Van Holt glowered but went over to the wall and allowed me to tie his hands behind his back to the pipe. My hands shook as I did it, worried that the innate magic would keep me from pulling the rope tight—would that be seen as an act of violence? It seemed the answer was no, since I was able to tie the knot.

"Now we'll tie Fairweather to the chair," Oberon said. There wasn't enough rope to tie Fairweather to each arm of the chair like I had been, so I tied his wrists to one of the chair's back slats.

"All right, let's go," Oberon said.

"You should crawl back into whatever hole you came from, Myers," Van Holt said. "It's the only way you'll be able to survive." He turned to me and some of the fire flickered in his eyes. "Gallagher . . . we've still got a gentlemen's agreement, yes? I'll keep to it if you do."

He sounded pretty tough for a man tied to a radiator pipe, but there was a desperation in his voice that was clear under the bluster.

"Yes." I didn't really have the energy to say more. Oberon grabbed hold of my shoulder and pulled me out of the room.

CHAPTER 21

About an hour later I was sitting in a houseboat, bobbing in a Camden canal. It was a cosy place, windows on all sides to let in the light from the streetlamps that lined the banks. On the bow of the boat a small generator puttered along, powering the dim lights inside the cabin, small bulbs that shone behind colourful paper contraptions made to look like stars.

I sat on a bed, holding my still-throbbing hand. Oberon had bandaged up each of my wounded fingers and was moving around the small space looking for a teakettle. We hadn't spoken as he had tended to my wounds. Even now it seemed like he was purposefully keeping himself busy so he wouldn't have to look my way.

"Aha!" he said, lifting up a small kettle while still keeping his back to me. From a jug he poured some water into it, then set it on a small, single-burner stove that was in the corner of the cabin. He turned a dial and the gas stove clicked on. Oberon stared down at it as though he were trying to read a message in the flame.

"It makes me queasy to see fire on a boat," I said. "Growing up in Liverpool, all the sailors I talked to always said they were more scared of fire than water."

Oberon tilted his head towards me, a small smile on his face. "Is that so? I've never spent much time on boats."

"Me either," I said. That conversation seemed to come to its natural end but Oberon kept it going.

"This isn't my houseboat," he said. "When I decided to come back to England, a friend of mine lent it to me."

"How bohemian." The quilt I was sitting on was made of faded silk patches, reminding me of a circus tent. On the shelves mugs shaped like various animals hung from hooks, further adding to the circus imagery. There was a gentle bob to the boat but on the whole the canal waters were calm.

The kettle started hissing. Oberon poured some loose tea into little sachets.

"Is jasmine all right?" he asked.

I shrugged. My mind was a million miles away, still stuck on the sight of James Godfrey, walking and talking and moving about. I didn't really care about what kind of tea Oberon had on hand—he could give me a cup of hot tar and I'd drink it down.

Oberon took two mugs off the wall and poured in the water. He handed me a mug that had an elephant on it, its trunk curled to make the handle. As I took it from him, the heat from the mug went straight through the plasters around my fingers and set my poor raw nails aflame.

"Ahh!" I dropped the mug to the floor. The elephant's trunk broke off and tea seeped into the floorboards.

"No worry," Oberon said, as if in reply to an apology. He grabbed a tea towel and got on his hands and knees to clean up the mess. His humbleness irked me, adding irritation on top of pain.

"I guess I should thank you for saving my life," I said.

Oberon sighed and shifted so he was kneeling. "I'm sorry about your hand. I'm sorry I have to yet again be apologizing for hurting you. I didn't mean for it to play out like this."

"And yet you still did it." Beyond the pain in my nails was the phantom feel of Oberon's hand pressing down on mine, holding it in place while Van Holt tortured me.

"I wasn't after Van Holt and Fairweather," Oberon said. "I needed to find out who they were working for. It was unfortunate, but I had to play along until their leader showed up."

"And just how far were you willing to play along, eh?" I asked. "If Van Holt had wanted to start cutting off my fingers, would you have handed him the shears?"

Oberon looked shocked. "No, of course not."

"Oh? Then what would you have done instead?"

"Well, I suppose I would have revealed myself and my true intentions and kept them under the gun until this Godfrey character arrived."

"So why didn't you do that when Van Holt decided he wanted to torture me some more?"

Oberon didn't have an immediate reply to that.

"It would have been risky," he said slowly. "What if one of them were armed in some fashion? In the moment, I went with what seemed like the safer option."

"For *you*." The pain was receding but present enough to make tears prick at the corners of my eyes. "Well, anyway, thanks. At the end of the day, I'm glad you got me out of there, even if you took your fucking time."

"I told you," Oberon said, "I had to wait to see who was behind it all. I needed to avenge my father."

I let out a cackle at that, one that made Oberon flinch.

"Mate, he wasn't your father and you didn't avenge him," I said.

Oberon's face hardened and for a moment he looked more like the Oberon of old, a hotheaded young man who hated more than anything other people's laughter, specifically when it was aimed at him. And I felt bitterly glad about that, that there was still some spark of the man who scared me, so I could continue to hate him. I hadn't even meant the jab about his dad; I'd just known it would needle Oberon further.

My eyes went to his hands, watching to see if they would clench into fists. They didn't.

"I understand that Godfrey was just one man and part of a larger organization," Oberon said. "I know that killing him alone doesn't mean that I've obliterated all the forces responsible for my father's death—"

"No, no, that's not what I meant," I said. "I mean you didn't avenge your dad because you didn't kill Godfrey. You *can't* kill Godfrey. He's already dead."

Oberon stared at me, waiting for some follow-up explanation.

"Gallagher, I know I've been out of the country for a few years," he said, "but I like to think some things stay the same. You shoot a man in the head like that, he stays dead."

"Not *this* man," I said. "He's not . . . he's, like, a construct. A jar of clay without a treasure."

"You're not making sense." Oberon got me a glass of water and carefully handed it to me. I didn't know how thirsty I was until I started drinking it.

"Years ago I did something foolish and I brought a man back from the dead," I said once I'd emptied the glass. "Godfrey was the man. Then Thomas shot him, just like you did tonight. I thought it was all over and done with, but I was wrong. When I brought him back, it wasn't . . . something's not right. That's why your cloth magic didn't work on him. You need a soul to practise magic and to have it work on you."

Oberon stood, ducking out of the way of the hanging light fixture. "This is . . . do you think my father knew?"

"Yeah. He knew Godfrey from before, right? Probably helped him reestablish his power behind the scenes."

"And then he turned on Godfrey? Why?"

"Sounds like Godfrey and his cronies were leaning on him to hand over Sabina."

"Yes, Godfrey mentioned her. But why would the government care about my cousin?"

Oberon spoke with what sounded like sincere puzzlement. He seemed on the level but I still wasn't sure if I could trust him—what if his whole rescue of me had just been part of a larger ploy to help him earn my trust? Maybe he was actually a member of the Virtuis Party. But that seemed quite convoluted when they could have just stuck to their original plan of torturing the information out of me.

"How close are you to Sabina?" I asked. Oberon sat in a chintz-upholstered chair and drummed his fingers on the arms. He stared at me and I realized that he was making the same calculations that I had been making a second ago: *Can I trust him? How much does he already know? Do I reveal more to him?* It seemed to me that we were both dancing around the same information.

"I'm very close to her," Oberon said. "We were both only children, and growing up we were like brother and sister."

"And as adults?"

"We stayed close."

"So then you know about her and Arthur?" I said.

"Oh, Paul, everyone knows about the two of them," Oberon said. "That's not some big secret."

"Did you know they are married?" I said.

Oberon startled at that. "How did you know about that?"

"Sabina told me."

Oberon nodded. "My father told me. He was the only witness at the ceremony. He was one of the few relatives Sabina ever trusted, and I think he felt chuffed being let in on such a big secret. So the Virtuis Party has found out about the marriage, hmm?"

"It's worse than that," I said. "They found out that Sabina's pregnant."

Oberon had just sipped from his mug of tea. Upon hearing my words he nearly spewed hot tea over me.

"What?!"

"Sabina told me too. I also put on this magic coat, which confirmed it."

"I see, I see," Oberon said. "And the Virtuis Party doesn't want a mixed-race child on the throne, so of course they're searching high and low for Sabina." His initial surprise gave way to something more reflective. "It's going to be a boy child."

"Well, I suppose you got a fifty-fifty chance of being right—"

"No, I can feel it—I *know* I'm right. Old Reginald, my grandfather, he went and saw a fortune-teller as a young man—rumour has it was a young Lady Fife he talked to, back before anyone even knew who she was. She told him a prophecy, that the next male born into his family line would reach greater heights than he could even imagine, that the child would restore his family to greatness. Reginald was enthralled with this prophecy, but as the years went by and his wife bore only daughters he grew quite bitter about it. He decided to take the fortune quite literally: he stipulated in his will that only a male descendant would inherit his wealth. It wasn't a magic spell or anything of the like, just the bitter act of a man angry that he himself had sired no sons. When I was born . . . I fulfilled part of the prophecy in a sense that I inherited Reggie's fortune. It was shared amongst my aunts and uncles in order to pay off family debts. I grew up being told that I saved my family, that I was destined for great things. But there always seemed to be something left unsaid, some doubt. And when Verity told me that I wasn't my mother's child at all, it made a scary amount of sense. Deep down I'd always known I wasn't the one everyone was waiting for."

I tsked at that. "See, this is why fortune-telling is such a load of bunk. All it does is mess with your head—"

"But Sabina's child . . . ," Oberon said as if just continuing his own ruminations, "if the child is in fact a boy, it will be the first male child born to old Reginald's line in three generations. He's the one." Oberon looked to me. "Can't Arthur protect them?"

"He's tried. But even if he's not with the Virtuis Party, he's a dangerous man anyway and Sabina's right to want to stay away from him. Plus, it seems like Godfrey's got a web bigger than even the prince's. He has the Court Magician in his pocket, as well as control of the government."

"Well, then why is he so threatened by one woman and her child? Parliament needs to certify royal succession. If they don't want someone on the throne, they have the votes to block such a thing."

"Yes, but that's still a big rigmarole. Much easier just to kill them." I yawned. My right eye itched. Out of habit I reached up with my right hand to rub it and was met with the rough feeling of cloth. Through the bandages my fingers twinged in pain.

"I'm sorry. I don't think I have any recoup cloaks handy that can help you," Oberon said. "The best thing you could do right now is rest. You take the bed; I'll take the floor."

"I'd rather sleep in my own bed, thank you very much." Though as I spoke, I wondered which bed I meant—my bed in the gardener's cottage? The guest bedroom at Andrew's? My cot in the studio? The bed in the town house that Tonya and I used to share?

"Any place you'd go is probably under watch right now," Oberon said. "You're in rough shape and need to rest."

A wave of sadness washed over me, making me feel tired indeed.

"I suppose." I didn't offer to take the floor or even try and share the bed with Oberon. I knew he was trying to do right by me, yet I couldn't help but resent the man. I flopped down onto the bed, undressed under the covers, and was soon asleep.

~

The next morning Oberon and I went to a nearby restaurant. We each ordered a full English breakfast. While the cook was serving it up I ducked out to a phone box to call Laura.

"Oh, Mr Gallagher! It's been over a week since I heard from you. I was beginning to get quite worried."

"Sorry for that, Mrs Spratt. I'll be away from Hillcrest for a while yet, but I've given the November rent to Prince Naveed and asked him to deliver it to you. Sorry it's late."

"I wasn't worried about the rent! I was worried about *you*, Mr Gallagher!"

It felt good to hear her voice, even as her words made my guts twist with guilt.

"I was also worried about you," I admitted. "Everything's all right up there?"

"Well, yes. Why wouldn't it be?"

So it seemed that Van Holt hadn't sent goons over to Hillcrest to round up Mrs Spratt and Beatrix. That was good. Maybe Van Holt was in fact a man of his word, or at least pragmatic. Sure, he could have used the two Spratts as leverage against me, but then there'd be nothing to stop me from revealing to the world at large that Van Holt was a man living two lives, one where he was the Court Magician married to one woman, another where he was a British man named Shipwright married to another. Even if the Virtuis Party was able to smother the story and keep it from being reported in the press, they'd probably demand that Van Holt abandon Olena and Gayle. And he seemed terrified at the prospect of that.

Which seemed to imply that he actually loved them. It was hard to reconcile the image of a loving husband and father with the man who'd joyfully taken my fingernails off.

"Don't tell me you are still worried about Harriet," Laura said gingerly, as if wary of bringing the girl up after our row.

"That is . . . this is bigger than even her. I can't explain it all over the telephone—you never know who might be listening," I said. "I just wanted to tell you I was all right and . . . to hear your voice." Jesus, I was getting too sentimental. What if Laura's phone was in fact tapped and I'd just given myself away? "I hope I can come home soon, but if I don't . . . in December feel free to rent the cottage out to someone else."

"No, Mr Gallagher, please, wait. I don't know what's going on, but please come ho—" I hung up the phone, not wishing to hear Mrs Spratt's worried voice any more than I had to. I was scared that if I let her say the word *home* my resolve would break and I'd return to Hillcrest, putting both her and Beatrix in danger.

Feeling rather glum, I went back into the restaurant where my breakfast was waiting for me. Oberon had grabbed us a small booth in the back. Aside from a couple of old men sitting near the front window, we were the only customers in the place. For a few minutes we ate in silence.

"So," Oberon said. "What do we do next?"

"What do you mean, 'we'?" I said, speaking around a mouthful of beans.

"Well, if what you say is true, then I'm far from avenging my father," Oberon said. "And they're not going to let up on you either. We may as well work together."

"This is where your help got me last night." I held up my hand to show off my bandaged fingers.

Oberon huffed. "I said I was sorry. I know it was a ghastly thing to go through, but I wish you'd weigh those four fingernails against the fact that you're still breathing. Look, I'll admit that I'm late to the show here. You have a far better handle on what's going on than me. But if you can put aside the past—"

"The recent past?" I said. "Or the *past* past?" My voice was rising and the two old men spared us a glance. "Should I weigh my four fingernails against the fact that you once *nearly beat me to death*?"

Oberon looked downwards.

"You said you forgave me for that," he said in a small voice.

"What? I did? Oh, back when you showed up unannounced at my dad's place in Liverpool, while I was home alone and still recovering? Oh yes, I wonder what *compelled* me to say that."

Oberon winced. "Really? At the time you sounded genuine."

It was strange to see such a burly man so uncertain. Since Oberon wasn't defending himself, my anger started to flag. I felt like an engine that was sputtering out.

"Look, it's complicated," I said. "I do want to forgive you, and on some intellectual level I do. Just . . . last night I came very close to dying, and so it's brought up old feelings."

That was as big an olive branch as I was willing to extend to Oberon. He nodded and started to eat his breakfast again.

"Do you think Gabriella would come and help us if you asked?" Oberon said. "She owes you one, doesn't she?"

"Why do you say that?" I asked.

"Oh, it's just, I heard the rumours about the two of you, that she'd cheated on her husband and that you were 'the other man.' But I had my doubts." Oberon had the shadow of a smirk on his face. "You're just covering for her, aren't you?"

"Jesus, Oberon, what are you going on about?"

"It just seems a little too convenient for her," Oberon said. "She's always had you wrapped around her finger, so I could believe that you had an affair with her . . . but I could also believe that you were helping her cover for something even bigger."

I sipped my coffee. "You know, mate, you sure talk a lot for a man who knows nothing."

Oberon bit off a corner of toast.

"I *do* know Gabs. I dated her for a good chunk of second year, remember? We had started to get pretty serious, so I figured it was time to be up front with her about my family's so-called fortune. I told her it was gone, spent long before my own birth. A week later she dumped me. I didn't make the connection at the time; I was too heartbroken.

But now I see that Gabs always had her own welfare foremost in her mind. You and I, we're just dupes to her."

He chuckled at that. I felt a swell of anger. Not at being called a dupe—Oberon probably had the right of it there. He was probably even right about Gabs. There was a summer when she and I had been an item, going to parties at night and exploring the city and surrounding countryside by day. We even took a trip to Cornwall to visit her family. It was a deliriously happy time, a heady combination of childhood freedom and adult agency. It was just after our first year of college, so we felt very grown up, but were still young enough to run wild. Then, a few days before school was due to start, she cut me loose. "Oh, dear heart, you'll always be my number one guy," Gabs said to me, "but if either of us are going to make something of ourselves, we're going to have to marry up." A week later she'd been on Oberon's arm.

So yes, I could believe that she'd dumped him merely because she'd discovered he was broke, but if Obie thought he could cosy up to me by bad-mouthing our mutual ex, fuck him. Fuck him, fuck him, fuck him.

"That's funny," I said. "Gabs told *me* she dumped you because you were a bore both in and out of bed."

Oberon paused, toast halfway up to his mouth.

"Oh, did she? Perhaps she left that out in order to spare my feelings," he said, unruffled. "Well, in a roundabout way I suppose I answered my own question: Gabriella won't come to help us because there's nothing in it for Gabriella. Shame. So who can we rely upon?"

Not Andrew. Not Lady Fife. Ralph? He was involved in a lot of local politics and a fierce opponent of the Virtuis Party. He'd want to help us, but I wasn't sure how much he could actually do.

"Have you talked to Princess Katherine since the picture was published?" Oberon asked warily.

I shook my head. "Haven't had a chance to." Which I felt grateful for—it wasn't a conversation I was looking forwards to having.

"Maybe the sooner the better," Oberon said. "Tell her about everything going on. Maybe she can help Sabina hide somehow."

"Even if she can, so what? Virtuis will keep looking for them. Arthur, as well," I said despairingly. And with Godfrey at the helm, they could afford to bide their time.

Oberon sighed, an impatient twitch by his eye. "Look, it's better than nothing. Right now we need to take immediate action and worry about the long term later. You say you brought this Godfrey character back to life? I'm sure you can likewise come up with some way to undo him."

CHAPTER 22

It was still early enough that I was able to call Cobalt and catch him before he left for work at the palace. It took a mix of criticism and flattery, supplication and guilt-tripping, but eventually he said he could arrange it so I could have a word with Kitty. There was some kind of charity event at the Tower of London that very night. The plan was to sneak in and meet with Kitty alone somewhere.

It had been ages since I'd been to the tower. Sometimes when I thought about London, I thought of it as a book of history. Right now, the book was open to the year 1958, but there were places in the city where previous eras broke through and upwards, like the old Londinium wall snaking its way through the financial district. The Tower of London was another place where the past had seemingly spiked upwards through the pages of the Book of London. It was a medieval castle built in a time when things had been made to last. Its walls were dark at night, though from outside I could see the floodlights that were used to illuminate the courtyard where the party was going on. The castle sat on a gentle slope, and downwards the river Thames flowed out into the ocean. Once upon a time traitors and kings alike had been rowed down the river to be locked up here. So many powerful figures had walked through the gates and never emerged.

What if this was a trap?

"Should you take my arm?" Oberon said to me.

"What? Why would I do that?"

"Well, we're supposed to be on a date . . ."

I'd managed to sneak into my studio and grab some of my magic clothes, including my snakeskin dress. Oberon meanwhile was wearing a nonmagic tux—he didn't have any magic clothes that would work as a disguise, so we just had to hope that styling would help him blend in. We were on the large square that was in front of the tower. Around us various well-dressed aristocrats made their way to the castle entrance. I huffed but took Oberon's arm. We stood awkwardly in the queue until we were at the front.

"So what have you been up to these last four years?" I said, the silence getting to me. "You still practise cloth magic, eh?"

"Yes," he said. "Though I rarely make clothes for parties like this anymore. I mainly make clothes that help patients recover from wounds or other ailments."

"Like a cloth magic doctor?"

"Exactly. I've spent the last few years seeking out war and battlefields, not so I could take part in the fighting but so I could tend to the wounded."

"How noble."

"Hardly. My reasons are more academic than altruistic. The battlefield provides wounded, desperate people, and they allowed me to practise cloth magic techniques on them. But I'll admit it: I do like to think that I've done some good in the world." There was a small upward climb in his tone, as if he was asking me a question. I didn't know why he sought my approval: I hadn't been with him these last few years, hadn't walked next to him on the battlefields, seen his supposed good works. He coughed, clearing his throat. "Anyway, about a week ago I received a letter from my father. It was a shock as I didn't even think he knew where I was. He told me that my family would need me very soon."

"And ever the dutiful son, you came back," I said. "I thought you'd cut ties with that man."

Oberon looked down at the cobblestones. "The letter was just so ominous; I had to see for myself what was going on. And as soon as I set foot on this island I learned that my father had died."

That did make me feel a pang of sympathy. I thought of my own dad up in Liverpool, spending his days in bed, rarely waking from his stroke-induced slumber. How many more years did he have on this earth? When all this was sorted out, I'd go up and visit him.

Finally we reached the castle entrance. A man with a clipboard stared expectantly at us, a couple of burly guards behind him, eyes watching the crowd.

"Princess Katherine put us on the list," I said, trying to sound both bored and authoritative. "Marsha Collins and George Sullivan."

As the guard looked over the list I realized that I was holding my breath. I sighed through my nose, and the guard must have taken it as a sign of impatience because he flicked through the list faster.

"Ah, here you are. Looks like you two were added just earlier," he said by way of apology and waved us on towards the drawbridge. We crossed it, heels and dress shoes clopping on the wood, the sound drowned out by both the chatter around us and the burble of the stream below us, rushing downwards to join the water of the Thames.

"Smile, love," Oberon said. He had brushed and trimmed his beard earlier today and I had cut his billowy hair short, but he still had the air of a vagabond.

"Don't call me 'love' and don't tell me to smile," I said.

"You're a pretty lady at a posh party," he replied. "You'll look out of place if you keep frowning like that."

We had entered the tower's courtyard, and a glance at the crowd proved Oberon's words right. The men were smiling, sure, but many were frowning or bored. Men, it seemed, were allowed to act disinterested. The women, however, were all smiling, laughing, doing their best to look like there was nowhere else they'd rather be. Sometimes I'd catch flashes of frowns from them, but only when they thought no one else was looking.

I plastered a smile onto my face.

"I hate this," I said. Oberon shrugged.

"This disguise was your idea. Now, how are we supposed to meet up with Princess Katherine?"

"Oh! It's you!"

The voice came from a few feet behind Oberon. Obie's shoulders hunched up and froze at the sound. It was Fairweather, his lanky form making his way through the crowd towards us. When our eyes met he gave me a big smile.

Right—he'd seen this disguise before. Luckily he had not yet seen Oberon's face. I doubt he'd have forgotten it already, considering just last night Oberon had held him at gunpoint.

I stepped forwards to meet Fairweather.

"Deputy Prime Minister Fairweather!" I said, shaking his hand enthusiastically. I could sense Oberon moving off, disappearing deeper into the crowd. Good. We'd have to meet up later, but at least for now our cover wasn't blown.

"Hello there, Ms Holden," Fairweather said, grasping my hand with both of his. I was impressed he had remembered the fake name that Dr Myers had given me—I myself had forgotten it. "I didn't know you'd be here tonight! Are you covering it for the newspaper?"

"Yes. Yes, I am." Fairweather had yet to let go of my hand. He used his grip to pull me in closer.

"Such a shame about Minister Myers, hmmm? Not the sort of chap I expected to top himself. But I suppose now with him gone, I could be your main point of contact at the Virtuis Party. Perhaps I can offer you a drink? If you wish, I could show you the room where they say the little princes were murdered all those years ago."

He leered at me. It seemed like offering to show off the murder site of two young boys was an odd way to hit on a girl, but I found myself both physically and socially unable to disentangle myself. He grabbed two glasses of white wine from a passing waiter and handed one to me, then pointed over my shoulder. The inside walls of the tower were lined with buildings, most of them in the Tudor style.

"That is where the two little princes lived, back in 1483," Fairweather said with relish. "You know the story, yes? The two little boys, Edward and Richard—"

"Were next in line to the throne, but the boys went missing and their uncle Richard ascended the throne," I said. Every schoolchild learned about it in school.

Fairweather looked delighted. "My, you really do know your history, Ms Holden!"

Thinking about the murdered princes of old made me think not only of Sabina but of another murdered child—little George McKenzie, the supposed illegitimate child of King Harold's now-dead brother Eddie. Tonya believed that George had been killed by her father on orders of the royal family, and I believed it as well. I felt my disgust with Dr Myers arise anew—rather than killing himself he could have used the rest of his life to help us, to make sure that what had happened to little George didn't happen to Sabina's child.

"Are you all right, my dear?" Fairweather asked, leaning in close. "Oh my, I'm sorry for bringing up such gruesome topics. Why don't you and I go somewhere quieter and—"

"Marsha!"

Cobalt bounded up and inserted himself between me and Fairweather. He took a deep breath, straightening his shoulders and acting as if he had just leisurely walked into the room.

"Ah, there you are, Marsha," he said, still winded. "I've been looking all over for you."

"Marsha?" Fairweather said in surprise.

"Jane Holden is my pen name," I improvised quickly, eager to be away from this man's dank breath and papery hands. "Sorry, Deputy Minister Fairweather, but I gotta go."

Cobalt and I started to walk away, but not before Fairweather reached out and grabbed my right hand. I winced as he squeezed my injured fingers.

"Oh, please, my dear, promise me that we'll meet later tonight to talk more—" He stopped, noticing the bandages on my fingertips. "Whatever happened here?"

His grip loosened enough for me to pull away. "Yes, we really should talk some more. I'll find you out in the courtyard before the night is over, Deputy Minister."

"Please, call me Peter," he said, but his face was troubled. His eyes lingered on my bandaged fingers, and I could imagine him thinking about how Paul Gallagher had lost his fingernails on *his* right hand.

Cobalt tugged me away from the party and down around a corner of the building—well, to call it just a building wouldn't be doing it justice. It was the White Tower of the Tower of London. Each corner of the building had a turret, three square and one circular.

"What *did* happen to your fingers?" Cobalt asked gingerly. He had never really had a strong stomach for blood.

"I'll explain it all to Kitty first," I said. "How is she?" And now it was my turn to be the gingerly one.

Cobalt shook his head, fringe swaying side to side. He had the best hair of anyone I knew—I suspected that he trimmed it every day to keep it at a perfect length. "It's been hard since the picture of you and Andrew was published. Her father has not been kind. Says she should have endeavoured to avoid such an embarrassment."

"*She* should have endeavoured?!" We were walking slowly down the castle lane. I didn't see anyone else around but I kept my voice low just in case. "This isn't her fault at all!"

"You and I both know that, but Princess Katherine's always been the whipping boy of the royal family," Cobalt said. "They weren't going to let her come tonight, since this scandal just broke yesterday. Too many questions and wagging tongues. But when I told her you wanted to meet, she insisted."

"Thank you, Cobalt," I said. "Really."

Cobalt ducked his head. "No need for thanks, Paul. You've done a lot for me too." He hesitated for a beat. "And . . . and after what I did, I want to make things up to you."

In the back of my mind I heard Lamb's voice: *I did warn you about him.* But I shook it off.

"Well, you've gone a long ways tonight towards that," I said.

Cobalt nodded, a wan smile on his face. "Thank you." He cleared his throat.

We were now several yards away from the courtyard but I could hear the festivities from around the corner. Cobalt turned sharply towards a nondescript heavy wooden door. He took hold of the handle and opened it, revealing a spiral staircase heading up.

"She's waiting on the roof," Cobalt said. "I'll stay down here and guard the exit."

I put a hand on his shoulder in thanks and then went up the stairs. Climbing them in heels was torture and I gave up after the first storey, taking them off and going the rest of the way in stocking feet. The building was luckily only about four storeys tall but with each step I felt like I was sinking lower. I needed to talk to Kitty about James Godfrey, but first we'd have to talk about the fact that I'd slept with her fiancé. Cobalt had made it sound like her family had reacted badly, but what about Kitty herself?

Finally I emerged from the stairwell and back out into the night air. The middle part of the roof was taken up by two peaked skylights and light shone up through the glass. I was facing south and could see the glitter of moonlight on the Thames, the lights of Tower Bridge just to the left, and lingering smog from the factories and railways that cluttered South London. Then I saw Kitty. She sat on what looked to be an overturned bucket, an odd throne for a teen girl in such a fancy gown. It was silver with a cream sash across the waist (I recognized it as Cobalt's design). She was looking out at the cars and buses beetling over the bridge.

As I stepped forwards the gravel spread over the roof pricked at the soles of my feet. I slipped on my shoes and Kitty looked over.

"Oh!" she said, standing. "Hello, Miss . . . ?"

"Don't worry, Kitty, it's me. Paul."

"Gally?! I wasn't expecting you to be wearing *that*!"

"We make quite the pair, eh?"

She gave me a half smile. "You look very chic. Is that part of the dress's magic?"

"Not really, Princess. I'm just comfortable in my own skin."

She slowly sat down on her bucket.

"That seems very much beyond me most days."

She had her hands folded in her lap, her chin tilted downwards with a tremulous quiver.

The roof was enclosed by a low wall that came up to my hip. I leaned against it.

"You're a lovely girl, Kitty, with a kind and caring soul. And every bit of it shines through."

Now she was crying.

"Oh, Gally," she said as she wiped tears away. "Why didn't you tell me you liked Andrew?"

"What?" I said. "I don't. I mean, not like that."

"Then why did you kiss him?" she asked, looking up at me with glistening, wide eyes.

"Well, it just kind of happened—"

"I wouldn't have minded," she said. "I consider you my dearest friend, and Andrew has always been so kind to me. If you two had wanted to be together, I would have gladly given my assent."

"Really?" I had always thought of Kitty as rather sheltered and conventional, but now she sounded like some kind of free-love advocate.

"Yes!" Kitty said. "You *know* that I have no interest in men. You know that my marriage to Andrew was merely one of convenience, and if there was a chance for at least one of us to be happy . . ." She stopped talking and started sobbing. I knelt down on the gravel of the roof and embraced her. She threw herself into my arms, hands gripping my shoulders as she cried.

"I'm sorry," I said. "I never meant to hurt you like this."

"No, that's not it," she said. "My parents are calling off my marriage to Andrew. They'll find me some other husband, some horrid man who I hate and I'll have to spend the rest of my life with and . . . and . . . and . . . oh, Paul, what if they have me marry Deputy Prime Minister Fairweather?"

"Kitty, we won't let that happen."

The conviction of my voice stopped her midsob.

"We won't?" she asked.

"No, we won't." I'd help her run off and leave the country before it came to that. "Kitty, I'm sorry. I know these last few days have been incredibly difficult, but I need you to stay strong for just a little longer. I've discovered something about the Virtuis Party, and something needs to be done to stop them before it's too late—"

There were faint echoes of footsteps coming up the stairwell and then the loud clang of the door being thrown open.

"You two!" It was Prince Arthur. He strode over, mouth a grim line. He was wearing a null cloak, the same one I'd seen him wear at past parties and events. As he strode towards us his hands were clenched and torso tilted forwards, as if he wanted to reach us that much faster.

"Katherine! So this is why you wanted to come here tonight?!" Prince Arthur whirled to face me. "You have some nerve, Gallagher. My sister might be a deformed degenerate, but she still deserves better than having her fiancé stolen away by her best friend."

At his words Kitty shrank in on herself, hand coming up to cover her lazy eye. Any fear or shock I had felt upon being discovered melted away, replaced with anger.

"And she deserves a better brother than an asshole like you," I said. Before Arthur could reply Cobalt appeared at the top of the stairwell. His bow tie was askew and his eyes were panicked.

"Paul! I'm sorry! He hit me and came up here!"

"It's all right, Cobalt," Arthur said, not looking away from me but calmly holding up a hand. Despite the serenity of his gesture, his face was red with anger, nostrils flared. "Everything will be fine. I can smooth things over with Mother and Father. Paul, you can come and work for the royal family again. Hell, perhaps with time, Kitty, you can even marry Lord Fife once this scandal fades from the public memory. But in return, Gallagher, I need you to tell me where Sabina is."

He spoke calmly but firmly. Kitty stopped covering her face to look up at me. She seemed hopeful but confused.

"What?" she asked.

God, if only we had gotten a minute more to talk before Arthur had barged in.

"All right, sure thing, Artie," I said. "How 'bout I come to the palace tomorrow and we'll talk?" If I agreed to his terms, maybe he'd bugger off and I'd be able to finish talking with Kitty.

"No, that will not do," Arthur said. "Tell me where she is *now*."

He stood there, less like a man on a roof and more like an oak rooted into the ground. Both Cobalt and Kitty were looking at me, entreating me to find some way out of this.

"Well, okay," I said, mind scrambling. "She's in Kingston. Kingston, Jamaica."

It was a plausible lie—Sabina's grandfather was from Kingston. It made sense that she might seek refuge with distant family, in a nation where she wouldn't stand out the way she did in Kington, England.

Arthur scowled. "As if I haven't already checked there! I've hired private investigators to look for her there and they turned up nothing. Why are you lying to me, Gallagher? We're all on the same side here."

I was caught a bit off guard by how quickly and completely Arthur had called my bluff, making me flounder.

"Did the goons from the Virtuis Party threaten you?" Arthur said. "Look, I also hate those bastards. I know Sabina and I have had our troubles, but she's my wife and the soon-to-be mother of my child—"

"She's what?!" Kitty interjected. Arthur continued on without pause.

"—and I will do whatever it takes to protect the both of them. Trust me. Tell me where they are. Let's join forces and finally root out the rot that the Virtuis Party has sown in this country. That's all I want. That's all any of us want."

He spoke so persuasively that for the first time I could imagine him as king someday. And despite my personal distaste for the man, he was right. He'd be a strong ally against Godfrey. Getting him on board might be the political and societal power to dislodge the Virtuis Party from power. And all I had to do was give up the location of one woman.

But the woman in question had explicitly told me not to do that. She'd made me promise.

"I'm sorry," I said. "I can't tell you what you want to know."

Arthur gave a little bob of his head and for a second I thought he was going to let it go. But instead he reached out and grabbed my shoulders to toss me onto one of the roof's skylights. My body hit it with a loud thud and I was terrified that the glass had cracked under me. That fear grew as Arthur started hitting me, his face immobile but his punches wild, hitting the glass as often as he hit me.

I was trying to get out from under him, but the innate magic spell upon me kept me from lashing out. The best I could do was try and duck his punches as they came. Kitty screamed. Cobalt stepped forwards and I could see him hesitate—dare he lay a hand on the crown prince? And amazingly, he *did* dare, grabbing Arthur's arm as he readied another punch. Arthur was surprised for a half second before standing and backhanding Cobalt, sending him stumbling.

Arthur grabbed me and hauled me to my feet, throwing me against the roof's low wall. The edge of it hit the small of my back in a way that made my heart lurch. A four-storey fall would kill me. The partygoers would hear me hit the cobblestone and find me splattered. They'd know it was me because, with me dead, there'd be no battery powering the dress and it'd no longer obscure my identity. Everyone would think I'd taken my own life because of all the recent scandals.

Arthur had both hands on my throat now, pushing so my upper body was out over the edge.

"Tell me where my wife is, Gallagher," he said. "Tell me or I swear I will drop you off this roof."

"Artie, stop!" Kitty had been helping Cobalt to his feet but now she rushed over. Arthur let go of my throat to turn towards her, moving to backhand her the same way he'd hit Cobalt just thirty seconds earlier. But this time, something else happened. Just before the slap was about to connect there was a flash of light. It was like some act of physics exerted itself on the prince and the prince only. He flew back over the roof's wall.

His foot clipped my shoulder and I almost fell with him. Cobalt saved me, grabbing my upper arm and yanking me back so hard I thought my shoulder might disconnect.

From below came a wet, almost hollow thunk sound.

CHAPTER 23

"Oh my dear Lord," Cobalt said. The noise of the party continued, both in the courtyard and in the building below. For the first time, I noticed that the courtyard had a string quartet, lively notes blending in with the general hubbub. No one seemed to have heard the thunk, even though it was still echoing in my ears.

"Artie? Arthur?" Kitty said, eyes searching the empty air. She ran to the edge of the roof. Her face took on a boneless quality as she looked down, her mouth dropping open and eyes so large you could see their curve. She drew in a breath for a scream. Cobalt ran forwards to cover her mouth but there was the flash again, and the same force that had thrown Arthur over the roof now sent Cobalt flying back. Luckily, Cobalt merely fell against the skylight. Kitty's scream died before it even left her mouth. She looked at Cobalt with shock.

I could still feel where Arthur had grabbed my throat and bare shoulders. I took a step forwards, hands on the low wall as I peered over the edge.

Some of the path was illuminated by light spilling over from the party in the courtyard, but Arthur seemed to have landed in a shrouded patch, a triangle of darkness where the wall of the building cut off the light. I thought I could see something that looked like a torso, though I couldn't make out a head, and the way the limbs were it was hard to tell what was an arm and what was a leg. Some blood was pooling around him, but aside from that nothing moved.

What if one of the partygoers decided to walk down that dark path? They'd see the prince, and they'd look up and see us. I stepped away from the edge of the roof.

"What just happened, Paul?" Cobalt said. He'd gotten to his feet and rejoined us. Kitty was holding on to him as if he were a life preserver ring.

"Innate magic," I said, wonder cutting through my horror. I turned towards the princess. "Kitty! It worked! That's what did this! Your brother tried to hurt you and so the magic reacted! And it did again just now with Cobalt!"

Both of them just stared at me.

Right, maybe it wasn't the time for it.

"Cobalt, you have to take the princess far from here. She can't be nearby when Arthur is found," I said.

Cobalt nodded. "Yes, of course. But what about . . ." He nodded towards the edge of the roof.

"I'll . . . see how bad it is." Such an insipid statement—even from four storeys up it was clear that things were pretty bad. "But no one knows I'm here, and if the princess is away from the scene no one will suspect us."

Cobalt nodded again. He let go of the princess and blushed slightly, as if only just now realizing how closely he'd been holding her. "Princess, let's go."

Kitty was still staring at the edge of the roof. Cobalt took her hand and they started towards the stairwell. I raced ahead of them to hurry down to the ground level, taking off my high heels as I went so I didn't fall to *my* death. As I emerged out of the stairwell I crashed into a large man.

"Gaah!" I yelled in surprise.

"Paul!" Oberon said. "I've been looking for you! I saw the prince head this way and—"

"He's over here," I said, lowering my voice. Still barefoot I ran a few yards down the length of the wall to where Arthur was lying. Oberon's thundering steps followed.

"Oh God," he said, his voice thick as if gagging. It was bad. Very bad. Arthur lay facedown, limbs sprawled out in a way that no living person would find comfortable. *Facedown* was a misnomer, because he didn't have a face anymore. He didn't even seem to have a head. My first thought was that somehow the fall had decapitated him; where his head should have been there was only a bloody stump emerging from the top of his shoulders. But as I stared I realized that I could see familiar blond hair atop that bloody stump. It *was* his head. Arthur had hit the stones crown first and it had driven his skull into his chest cavity.

Behind us I heard the stairwell door open and then the clatter of Kitty's heels as she ran towards us.

"No, Kitty, don't look!" I spun around and held my arms out wide. Kitty stopped a few feet away, Cobalt racing to catch up with her. Her eyes strained to look past me, darting around as if trying to make sense of the mess that was her brother's body.

"Paul." Oberon put a hand on my shoulder. I spun back around, arms still out like a scarecrow's.

Oberon wasn't looking at the corpse. I followed his gaze to see Court Magician Peter Van Holt leaning against the castle, unlit cigarette in hand. Even in the darkness I could see how pale he was, the whites of his eyes on all sides of his irises. He stood stock still, as if trying to blend into the wall. If I hadn't been so distracted by the prince I would have spotted him easily, but with everything else going on I had missed him.

Having been spotted he lunged from the wall and made a break for it. At first it seemed like he was trying to run back to the party, but he quickly realized that was a mistake; all of us were standing between him and it. So he pivoted and ran down the tilt of the path, into the darkness.

Oberon took off after him, moving surprisingly fast.

Van Holt looked over his shoulder to see Obie gaining on him, and this moment's inattention caused him to trip. He fell face-first, hands clumsily breaking his fall, but before he could get up Oberon was on him, knee on Van Holt's back and hand fisted in his hair. Oberon then slammed his head down, forehead bouncing off the stones.

Seeing this show of violence made all my joints lock in place. For a second, time and space melted away and it was *me* under Oberon, panicking as death set in.

But Van Holt wasn't dead. He was groaning quietly, like someone trying to wake up from a nightmare. Oberon let go of his hair but stayed kneeling on him. He looked to me, face grim as if waiting for further instruction.

I turned to Cobalt.

"Get the princess somewhere safe and stay with her," I said. "We'll handle this."

Cobalt shook his head. "No, you need me. There's a small staff room at the end of this lane. Bring Van Holt there and wait for me."

Cobalt turned and gently took Kitty's forearm, leading her away from the horrible scene. She moved unthinkingly, her face still slack and eyes wide, staring at the mess that had once been her brother. I waited until Cobalt and Kitty disappeared around the corner and into the light and gaiety of the party.

I walked down to where Oberon was holding Van Holt.

"There's a space we can take him," I said to Oberon and relayed what Cobalt had told me. Oberon nodded and got to his feet, bringing Van Holt up with him. Van Holt was awake, blinking stupidly at us, but his movements were dazed.

"Help me with him?" Oberon said. I wasn't sure if my innate magic would allow me to, but I gave it a go. I was able to slip Van Holt's arm around my shoulder and help carry him down the path.

We reached a door that I presumed was the one Cobalt had talked about—either way it was unlocked, which was good enough for me. The door revealed an old stone staircase, one that went up just a few steps before opening to a room that was a mix of medieval and modern. The walls were stone and the windows peaked and filled with small panes of glass held together by a grid of iron. But the floors were linoleum, the cupboards lining the walls made from plywood. There was a table in the middle of the room. Oberon and I laid Van Holt on it. His head lolled around as he tried to focus his eyes. I found a light switch and flicked it on. Van Holt cried out softly as the fluorescent lights snapped to life.

"We should take off his jacket, shirt, and trousers," I said. "They're magic. I don't know how, but I don't really want to find out."

Oberon's expression was grave, but he was quick to strip the still largely unresponsive Van Holt.

"Paul," Oberon said, voice remarkably level, "what exactly is going on?"

It was amazing that it had taken him so long to ask. I was grateful for it actually—everything up until now had been too frantic and horrible to summarize.

"There was an incident on the roof," I said. "Prince Arthur attacked Princess Katherine and ended up falling over the side."

Oberon cast a glance down at Van Holt, as if to warn me against saying too much, but did it really matter? Van Holt had already seen the prince's body and the lot of us standing over it. Hell, maybe he had even seen the prince hit the ground, which might help explain his shocked state.

I needed to clear my head. I walked over to look out the window. The room faced the Thames, so close it felt like we were about to fall into the water. It was somehow calming to watch the river water flow out towards the ocean, the lights of Tower Bridge catching currents.

The door creaked open and both Oberon and I jumped a foot in the air. It was only Cobalt.

"Good, you're here." He locked the door behind him. Cobalt was pale but his movements were sure. He stood next to Oberon, hands on hips, and the difference in their stature was comical only because of how serious they both looked. "What are we going to do about *him*?"

The "him" in question was starting to look a little more lucid and, with that, a little more worried. Van Holt was still lying on the table but he had pushed himself up on his elbows.

"I . . . I didn't see anything," Van Holt said. "Please."

"No, that won't do," Cobalt said. "It's obvious you saw *something*. So what did you see?"

"I . . . I saw Prince Arthur fall to his death," Van Holt said. "That's all. A tragic accident. Maybe one brought about by too much drink. Still, tragic."

"Yes, that's plausible," Cobalt said. "Artie had been deep into his cups tonight. Lots of people would attest to that. We could spin it that way."

"Yes, exactly!" Van Holt said. "And I'll help!"

"Why would you help us, Van Holt?" Tiredness crept into my voice, the weariness that comes from having to play out a conversation when you already know how it will go.

Van Holt squinted at me in confusion as if trying to place me. But of course he didn't recognize me—I was wearing a magical dress that disguised my true identity.

"Well, b-because I'm the Court Magician," Van Holt said. "I wasn't able to save Prince Arthur, but I can still at least save Princess Katherine from being associated with his death. There's no need for her to be dragged into all of this."

Oberon, Cobalt, and I all traded glances. They looked as wary as I did.

"Please!" Van Holt said. "I swear on . . . on my . . ." He stumbled, tongue trying to conjure up something sacred, something we'd believe he actually valued.

"Don't embarrass yourself, Van Holt," Oberon said. "Just stop this." Obie turned to Cobalt. "Can you get some rope? And something heavy?"

"Something heavy for what?" Van Holt asked, words coming out in a rush.

Oberon spared him a glance. "To weigh your body down when we toss it in the Thames."

Van Holt yelped at that and I might have too. I definitely found it unnecessarily cruel to speak such things aloud.

"Miss." Van Holt looked to me. "Miss, I do not know who you are or how you came to be in league with these two criminals, but please, stop them before they do something awful."

Van Holt did sound truly desperate, and it got to me. "Hey, Oberon, knock it off."

A flicker of heat rose in Oberon's face at my words but it died down as quickly as someone adjusting the flame on a gas stove.

"What else are we supposed to do with him, Paul?" Oberon asked. He didn't sound accusatory, just resigned.

"Paul?" Van Holt said, confusion overtaking fear.

I reached up to run my hand through my hair, but I got snagged on two uncomfortable sensations: my raw fingernail beds pressing against their plasters and my hand snagging on my wig.

I pulled the wig off and threw it down on the floor. Next, I started unzipping my dress. I was tired of wearing it, of appearing like a woman when I wasn't. In the past this dress had always been a fun outfit, a chance to have an adventure and just be someone else for a bit. But now I'd always associate it with the night Prince Arthur died.

"Cobalt, can you unzip me?" I said, unable to pull the zipper down myself. As Cobalt did so I looked at Oberon. "Can you lend me your tuxedo jacket?"

He handed it to me. The shoulders were much too broad for my frame but I didn't mind since it gave me more cover. I was left wearing nothing but stockings, pants, and a too-large jacket, my hair mussed from the wig and makeup smeared on my face, but I felt like I could breathe again.

Van Holt stared at me, wide eyed.

"Gallagher?"

"Well? What are we going to do?" Cobalt asked, my dress draped over his arm. He spoke evenly but looked away from me, perhaps embarrassed by my half-dressed state.

Van Holt was quick to get over his surprise. "I won't speak of this! Let me leave and I swear I'll keep my silence!"

"Easy to say that now," Cobalt said.

"What's to stop you from telling everyone once you leave here?" Oberon said, as if he and Cobalt were just one person speaking in two different voices.

"Gallagher!" Van Holt swung his head towards me. His eyes had a new light, one fuelled by revelation rather than fear. "You know I won't tell anyone! You have dirt on me, just like I have dirt on you! You know about my family; you know I'd do anything to protect them."

Of course. I was the only other person who knew that Van Holt was a bigamist. We had our little gentlemen's agreement not to go after each other's loved ones, but could I really trust it to stretch this far? Could Van Holt really be expected to keep his silence now that regicide was in play?

Cobalt and Oberon looked to me for an explanation but I didn't bother. I turned the matter over in my head, trying to find an angle I hadn't seen before. I felt no love for Van Holt—hell, he was high up on a short list of people I could genuinely say I *hated*. Just a mere twenty-four hours ago, he'd been laughing like the devil as he'd tortured me. And yet despite that I didn't want Van Holt dead. I didn't want to go through with his murder, for such an act to stain Cobalt's and Oberon's souls, no matter how resigned they already were to it. I didn't want to have to watch as the life was choked out of him or as his body sank in the Thames. And I certainly didn't want to have Olena and Gayle on my conscience, always wondering where their beloved husband and father was, adrift in the world like Harriet Hollister and her brother.

The idea came to me so fast that out of habit I snapped my fingers, then winced because I'd done so with my injured hand.

"We don't have to kill him," I said.

"That's right," Van Holt said, but he seemed as confused by my statement as the other two men in the room.

"Paul, not that I'm looking to spill more blood tonight, but why *wouldn't* we kill him?" Cobalt said.

"Because we can do innate magic instead," I replied.

CHAPTER 24

The three stared at me as though I'd just opened a third eye in the middle of my forehead.

"It's not that amazing. I've done it before. Cobalt, you saw the results of it tonight," I said. "I can change Van Holt into someone else. Someone who didn't see what happened here tonight. I've read about it in ancient texts. By breaking certain bones you can not only wipe a person's memory but change their very identity. There are stories of tribes in South America that used to do this. The leader of the tribe would undergo the ritual and therefore effectively be the same person each generation."

"What exactly are you proposing here?" Van Holt said. I noticed that even though he was speaking quietly his Afrikaans accent was coming on strong.

"Deep down, isn't there a part of you that's always wanted to fully live as Shipwright?" I asked.

Van Holt paled.

"That's your plan?" he said. "Magically make it so I *am* truly him?" He shook his head. "It won't work. Innate magic relies on consent, and I'd never consent to having half of my identity wiped away."

"Really? Even when the other option is having your life wiped out completely?" I held up my hands, palms up, as if they were two scales. "See, magic, if we're to treat it like an entity with wants and needs, it doesn't care so much about motive. Maybe you don't truly want this but you agree because it's preferable to dying. As far as the magic is concerned, you still agreed to it."

Van Holt was quiet, eyes boring a hole into the wall as he thought his options over.

Cobalt came around the table to stand next to me. "Is it really worth it?" he said, quietly but Van Holt no doubt still heard us.

"Yes. It is worth it," I said. "I made a promise and I'm doing my best to keep it."

That seemed to snap Van Holt out of his stupor.

"Yes, yes, all right, fine," he said, as if he were merely agreeing to a faulty charge on his dry-cleaning bill, rather than a dangerous magical ritual. "Let's just get this over with."

"Fab. Cobalt, you seem to know your way around this place. Could you get me some tools? A hammer and mallet, some wooden stakes, rope. Whatever you can get and get quickly."

Cobalt nodded. "Lock the door after me. I'll knock four times when I come back."

After he slipped out Oberon looked over at me.

"Innate magic, Paul? Really?"

"Yes. That is quite the ace up your sleeve," Van Holt said, going for a conversational tone, but there was a quaver to his voice. "However did you pick that up? Please, I am very curious. You may as well tell me. I won't remember it anyway."

"I don't rightly know, to be honest," I said. "But it's nothing you need to be worried about."

"I rather think it is!" Van Holt said. "If you're some kind of fraud, you'll kill me! One way or another!"

"I won't kill you," I said. "This will work—"

Four quick raps at the door. Oberon went over to unlock it, opening it just a crack first to see who was on the other side, then opening it all the way to let Cobalt in. Cobalt bustled into the room, rope in one hand, hammer and a pack of nails in the other.

"What do you need the nails for?!" Van Holt exclaimed. For a brief, exhilarating second I imagined driving them under Van Holt's fingernails. The image flickered out as a wave of disgust washed over me.

"Yeah, I don't think we'll need them," I said.

Cobalt shrugged. "I wasn't sure." He handed over the items to me. "They discovered Prince Arthur's body out there. It's quite a commotion."

Now that sounded like an understatement.

"We should do this quickly." The castle grounds were going to be hopping with activity as people tried to figure out how the crown prince had fallen to his death, and I didn't want someone placing me and the others at the scene of the crime. "All right, Oberon, tie Van Holt's ankles and arms to the table legs. Van Holt, let him do it."

I tossed Oberon the rope. Van Holt glanced around the room, looking for an exit. Cobalt went and stood against the door, arms folded as if he were a bouncer at a bar.

"Are you sure you know what you're doing?" Van Holt asked.

"Well, admittedly, I am largely self-taught." I couldn't help but be pleased by the jolt of fear that passed through Van Holt's eyes.

"What bone will you break?" Van Holt asked.

A good question. From my research into innate magic, bigger bones were better for bigger changes, but smaller, more delicate bones allowed for more specific results. For something like this, I felt like I needed something that gave me both specificity and grandiosity.

"Why not crack his skull?" Oberon suggested as he tied Van Holt's ankles to the table legs. "They say that a man's personality is housed in the frontal lobes. Give them a good whack and I'm sure that will do the trick."

"Mm, that doesn't really sound like magic so much as a lobotomy," I said. "What do you suggest, Van Holt? You've got a pretty vested interest in this, so maybe you should weigh in."

Van Holt shook his head. "I've never done anything like this before. You might not think well of me, Gallagher, but I'd never use innate magic in such a vile way."

Oberon tied Van Holt's arms to the table legs. Fear overtook Van Holt as his chance of escape slipped further away. He tried to jerk out of Oberon's grip but Obie merely grabbed him by the forehead and slammed the back of his head against the table. Cobalt strode forwards and pulled a silk handkerchief from his inner coat pocket. He stuffed it in Van Holt's mouth and tied a piece of rope around his head to make sure the cloth stayed in there. While Van Holt was still dazed Oberon finished tying him down.

"Well," Oberon said, standing back to examine his work, "now what, Paul?"

I stepped forwards. Van Holt glared at me. I tried to think of what made him and Shipwright different from each other. Shipwright had a pitch-perfect London accent, just a little bit posh. Did that signify the biggest difference between them in Van Holt's mind? How they spoke? If I broke his jaw, would that be enough of a connection to change his whole personality?

Van Holt's fists were clenched, and for a second I worried that Oberon had tied the ropes too tightly around his wrists—his hands were already turning red.

Then I noticed something about Van Holt's right hand. His middle finger had an odd bend to it on the lowest joint, much like mine did on my left pointer finger.

"Is this the break that made you a mage maker?" I asked. Van Holt said nothing—granted he was gagged, but I got the feeling he would have stayed silent anyway. I put my hand on his upper arm, gently feeling along. I could sense the disruption of magical energy flowing through him, not only from the break in his finger but from two breaks in his arm. I knew these breaks well. They were the same old injuries that all prospective mages studying in England got from the nation's mage maker, one for becoming a Book Binder, the other for doing cloth magic.

Shipwright was left handed. All of Van Holt's magic and his history as a mage were centred in his right hand and arm.

"All right, I think I know what I need to do."

"You 'think'?" Cobalt asked sceptically.

"I *know*," I said. "Hand me the hammer." Cobalt did so and I turned to stare in Van Holt's eyes. "Magic is all about intention, right, Van Holt? So I need you to act in concert with me for this to work, yeah? I need you to think hard about your wife and child. Think about how happy they will be to see you again."

Some of Van Holt's fury dimmed at that. I thought about Olena and Gayle, about how I'd promised Van Holt I'd keep them safe. Images of Laura and Beatrix bled into my thoughts. Were they thinking about me? Did they miss me?

"Oberon, hold his upper arm here," I said. Oberon did so. I summoned up my strength and brought the hammer down on Van Holt's right upper arm.

His scream escaped from around the gag. Both Oberon and I stepped back but Cobalt seemed unbothered.

"Don't worry. The walls are thick here. No one would have heard that."

I stepped forwards. Van Holt was still thrashing around on the table but I was able to place my hands on him to try to feel the magic energy within. I hadn't managed to break the bone.

"Oberon, I need you to hold him again," I said. Oberon did so. I brought the hammer down again and this time I felt the force of it ripple through Van Holt's skin and muscle to connect with the bone held tight within. The crack was so sudden and sure that I swear I felt it reverberate back up through the hammer to me.

"GAAH!" If Van Holt's scream before was loud, it was nothing compared to this one. Even Cobalt looked a tad worried. But I could not let it faze me. I placed my hands on Van Holt's arm, one below the break, the other above. I could feel the magic within him trying to complete the circuit, to continue flowing through his body. I needed to redirect it a smidge. I gripped his skin tightly and gave his arm just a little torque.

This action made Van Holt cry out anew. But as Van Holt screamed his hair changed colour, going from dark brown to blond. There were also more subtle changes in his physiognomy: his cheeks filled out somewhat, and his shoulders grew broader. When he opened his eyes they had gone from brown to blue. There was no anger or fury in them, just pain and confusion.

"Untie him," I said.

"Paul, are you sure—"

"It's fine. Do it."

Oberon and Cobalt didn't protest any further, just set to untying Van Holt's limbs. But I knew he wasn't Van Holt anymore. I knew it before the gag was out of his mouth and he spoke.

"What is happening here?" he asked, his voice strained with pain. Yet even through that his upper-middle-class British accent was clear. He blinked away tears as he cradled his arm. "Gallagher? Did you break my arm? What the devil has gotten into you? And why are you wearing nothing but your pants and a jacket?"

"He might be faking it," Oberon whispered.

"But his whole being changed," Cobalt pointed out.

"Hey, Shipwright," I said. "I'm sorry about this. There was an accident, and your arm got broken. But my friend here can patch you up."

Oberon realized I was talking about him.

"Is it okay to put a splint on the arm?" Oberon asked. "Will it affect the . . . you know?"

"No, it's done. You can treat him now."

Oberon nodded. Using brute strength, he ripped Van Holt's jacket into strips and created a splint for Shipwright's upper arm and after that a sling.

"Why am I not wearing trousers?" Shipwright asked.

"Here, put them on," I said, holding out Van Holt's trousers. Shipwright needed help getting into them, partly because he only had one hand and partly because they were a snug fit now that his frame was slightly bigger.

"Here, you can wear this," I said, taking off the tuxedo jacket. It fit him better than me, though he couldn't put his broken arm through the sleeve: instead he let that side of the jacket drape over the makeshift sling Oberon had crafted. The fact his arm was in a sling nearly hid that he was shirtless, but he was still a sight: a confused man with a broken arm. How were we to get him out the tower? Especially now that the place was on high alert after the prince's death?

"Tide's low right now. There's an exit we can use that goes out to the bank of the Thames," Cobalt said, as if reading my thoughts. "Though where we take him after that, I have no idea."

"Cobalt, how is it that you know the Tower of London so well?" I asked.

"I was raised here," he replied simply. I stared at him. Raised in the Tower of London? I had always joked about him looking like a kind of fairy prince, but growing up in an actual antique castle? That was too interesting of a tidbit to just drop like that, and if things weren't so dire I'd have a million questions. But they would have to wait.

"Right. I do know where he lives, so once we get out of the tower I'll take him there," I said.

"Where *he* lives?" Oberon said, voice high with disbelief. He gestured at Shipwright, hands loose as if the gesture was trying to encompass more than just a man. "*He* didn't exist five minutes ago!"

"That's not true," I said firmly. I turned to Shipwright, who was sitting on the table, eyes darting around nervously as he cradled his broken arm. "You know your address, don't you? I've been to your home, broken bread with you and your wife in St John's Wood. I met your daughter."

For a moment he just blinked at me and my heart pounded. I was terrified that I had gone too far, wiped all his memories and not just his ones as Van Holt. Then Shipwright smiled, a flickering but genuine smile.

"Yes, of course. You've been there, Gallagher. I live up in St John's Wood."

I breathed out.

"Yes, that's right."

Oberon threw up his hands. "I don't understand any of this."

"You don't have to," I said. "Just help me get him out of here."

Oberon huffed but didn't raise any more complaints. I put a comforting hand on Shipwright's shoulder. "Listen, mate, we're going to get out of here and bring you to your wife and child and then after that this night will all just be a bad dream. For all of us. All right?"

"All . . . all right," he said shakily. I could still see some resemblance to Van Holt in the shape of the mouth and the far edges of the eye sockets, but it was a familial resemblance, not identical. I patted him on the shoulder once more before gathering up my dress, wig, and heels. I stepped outside in the stairwell and changed back into them. I wasn't thrilled about having to put on this getup again, but at the very least it was still a disguise.

I stepped back into the room.

Shipwright looked at me, eyes wide. "Who are you?" he asked.

"I'm a friend of Paul's," I replied. "My name is . . . Mary." I thought it best to use a different name than one I'd used before, and it was the first one that popped into my head. "Paul asked me to make sure you got home all right." I turned to Cobalt and asked him to lead us out of there.

He brought us back down the small staircase that led outside. Oberon helped support Shipwright, letting the man put his good arm around his shoulders and going down the steps slowly so as to not jolt his broken arm. I brought up the rear, trying not to fidget even though I was getting impatient. Every second we stayed on the tower grounds put us in more and more danger.

That was especially clear once we were outside. Farther up the castle lane there was a crowd of people gathered around the prince's body. They were so far away that they looked like nothing more than a shadowy mass, their words indistinct but panic and distress clear in their voices. Some people were still coming over from the party, others rushing around to get help or, more likely, to spread the word. One of those figures was probably a member of the Virtuis Party. Had word already reached Godfrey? How would Arthur's death factor into his plans?

"This way," Cobalt whispered. No one spared us a glance as we hugged the wall and walked away. Soon we disappeared around a corner.

"What was going on back there?" Shipwright asked. "Why were all those people so upset?"

Before I could answer Cobalt opened an old wooden door, one that creaked loudly.

"My apologies," he said. "So close to the water, the hinges always need oiling, and the wood of this door is always getting warped out of shape—"

"Let's just go," Oberon said, practically hauling Shipwright through the doorway. I followed and Cobalt darted in after us, pulling the warped, creaky door closed.

When Cobalt had said we were "close to the water," he hadn't been fibbing. We were in an old stone room with a round opening that looked out on the Thames. We were standing on a little wooden bridge that led to another door. Below us were dark, smooth riverbank stones. With the tide being low the water's edge was still a few yards away from the entrance.

"Just climb over the side. With the waterline low, you can walk along the castle wall. Keep heading back towards the city and eventually you'll reach some steps that go up to the road," Cobalt said.

Oberon climbed over the railing first, then dropped down to the stones with a huff. Shipwright went over after him, with Cobalt and me helping him in place of his right arm. Once he had dropped down into Oberon's waiting arms I turned to Cobalt.

"Once we're gone you should go back to the princess," I said.

Cobalt nodded as if that was already his plan. We looked at each other, clearly sharing the same thought: if our part in the night's events was discovered, we might never get the chance to speak again.

"Take care," Cobalt said.

"You too," I said. "When things calm down, I want to hear all about growing up here."

Cobalt smiled at that. I climbed over the railing of the bridge and dropped down with some grace, my childhood tree-climbing skills coming back in full force. Shipwright, Oberon, and I went out through the opening facing the river and followed Cobalt's directions. The old stone of the tower soon gave way to the more modern retaining walls that kept London from falling into the sea. It was dark and cold down on the banks of the Thames, wind skimming over the water as if solely to chill us.

We passed under the city's aqueducts, drainage-pipe openings shaped like open-mouthed lions. These existed not only to drain excess water in the city's sewers but also to give the many rivers of London some way back to the sea.

"Oh, the lions," Shipwright said, the first words spoken between us since we'd left the tower. "I was teaching Gayle the rhyme about them the other day: 'If the lions are drinking, London is sinking. If the lions are ducked, London is—'"

"Fucked," Oberon cut in, flatly.

"Well, I told her 'underwater.' No need for such blue language at her age."

We finally saw the stairs. We climbed up them and immediately felt the warmth of the city, of streetlamps and shelter from the elements. I flagged down a cab and haggled with a driver until he agreed to be paid in American dollars rather than by Book. It was going to be a hefty fee, not just to keep things off the record but because we were going all the way from the Tower of London to St John's Wood. I grabbed the front seat and chatted with the driver while Oberon and Shipwright sat in the back. Maybe it was a bad idea to be so friendly when we were trying to be incognito, but I was feeling pretty frazzled and chatting with a stranger about American music for thirty minutes helped me think about something other than Arthur's blood smeared on the stones.

Finally we arrived at Shipwright's home. It was coming up on eleven at that point, and the residential street we were on was quiet. Shipwright had been unsure and nervous the whole car ride, but now his face broke out into a big smile and he got out of the car before I had even finished plying the driver with bills.

Oberon and I hurried after him.

"Should we just leave him here?" Oberon said. "This is his home, right?" He still sounded so confused.

Shipwright had taken some keys out of his trousers and unlocked his door. As he stepped in I hurried after him.

"Adam?" It was Olena, clad in her nightgown as she hurried downstairs. She stopped when she saw me and Oberon. "Hello," she said hesitantly.

"Olena, it's all right," Shipwright said. "They were just seeing me home."

"What happened to you?" She came closer, putting her palm to his cheek, the other hand lifting up the part of the jacket draped over his broken arm.

"There was an accident," he said, and I was so grateful he was the one telling the story rather than leaving it to me or Oberon. "I don't know exactly what happened, but these two were able to help me and make sure I got home safe."

"Thank you," she said to us, but her eyes were still doubtful.

"My name is Mary," I said, offering a hand to shake. Olena shook my hand but of course there was no spark of magic—we had already met after all. Though that raised an interesting question in the back of my mind: Would my magic even work if I was meeting someone while in disguise? "Could I trouble you for a cup of tea?" I said. Oberon gave me a look that made it clear he thought I was starkers for wanting to stick around in that house, but I ignored him.

"Yes, of course. I'm Olena Shipwright, Adam's wife. Please come with me."

Adam sat down in a chair in the living room and Oberon went over to check on the state of his splint. I followed Olena into the kitchen, where she put the kettle on.

"What happened to him?" Her accent was heavy, but she spoke carefully, concentrating to get each word across clearly. She didn't seem nearly as shy as last time I'd been here. I wondered if it was the extraordinary circumstances of the night that had made her come out of her shell or the fact that, as far as she could tell, she was speaking to a fellow woman.

"There was an accident," I said. "He fell from a great height, broke his arm and hit his head. My friend and I were nearby, and we wanted to make sure he got home all right."

"What happened to his clothes?"

"They . . . they were torn up and there was a lot of blood. My friend lent him his jacket." I was on the verge of babbling. I heard how ridiculous my words sounded, and from the way Olena was staring at me, she heard it too.

The kettle started shrieking. With a steady hand she filled the teapot.

"Is he in danger?" she asked me once she set the kettle down. "Are *we* in danger?"

"What? No. He just broke his arm—"

"I know my husband has secrets. Maybe you are one of them," she said, giving me the once-over. "I know he has them even if I don't know what they are. But he has always kept us safe. If there is something I need to know to keep him safe, please, tell me now."

Her voice was calm but I noticed how tightly she clutched the kettle handle. I certainly couldn't tell her the whole tale, but I could see she was hungry for answers.

"How well do you know your husband? What he does when he's not in this house, inside these walls?" I asked, trying to see just how deep the water was.

"I know who he is within these walls," she said, then hesitated. "But I don't know him as well . . . as well as a wife should know her husband." She actually blushed at that, and I realized what she was referring to. Had she and Shipwright never been intimate? It made sense—if Peter Van Holt was only Adam Shipwright when he was wearing his magic outfit, then of course he'd never let anyone see him out of it.

"Your husband . . . when he's out in the city, he's not the man you know."

Olena nodded tiredly, and I suspected she was taking my words metaphorically rather than literally.

"Yes, I do know that. He works for that awful cousin of his, the one who works him so hard." Her mouth pulled down in distaste, and I wondered if Van Holt / Shipwright spent his evenings bad-mouthing himself to his wife. Jesus. What a warped soul that man had. He should have unloaded his burdens to a priest or, better yet, a psychiatrist.

I supposed it was too late for that now.

"Your husband will be fine," I said. "He got mixed up in some bad business and should lay low for the next little bit."

She frowned. "He should lay down?"

"No. No, he should stay home, stay quiet. Not go out into the city. Not be . . . seen by people."

This she understood. She nodded but fear was back in her face.

"It'll be fine," I said. "Though . . . he might seem a little off, not quite the man you remember. But know that he deeply loves both you and your daughter, and it's that love that brought him back here. Soon you'll be closer than you ever were before."

She nodded and, with a stiff upper lip, took up the tray of tea and brought it out into the sitting room. Oberon was there, standing near Shipwright, who was still sitting in the same chair we'd left him in. But also there was Gayle, in her nightgown, looking more with curiosity than fear at her father's broken arm.

"And it hurts lots?" she asked.

"Oh yes," Shipwright said. "But broken bones heal, so your old da will be right in a month or so."

"Please, take it easy while it heals, okay, mate?" I turned to Gayle. "Please, look after your father and help your mother until your papa's arm is healed, all right? They'll both be needing your help."

Gayle nodded solemnly. It reminded me so much of Beatrix, and I felt my heart clench.

CHAPTER 25

The early-morning papers announced that Prince Arthur had died after a tragic fall from the Tower of London. They ran an official royal press corps photo of Arthur, bright eyed and smiling for the camera. I thought of him now, head shoved down into his torso. The article made no mention of that. It just said that his body had been found by other partygoers ("some of whom had even heard the sound of the prince's body hitting the ground") and that he'd been dead before a doctor could attend to him. Another guest claimed to have seen the prince go to the roof. Several talked about having drinks with him earlier in the evening. The reporter obviously didn't want to come right out and say that Prince Arthur had gotten sloshed and then fallen off to his death, but it was there between the lines.

"I suppose this is good," I said, not quite sure how to parse this. I had never liked Arthur, but that didn't make his death any easier to stomach. It felt wrong to feel relief that we were seemingly getting away with murder: How could I ever seek God's forgiveness for my crimes if I shirked the earthly repercussions?

"Yes, it is," Oberon said firmly. He had brought a couple of apples along with the newspaper and was eating one. I'd started to bite into the other but I felt too nauseated to finish it. Oberon started speaking again. "This isn't just about protecting us but also Princess Katherine and Cobalt. And staying free to take down the Virtuis Party. What happened to Arthur was an accident at worst, self-defence at best. You understand that, right?"

I shrugged.

"Look, Paul, don't throw our lives away over a guilty conscience," Oberon said. "You'll have the rest of your life to make up for Arthur's, all right?"

"It doesn't work like that," I said, but Oberon had no more patience for me. He took the newspaper and was peering at the article again even though he'd already read it multiple times.

"Odd that they don't mention Van Holt at all."

In the next twenty-four hours a dark cloud descended over the city, with people wearing either black clothes or black armbands in mourning for the prince. People put his picture in storefront windows. Talk on the street was hushed and about one subject: Artie's death. From the little bits I caught while eavesdropping, the big debate seemed to be whether the prince had in fact fallen while in a clumsy stupor or if he had jumped. I was shamefully relieved that no one considered he might have been murdered.

Before his death, it would have been a stretch to say that people *liked* the prince. It was more like they'd enjoyed his antics and occasional off-the-cuff inappropriate remarks. He had been like a temperamental jungle cat housed in a zoo, one that was likely to bare its teeth and growl at you, to the crowd's fear and delight. Maybe that was how it had felt for the prince as well.

But the next day the narrative changed yet again.

Court Magician Sought in Death of Prince Arthur

The article talked about how the Court Magician himself had been missing since the night of the prince's death. The police stressed that they only wanted to talk to Van Holt, and a spokesman from the royal family wished for Van Holt to get in touch so the king and queen could be reassured that he was all right.

"Jesus Christ," I said, once again hiding out in Oberon's boat. "They think Van Holt did it."

"Perhaps," Oberon said. "But we still have to be careful. We can't give them cause to think otherwise."

I was tired of living on this boat and having to share such a small space with Oberon. All I wanted was to get back to my cottage at Hillcrest.

"Lay low for just a few more days," Oberon said. "Believe me, I want as much as anyone to get back into the fight against the Virtuis Party, but things are too hot right now."

It did seem like the country was in disarray after the prince's sudden and shocking death. On the radio they debated whether Princess Katherine should be the heir apparent or if the crown should skip over her to the next male heir, the king's cousin. They debated whether Van Holt had been killed by spies or if perhaps he was a spy himself. Over the course of the day more and more suspicion grew against Van Holt, largely based upon his mysterious disappearance and the fact that "he isn't even British, after all." People suggested he was a spy for the Dutch, for the South African government, for the Americans, for the Russians. Regardless of who he was spying for, the public at large agreed that he was probably the one who had pushed poor Artie over the edge of the roof.

But that almost seemed beside the point, at the end of the day. The country was down a prince, but even worse, it was down a Court Magician. What would the nation do when it was time to create new mages? Since Van Holt was so young and new to the role, there wasn't an apprentice mage maker already in line to take his place.

And then on the third day King Harold announced that, in Van Holt's absence, he would be appointing an interim Court Magician: Gabriella von Melsungen.

~

Oberon had a small wireless on the boat, and we sat inside to listen to Gabs's first public interview on the BBC, Oberon in the chintz chair, me on the floor, back resting against the bed.

"I must say, Interim Court Magician, I never in my life thought we'd see a woman in the role," the interviewer (a man with a plummy accent) said. Even through the radio I could imagine Gabs's smile.

"It is indeed an honour. When His Majesty sent word asking me to take on the position, I was surprised yet delighted. Out of all the mages in this country, that he should ask me, a woman, really shows just how progressive Great Britain is."

"Quite, quite. But what does your husband think about you taking on the job? He's all the way back in Germany, isn't he?"

A beat of silence from Gabs, even though she must have known this question was coming. There was a good chance that the listeners at home might have known about Gabs from seeing her picture in the society pages, but unless they listened in to the right grapevines, they would not have heard about her affair with me. From his cloying tone though, it seemed the interviewer had.

"Oh, of course he misses me dearly," Gabs said. "But he also understands that my duty to this country comes first. If the king himself has asked it of me, how could I say no?"

"Yes, and it's not as though you're going to be in the role forever," the interviewer mused. "You are, after all, the *interim* Court Magician. You don't have the ability to make new mages, correct?"

"Yes, that is correct. But my cloth magic has won awards in both Italy and France and—"

"But making new mages is the core purpose of the Court Magician, is it not?"

"The core purpose of the Court Magician is to protect the royal family." Gabs would never grit her lovely teeth, but I imagined right now she was bearing them in a sharp smile. "Something I am more than capable of doing. I will see to it that we do not suffer another tragedy like the untimely death of Prince Arthur."

"Yes, yes, it's very good that we have an accomplished mage like yourself standing guard," the interviewer said. "But what will the nation do when it's spring and time to make new Book Binders? And with the prison population rising, we are in need of cloth mages as well. Are there plans to seek out a replacement Court Magician from somewhere else in the Commonwealth? Have the deputy mage maker of Canada or Australia come here and do the ritual?"

"That has certainly been discussed, but nothing has been decided upon yet," Gabs said, some of the sparkle gone from her voice.

"Yes, I suppose there's a lot to consider. But it makes sense that you'd only want to stay in the role for a short time, Mrs von Melsungen. I'm sure you're eager to get home to your husband and start having children. Being Court Magician would just get in the way of motherhood, after all!"

"I . . ." It was rare to hear Gabs at a loss for words. The interviewer didn't seem to notice.

"Well, I certainly look forwards to talking with you more in the near future, Interim Court Magician. But it's almost top of the hour, so time for global news—"

Oberon switched off the wireless.

"Well, looks like Gabs has done pretty well for herself," he said. "Even after that whole scandal with you, she's managed to snag the role of interim Court Magician? It's a bit much. Do not misunderstand me—she's a gifted mage, but something about this smells fishy."

"Yeah," I agreed, but I was distracted, thinking about the first time I'd met Gabs. It had been in the week before our cloth magic classes were due to start, and Dean Abernail was having a party in the flat of one of the programme's financial benefactors. When I saw Gabs at that crowded party I was struck by her flawlessness—compared to the rest of us, she looked like a sculpture amongst mounds of clay. The first time our eyes met we smiled like we were old friends seeing each other after a long time apart. We chatted for a little bit before stealing a bottle of wine and hiding ourselves away in the closet. I had thought we were going to kiss then, but instead we ended up drinking and rating the other partygoers on their attractiveness, men and women alike.

"Oh yes, I like girls just fine," Gabs had said drunkenly. "But where will liking girls ever get me?"

"Do you think she knows about Godfrey?" I asked Oberon. He frowned, thinking it over.

"She may just be a pawn in this whole thing," Oberon said. "Maybe specifically to draw you out. She could be in the dark about the real power of the Virtuis Party, but even if so . . ."

He paused, as if wary of speaking ill of Gabs in my presence.

"Spit it out, man."

"Even if she's not with the Virtuis Party, I don't think she's necessarily on our side either," Oberon said. "Gabs is only on her own side."

He winced, as if waiting for me to bite his head off. But for once, I had to agree with Oberon.

~

I was taking a piss when I heard Gabs's voice behind me. When I turned to see her peering at me from the bathroom mirror, I jumped and nearly hit my head on the roof of the boat. Once I got over my shock she looked away so I could button up my trousers and wash my hands.

"Jesus, Gabs, you scared the life out of me."

"I'm sorry, dear heart. I tried calling, I tried visiting your studio, I tried everything. In the end I had to use magic." Her dress had a large neck ruff made of silver silk panels. Maybe that was what allowed her to speak through mirrors? Did she need to know my location, or did it just allow her to peer out of any mirror while searching for one person?

Could she figure out where I was from what she saw in the bathroom? There was a tiny porthole above the mirror, letting in some air and light; could she use that to piece together that I was on a boat?

It felt odd to be so suspicious of Gabs—we used to be each other's closest confidants. But now that she was moving in the upper echelons of power, I wasn't quite sure where we stood.

"Well, Madam Interim Court Magician, a lot has been going on while you were abroad," I said. "I've decided it was in my best interest to lay low for a bit."

"I know more than you think, dear heart," Gabs said. "I wish to speak to you in person. Talking to you through a dingy bathroom mirror is beneath both of us, and I want to see your lovely face up close."

"Well, Gabs, if anyone could get me out of hiding, it'd be you, but surely you won't take it personally if I turn you down."

"What if we met somewhere that guaranteed safety?" she said. "Tomorrow is the prince's funeral. Let's meet afterwards in some corner of Westminster Abbey. No one, not even our most base enemies, would attack us in that place or on such a solemn day."

I noticed her use of *us* and *our* and even though it was a blatant attempt to make it seem as though we were on the same team, it still made me feel warm and relieved: if Gabriella von Melsungen was with me, I had nothing to fear. I wasn't so naive to believe that she *was* with me, but it was a nice feeling to experience briefly. I didn't know how she had ended up getting the plum job of fill-in Court Magician, but for all I knew it meant she was already on Godfrey's side.

The offer to meet at Westminster Abbey was clearly meant to appeal to an ex-choirboy like me. But I'd read history books as well as the Bible—in England being in a church was no guarantee of safety, not if the Crown was against you. I did not want to be Becketed.

But *was* the Crown against me? The Court Magician was supposed to serve the royal family first and foremost: the split between Prince Arthur and Van Holt had come because Van Holt had decided to align with the Virtuis Party and follow Godfrey's directives rather than Artie's. But what if Van Holt *had* been serving the royal family? Specifically, the king himself? The king was supposed to be above politics, but what if he was a shadow member of the Virtuis Party?

"We could also meet at a Catholic church, if you'd prefer that," Gabs offered.

I shook my head. I *did* want to meet with Gabs—in person I could get a better feel for where her loyalties lay. But I needed us to meet somewhere even the king's reach couldn't grasp me, somewhere starting trouble would really be a bad idea.

"No, no churches," I said. "But I do know somewhere we can meet."

~

"Mr Gallagher, I said this before but I will state once more that I am truly astounded by the outright cheek of your request. Asking me to host your little peace talk with your old lover, a mere week after you did my son such an ill turn. I had thought there was no end to your self-absorption, but you are a veritable black hole of self-regard."

Lady Fife and I had entered a new era of our relationship, one where she plainly told me how I was just the worst. She sat on a chair in her living room, hands in her lap while she rattled off her litany of complaints against me. And she didn't even know the half of it—she was angry I'd broken her son's heart, but it seemed she didn't know that I was the one who'd outed him. Small mercies, even though it just made me feel even more guilty.

"You didn't have to say yes." I stood on the other side of the living room, looking out the window at the backyard garden. There had been a chill last night that had sapped all the plant life of its vigour. Even though it was a grey day, I yearned to go outside to stand in the muddy ground and damp air. It would be better than listening to Lady Fife's eerily calm tirade against me.

"Even after what you did to him, it would kill my son if something happened to you," Lady Fife said. "So yes, despite my own reluctance, if this will give you a chance at survival, I felt obligated to assist."

"How . . . how is Andrew?" I asked.

Lady Fife looked away. "He's left the country. One good thing about Prince Arthur's demise is that it very much overshadowed the scandal between you two."

"Right." I'd noticed that myself. The photo of the two of us hadn't been reprinted since Arthur had died—it just seemed like such a tawdry, tedious scandal to dwell on in the face of a royal's death, and so it had faded from public consciousness.

"Still, I've advised him to stay abroad for now," Lady Fife said.

A silence filled the room as Lady Fife's mood shifted from wrathful to mournful. I knew I should apologize for my part in all this, for being the reason Andrew had left the country, but I feared to speak, afraid that by owning up to it I'd give Lady Fife licence to once more list all my faults. And perhaps I deserved it, but that didn't mean I was brave enough to seek it out.

"Be careful when speaking to her," Lady Fife said. "Let Gabriella do most of the talking. Don't open your heart to her."

"Oh, Lady Fife, believe me, I think I might just be closer than anyone to Gabriella." I meant it too. No matter which guy she was dating, I always felt smugly above them. Gabs and I were more than old lovers: we were friends. Even when she'd married one of them, I'd known she'd keep him at arm's length, at least emotionally, and not let him in the way she did with me. "I know what she's like."

Lady Fife seemed like she was about to contest that when something outside caught her eye. I turned to look and saw a large black mist creeping up over the garden wall. It was a mass of curling grey tendrils, and once it was done falling over the wall it formed a cloud. The cloud condensed into the form of a woman: Gabs. She wore a long black dress, made from taffeta that billowed around her. The dress blurred the line between air and solid—when she moved, wisps of darkness followed after her. She wore sleek black gloves, and the only skin visible was her pale, lovely face. Her broad-brimmed black hat sat upon her perfectly coiffed blonde hair at a severe angle. When she tilted her head up she saw me staring at her through the window. She blew me a kiss. I made a show of plucking it out of the air and putting it in my pocket.

She started walking to the house. I went to the back door to meet her.

"Paul!" she said, her delight at odds with her funeral attire. "And Lady Fife." Gabs went down into a deep curtsy, wisps of dark cloud around her like silt being disturbed at the bottom of a riverbed. "Thank you for your hospitality."

"Don't thank me just yet," Lady Fife said. "I'm not a neutral party here. I still have friends in the government, and I've heard how the Virtuis Party was instrumental in you getting this position. They have harmed both myself and my family. They are the reason my son had to leave the country."

"Lady Fife, that was a tawdry business indeed, and done before I was ever involved with matters," Gabs said, standing up slowly. "And it's true that a Virtuis Party operative took the incriminating photo. But it's Paul who sent it to the newspapers."

Lady Fife was at a loss for words.

"Mr Gallagher," she finally said. "Is this true?"

I turned to her. "Yes," I said. "I'm sorry. I couldn't let it be used as blackmail leverage against me."

Even after I spoke she still seemed to be waiting for more, eyes searching over my face, like if she could just see me from a slightly different angle it would all make sense.

Then her disbelief fell away and was replaced by her usual icy primness.

"You two may talk and then leave," she said. "Both of you."

She turned and went down the hall before taking the stairs up to the second floor. Gabs and I waited until we heard the floorboards overhead creak before looking at each other.

"Nice to see the old seer surprised, eh? Poor girl's missed quite a few tricks since she lost her foresight." Gabs stepped forwards and I drew back to let her into the house. She chuckled and took my arm as we walked together to the sitting room. "You know, she's indirectly responsible for ending things between Andrew and me. Remember when he and I were an item back in first year?"

"I do," I said. Part of my mind was still dwelling on Lady Fife's words, about how the Virtuis Party had been instrumental in Gabs getting her current job. I wanted to ask what exactly that meant but Gabs had already sat down on the couch and was still talking about our school days.

"It was going grand between Andrew and me. All right, so not really: Andrew knew as little about girls as a fish knows about the sky. But he was young and rich, so I could forgive that. Then one day he said to me, 'Gabriella, you are truly a stupendous woman! Intelligent, beautiful, and a deeply gifted mage . . .'"

I couldn't help but smile—I knew where this was going, having heard the story from Andrew's side.

"'. . . you're just like Mother in every way!'" We both laughed, loudly and then quietly, in case Lady Fife heard us.

"He thought he was paying you the highest compliment," I said.

"I'm sure he did, but it's not what a girl wants to hear. So I ended things. It was probably for the best in the long run."

The feeling of mirth faded from the room.

"I'm sorry just now for snitching you out to Lady Fife," she said.

"You had to. She only let you in because she was mad at both of us."

Gabs nodded, as if relieved that I could see her reasoning. "Exactly. My, things have gotten complicated since I was last in England! And a murdered prince at the centre of it all!"

"Murdered?" I said. "I thought there was still a chance it was all an accident."

Gabs gave me a pitying look. "Oh, dear heart, I know you want to see the best in people, but it's pretty clear something happened on the roof and that Van Holt was involved. It's well known that the two didn't get along. Perhaps they came to blows and then . . . well, it's conjecture, but the only one who knows the truth now is Van Holt, and he's missing."

Gabs seemed to be sincere about blaming Van Holt for Arthur's death, which made me feel both guilty and relieved—maybe we really would get away with it after all.

"But with Van Holt on the run, Britain's out a Court Magician," I said.

"Well, Great Britain has me now," she said. She leaned in. "Can I tell you a secret, Paul?"

"Sure," I said. What was one more secret to carry?

"I'm glad Prince Arthur's dead," she said. "He was a prick, and he'd be a horrible king. And I'm glad Van Holt was stupid enough to be the one to do him in. It's this unlikely combination of things that have made it so that I, a girl from Cornwall, a mere woman, can be made Court Magician."

"How did Kristoff take your new appointment?" I didn't mean to echo the BBC interviewer; it was just, I knew Kristoff and while things had always been somewhat awkward between us even before the scandal, I liked the guy and wondered how he was handling all this.

Gabs leaned back. "We're not really speaking right now," she said, her voice wavering slightly. "He found out about me and Klaus."

"What?" When I had agreed to help Gabs cover up her affair, I had done so because she'd said it was the only chance of saving her marriage. Gabs's reasoning had been that while Kristoff could forgive her a one-off fling with an old flame, he wouldn't be able to forgive her sleeping with his own brother. Now she was telling me that Kristoff had found out the truth anyway and me torpedoing my reputation had been for nothing.

She looked away, eyelashes so low they almost touched her cheek. "He won't file for a divorce. So we're just living this public fiction that we're still together. But after he found out, he told me I should leave, give him space. I went back to Cornwall and was living there in secret with my family. It was really quite a low point for me, I hate to say. I didn't know where I'd end up."

"That doesn't sound like you," I said. "You know, you could have reached out to me."

She gave me a smile, the motion of her head almost shaking loose the tears from her eyes. "But I'd already asked so much from you, Paul. Verity left you because of me. And I know our so-called affair was high gossip here in London. How could I tell you that it had all been for nothing, that Kristoff had discovered the truth and thrown me out?" She sat up straighter—a tear slid down her face but it seemed like a revenant from a past sadness, her mind already moving on. She carefully wiped at her eyes. "But while I was in Cornwall, I suppose I wasn't as hidden as I believed myself to be. An agent from the king came to my door and asked if I would agree to be the interim Court Magician. So in a way, everything worked out for the best." She smiled. "Well, pet, as much as I'd love to continue to catch up, we've got much more serious matters to discuss."

"Yes, I suppose we do."

"I'm told that the former Court Magician and the deputy prime minister were not very kind to you."

"You mean they tortured me?" I held up my hand. Oberon had replaced the large cloth bandages with smaller ones, but it still looked bad to have four fingers bandaged up. Gabs looked at them, a frown on her face, a hint of anger behind her gaze.

"There was someone else there," I said, keeping my hand up.

Gabs brightened at that. "Oh yes! I hear Oberon's in town. And that he's grown a great bushy beard! How is he? I—"

"I'm not talking about him," I said. "I'm talking about James Godfrey."

Gabs cocked her head to the side. "Who?"

"Come on, Gabs!" I said, letting my hand fall down to rest by my side. "Just tell it to me straight. Are you working for the royal family, like a good Court Magician should, or are you in league with the Virtuis Party?"

Gabs poured herself some tea. "I have no idea what you're talking about."

"Oh, Gabriella," I said. "You don't have any idea the evil you've mired yourself in. Look, I've been thinking about this. Court Magician is supposed to be an apolitical appointment, right? But Van Holt was in deep with the Virtuis Party, which would be at odds with his directive to serve the king and the rest of the royal family, yeah? *Unless* he was in fact serving Virtuis and the king, because the king is a shadow member."

"Paul, you sound like a conspiracy theorist."

"Gabs, listen to me. Maybe you don't know just yet what you've waded into, but I know you. I know you don't agree with what the Virtuis Party champions. Don't sell your soul for worldly gain."

A brief flash of anger showed on Gabs's face but she quickly controlled it.

"I know more than you think I do, pet," she said, suddenly all business. "King Harold asked me to convey a message to you. See, that's one of the reasons I was chosen for this job, beyond my own qualities. They knew I could successfully broker a peace treaty."

"You want me to accept an olive branch from those bastards?"

"At least hear out the terms," Gabs said, setting her cup down. "King Harold asked *me* to tell you to please tell Sabina that she and her child are no longer in danger. Yes, I know about Sabina—I'm not the ignorant girl you seem to think I am. Tell her that as long as she never makes any fantastic claims about her child's royal parentage, the two of them can live in peace. With Arthur dead, there's not anyone who can truly back her up, so she may as well drop the whole thing."

"I see." Privately I did not think that Sabina would be pleased with such an offer. "She might want some financial compensation."

"I suggested that as well, but the king was firm. All she gets is assurance that the Crown will not move against her," Gabs said. "But surely that's better than living in hiding for the rest of her life?"

I was quiet. Maybe Gabs didn't know that the one pulling her strings was an undead zealot, but she *did* know that her new employers were willing to kill a child. I was so disappointed in her.

"And this extends to you as well, Paul," Gabs said. "The goons from the Virtuis Party will no longer hunt you. The prince's death has changed a lot of things. With him gone, who will champion his bastard child's claim to the throne? Not a soul. So there's no reason to hound Sabina's location out of you. The powers that be are prepared to drop the matter."

"How kind of them."

"Pet, don't be so surly. Everyone involved just wants a clean slate. Things are bad enough right now with a Court Magician straight up murdering a royal. The nation's been through enough already. Everyone just wants calm. You do too, don't you?"

I did. The Virtuis Party disgusted me, but I was still afraid of them. The fact that they believed that Van Holt had killed Arthur was the only silver lining in this situation: it let me, Kitty, Cobalt, and Oberon off the hook for his death. Also, it meant that Godfrey and Fairweather would have to play things carefully for the next little while to avoid bringing too much scrutiny their way.

I could get on with my life. I could be with Laura and Beatrix again.

"All right," I told Gabs. "Tell the king I accept his terms. I'll get word to Sabina."

CHAPTER 26

One person who *didn't* accept these terms was Oberon.

"Why would you agree to such a thing?!" Oberon said, pacing the small length of the houseboat while I packed up my clothes.

"Mainly because I was tired of living on this fucking boat," I said. "God, I don't know how Noah stood it for forty fucking days." I was beyond eager to get home to the gardener's cottage. Already I could hear the wind rustling the trees and feel the long grass under my hands.

"And what about undoing the Virtuis Party?" Oberon said, stopping midpace to loom over me. That made me lock up in a flash of fear—I didn't think he was trying to physically intimidate me, but he was doing it nonetheless. When he saw the look on my face he backed off.

"It can't be done," I said. "They're more entrenched than I first thought. Not just the prime minister but the *king* is in on it."

"So?! There are still things we can do! You're best friends with the crown princess!"

It wasn't the first time I'd heard someone refer to Kitty as "the crown princess," but it still came as a shock. With her brother's death, she was now next in line for the throne. Already the world was looking at her differently, sizing her up as a future ruler. That would be a lot for a teenage girl to take on suddenly at the best of times, but this wasn't the best of times: Kitty had just lost her brother. Worse than that, she'd had a hand in his death. She was such a sensitive girl. What if the Virtuis Party tried to get their claws into her? Sure, they had King Harold on their side, but Godfrey clearly had the long view of history. What if Kitty didn't fit into his plan?

"I can't be seen with the princess right now. As far as the world at large is concerned, she's still mad that I shagged her fiancé."

"So you're just going to let Godfrey and his ilk steamroll this country into a hellscape?" Oberon said. "The longer things go without someone standing up to them, the bolder they'll get! Don't you care?"

"Big talk, considering you didn't care until your dad died." I stood and Oberon blocked my way. I felt anger heat up my cheeks. I was so angry that Oberon would use his bigger frame to try and stop me, even though he *knew* better.

"You're right. I didn't care until it affected me personally. But I didn't think you were like that. I had always thought you were the better man, Gallagher." He stepped aside. I waited, trying to think if I had some comeback, but none came, so I walked out.

~

It was dark when I reached Hillcrest, the sun down and moon in the sky even though it was only six o'clock. I could have gone right to my cottage, but after parking by it I walked up to the main house, thinking that I should tell Laura I was back. But I hadn't figured out what exactly I'd do when I was face to face with her. Last time we'd seen each other we'd both said harsh things. Should I start off with an apology? But I'd been trying to warn Laura about a danger in her home, and she'd said some pretty rotten stuff to me too. Should I wait for her to apologize first?

I was still going over my options when I felt a small hand in mine. I looked down to see Beatrix standing next to me, a solemn look on her face. Still silent, she leaned her head against me. I felt a little like David in the lions' den, awestruck that this wild animal was acting so gentle.

"Please don't go again," Beatrix said, voice muffled by my coat. I think it was the first time I'd ever heard her say *please*.

This was exactly what I'd hoped and feared would happen. Was I going to be one more adult in Beatrix's life who disappointed her? I wanted to promise her the moon, but I was scared, scared of not living up to my word.

Before I could fumble out some kind of assurance, Beatrix spoke again.

"Pick me up and carry me inside the house."

I did as I was told. When Laura saw us, a bright relief filled her face. "Mr Gallagher!" she said, then saw her daughter in my arms. She took her from me, tsking as she saw how dirty the child was after a day of playing in the woods. She was quickly caught up in telling Beatrix off, but between admonishments she shot smiles my way. I wanted to stay but Beatrix was rubbing her eyes and Laura was busy looking after her, so I eventually slipped away to my own little home.

~

The next day I got in touch with Brennan and told him to relay the king's message to Sabina. After the phone call I lay on the couch in the living room of Hillcrest and closed my eyes. An uneasy calm settled upon me. I felt simultaneously relieved and disquieted, glad to be done with the whole matter but also unsure if I had done the right thing. I didn't think I had acted wrongly: at no point had I played the Judas and betrayed Sabina or her unborn child. No, I was just washing my hands of them.

"Are you all right, Mr Gallagher?" Harriet asked, standing once more upon the stair, a wince on her face.

"Ah, Harriet." Hopefully the girl would report to Fairweather that I'd done my part and tried to get word to Sabina about Virtuis's peace agreement. "I didn't know you were still here. Are you planning to go back to your fiancé?"

She came down the stairs slowly, as if she were walking on fragile glass.

"I don't know." She sat in a chair that was on the other side of the room, as if afraid of getting close to me.

"What, haven't you reconciled with Peter yet?" I figured she would have dropped the whole pretence about having broken up with him—did Fairweather really need her spying on me at this point?

Harriet looked down as she twisted her hands in her lap.

"I'd like to stay here. And . . . and I'd like to study cloth magic alongside you and Rosemary and Naveed as well."

"Really? You three don't always seem to get on."

"Oh, it's nothing serious. We're just . . . fraught friends."

Fraught Friends. I found the phrase quite charming, and I couldn't help but turn it into a proper noun. Mischievous Rosemary, boisterous Naveed, and flappable Harriet: the Fraught Friends.

"But if you want me to go, I will," Harriet said. "I feel like I owe it to you, Professor."

"What?" I said, confused. "Why would you owe me?"

"Well, one, you never charge me for the tutoring sessions," Harriet said. "And even more than that, I know you stayed away for a while because I was here. Mrs Spratt, she missed you something terrible. The whole house seemed so gloomy without you here, and I could see what a toll it took on Beatrix and Mrs Spratt. I felt so guilty . . . but even so, I so wanted to stay here. I know I'm a bother, but Mrs Spratt is so kind that she's taken me in anyway. This house, it's one of the few places I've ever felt safe."

Harriet's words sent me on a teeter-totter of emotions—a surge of elation that Mrs Spratt had missed me, then guilt about begrudging Harriet's presence at Hillcrest.

"You're not a bother to Mrs Spratt," I said. "I know she's very happy to have you here. She told me that in return for room and board, you look after Beatrix and help around the house."

Harriet nodded eagerly. "And I help with the washing and mending and sometimes the cooking," she said, then faltered. "But for Mrs Spratt's sake, I'd rather you be here than me. So if you won't have me as a neighbour, I'll leave."

Admittedly, when I'd come back to Hillcrest, I hadn't expected Harriet to still be hanging around. But here she was.

Maybe the wallflower act was just a ploy to make me lower my guard so that she could avenge her father. But she was my neighbour, in both the literal and spiritual sense, and I'd be damned once more if I didn't extend kindness to her.

"I think there's room at Hillcrest for both of us, don't you think?"

She looked up and, after blinking in surprise, gave me a wide, relieved smile.

~

The next day Laura and I were doing the washing up together while Harriet put Beatrix to bed. The two of us stood by the sink, hip to hip as I washed the dishes and Laura dried. We'd had a grand feast to celebrate my return, a full Sunday roast. I'd felt guilty to see so much money spent for my sake, but the mood was so joyful that my guilt hadn't lasted long.

Now, alone in the kitchen together, the two of us engaged in such a domestic scene, we both suddenly felt bashful, at a loss for words.

I went first.

"I'm sorry for raising a stink about Harriet. I know she's been a big help to you here." Maybe Harriet would in fact shank me as I slept one night, but I probably deserved it.

"Well, I still don't quite understand your paranoia around that girl, but with so much going on in this country . . . I suppose I can see why you might get worked up," Laura said. "And I must apologize too." She blushed, gaze fixed on the plate in her hands. "I'm sorry for being so curt with you, for saying you were just a tenant."

"Oh?" My heart was beating so loudly I was terrified that Laura might hear it. I splashed some water around in the sink to cover up the sound.

"Yes. That wasn't fair to you. You've been a good friend to both myself and Beatrix. It was very unkind of me to act otherwise. I'm glad you are back."

"Me too." I smiled at her. Laura returned my smile but still seemed unsure of something.

"So . . . while you were away, you stayed with your friend Duke Fife?"

I could see what was on her mind as clearly as if it were being projected onto the wall: the newspaper photo of Andrew and me snogging.

"Mrs Spratt—"

"You may call me Laura," she said, voice bold even as she started blushing. "When we first met you said I could call you Paul. I hope that's still the case."

"Yes, yes, of course," I replied. "Please. Laura, what happened between me and Andrew . . . it's over now. There really wasn't too much to it in the first place," I said, not wanting to talk about it further. She seemed to pick up on that, because she didn't ask anything more about Andrew. She did, however, choose an almost equally uncomfortable track.

"And I see that Gabriella von Melsungen has been named the interim Court Magician. I've seen articles speculating that she came back to this country so the two of you can be together. If so, that's awfully romantic." Her tone was a strange mix of wry and wistful.

"It would be, but that's not the case," I said. "We're just friends nowadays. The papers like to make it out that we're these star-crossed lovers, but that's just because it helps sales—"

Laura laughed. "Oh, Mr Gallagher, you don't have to explain that to me. They've used me plenty of times to sell copies." She smiled and whatever nervousness had been there before was gone, replaced by a relaxed happiness. "I'm sorry, I must sound like one of those nosy landladies, always sticking her nose into other people's business. I didn't mean to pry. I've just been worried about you. It's been such a tumultuous time, with the prince's death. With everything going on, I was worried you might get caught up with it somehow."

I was sure she was speaking the truth, but from the way Laura's blush was deepening I couldn't help but think that there was another reason she was asking about my various lovers. I wanted to tell her that I was a free man, my options open. But I didn't. Even if it was true for me, it wasn't for her. She was still married to her husband and in the middle of a messy divorce. Declaring my feelings would just make her already complicated situation even more precarious.

"No need to worry, Laura," I said. "Everything's going to be fine from here on out."

~

And for a few weeks, it was. I continued to stay in the cottage, though I ate my meals at the main house with the girls. I started tutoring the Fraught Friends again, and sometimes the lot of us—Laura, Beatrix, Harriet, Naveed, Rosemary, me—would have indoor picnics, dining on a blanket spread out in the living room.

I sent a formal condolence card to Princess Katherine in the wake of Arthur's death and privately reached out to Cobalt to see if she would meet with me.

"She doesn't want to see you right now, Paul," he told me. "Considering what happened last time . . . well, she's not too inclined towards another rendezvous."

"Please. Tell her it's important." I needed to tell her not to trust her father, that he was in league with evil men who didn't have her best interests at heart. Even though we'd been through a horrible ordeal together, even though Cobalt had come through for me with flying colours, I wasn't sure if I could trust Cobalt with that information. What if he just used it to advance his own position?

"It really isn't a good idea for you to talk to her right now," Cobalt said, and his voice changed from that of a prim, gatekeeping secretary to that of a sympathetic mate letting you in on the real story. "She blames you for Arthur's death."

That was horribly unfair—I'd only been trying to protect her.

"I know," Cobalt replied when I protested. "And I'm trying to protect both of you. I'll try and be your champion here, but . . ."

But not at a cost to his own good standing with the princess.

"I will be by her side day and night, watching over her," Cobalt said. "Believe me, I know there are still evil forces in this country. This calm can't last forever."

But for a few weeks it did. That November not much happened. For once I could actually note daily how the leaves changed. A side benefit of being in the country was being able to experience the seasons.

And then in December my father died.

My brother Patrick called me to tell me. I felt a series of losses all at once: the loss of my father as I'd known him before the coma, the loss of hope that he might rouse from it, the loss of my strongest connection to my roots. Then Patrick started talking about funeral arrangements, and that cut through the haze of my grief, at least momentarily. I agreed to everything he said. It was probably one of the most civil conversations the two of us had ever had, and all it took was our father dying.

Laura was standing in the entrance to the living room when I hung up the phone. When the call had come in, instead of sending Beatrix to fetch me she had come to the cottage herself, perhaps sensing something in my brother's voice that implied this wasn't a frivolous social call.

"My father's dead," I explained to her.

She insisted I sit down. She sat next to me on the couch—actually next to me, so close our thighs were touching.

"I'm so sorry for your loss," she said.

"Thank you. It's odd: I've had months to make peace with the fact that he was dying but . . . it still comes as a blow," I said. "I don't really feel like I have any family left in the world now."

She nodded. "I know that feeling quite well." As soon as the words were out of her mouth she looked away, aghast, clenched fists pressed against her forehead. "Oh, Laura, you stupid bint! God, I can't believe I'm comparing myself to someone who's an actual orphan. I'm so sorry, Paul."

I couldn't help but find her consternation quite cute. "No, please. I want to hear all about it. It'll take my mind off my own pain for a bit," I said.

"Oh, well, it's just, some days it seems I'm not just divorcing my own husband but my own family," Laura said. "They set up the match, you understand. And I didn't fight them. I was a nineteen-year-old girl who'd been raised on a steady diet of fairy tales, so when I met this handsome, roguish lord-to-be, I fell head over heels."

I felt a twinge of jealousy at hearing Laura talk up her ex but tried not to let it show.

"But when I grew older and the fairy tale faded away . . . they made it clear that if I left Jack, I could expect no help from *them*." She looked away to briefly rub her eyes. "So even though my family is still alive . . . I'm dead to them."

"I don't get along with my brothers," I said. "Even though they're the only blood I have left in this world, I don't want to see them." A sudden realization knifed through me. "I don't even want to go to my father's funeral."

"Then don't," Laura said, reaching over to grab my forearm. "Stay here with me and Beatrix. Tell us stories about your father. You can grieve just as well here as in Liverpool."

I wasn't quite sure if that was true—there might have been some cathartic value to walking the same streets I used to walk as a tyke, speaking to his old friends, maybe even shoring things up with Patrick and Mikey. I could go visit the same cathedral where I'd had my first Communion.

Visit my parents' graves.

The realization came then that it wouldn't just be my mother in the ground from that point on. I didn't respond to Laura's plea for me to stay, just cried there on her couch as she held me.

I *did* end up staying at Hillcrest. When I told my brothers they took turns chewing me out over the phone, calling me all the old usual insults and some new ones as well. I replied in turn, hung up with my blood boiling.

I wrestled with whether I had made the right decision in staying in London, but usually only when I was by myself, lying in the dark and staring up at the ceiling. The rest of the time, when I was teaching the Fraught Friends or romping around the estate with Beatrix or just talking to Laura, I did not feel any doubt at all.

Laura was true to her word, listening to my stories about my mother and father. I ate dinner with them every night, simple meals we managed to cobble together but enjoyed all the more for having made them ourselves. I started to remember recipes that I'd helped my mum cook. Beatrix became my assistant in the kitchen, helping me the same way I had helped my mother many years ago. We started to get ready for Christmas, cutting down a tree and making paper chains to decorate it.

I knew things were still bad beyond Hillcrest. The Virtuis Party was still in power, and every day in the papers there was more news about massive arrests, about rumblings of war between America and Russia. But since it didn't touch me directly, it was easy to ignore it. Until it wasn't.

CHAPTER 27

On December 21, Harriet got a phone call right after dinner. We were sitting at the table having coffee when the phone rang. Laura went to answer it, and when she came back she looked to Harriet with a frown.

"Mr Fairweather is on the line for you," Laura said. "Should I tell him you're unavailable?"

"N-no, I'll speak with him," Harriet said, trying to stand before even pushing her chair out, causing her to almost overturn the table. Even though I knew that Harriet was probably still spying for Fairweather, it was odd for him to call the house. He had once or twice called the main house early on in Harriet's stay, but I thought he'd realized how suspicious it would be if he stayed in such contact with his estranged fiancée. Instead, Harriet had taken to going on evening bike rides. Once I had passed her in a phone box by the nearest petrol station, talking on the phone to someone—Fairweather, presumably. Harriet was so awkward and unassuming that it was easy to forget at times that she was aligned with my enemies.

She came back from the phone call, pale. Instead of sitting back down at the table she stood in the doorway to the dining room for an agonizing thirty seconds as Laura and I tried to chat normally.

"Professor Gallagher, I *must* speak with you now," Harriet finally said. "Can we step outside?"

We stepped out into the back garden. It was dark but the light from the house illuminated the light snow that had fallen on the downward slope of the backyard. In the distance we could see the London city lights.

"Mr Gallagher, there are many things I need to tell you," Harriet said, speaking rapidly. "I'm sorry to you and Mrs Spratt, but I've been living here under false pretences. I did not have a fight with my fiancé. I'm here because he asked me to live here so I could keep an eye on your comings and goings. And . . . for my own part, I also wanted to get closer to you, to see what kind of man you are. To see if you really were the man who killed my father."

Well, it was all coming out now.

"Harriet—" I said, words getting caught in my throat.

"Mr Gallagher, we don't have time to talk now," Harriet told me, which was fine enough for her to say after *she* had already gotten a chance to talk. "You must leave here now. They are coming to arrest you."

"What? Who?" Things were moving too fast.

"The police," Harriet said. "They are coming to arrest you for the prince's murder."

"What?! But they have no proof!" As soon as it was out of my mouth I realized what a stupid thing that was to say.

"Peter said they found Van Holt," Harriet said. "Van Holt says it was you. Peter called me to ask if you were home. I . . . I said yes but I lied and said you were at the cottage."

I barely took note of Harriet's words beyond the first sentence. They had found Van Holt? How was that even possible? Van Holt didn't even exist anymore.

"Is something wrong?" Laura asked, stepping outside.

There was the sound of a car pulling up on the front side of the house. Harriet's eyes widened.

"I'll go stall them," she said. "Run, Professor Gallagher!"

She hurried off to the front of the house.

Laura stepped close enough to take my hand and I noticed a slight tremble when we touched.

"Paul, what is going on?"

"You need to grab Beatrix and go," I said. "You need to hide."

"What? Why?"

If Fairweather had in fact found Van Holt, then not only was I in danger, but Beatrix and Laura were too. Van Holt knew the secret behind Arthur's death, but on a more personal level he knew how I felt about Laura. If he told Godfrey, then Godfrey would do the exact same thing that Hollister had done: he would use the person I loved against me, forcing me to perform horrible miracles in order to keep them alive.

"They've found the Court Magician," I said. "He knows I was there the night Prince Arthur died and is saying it's my fault. And it is, Laura. The prince died because of some innate magic that I cast. I can do things that most mages can't or don't dare. And my enemies wish to either destroy me or compel me to use that power in their service. That's why you and Beatrix need to hide. Van Holt knows that I love you."

Laura stared at me, surprise clear even in the dark moonlight.

"Hey, lovelies!" Naveed strolled around the side of the house, Harriet and Rosemary on either side of him. I let out a sigh of relief.

"So I don't know if you've heard the latest, but some of the royal guard tried to arrest sweet little Princess Kitty and her pet mage Cobalt for the murder of her brother," Naveed said. "But when they went to grab Her Highness, some tricky magic tripped them up. Kitty and Cobalt were able to make an escape, but the coppers are on their way here right now for *you*, Professor."

"Yes, I know. We have to get out of here."

"Correct," Naveed said. "Don't worry, there's a place we can go to meet up with Kitty. We'll take my car." Naveed spoke as breezily as if arranging holiday plans. I turned to Laura.

"You can't stay here," I said. "When they find I'm gone, they'll try and get information out of you. That and . . . what we were talking about before."

I was referring to my blurted confession of love. It had been awkward enough the first time; I didn't want to repeat it with the Fraught Friends watching like they were an audience at some melodrama.

Laura nodded. "I understand. We'll go." She looked to Harriet and Rosemary. "Can you girls go fetch my daughter and pack a few of her things? She'll only need a couple outfits."

"I'll grab some of your things as well," Harriet offered helpfully. She rushed back into the house. Rosemary looked more reticent, clearly wishing to stay and continue watching whatever was unfolding, but eventually, eyes still on us, she slunk into the house.

"It will be a tight fit getting all of us into the car," Naveed said, "but we can make it work."

"No, I'll take my own car," Laura said. This surprised me, since Laura was still only a fair-to-middling driver. I'd been giving her lessons, and just the other day she'd almost reversed into a ditch.

"In that case, Mrs Spratt," I said, "I could ride with you and drive—"

"No," Laura said. "We're not going to the same place. I'm taking Beatrix and going back to my husband."

Naveed covered his mouth in surprise. I gave him a look and he stepped away, giving Laura and me the illusion of privacy while still staying close enough to eavesdrop.

"Laura, what are you talking about?" I said. "Why go back to your husband?"

"You've made it clear that if my daughter and I stay here we'll be in danger from your enemies—"

"Then come with us!"

"And live like fugitives? Paul, if it were just me, just my life at stake . . ." She reached out to briefly touch my cheek before drawing back. "But it's not. I have Beatrix to look after, and I can't put her in that kind of danger. Do you even know what you're going to do next? Or where you're going to go?"

"There is a plan," Naveed interjected, unable to remain a silent observer. "There's a meeting space we're all going to head to, but . . ."

"But after that you'll be enemies of the Crown, and who knows where things will go from there," Laura said. "I'm sorry, I can't go with you. It's too uncertain."

"I know everything's all gone to pot," I said. "I know I can't promise yours or Beatrix's safety, but your husband—"

"Can," Laura said. "If there is one thing this divorce has taught me, it's that both Jack and his family will fight hard to keep their control over me. Me *and* Beatrix. The Spratts, for all their faults, are not part of the Virtuis Party. They won't turn me over to them."

"But Laura, you told me . . ." *That your biggest regret was not getting out sooner.* And now she was going back to him. The life she'd managed to claw out for herself was crumbling and it was all my fault.

Laura smiled at me briefly. "Don't fret, Paul. I always knew this was a possibility."

"I think it's a good plan," Rosemary said as she stepped into the backyard. She was holding Beatrix's hand. Beatrix was rubbing her eyes, nightgown on under her hastily buttoned coat. Behind them was Harriet, carrying two small suitcases.

"Mama!" Beatrix ran over to Laura. Laura scooped her up in her arms and buried her face in the girl's hair, eyes squeezed tight. Up until that point I had been impressed with how quickly and calmly Laura had come to a decision. Only now did I see what it was costing her.

Rosemary came up to me.

"Don't worry, Professor Gallagher," she said. "I'll ride with them and make sure they get to her in-laws unharmed. Later on I'll rejoin you all."

This did actually make me feel better. Of all my three students, Rosemary was the most fearless. If she said she would protect Laura and Beatrix, she'd do it.

Cars went by on the main road. We all froze, but they passed the house and continued down to the road that led to the gardener's cottage. We could just see their lights through the trees as they pulled up to the building.

"We should go," Naveed said, fear making his voice take on a high, singsong quality. Quietly but quickly the others started making their way to the front of the house. Everyone but Harriet.

"I'll . . . I'll stay and stall them," Harriet said. "For real this time."

Carefully I took her hand. "Harriet, you've done enough. Do you *want* to stay here? Or do you want to come with us?"

She seemed paralyzed.

"I'll put it this way: Do you *really* want to marry Peter Fairweather?"

A trembling started in her toes and built upwards until she was shaking her head violently.

"All right then, let's go." I tugged on her hand and we followed the others to the front of the house. Laura and Beatrix were bundled into the back of Laura's car while Rosemary slid into the driver's seat. I wanted to go talk to Laura, to apologize once more about everything that was happening, but Harriet was tugging on *my* hand now, pulling me over to Naveed's car. He was standing by the driver's side as he impatiently waited for us. Part of me was surprised he could even drive—in the past he had always been chauffeured to Hillcrest.

"You should get in the back, Professor," he said, settling into his seat. "Less chance of being spotted."

I followed his advice and Harriet sat beside me. It occurred to me just then that while Laura and Beatrix had grabbed clothes, I had nothing but what I had on me—none of my magic outfits, not the big wads of American dollars I had stashed away for safekeeping, not sentimental things like photos of my family or my onyx rosary. I was still cataloguing things when Naveed started the car. We were too far from the cottage to hear the sounds of the men who'd come to arrest me, but surely they'd heard *us*. We pulled out of the driveway and onto the main road before reaching the motorway with no sign of our pursuers.

CHAPTER 28

We stayed behind Laura's car for twenty minutes before they took the exit that would bring her to her in-laws' home. Watching the car disappear from view was a relief and a gut punch. I knew Laura and Beatrix would be safer away from me, but that didn't change the fact that I wanted them with me.

Without another car to keep pace with, Naveed pressed down hard on the accelerator, causing us to fly down the road.

"Where are we going?" I asked.

"Somewhere safe," Naveed replied, eyes flicking up to the rearview mirror to glance at Harriet.

"She's all right," I said. "Harriet warned me that the police were on the way before you even showed up."

"It's true, Naveed," Harriet said. "All I want is to help Professor Gallagher to get away a-a-and . . . I just want to get away too. I want to get away from Peter and his horrible aunt and horrible friends and I don't want to marry him or anyone, so please, wherever you're going, please, take me with you."

She was crying by the end of it, leaning across me to grab the back of the driver's seat, as if trying to clutch at Naveed to make her appeal.

"Harriet, sit down. It's all right. We're not going to leave you behind," I said. She seemed horribly relieved and let go of the driver's seat in order to throw her arms around me, crying into my shoulder. I comforted her with a few pats on the back and made no effort to remove her even as tears soaked into my suit jacket. I met Naveed's eyes in the rearview mirror. He still looked sceptical, but Harriet's words seemed to have softened him up somewhat.

"Where are we going?" I asked again, this time a little more forcefully.

"Slough."

"Slough?" I repeated back to him. "What in Jesus's name are we going to *Slough* for?"

"Yes, pet, why indeed?" Gabriella looked back at me from the rearview mirror. I jumped in my seat, jolting Harriet off me.

"Gabs!" Oh, Jesus, how much could she see? Could she figure out where we were? Well, maybe that didn't matter so much since she knew now where we were going.

"What about her?" Harriet asked. I pointed to the mirror. Harriet and Naveed looked but just seemed confused.

"They can't see me, pet," Gabs said. "It's *you* I want to talk to. Running is a very bad look, Paul. You should turn yourself in before things get too messy for me to clean up. I'm on your side."

"Then you could have warned me that the police were coming," I said, leaning forwards between the front two seats so I could stare into the rearview mirror.

"You haven't been totally forthcoming with me either, dear heart. You never told me that you could do innate magic, of all things."

Her reference to innate magic made my heart sink, since it confirmed that they really had found Van Holt. Part of me up until that point had believed it had been a bluff, an excuse to go after me and the princess, but now it seemed to be the truth.

I reached out and grabbed hold of the rearview mirror. It took several tries, but eventually I yanked the mirror loose.

"Hey! I need that!" Naveed said.

"Sorry. No looking back now." I turned to Harriet. "Can you roll down your window?"

She got to it, using both hands to turn the crank.

"Really, Paul. Be sensible," Gabs said from the small mirror. "You've been a bad boy, but that doesn't mean I want to see your pretty face at the end of a rope. I'll protect you from that. We can work out a solution for this. A way where instead of dying for your crime, you make amends."

"I see. Just like all those prisoners across the nation right now?"

"Oh, that would be such a waste of your talents," Gabs said. "I'm talking about something much bigger."

"I know you are," I said. "Which is why I'll have to decline." I tossed the mirror out of Harriet's window. I looked back to see the mirror shards scatter on the road and disappear into the darkness.

"What was all that about?" Naveed asked.

"The interim Court Magician knows we're going to Slough."

"Fuck!" Naveed said. He sped up, going even quicker down the dark motorway.

"Maybe we should go somewhere else, then," Harriet suggested. "Hide until we get a chance to move undetected."

"No, we have to keep going," Naveed said. "The others are already waiting for us at the castle."

"The castle?" I asked.

"Well, yes. Windsor Castle."

Of course—*that* was what was in Slough. But if we were enemies of the Crown, why would our rallying point be a royal stronghold?

"The others have already taken refuge there," Naveed explained. "The princess, Cobalt, the queen."

"The queen?" I hadn't expected Queen Andriette to be on our side, considering we were responsible for the death of her son.

"Yes," Naveed said. I noticed how tightly he was clutching the steering wheel. "Also, my entire family is there, so if you don't mind I really want to get there PDQ, hmm?"

"But—" Harriet said before Naveed cut her off.

"Look, Harriet, the Virtuis Party is bringing down the hammer tonight. The prince's death has given them free rein to go after whatsoever they wish—look at the outrageous slander they've concocted against Professor Gallagher! The only advantage we have right now is that everything is chaotic enough for us to slip through their net. If we slow down now, we'll lose that."

Harriet had no reply. I turned over Naveed's words in my mind. If he was right, then countless friends of mine were in danger. Ralph was very openly against the Virtuis Party, Oberon had his personal grudge, and Lady Fife, though diminished in power, was still a threat.

We were silent as we zoomed down the motorway, a kind of grim quiet in which everyone was aware that this might be their last hour on Earth, so why clutter it up with needless words?

Naveed took the exit for Slough. Immediately as we came off the ramp a military checkpoint came into sight. Both Harriet and I tensed up but Naveed actually relaxed, rolling down the window to wave back at a soldier after the lad waved us through.

"What the hell?" I asked.

"There's a faction of the military that's on our side," Naveed said.

"A faction of the military"? "On our side"? I hadn't even known "we" had a "side." A few hours ago I'd been having a late supper at Hillcrest, living more or less alone with the secret of my crimes bearing down upon me. Now the whole world had flipped and suddenly everyone knew what I'd done.

Finally the castle itself came into sight. The castle walls sloped along the hill it sat on like a lopsided cake, a round tower at the apex, square grey stone buildings at the base. I'd never been to Windsor Castle before, only ever seen pictures of the place. It was bigger than I'd imagined, every building squat and sturdy.

We passed through the largest military checkpoint yet and then Naveed motored up the long drive to the castle, zoomed through the castle gates, and stopped with a screech in a large courtyard.

Naveed turned off the car and got out. A stampede of people ran to him, and it was easy to guess that it was Naveed's mother and father as well as two young women who were probably his sisters. They talked over each other to both praise Naveed for his daring and chasten him for not being quicker. He stood there proudly, a smile on his face, all the worry and tension from the last hour gone.

Harriet and I got out of the car as well, feeling like a bit of an afterthought as the crowd fussed over Naveed.

"Gally!"

Princess Katherine was running towards me, Cobalt hot on her heels. When she finally was in front of me she stopped so suddenly she nearly crashed into me. She steeled herself into a calmer countenance but struggled for a moment to figure out a proper greeting. "I am glad to see you are all right and made it here unharmed."

"Thank you, Princess," I said.

"I am also glad you're here," Cobalt said, somewhat stiffly. He had a bandage over his left eye and his right arm in a sling.

"Jesus, mate! What happened to you?" I asked.

"I am perfectly all right, just some minor abrasions," Cobalt said.

"That's not true. Cobalt fought valiantly to get me away from the interim Court Magician and was wounded deeply. Despite losing an eye, he was still able to get me away," Kitty said, placing a hand on his uninjured shoulder. I took in Cobalt's bandage anew—*Gabs had taken his eye?*

Kitty looked past me to Harriet.

"I'm sorry, I don't think we've met."

Harriet was gawking at Kitty, though once the other girl spoke directly to her it seemed to snap her back to her senses. Harriet clumsily did a curtsy.

"Princess Katherine, my name is Harriet Hollister. I'm a student of Professor Gallagher's."

"I see." Kitty looked at me askance, as if trying to overlay the title of *Professor* onto me. When she wasn't able to, she turned away. "We should go inside. We have much to talk about."

"Yes, of course." I followed after her but when Harriet did likewise Kitty stopped. "I'm sorry to be so curt, Ms Hollister, but could you please wait with Naveed? There are some things that need to be discussed in private."

"O-o-of course, Your Highness. Pardon me," Harriet managed to get out. She looked around the courtyard, full of soldiers and Naveed's family, and looked very much like a guest who had shown up at a party where she didn't know anyone.

Kitty led us into a large building, moving as though she owned the place. Which, of course, she did: she was a princess, and this was one of her family's many homes. There was a coldness in the rooms that went beyond merely it being December, a historical chilliness steeped into the stones, something that not even electricity and indoor plumbing and all the mod cons in the world could banish (though it was clear that generations of royals had tried). We walked through several sitting rooms festooned with full-ceiling murals and walls decorated with elaborate portraits. Even something as simple as a tea caddy was embellished with ornate cut glass. Windsor Castle was like a geode, a rocky and rough outer shell with glittering insides.

As we walked I drew up next to Cobalt.

"Cobalt, mate, you went up against Gabs?"

"Yes. After the palace guards were . . . dispatched . . . by Kitty's magic, the interim Court Magician tried to stop us from leaving,"

Cobalt said grimly. "I was wearing this." He gestured a gloved hand towards his outfit—I recognized it as a suit that had various parts of it transposed, the effect allowing him to walk on walls or the ceiling. "I had a knife and I figured if I could attack from above I might distract von Melsungen long enough for the princess to get by her. But before I could drop down she looked up at me and I was mesmerized by her dress. It was flowing, seafoam green with what looked like a peacock-eye pattern on it from far away. But once I was up close I saw they weren't peacock eyes at all. They were human eyes. And then I felt my own wrenched out of its socket."

"She really pulled your eye out?!"

"It was the magic of the dress," Cobalt said. "The pain made me lose my focus, and I dropped from the ceiling to the floor. If the princess hadn't distracted von Melsungen, I'm sure she would have killed me right then."

"Distracted her how?" I asked, looking to Kitty. She actually blushed.

"It was silly, but I grabbed a painting off the wall and whacked her with it."

That made me smile briefly. "I'm sure that did surprise her."

"It seemed like von Melsungen knew better than to try and attack the princess," Cobalt said. "Princess Katherine helped me up and we were able to get out of the palace. So really, I have not been much of a protector tonight at all."

"Nonsense, Cobalt. I would have fallen apart long ago without you," Kitty said. We were going up a winding flight of stairs. On the second floor we entered a meeting room. Stone walls with small, peaked windows gave the room a medieval edge even though the furnishings were modern—well, modern in that ornate, fussy, old-style aristocratic sense.

Sitting in the room was Lady Fife.

"Lady Fife!" I exclaimed, like someone yelling, *Snake!* She stood and for the first time since I'd met her I saw she was wearing trousers, tweed knit. Her top was more of her usual style, a frilly chiffon blouse. She still looked past me to give a curtsy to Katherine.

"Crown Princess Katherine," Lady Fife said. "I'm so grateful that you made it here safely."

"Only at a great cost to one dear to me," Katherine said, hand upon Cobalt's shoulder.

Lady Fife nodded, straightening up. "Indeed. Mr Cobalt, your fidelity to the princess is an example to us all."

"Thank you," Cobalt said, shoulders hunched and teeth clenched, "though if we had gotten a little more warning, perhaps I might not have lost an eye."

Lady Fife nodded. "I warned the queen as soon as I got word. I'm sorry it was not sooner."

"How exactly did you know all this was going down, Lady Fife?" I asked.

She tilted her head to the side. "Mr Gallagher, did you truly think I was doing *nothing* these last few years? I've been getting ready to act when the time was right. And I'll admit, the impetus for change came upon us all very quickly, but we shall just have to act quickly in turn."

"To do what?" I asked.

"Why, to dislodge the Virtuis Party from their seat of power, of course," Lady Fife said. "Even if it means usurping the crown to do so."

Kitty tensed at that.

"You'd have me become exactly what they accuse me of being?" she said, sounding out the words carefully, as if in disbelief. "When the guards came to arrest me, they said it was for the murder of my brother, that I killed him in order to have the throne for myself. Do you also think that of me, Lady Fife?"

She shook her head. "No, child. I'm sure the prince's death was an accident or even a case of self-defence. But there's no bringing him back from the dead so—"

"So we may as well treat his death like some chess gambit?" Kitty said, anger causing her words to speed up. "Treat him like nothing more than a political opportunity?"

"That is how our enemies will treat it, so yes," Lady Fife said.

"'Our' enemies, Lady Fife?" I said. "Are you really willing to make a stand against the king himself? I had thought you were staying neutral in this whole thing."

Lady Fife smiled serenely. "And I had thought you weren't so naive." Her smile dropped. "The road from here on out won't be easy, but it is the path we must take, not just for ourselves, not just for Britain, but for the wor—"

Her spiel was interrupted by a knock on the door. A second later the door opened and Oberon stepped in. He looked unharmed, though his clothes had a dampness to them as if he'd gone swimming earlier in the night. We exchanged curt nods—with everything happening it made sense that he'd be here.

What surprised me was when another man followed Oberon into the room. The man was short, shorter than even me, with wavy dark hair. He wore a belted suit that gave him almost a military air. Above his lip was a light moustache.

The man was Thomas Dawes.

"Thomas?" I stumbled towards him, my gait unsteady, like an apostle stumbling towards an empty tomb, eyes wide in amazement. Thomas looked at me, a mix of emotions on his face but chief amongst them regret.

"Hello, Paul." Years later his voice hadn't changed one whit. "Sorry we couldn't talk earlier."

"We can talk now!" I said. "Jesus, mate, I—!" I wanted to reach out and grab him but I stopped since every eye in the room was on us. All I wanted was to hug the little bastard.

"You'll have plenty of time to catch up later, Mr Gallagher," Lady Fife said. I gave an indignant squeak at that, gesturing at Thomas. It felt like something miraculous had just happened, but I was the only one who even saw it. Part of me had come to believe that I'd never see Thomas again in this life, and yet he had just reappeared.

Thomas lightly touched my arm.

"Paul, listen to her," he said.

"Thank you, Mr Dawes," Lady Fife said. "As I was saying, we are acting not for our own advancement but to save the world from destruction. Spies from the Virtuis Party have been working hard these last few years to fan the flames of war between the United States and the Soviet Union. They believe that if World War Three happens, those two great powers will wipe the other out."

"Wouldn't Britain be wiped out as well?" Kitty asked.

"They believe that their prisoner-generated shield would protect the nation from both nuclear and magical attack," Lady Fife says. "In the aftermath, they believe that Great Britain could emerge as *the* world power. With the rest of the world in ruins, they would revive the British Empire and rule over all."

We were silent at that. Lady Fife let it linger for a moment before pressing on.

"I've been trying to stop them from the shadows, and I like to think we've managed to keep the worst at bay up until now. But such moves are merely stalling tactics. Now is the time to move in the open. We will give the British people a different option than that fascist regime they've been living under. We will offer them a new ruler." She gestured to Kitty. "And a new Court Magician." Now she gestured to me.

Court Magician. A long-ago dream raised its head yet again. Despite the fear and tension that still tinged my thoughts, I couldn't help but feel a jolt of want.

"No. No, no, no," Kitty said, shaking her head. "How dare you? I will not take part in such a scheme." She turned to Cobalt. "Let us go and speak with my mother. I am sure she would never agree to any of these evil machinations." Kitty turned to leave.

"She has," Lady Fife said. "She knows Arthur's death wasn't your fault, Princess. But she also knows that going forwards means going against her husband. She's accepted that, so it is best you do as well."

Kitty stood there, hands clenched and shaking.

"Word is that Van Holt has named the four of you as conspirators and actors in the prince's death," Lady Fife said, looking at Oberon, me, Kitty, and Cobalt. "For us to succeed, we must decry this as fiction, an untruth used to slur Princess Katherine and Mr Gallagher in particular. Our official word is that none of you were anywhere near the prince when he died, that Van Holt is spewing nonsense."

"You said my mother already knows the truth," Kitty whispered.

"Yes," Lady Fife said. "And besides her and the people in this room, no one else must ever know."

Kitty said nothing more, just left the room with Cobalt hurrying after her.

Lady Fife frowned as the door shut behind them.

"You'll have to talk to her, Mr Gallagher. Convince her this is the way forwards," she said.

"Convince *her*? I'm hardly convinced myself!" I said.

"Well, I'll leave that to you, Mr Dawes," Lady Fife said, straightening her clothes as if about to leave.

"I'm sorry, do I need to even be here?" Oberon said, cross. "I was shot at tonight and no one's even asked me how I am."

"I'm sorry, Mr Myers," Lady Fife said. "I don't mean to be brusque; I'm just very tired. Come with me to the banquet hall and we can talk. I can tell you about what your father had been up to in the last few years of his life."

That caught Oberon's attention. He followed Lady Fife out of the room, leaving Thomas and me alone with each other.

CHAPTER 29

"You look well," Thomas said. I was fixated on the part of his hair. He had never bothered to part his hair before, just letting it go whichever way it wished on his head, like he and his hair were two entities that grudgingly shared the same space and tried to have as little to do with each other as possible. But now it was, dare I say it, "neat," parted to the left in a disciplined line. Granted, aside from that part it was still near-untameably wavy, but that left part spoke of years of styling and attention, of change in a person.

"That's all you have to say?" I said. "I haven't seen you in four years and all you can say is that I look 'well'?" I plopped down on a couch. "Jesus, mate. And you had the benefit, I assume, of knowing you'd be seeing me tonight. You could have come up with something better."

Thomas dithered in the middle of the room.

"How long have you been in the country?" I asked.

"I arrived soon after Prince Arthur died."

So he'd been in England for almost two months.

"You could have come and said hello to me," I said.

"It was clear that you were trying to lay low," Thomas said. "I didn't want to ruin that by popping out of nowhere."

Now, *that* sounded like a rehearsed line.

"You must have heard that Dad died," I said.

"Yes, I'm sorry," Thomas said, faltering slightly.

"That would have been a fine time to come visit."

"I know," Thomas said. "I wanted to."

And there was such a clear current of pain in his words that I stopped pitying myself and remembered that Thomas was still my little brother, that our fortunes were tied together, and that the main difference between us was that he was more likely to suffer in silence.

"I'm sorry," I said. "He loved you like his own son, Thomas. We both lost a father with his passing."

"No," Thomas said, a tired edge to his voice. "Sean was always there for me, but my own father died when I was twelve."

"What?" I shot a look at him. "What are you talking about, mate?"

"Do you remember Mr Erlich?"

"Of course I do. He was the old man who ran the sweetshop and let us hang out in the back room on rainy days and oh sweet Jesus, he was your father." The last part came to me in a rush of understanding. No wonder the old man had always been so nice to us—at the time, I'd taken it as proof that my innate magic worked even on adults. It had never occurred to me that maybe the man hadn't been kind to us because of me but because of Thom.

Thomas looked at me, waiting for me to get over my shock. But now that the surprise was ebbing away, a kind of horror was welling up within me. Joshua Erlich had been a Jewish man. I remembered how some of the adults around me, not my mum and dad but priests and teachers, would say some awful stuff about Jewish people. As an idiot child, had I unthinkingly repeated some of that shit? Had I ever said something awful to Thomas, all while he internalized it? The fact that I was worried that such a thing had happened wasn't a good sign.

"Thomas, I never knew," I said.

"No one did," Thomas said. "My mum asked me to keep it a secret, so I did. But I wanted you to know." He looked down at his shoes. "I wanted you to know that I know what you're going through."

I'd missed him so much.

"Come over here and sit down already," I said.

He did so, sitting on the far end of the couch. When we were younger he had always favoured suits and cloaks with wide shoulders, going in for flourishes like caplets in an attempt to make his small form look bigger. The suit he wore now was more fitted with sharper lines. It didn't make him more imposing physically but he did seem more at ease in his own skin.

"How have you been?" I asked with a put-on casual air. Thomas half smiled.

"I've been busy," he said. "Like Lady Fife said, we've been trying to avoid World War Three."

"Are you telling me you're a spy now?" I said. When Thomas had gone away, I'd imagined all kinds of possibilities: That he'd become a pirate. That he'd gone off in search of rare animals. That he had become a spy. Who would have thought that one of my crazy guesses had actually been correct?

Thomas shrugged.

"It feels a little much to call myself that," he said. "It's not always the nicest work, but it's important. Mainly I've spent the last few years working against the Virtuis Party, keeping their agents from kicking up shitstorms, keeping dangerous magical artefacts hidden—"

"Killing people?"

"If need be, yes," Thomas said, voice level. "But that's usually a last resort, not just from a moral standpoint but a practical one."

"Right. I suppose dead bodies pile up in a way that live ones don't." I thought of Godfrey, the undead corpse running the country. Thomas hadn't managed to kill *him*. "Do you know about Godfrey?"

Thomas nodded. "I only found out recently when Lady Fife showed me a picture."

"I saw him in person," I said.

"You saw him?!" Thomas said, sitting up straight. He looked me over as if amazed I was still alive.

"Yeah. Van Holt and Fairweather were trying to torture some information out of me but I wasn't talking. So Godfrey came to take a crack at it. He looked like just another bloke on the street but he felt *wrong*."

"How did you get out of that?" Thomas asked, amazement still tingeing his voice.

"Oberon showed up and held them under the gun. He even shot Godfrey, for all the good that did in the long run."

Thomas nodded. "Good man, that Oberon."

That caught me by surprise. Back when we'd all been at school together Thomas had *hated* Oberon Myers and Obie had rightfully been afraid of Thomas. But now Thomas was complimenting him. Not just that—his tone sounded like he was talking about a close friend, not a schoolmate he hadn't seen in years.

"So what exactly are you doing here *now*, Thom?" I said.

"Well, things have changed," Thomas said. "Obviously. I mean, with Prince Arthur dead there's a power vacuum. The throne is up for grabs—"

"But it's not!" I said. "With Arthur dead, Kitty's next in line—"

"And a lot of people don't want her to be queen," Thomas said. "Not if they can put their own patsy up there. If Kitty is unable to inherit the throne from her father, next in line is the king's cousin, George Quingate, who like the king is very much a Virtuis Party man."

"But why are they so dead set on capturing the crown?" I said. "This is the twentieth century. The royal family are figureheads. They don't have any serious political power."

"They still have some," Thomas said. "Not to mention the influence they have over the country as a whole. But the real prize is having the Court Magician in the Virtuis Party's pocket, and it's hard to do that if you don't already have the royal family in line with your views. And once they manage that, it will be generations before we can get them out."

Thomas had a point there, especially the bit about generational power. Godfrey had made it clear he was playing the long game, thinking of decades in the future, whereas we just had our lifetimes to deal with his shit.

"So in order to keep the Virtuis Party from entrenching itself further, you think we should stage a government coup to not only replace the prime minister but the king?" I said. "You want me to move against *Gabs*?"

"Gabs, who just took out Cobalt's eye? Gabs, who tried to kill Princess Katherine? Gabs, who has apparently become a bootlicker for a bunch of power-hungry monsters and now likes the taste? She'd have no qualms about killing you, Paul, especially if she thought it might help her go from being the 'interim' to being the permanent Court Magician. Don't be soft on her, because she will not do the same for you."

"But the deck is stacked against us here," I said, trying to appeal to Thomas's pragmatic nature. "You really think we can take on the king and his followers? All that will accomplish is getting everyone in this castle killed."

"No, fighting back is the only way everyone here *survives*," Thomas said. "This is war now, Paul, and the Virtuis Party will scourge anyone against them if they are able to. Princess 'Kitty' will be beheaded. Cobalt, Oberon, all of the Parkeesh family will be shot. As will myself and Lady Fife and the girl you arrived here with, whoever she is—"

"She's Harriet Hollister," I said and that threw Thomas off his game for a second.

He looked at me, his eyes wide: "Shit." Then they narrowed again and he continued. "She'll be deader than her dad if the Virtuis Party wins out. And you, Paul, you—"

"Right, right, I'll be garrotted or something on Tower Hill?"

"No. You'll only be able to wish for death," Thomas said. "Godfrey is one of the few people in the world who knows what you can do. Godfrey is banking hard on magic to bring back the glory of the British Empire, and he'll want whatever you have. And they will get it from you. So instead, let's stand up to them. You can use that power to—"

"Use that power?!" I said. "Thomas, you were *there*. You know how horrible it is, what it costs! You—"

Thomas held up his hands in a placating gesture. "Sorry, that came out wrong. What I'm saying is, Gabs is a fantastic cloth mage, but you've got *innate magic*. That's what makes a Court Magician."

I clenched my hands into fists.

"I . . . I barely know how to use it," I said. "The things I've done . . . the ritual with Hollister, or even when I broke Kitty's ribs . . . it's all just me doing my best guess based on a mix of research and gut feeling. I don't know if I'm truly a better fit for the role than Gabs."

"What the hell? You used to talk about becoming Court Magician all the time," Thomas said.

"I also said I couldn't do it without you," I replied.

Thomas inched a little bit closer but stopped, as if he wanted to reach out but wasn't sure how.

"I'm here now," he said. "You don't have to do this without me. I'll be with you through every step to make sure that you become the official Court Magician for Great Britain. We'll figure it out. There's gotta be some way for you to learn how to make mages. We'll just take it one day at a time."

"I wish I was as sure of this as you," I said. "I wish I was as sure of things as when I was younger. But one thing I do know is that I'm glad you're here."

And because he couldn't do it I reached out and squeezed his shoulder. His own hand came up to squeeze mine, before he stood.

"Anyway, it's been a long night. There's a room set up for you. Don't worry, you'll be safe here. Nothing will happen while you sleep."

"I know," I said. Thomas nodded, relieved that I believed him.

"Yes, the castle's very secure," he said.

But it wasn't the castle security that reassured me. It was the fact that Thomas was there.

CHAPTER 30

I found Kitty the next morning in the banquet hall, having breakfast with her mother. The two were talking low and earnestly, and when I walked in they both looked up with alarm, as though worried that I was a battalion of the king's soldiers, there to drag them back to Buckingham Palace. When she saw it was just me, Queen Andriette relaxed.

"Oh, Mr Gallagher, good morning." Even decades after coming to England she still had the lightest Danish accent.

"Good morning, Your Highness, Princess Katherine," I said with a slight bow. "May I join you?"

Queen Andriette stood. "I'm sorry to be so rude, but I actually have a prior appointment I must keep. But I do wish to speak with you later, Mr Gallagher. Could we have tea together tomorrow?"

By teatime tomorrow we might all be dead, I thought. But surely Queen Andriette knew this as well as I did. Everyone here was in a state of rebellion against the Crown, but the queen had done us all one better: she had rebelled against her *husband*. I didn't know this soft-spoken woman well, had never had a chance to speak alone with her. I didn't know what her reasons were for joining in this coup, but as I watched her say her goodbye to Kitty I got a hint from the softness in her face. Andriette had outlived two of her children already: Arthur, as well as Arthur's little brother Maxwell, who'd been a crib death.

Perhaps she was here simply because she did not want to see her last surviving child dead. She and Kitty spoke briefly in Danish, and then the queen left.

I was hesitant to sit down next to Kitty. The princess hadn't relaxed when I came in. Even now she looked like a child sitting in the headmaster's study awaiting a lecture or, worse, the strap. If I went closer to her, I worried she'd just cringe more from me.

"I didn't know you spoke Danish," I said.

"Not very well," Kitty said. "My mother tried to teach us when we were young. She rarely got to see us growing up, but whenever we spent time together she'd teach us a few words. When Father found out he forbade it, saying it would warp our young minds learning different languages at such a young age."

"I see."

Kitty sighed. "You may as well sit down, Gally."

I did. Kitty fidgeted, fingers tapping and twitching together in her lap.

"You're here to tell me that I must usurp my father and take the crown, yes?" She laughed but there was no joy in it, just fear and nervousness. "Surely more than anyone you can see what a horrible idea that is."

"Why would I ever think that?"

"Because of how well you know me. You know I'm a stuttering fool, a flibbertigibbet with no grace or charm, an idle child who could not even get a dog to follow her commands, let alone a nation," Kitty said. "You know that."

"Far from it," I said. "I know you as a kind person, a caring individual who thinks about and feels deeply the suffering of others, a curious mind who is unafraid to venture forth and see the world for herself. I see someone who's very brave and intelligent. I'm frequently humbled by you, Kitty. If that's not queen material, I don't know what is."

Kitty shook her head as tears welled up.

"Oh, no. See, Gally? I can't even take a compliment without causing a scene. Even if what you say is true—and I'm not calling you a liar, I'm touched that you believe your words even if I don't—even if that's all true, I can't do this. I can't, I just can't, I can't—"

We were not alone in the banquet hall—there was a handful of army officers having coffee, and the two Parkeesh sisters were also having breakfast a few tables away. Kitty, always aware of the public eye, managed to calm herself down.

"I'm sorry," Kitty said. "It's been a trying time."

I let out a short laugh at that understatement. Kitty smiled, but it quickly dropped.

"I never liked my brother, but I still didn't wish for his death."

"I know, Kitty. It was an accident, a horrible—"

"But while he was alive, his existence did provide me some comfort," Kitty continued, as if I hadn't interrupted her. "I knew that as long as he was around, I'd never have to be queen. Even if I lived my life under the scrutiny that comes with being a royal, I'd never have to deal with the crushing weight of being this nation's ruler. Arthur could not escape that lot, but I was spared."

She went silent. I likewise stayed quiet, sensing she had more to say.

"As the crown prince, there was pressure upon Arthur to marry and produce an heir," she said. "I knew that as a woman, a similar pressure was upon me. And I really do appreciate that you tried to help me. I thought that with Andrew, I could perhaps get over my distaste for men to at least live peacefully alongside him. But when the scandal broke with that photo . . . when my parents told me the engagement would be called off, I felt relieved. Although I knew Andrew was my best possible match, I couldn't help but dream of an even more appealing option: Never having to marry a man at all. Never have to bear his children. Never have to experience the distortion of pregnancy and pain of childbirth."

I suddenly had a suspicion of where this was going. Kitty took a shuddering breath and continued.

"So you see, Gally, by becoming the queen of this nation, not only would I carry the burden of leadership but the expectation that I marry and produce an heir—multiple heirs, preferably—in order to consolidate power. Even our allies here in Windsor Castle expect it of me."

She was right. Part of the reason Lady Fife wanted Kitty in power was to keep the king's cousins from taking over the throne. Even if Kitty were to become queen, if she died without an heir then power would still end up in the hands of the Virtuis Party.

"Kitty, you don't have to worry about that," I said. "I have a plan, one that will honour your brother and will spare you from having to marry and produce children."

She looked at me, hope in her eyes as she clutched my hand.

"Truly, Gally?"

"Yes," I said. "You see, there's already another heir to the throne."

~

"You'd put a dead man's bastard on the throne?"

That was unusually uncouth for Lady Fife but to give her due, it had been a trying day: tanks had rolled down the motorway from London to Slough but had been unable to get past our forces situated strategically around the off-ramp. In the skirmish two soldiers on our side had died. While that had been going on those of us in the castle had been instructed to take refuge in the bomb shelters on the grounds. I'd spent an hour sitting next to Naveed's pregnant sister Marion, so close I could feel her baby kicking. Maybe it had been as scared as we were.

With a stalemate in place for now, we had come out of the shelter as evening fell. I'd sought out Kitty and we'd gone to Lady Fife's office as a united front, ready to declare our demands.

"Not just any dead man and not a bastard," Kitty replied, unusually forceful for her. I supposed these extreme circumstances were bringing new sides out in everybody. "Sabina's child is the crown prince's heir, born out of a marriage between them. My brother would have wanted his child to ascend the throne, not me."

"Well, we're a little beyond one man's wants and needs at the moment," Lady Fife replied.

"Then how about the divine line of succession?" Kitty pressed.

Lady Fife laughed. "Oh, we are far beyond that as well. The divine line of succession is a quaint idea. Yes, royal lineage is an unquestionable, unbroken line ordained by God . . . until it isn't. With your brother's death, Princess, you are next in line. Yet our enemies are already introducing bills in Parliament that would sidestep you. They know that the next ruler will not be decided by blood or marriage but who has the power to stake their claim."

"Then we will have to win," I said. "Win so we can put Arthur's child on the throne."

"We won't go along with this rebellion unless you agree," Kitty said. She'd been doing so well but for the first time there was a waver in her voice.

Lady Fife drew in a deep breath. "A great deal depends on us," she said slowly. "If we lose, this country will continue along its path of being little better than a penal state. If we don't regain control of the government and crown soon, the whole world might be wiped out in another war. And just as the stakes are high, our odds of succeeding are exceedingly stacked against us. Our armed forces are barely enough to hold the city; our political capital is all in credit that will only be good if we win. Our only bet is to win the hearts of the British people. And we won't be able to do that if they learn that we are planning to put a Black child on the throne."

She fell silent, letting her words hang there. Neither Kitty nor I had an immediate rejoinder. British xenophobia was an all-absorbing thing and compounded by racism. Would the majority of Britain ever accept a mixed-race prince? Not just accept but embrace him to the point where they'd help us overthrow the current king and his relatives?

"I don't think you give the British people enough credit, Lady Fife," Katherine said. "They have suffered these last few years under the Virtuis Party. They will see that we are offering a better world, and they will accept that having a new ruler is part of that. The people are willing to move towards a different future than the path to destruction we are on now."

Lady Fife cocked her head to the side. "I never imagined you'd be the voice of the common people, Princess Katherine."

"I'm not, but I have spent more time amongst them than you may realize," said Kitty. "Mr Gallagher has seen to that. We have spent many evenings out amidst the people of London. I've heard their complaints over a pint in the pub or on a bus after a twelve-hour day. I spent a night in Trafalgar Square with Mr Gallagher keeping watch so I could see what it was like for the rough sleepers of London. I know that one night in the cold does not approximate a lifetime. But I think if we give people the option to do better, they will take it."

Lady Fife leaned back in her chair.

"I want to think you are right, Princess. It's quite the conundrum, isn't it?" Lady Fife was quiet for a few seconds before speaking again. "The child's mother is royalty in her own right, isn't she?"

"Yes. She's descended from the Dahomey ruling class," I said. "Her people were wiped out by a neighbouring tribe—"

"Who had gotten the firepower to do so from the British Army. Yes, I remember the story now. We had sent our armed forces there to set the various factions against each other," Lady Fife explained. "It was a massacre. Sabina's grandmother was the only survivor of her people. I always assumed that Brennan, the military man who'd rescued her, did so partly out of guilt over murdering her whole family." She frowned. "Well, and so Britain could use the girl as a political pawn. Easy to keep the conquering tribe in line if you have a replacement ruler in your back pocket. But that was generations ago. Sabina herself is of a royal lineage, yes, but not in any meaningful sense."

"Sabina brings other things to the table," I said. "Her family is still very close to Brennan's, including General Brennan."

Lady Fife looked intrigued. "Go on."

"His family is sworn to protect hers," I explained. "So—"

"So by taking on Arthur's child's case for the crown, we gain a strong military ally," Lady Fife said, seemingly warming to the idea. She fixed her gaze on Kitty. "But this child is yet to be born, and even when they do arrive in the world someone will need to rule until they come of age."

Kitty squared her shoulders. "I would do so. But once the child is old enough, I will abdicate and have nothing more to do with ruling this nation. I want to live as a private citizen, free to do as I please."

Lady Fife laughed. "Don't we all? But yes, I can agree to those terms." She stood and came over as though to shake hands with Kitty. Kitty even extended her hand, but then to both our surprises Lady Fife drew Kitty into a hug. I had never seen Lady Fife be physically affectionate with anyone. Plus, you just didn't touch royalty like that.

Kitty meanwhile was frozen, one arm still bent at a ninety-degree angle, waiting for a handshake that would never come.

"I'm sorry that you must take on so much, Princess," Lady Fife said, holding her tight. "I did not wish for it to be such a hard road for you. Even when you and my son became engaged, I knew it was a mistake that would lead to unhappiness for you both. But I let it happen, because I thought it might be a better way forwards. And for my own selfish reasons too—I'd always wanted a daughter."

Lady Fife drew back and just like that, her expression reset to its usual placid half smile, as though the burst of emotion from a second ago had been a hallucination on our parts.

My mind was still turning over Lady Fife's words: *I thought it might be a better way forwards*. Just how long had Lady Fife been planning this sedition? If Andrew and Kitty had gotten married, had Lady Fife been planning to use that relationship as a starting point for launching a coup against the rest of the royal family? Just how many plans and fail-safes did she have in place?

"We still need to keep Arthur's child under wraps," Lady Fife said crisply. "We will reveal them to the world only *after* we've gained control of the nation. Mr Gallagher, please get in touch with General Brennan. Tell him his services are needed."

CHAPTER 31

On Christmas Day, as he did every year, the king addressed the nation. This time, it was guaranteed that it would be a bit different from his usual staid speeches for two reasons: (1) the nation was on the brink of civil war; (2) it was the first time the Christmas address would be televised.

Thomas and Oberon rolled a large television into Lady Fife's office. Gathered there were Kitty, Lady Fife, and me. Everyone else in the castle was either in the banquet hall or in their rooms, listening to it on the radio.

Black-and-white static crackled through Lady Fife's office. Thomas adjusted the dials until eventually the wavering lines snapped into place, becoming a BBC News title card. We stared at the screen as if it were a basilisk egg about to hatch.

A flicker of white and then the title card was replaced by the image of Deputy Prime Minister Peter Fairweather, sitting on what looked to be some kind of talk show set.

"Hello, good people of Britain. Deputy Prime Minister Fairweather here. I know that the past few days have been an upsetting time for the people of this nation, with soldiers on city streets and tanks on the motorways. And at Christmas! Please believe me that we would not be taking this kind of extreme action if not for the fact that the very soul of our country is at stake. There was a plot to overthrow the king and the conspirators killed Prince Arthur as part of their ploy to gain power. Even now, these criminals are holed up in Windsor Castle. Of course, it is only a matter of time before they are brought to justice, but in the meantime certain measures must be brought in to protect the nation. King Harold himself will speak more on this at the end of this broadcast, but first you will hear from a witness to Prince Arthur's death, one who can speak to the wickedness of our enemies. I am speaking of former Court Magician Peter Van Holt."

There was a change of camera shots, and both the quick cut and the sight of Van Holt made me hiss in surprise. He was vastly changed. If Fairweather hadn't just introduced him, I might have not guessed who he was at first. He did not look like the Van Holt from before or Shipwright. He had Van Holt's face, though it was haggard looking, a thinness to his cheeks that hadn't been there before. His eyes were heavy lidded and fixed downwards, as though he were trying to see to the bottom of a very dark, deep hole. Most shocking of all was his hair. In the black and white of the TV it was clear that it had gone pure white, so bright that it glowed on the screen.

Van Holt sat there, unblinking. Off-screen, Fairweather cleared his throat.

"Former Court Magician?"

Van Holt looked up and blinked at the bright studio lights.

"Yes, hello, Deputy Prime Minister." His voice was familiar, the soft-spoken, slow Afrikaans accent to his words present. How was this possible? I'd used innate magic to change this man into someone else. How had he reverted back? "Thank you for this chance to address the public."

"Of course!" The camera flipped back to Fairweather. "We were all so worried about you. You were missing for over a month! Can you please explain to the British public where you were?"

There was a third camera present, one that presented a larger view of the set to take in both Van Holt and Fairweather. Van Holt suddenly seemed so small within this larger frame.

"I was . . . I was with my family . . . no, I was . . . I don't know where I was. I was not myself." As he spoke his accent fluctuated, sounding more like a native Londoner's.

"You were under a magic spell, yes?" Fairweather prompted.

"Y-y-yes," Van Holt said, but it was less like he was agreeing and more like he had just received devastating and surprising news. "I spoke with a new tongue. I felt so pleased to hear the sound of my own voice, and I'd question why. Why did I feel so happy just hearing the way certain sounds unfolded in my mouth?" A new light of recollection started shining in his eyes. "Gallagher did this to me. Gallagher changed me and now I can never go back to how I was."

"He also made it so that you forgot what you witnessed the night of Prince Arthur's death, yes? Can you tell us what you remember now?"

"He killed me. He should have just killed me, but instead he *killed me*." Van Holt was getting worked up now, his left hand clutching the armrest of his chair. His wild eyes found one of the TV cameras. The shot changed so it looked as though he were staring out directly from the telly and into the nation's living rooms. "Gallagher, I know you are watching this! When I find you, you'll learn what it feels like to lose yourself! I'll watch the fucking light die in your eyes! You'll beg me to kill you! You'll beg me to kill the people you love—"

"Old boy, please. Control yourself," Fairweather chided. He reached out to put his hand over Van Holt's hand, the one still clenching the armrest. Van Holt looked at it, then with a great exhale let go. Fairweather drew back. He seemed to be looking at someone off-screen and he gave a slight shake of his head before turning to one of the TV cameras with a smile.

"The prince's death has obviously left a deep impact on the former Court Magician. I'm sure all of you watching at home understand."

Fairweather looked to Van Holt. "Can you tell us what happened the night of Prince Arthur's death?"

Van Holt nodded. His eyes became heavy once more and his accent returned. "Yes. That night there was a soiree at the Tower of London. I of course was there, as it is part of my duties to stay near the royal family and to protect them. I failed that night, and Prince Arthur's death stems from the fact that I failed to save him."

"Yes, but there are figures more directly responsible, yes?" Fairweather said. "Such as Princess Katherine and Paul Gallagher."

Van Holt nodded, head moving slowly like a buoy bobbing on the waves.

"Indeed. I was patrolling around the White Tower, looking for threats—"

"Such a lie!" I said. "He was ducking out to smoke a cig!"

"—when I saw Prince Arthur's body fall off the roof of a nearby building. I of course ran over to help him, but it was clear the prince had died on impact."

Next to me Kitty shuddered. She was probably remembering the same thing I was: Arthur's head shoved in between his shoulder blades. I took her hand. She was still trembling but managed to give my hand a squeeze.

"Then I heard some people coming down the nearby stairwell," Van Holt continued. "I drew back, unsure of who they were, but when they approached it was Paul Gallagher and Princess Katherine, as well as two of their associates, the magicians Cobalt and Oberon Myers. They didn't see me, and as they stood over the prince's body they began to discuss how they would cover up his murder, make it look like an accident. I didn't know what to do except stay silent, but still they spotted me."

Van Holt slowed as he was talking, as though his gears were grinding to a halt. As the dead air lingered Fairweather shifted in his seat.

"What happened next?"

"They abducted me and took me to a room in the tower. Once there, Paul Gallagher used illegal magic to erase my memory of that night. He made it so that not only did I forget what I had witnessed, I forgot who I was. For the last month I have wandered the city streets, oblivious to my true identity."

"Yes, and your prolonged absence gave us quite the scare, old boy!" Fairweather said, his jovial tone a jarring contrast to Van Holt's haunted expression.

"It was innate magic," Van Holt said, a slight shake to every syllable. "He broke my arm and made it so I was a new person. When I was told who I truly was, I was so confused. How could I be anything but who I was? How can I not be that person anymore?"

"But we were able to save you." Fairweather spoke earnestly, like someone begging a drowning swimmer to take hold of a rope thrown to them. Van Holt's head snapped up, eyes on Fairweather.

"Save me? You had to kill me to do it! You had to cut off my arm!" Dread pooled in my stomach as Van Holt leaned forwards. His right arm was gone, the shirt sleeve rolled up and pinned below his shoulder. "That was the arm that had my mage break in it! I can't even do magic now!"

"Yes, it was a dastardly thing that Paul Gallagher did to you," Fairweather said, leaning back in his chair as if afraid Van Holt was going to lunge at him. "It shows just how dangerous illegal magic can be in the wrong hands. Our country is ever so grateful for your sacrifice, Van Holt."

Van Holt, open mouthed, looked towards the camera in disbelief. He stood, and the sudden movement made Fairweather flinch. Van Holt's gaze went from one camera to another, as if looking for something in their gaze.

"You're all going to fucking die, Paul. You last and worst of all. You'll see what it feels like to—"

Before he could say something else, the cameras cut away.

Standing in an opulent room was Gabs. She wore a white dress festooned with filigree lace in such a way that it caught the light from every angle. It was a staggering piece of art but also looked organic, as if Gabs had simply risen from a field of moss and flowers wearing this amazing outfit. She smiled at the camera, and it was the same sensation as before when Van Holt had looked out from the screen: the feeling that she was looking out directly at me. Then it was gone. A slight shift in her smile and it felt more like she was addressing the nation.

"Good evening," she said, her voice level, as though trying to reassure viewers after Van Holt's outburst. "My name is Gabriella von Melsungen, though I was formerly Gabriella Wilkes of Cornwall. I was born in Herodsfoot and studied magic at the University College London. While there, I met my future husband, Kristoff von Melsungen, and after I graduated from the cloth magic programme we were married. I went to live with him in Germany, where we were very happy together." She did not stumble over those last few words, but I noticed how her smile widened even as her eyes dimmed. I knew well enough to know when Gabs was lying.

"Despite marrying a German man, I always retained my British citizenship and never forgot my duty to this country," Gabs said. "That is why I am stepping in now as the interim Court Magician. Former Court Magician Van Holt can no longer carry out his duties thanks to the spell Paul Gallagher cast upon him, so in his stead I will protect the royal family from conspirators. I may be but a woman, but within this womanly frame is a deep will to serve the Crown and an abundance of magical energy. I will serve in this capacity until a new Court Magician is found." Now here she faltered, just a little. Maybe it was because she was admitting on TV that her ascension was a temporary one. Or maybe it was a broader worry: How exactly were they going to find another mage maker? Van Holt couldn't create one, and it was illegal for anyone else in the country to practise innate magic.

She continued on: "And now, to end this broadcast, King Harold will address the nation."

The camera cut yet again. King Harold was centre frame, sitting upon his throne, ermine-trimmed cape flowing over his shoulders (the cape was a dark grey on the black-and-white screen, but even so I could imagine its bright-red shade). His pose and outfit were such a clear display of royal authority that my eyes went to his hands, half expecting to see them holding the royal sceptre, but they were empty—someone, maybe Godfrey, must have decided that would be too much. King Harold's face was stern, eyes hard.

"People of Great Britain, we are in an era of darkness. A vast conspiracy, led by the criminal mage Paul Gallagher, has sought to harm Crown and country. This malignant contingent would undermine us at such a pivotal point in world history, a time when the rest of the world is amassing power in a bid to preemptively win the next world war. We must stay strong. Great Britain must continue to be an isle of safety even if the rest of the world should turn to ash. We have put safeguards in place, a magical barrier that will protect this country, but these criminal forces would undo all that and allow us to perish along with the rest of the world."

King Harold was still for a moment, to the point where it seemed like they were broadcasting a static image rather than a live one.

"Amongst the conspirators is my daughter, Princess Katherine," he said. "In order to be first in line for succession, she took part in a plot to kill her older brother, the Crown Prince Arthur. She, like the rest of the conspirators, has been tried in absentia and declared guilty of high treason. She will face the same fate as the other traitors to the Crown: death at the end of a noose."

Next to me Kitty's legs buckled. I was able to catch her a split second before she hit the ground, her deadweight pulling me down to my knees. Others rushed over to make sure she was all right. On the telly King Harold continued to talk.

"This is a trying time for all of us, but we will get through it together. In light of the crisis this country is going through, we are decreeing that Parliament may not call for an election until the current state of emergency has been resolved. We believe that Gallagher's usurper faction has allies and sympathizers in the government, and until we have rooted them out, we cannot allow them to further destabilize this nation. I have utmost trust in Prime Minister Hywell, Deputy Prime Minister Fairweather, and the rest of the cabinet. They will lead the country to safety and cleanse it of all those with ill intentions. People of Britain, it will not be long before we are out of this dark age and back into the light."

A sudden cut to a news studio showed a couple of white, male BBC newscasters sitting behind a desk. They started summarizing what Fairweather, Van Holt, Gabs, and King Harold had just said. I was only half listening, one eye on the telly, the other on Kitty. Lady Fife waved some smelling salts under her nose and only then did the princess stir in my arms.

Kitty blinked awake and shakily sat up. Her hands went to her throat as if checking for a noose.

"Princess Katherine, are you all right?" Lady Fife asked.

Kitty's eyes looked past us all to the screen. The newscasters were reading out the names of coconspirators. They had just gotten through listing all of the Parkeesh family.

"Oberon Myers." A black-and-white photo of Oberon from our school days filled the screen. He was so young and smug looking, a stark contrast to the serious man standing a few feet away from me now. "Phillip Puce, also known as Cobalt." A photo of Cobalt was on the telly now. It was a picture taken at a fancy-dress party where Cobalt had dressed up like a 1930s American gangster. He was wearing a pin-striped suit and a bowler hat and was holding up a toy pistol.

"Do you think he's more embarrassed by that photo or by the fact that everyone now knows his real name is Puce?" Oberon asked.

The next photo on screen was Harriet Hollister. I felt a tightening in my chest—I had brought her into this mess after all. After Harriet the newscasters kept listing wanted criminals, some people I'd never heard of, a few that I had, like Ralph. Lady Fife seemed to know all their names and faces, though. Her mouth tightened into a hard line as they were announced one by one.

Finally, the fugitive roll call came to an end. The newscasters asked the viewers to stay vigilant and then wished us all a good night. The broadcast ended and a light-music programme began.

"My goodness," Oberon said, somewhat shaken. "Now what?"

"We make a broadcast of our own," I said. "We get our side of the story out to the people, make our case." I looked to Lady Fife. "Windsor Castle has a radio transmitter, right?"

"Yes." It was Kitty who answered. She blinked, looking away from the glowing screen to look at me. "Father's used it to make his Christmas speeches."

"Aces. Well, let's fire that thing up—"

"And say what, Mr Gallagher?" Lady Fife asked.

"We gotta say *something*," I replied.

"He's right," Thomas said. "Public opinion isn't set in stone yet, but by dawn it will be. Even an imperfect message from our side now is better than letting Buckingham Palace set the record."

Lady Fife seemed to take his words to heart.

"All right. Let us go address the nation."

~

Kitty, Lady Fife, and I hotfooted it to the northwest tower. Along the way Lady Fife stopped a butler and asked him to send someone named Clara up to the broadcasting room. The room was large and square—I had been expecting some kind of recording booth or even a set like on TV, but it looked very much like a regular sitting room save for a wall covered in wires and dials. A middle-aged woman stood in the centre of the space. Her dusky hair was swept up in what had probably started out as a sensible bun but had come loose as she had tended to the duties of the day. Next to her was a nervous-looking teenage boy. The two were white with dark hair and broad faces, a strong familial resemblance between them. The woman looked at us each in turn before doing a low curtsy to Kitty, keeping her wide grey eyes on the princess the whole time.

"Princess Katherine," she said.

"Clara, it's been some time," Kitty stammered. "I'm sorry we're meeting again under such pressing circumstances."

"Yes, your arrival was very sudden," Clara said, standing up straight. "We hardly had time to prepare. But then I suppose you couldn't have given us notice ahead of time that you were planning to overthrow your father."

Kitty was shaking, though whether from anger or fear I couldn't tell.

"Clara more or less runs Windsor Castle," Lady Fife said to me.

"Aye, with a skeleton crew," Clara said. "We hardly have the staff on hand to look after a dozen conspirators and fifty soldiers. This is not what anyone here signed on for."

"Clara also knows how to operate the broadcasting equipment," Lady Fife said, rather pointedly. I nodded and stepped forwards.

"Clara, is it? Thank you so much for your hospitality, even if it has been unwilling. I'm sorry about that. My name is Paul Gallagher." I held out my hand. She stared me down.

"I know who you are." She left my hand hanging there, leaving me with no option but to withdraw it.

"I don't want any of the servants here at the castle to feel like they've been press-ganged into a rebellion. Any of you may leave at any point."

"And then who would keep the larder stocked? Or launder the sheets? Or make sure the gutters don't get clogged up? Or fix the pipes when they burst? Or tend to the gardens?" Clara said, aghast. It seemed the only thing worse, in her mind, than being part of a rebellion was abandoning her duty. "We all have our jobs to do here, Mr Gallagher. I have been housekeeper for this castle since before you were born. And now you have put me in the position of either abandoning my life's work or helping to destroy it! And for what?! So the two of you can grab at power?!"

"That is not what's happening here at all," I said. "We've come here because we wish to tell the nation the truth. You've known the princess her entire life. Do you really think she'd kill her older brother? Or even be party to it?"

Behind me Kitty started sniffling. Clara's eyes clouded with doubt.

"Please. Turn on the broadcasting equipment. Let me talk to Britain through you," I said.

"Through me?" Clara said.

"Yes. We'll sit down and you can ask me anything you like."

"Why me?"

"Because if I can convince you, Clara, I can convince the nation."

Clara just stared at me for a moment, still with surprise. When she finally recovered she looked to the boy.

"Norbert, start the broadcast signal."

Norbert got to it, flicking switches that turned on various lights on the wall.

"This will send out a signal to the BBC and other radio stations that Windsor Castle is about to make a broadcast," Clara explained. "They may not pick it up. There's a good chance that no one will even hear you, Mr Gallagher."

I couldn't help but smile at that. "Oh, I doubt that." What listener wouldn't want a taste of the forbidden fruit we were sending out on the airwaves? News straight from the very bastion of deceit and villainy.

Clara brought me over to a little table that had a set of headphones and a microphone on it. She gestured for me to put them on. I did so and she adjusted the height of the microphone so it was in front of my face. She nodded to Norbert and he threw a switch, causing a light to go from red to green. Clara nodded at me. I realized that I was live on the air.

"Good evening, everyone," I said, already regretting my word choice. Why hadn't I said something grander? Or at least delivered it with more force? "My name is Paul Gallagher. I'm a mage who has long been in service to the Crown. As you can hear from my voice, I'm a Liverpool lad. I came to London when I was eighteen, looking to study cloth magic. I graduated a few years later and eventually was able to put my skills to work for the royal family."

I took a deep breath.

"The king and Virtuis Party would have you believe that I have misled Princess Katherine and killed her brother. That is an absolute lie. We did not murder Prince Arthur." I stopped there, holding Clara's gaze. I needed to believe it so she would believe it. And it *was* the truth—we hadn't meant to kill him. It had been an accident, one that had come about from him attacking *us*. If not for my magic, I'd have been the one smeared on the pavement. "Arthur was the victim of a conspiracy, but not one perpetrated by the princess. He was killed because he opposed the Virtuis Party and their bid to rule this country indefinitely. You heard what the king said tonight, that Parliament can't even call for elections! They say it's because there's a state of emergency, but just you watch; they will never lift it. The king and the prime minister will make it so their cronies are never called to account. They will continue to solidify power. They will continue to draft your sons into mandatory military service. They will continue to arrest and lock up people for petty crimes. They will continue to rattle sabres at the rest of the world in a bid to start yet another war. And anyone who opposes them will be killed like Prince Arthur or set up as scapegoats like the princess and myself. The princess and I did not set out to become rebels, but we have chosen to stand up against the rot that has grown within the country.

"People of Britain, you also have a choice. You can stand with us against the people who'd rule this country without your say in it. We demand that King Harold step down and Princess Katherine be crowned queen. We also call for an immediate election." These were points that Lady Fife and I had quickly hammered out on the way over. There was one more needed. "Also, Gabriella von Melsungen must immediately cease acting as interim Court Magician. The nation already has a Court Magician. Me." Clara's eyes widened at this. "Before his death, Redfield gave me the ability to do innate magic. He did this because he suspected that his apprentice, Peter Van Holt, was in league with the Virtuis Party and could not be trusted. Redfield gave me this power in case the nation was overtaken by Virtuis, and that is exactly what has happened. He wanted to make sure that there was someone in this country that could stand up to them."

It was a good cover story and one that I'd been working on ever since Redfield had died, God rest his soul. It was well known that Redfield hadn't liked the Virtuis Party or even Van Holt for that matter, so creating a backup Court Magician in secret would have been in character for him.

"He did *what*?" Clara asked. I heard her voice dimly relayed through the headphones. "But *how*? How could he have done another mage-making ritual in secret?"

It was a good question; to create the next Court Magician, the current one had to kill anywhere from a dozen to two dozen candidates before that magic took in one of them.

"He knew another way to do the ritual," I said. "A surefire way, one where the magic took immediately and didn't kill the person it was used on. That was the version he used to give me the ability to create innate magic. And he taught me how to do it."

This was a new kind of lie. It was one thing to say that Redfield had given me this power; the man was dead in the end, and it didn't matter so much how I'd gotten it. But saying that I could give others this ability . . . that was dangerous territory. It was an untruth that could actually be put to the test. But I felt like I had to say it. And part of me believed I did have that power, or at least it was possible—whatever that Irish mage had done to me as a child, it had seemingly given me powers similar to a mage maker, and she had done it flawlessly in one go. On the way over, Lady Fife had stressed to me that I had to make it clear that I was the superior mage—superior not just to Gabs but to every other mage in this country. One of the few advantages our side had over the lot at Buckingham Palace was that we had an innate magician: me. So what if I barely knew how to use this power? We had to work with what we had.

"The Virtuis Party and King Harold represent nothing more than a dead end for this country. They can't produce more mages, and their only vision of the future is one of destruction and draining the populace of their very life energy. We are offering a different path than that. We will be speaking more to the public over the coming days, but in the meantime please do not believe the lies coming from both the king and the prime minister's palace. Thank you." Again, I wished I could think of some grander sign-off, but rather than risk overdoing it I slipped the headphones off.

Lady Fife gave Kitty the slightest push forwards. She looked around frantically.

"Me? I really don't . . ."

I held the headphones out to her. "It's all right. I'll be right here."

Kitty took them from me and slipped them on.

"Good evening." Her voice was quiet but steady. She straightened her shoulders. "This is Princess Katherine speaking to you all from Windsor Castle. What Mr Gallagher said just now is all true. We have been set up, framed by my brother's true enemies for his death. As a member of the royal family, it is my duty to make sure this country does not fall into darkness. It will not be an easy fight, but it is a necessary one since it is for the soul and heart of this nation. Please stay strong."

She faltered there and finally just took off the headphones. She handed them to me before walking over to look out a window. Clara waited a second to see if I had anything else to say, then motioned to Norbert. He flicked some switches and the light went from green back to red.

I let out a breath that I'd been holding in, rocking slightly on my feet.

"So if the princess didn't kill Prince Arthur, then you're saying the king did?" Clara asked.

"You know the royal family better than anyone," I said. "So you tell me."

Clara shook her head. "Mr Gallagher, even if I do believe you . . . and I hate to admit it, but I fear I do . . . just because you are in the right doesn't mean you'll win out."

I smiled wearily. "I suppose I'll just have to convince both you and the nation that we will."

CHAPTER 32

Over the following days many of the servants did decide to leave—a little over half of them in fact.

"Well," I said, Harriet and Naveed at my side as we looked at a pile of dirty dishes left over after supper. "It's not as though we can't make our own beds and the like."

Harriet nodded eagerly and started rolling up her sleeves. Naveed looked at me as though I'd just suggested swimming back and forth across the English Channel.

But many of the servants stayed: Clara and her grandson Norbert, a butler who seemed more fatherly towards Kitty than her own father had been, a quartet of cooks and their assistants. The soldiers were given minor maintenance jobs to do alongside their guard duty, sweeping the courtyard and corridors. A couple of them were even apprenticed to the castle's ageing gardener, a wizened old man who seemingly stuck around more out of a desire to protect the lawns than out of any feelings for our cause.

The gardener, like many of the servants, did not live on the castle grounds but instead in the surrounding town of Slough. Slough itself was now seen by the rest of the country as rebel territory. Our soldiers were still posted on the roads and exits leading to and from the city. Trains still arrived at the station, and daily lorries with eggs and milk and other produce from nearby farms still trundled in. Thomas kept an almost obsessive count of what was coming and going; he was worried that the Virtuis Party might try to starve us out by blocking further supplies, but Lady Fife didn't think they'd make such a drastic move yet.

"It would turn the public at large against them, since it would be seen as an attack on the civilians living in Slough," she explained. "No one wants to see British soldier fighting British soldier—after the last skirmish, the prime minister was raked over the coals by the press. And to attack a national landmark like Windsor Castle . . . that would solidly cast them in the role of the villain. We are safe here for now."

Even as people left the castle and surrounding town, new faces arrived or sent aid, people who were targets of the Virtuis Party and wished to help bring them down. Most of them were sent home by Thomas after a thorough vetting, because he deemed them either untrustworthy or useless. But a few stuck around, including some cloth mages who had previously worked at prisons across the nation. They were able to use the things they learned in those places to help with our magical defences. They sewed multiple "shield" cloaks, the same as what prisoners wore, and Thomas created a rota so that there were always at least five people on the castle walls wearing them. It was a weak shield and wouldn't protect us if we were bombed, but it protected us from magical attacks and infiltration. Thanks to that we were able to uncover all the mirrors in the castle.

But despite our vigilance an intruder was still able to get in.

It was New Year's Day, and even with a civil war going on, there was a sense of drowsy peace over the castle. Since we had such a skeleton crew running the palace, the only set mealtime each day was dinner. Otherwise we were all left to scrounge up food for ourselves. (Well, the princess and her mother were still brought meals. I supposed if I wanted to be catered to I would need to throw my weight around as Court Magician, but I wasn't keen on that.)

I had managed to blag a blueberry scone from the kitchen and was looking for Thomas so I could share it with him. I did not find Thomas, but Rosemary did find me.

"Professor, why are you hiding out on the roof?" she asked. When I couldn't find Thomas, I'd ducked into a greenhouse that was on the castle roof, jacket drawn tight against the cold. Some days it felt warmer outside than it did in the drafty castle.

"Just eating lunch. What are you doing here?"

"Looking for you," she said. "C'mon."

I wrapped my scone up in a napkin and followed her into the stairwell. The stone steps were uneven and the ceiling low. The whole castle was full of spots like this, holdouts from the castle's early days in the Middle Ages. Moving through the castle almost felt like time travelling—you'd be in the 1300s in one room, then go next door and find yourself in 1777.

"Why exactly were you looking for me?" I asked.

"Because there's an assassin in the castle here to kill you."

She spoke as breezily as if she were relaying what was for supper.

"Sorry, there's a what?" I said, hurrying to keep after her in the spiral stairwell.

"Mr Dawes and I have both been looking for you. Don't worry. Now that I've found you, I'm sure we'll find the assassin." Rosemary's words were cut off by the sound of footsteps echoing in the stairwell, coming from both below and above.

"See? We just have to let them come to us." She stopped on a small landing, opened a door, and pulled me inside before locking it. We were in the billiards room of the castle, one of the rooms that would usually only be used by the royal family. Billiards seemed like such a low-class pastime, but I supposed that was why they usually kept this room private. The billiards table sat in the middle of the room, sunlight streaming in through the windows on the left. There was another door on the side of the room opposite us, but between us and it stood a figure.

It was a slight man with wavy, shoulder-length hair. He was wearing a loose-fitting white shirt and black pants and over that a capelet made of some shiny, silvery material. The whole ensemble made me think *The Three Musketeers* in space.

The man held up his hands (he was wearing black gloves). "I just want to talk."

He had an Irish accent and a higher-pitched voice than I was expecting. Something about him seemed so familiar, but before I could place it Rosemary spoke.

"Well, *I* just want to fight," she said. "Professor, stay behind me." She fixed the strange man with a stare. "Did you know that in Celtic, the word *Avon* means river? There are five River Avons in England. How silly to name something twice. Imagine them all spelled out on a map. River River, River River, River River . . ."

As she spoke the man's face took on a glassy cast. I took another look at Rosemary's dress—it was her usual lace, but this one had the look of an old faded tablecloth, like something that might sit under a crystal ball. It was black but woven through with silver thread and had white linen underneath. From the effect it was having on the mystery man, it seemed to be some kind of hypnosis-inducing magical dress. As Rosemary droned on, the man stood frozen in place.

Still talking, Rosemary picked up a pool ball. Her eyes were still locked on the man, so she didn't see what I saw: a shadow on the left side of the table, as if a figure was passing in front of the windows.

"Rosemary, on your left!"

She didn't hesitate, just swung her arm to the left at about head height. There was a flash and the man was suddenly there, stumbling backwards. He crouched down and seemed to stay there, but a second later Rosemary's head jerked back as though she'd just received a blow to the face. Another flash and the man was standing in front of me. He smiled, and recognition hit me. It wasn't a man at all but a woman. The same woman I had met as a child in the woods near Liverpool.

"You've grown," she said.

"You haven't changed at all," I said.

Rosemary, nose bloodied but eyes cool, pulled out a switchblade.

"Rosemary, it's all right! I know her!" I said. "She's not here to kill me." I realized that was maybe assuming too much. I turned to the stranger. "Tell her. Tell her that you're not an assassin."

"Well, I'm not here to kill anyone," the woman said. Rosemary rolled her eyes but relaxed somewhat.

"Then what are you here for?" There was a hint of annoyance in Rosemary's tone. Maybe she really had been looking forwards to fighting to the death.

"Like I said, to talk," the woman replied. "To Court Magician Gallagher, of course. But also to the princess and your other head coconspirators. You'll all want to hear what I have to say. I'm here to help you overthrow the king."

Rosemary kept the blade in hand and had the Irish woman walk in front of us as we made our way to Lady Fife's office. This made chatting awkward but I tried my best.

"You know, all those years ago, I never did get your name."

"Eimer," the woman replied. "Eimer Aucoin."

"I thought you said you knew her," Rosemary said.

"I do."

"Paul saved my life once," said Eimer.

"That's laying it on a bit thick. I got her some bandages for a wound, that's all."

We had passed by some servants in the hall who looked nervous once they noticed that the stranger with us was being escorted at knifepoint. I asked a servant to please round up Princess Katherine, Thomas, and Lady Fife as quick as he could. Everyone was already there by the time we arrived at Lady Fife's office.

Lady Fife had been sitting at her desk but when she caught sight of Eimer she rose slowly from her seat.

"You."

"Me," Eimer said, grinning. "Here to aid you in your hour of need, Lady Fife. After all this time, we finally get a chance to work together."

Lady Fife had the best poker face of just about anyone, but speaking as someone who was rather obsessive about sorting out Lady Fife's microexpressions, I'd say murder was on her mind.

"You know her too?" Rosemary asked Eimer.

"Oh, we go way back," Eimer replied. "But I didn't come here to merely catch up with old friends. When I heard what you were all up to, how could I stay away?"

"How exactly did you manage to get into the castle? We have guards, patrols," Thomas said. "And me."

"And me!" Rosemary chimed in.

"Well, congratulations, you caught me," Eimer said. "But we can go over the holes in your security system later." She turned to me. "First, we need to sort out your innate magic."

Thomas coughed. "Rosemary, good work. I'll come find you later."

Rosemary pouted at being kicked out. Still pouting, she snapped her switchblade closed and left.

Once she was gone Eimer smiled at me.

"It really is good to see you. You're more handsome than I would have wagered. You were quite the ugly duckling as a child."

Kitty raised her hand slightly.

"Excuse me, sir, but who exactly are you?"

Eimer looked her way. "Ooooh, so polite for a princess! Not going to order me to name myself?"

"Their name is Declan Rime," Lady Fife said tightly.

"I go by Eimer Aucoin nowadays," Eimer said. "Sorry, Lady Fife. Your spies need to keep better track of me." Eimer tilted her head. "Or maybe it's not your spies that are slipping but you? We used to have a lot of fun, before you lost your powers. What an unfortunate and unprecedented event. But not even you could have foreseen a dead man coming back to life, hmm? Things always get gummed up when the dead walk the earth."

"Wait, you know about Godfrey?" I asked.

Eimer nodded. "Yes, and I know his existence is the source of Lady Fife's inability to see the future."

That was news to me, but I supposed it made a kind of sense—Godfrey was an unnatural thing, so maybe his rebirth had been like a spiritual atomic bomb, changing everything that had come before. Or maybe because he had no soul, he was protected from Lady Fife's second sight.

"But you've still done well, even as a mere mortal. Got this little rebellion off the ground. Now, can you keep it in the air?" Eimer said.

"What do you want?" Lady Fife asked.

"I want you to succeed," Eimer said. "I don't want the Virtuis Party in power any more than you do. Rotten, they are. I want to help you be rid of them."

"And what do you want in return?"

"Well, how about a favour to hold in reserve? Say, a favour from the country's future queen and current Court Magician."

Kitty and I traded panicked looks. I felt like I was back in the basement of The Nail, watching as other people discussed me like I was a commodity rather than a person.

"No way. We don't just write blank cheques here," Thomas said.

Eimer shrugged. "What else can you offer? It's not like you have anything of value currently. People—not just me but everyone—will help you with the expectation of some kind of return on their investment someday when you're in power. All there is to it."

"Even so, you ask too much," Lady Fife said, and both Kitty and I let out a breath. "The two of us can negotiate your price later, Aucoin. But first tell us what you are offering."

"You told the people of Britain that Paul Gallagher is the country's Court Magician, the true successor to Redfield," Eimer said. "But is that really true? Can he *really* do innate magic?"

"Of course he can!" Kitty blurted out. Eimer raised an eyebrow in surprise, looking her over, her eyes lingering for a moment on Kitty's ribs.

"Is that so?" Eimer looked to me. "You've done a good job of finding your way in the dark; I'll give you that, child. But if you had a teacher, you could actually be the grand mage that you claim to be."

"And you'd be that teacher?" Thomas said.

"Indeed I am," Eimer said simply. "The public will need proof of your words, Paul. You've been able to do some spells on your own, but do you know how to create cloth mages or Book Binders? Or another mage maker for that matter? I can show you how and more."

Everyone seemed to be waiting for me to say something, but I was at a loss for words, afraid to say no but also afraid to commit to Eimer's offer.

"Or you can continue to feel your own way along," Eimer said. "But that is the path of trial and error, where *error* means numerous deformed and wrecked bodies at your hands."

"If you teach me, can you show me the true way to create a mage maker?" I said. "The one different from the one that British Court Magicians use?"

"What do you mean?" Eimer said, but there was a hint of a smile on her lips, implying she knew exactly what I was talking about.

"A way that works every time." I turned to the others in the room. "Eimer is the one who first broke my bones and cast innate magic on me. She gave me the spell that made me so charming."

"What?" Thomas said, clearly confused. "When did all this happen?"

"The day we first met."

"We were, like, six!"

I nodded and looked to Eimer. "But you did more than just that spell, didn't you? You cast another spell, one that allowed me to practise innate magic. I'm right, aren't I?"

Eimer tilted her head to the side and smiled. "Yes, it's true. Even though you were just a child, you already had a keen insight into how magic worked. I was impressed, so I gave you the ability to work innate magic as well."

"Including being able to make other mages?!" I said, excited to finally have some answers.

"Yes."

"And I didn't die!" I turned to the others. "She made me a mage maker in one go! She didn't have to kill a bunch of other people to get a winner; she just *did* it."

"Maybe you survived just through dumb luck," Thomas said heatedly.

Eimer shook her head. "The way I create mage makers is different from how your Court Magicians have done it. My way works every time."

"But there's a price, right? A consequence," I said. "Like with me."

Eimer looked confused. "What do you mean?"

"You know. You made it so that I couldn't physically hurt anyone, outside of when I was doing magic," I said. I'd told this to Thomas before but it was news to Lady Fife—she looked at me with great surprise, arched eyebrows coming down so she could frown at Eimer.

Eimer laughed. "Oh, yes. I had forgotten that I did that."

"You forgot?" I'd almost died multiple times because of it, been beaten bloody because I couldn't defend myself, been sick with fear as I watched people I love suffer, myself unable to do anything. And she'd forgotten?

"It was a long time ago," Eimer said.

"Really?" Lady Fife said, one eyebrow cocked.

"Well, I suppose not really, but I've been busy. You start to forget the little things. But it's not a consequence or a by-product of another spell. It's just something I did."

"Why put that on me at all?" I said, mentally scrambling for words. "I had just helped you. You'd just given me a gift in return. Why put a curse upon me like that? I was a little boy."

Eimer gave a shrug, palms up. "Well, that's all true, but the gift I'd given you was a considerable one. It only made sense to put in some kind of safeguard. After all, you weren't going to be a little boy forever."

No one spoke when she was done.

Finally Lady Fife cleared her throat.

"Mr Dawes, Paul, I'd like to speak with Eimer alone, please," she said.

Thomas looked from her to Eimer doubtfully.

"Are you sure—"

"Yes."

There was no arguing with that. Thomas came over and took my arm in order to lead me to the door.

~

Lady Fife asked me to have a drink in her office with her after dinner that night, so after eating with the Fraught Friends in the banquet hall and freshening up in my rooms, I finally worked up the nerve to go see her.

"You're late, Mr Gallagher," she said.

"My apologies, Lady Fife. I still get lost in this big old castle." I couldn't tell her that I'd dreaded seeing her, spending the last few hours feeling like a condemned man, waiting to hear my sentence. Just what exactly would Eimer want in return for her help?

"Hmm." She motioned for me to step inside. Over the last week the decor had switched from King Harold's taste to Lady Fife's: the military swords had been taken down as well as his portrait. In their place Lady Fife had put up a large ornamental fan. On several small tables around the edges of the room she had placed porcelain vases with winter bouquets of leaves and fir branches, giving the room a bit of a witchy vibe.

Lady Fife was wearing a rather smashing green wrap dress created out of an excess of fabric, enough that two dresses could have been made from it. It was designed in a way that it all flowed gracefully around her rather than bunching up. Her gold earrings matched the gold-and-emerald necklace resting across her collarbone. The magic of her dress was meant to help keep up the wearer's energy while they wore it.

I'd made the gown. It had been from a commission two years ago. Money was tight at the time—it was before I'd become friends with Kitty and was grappling with various debts. Tonya and I could barely afford the rent on our Islington flat. Then I received an anonymous commission to make a fabulous outfit. They would pay for the materials, naturally, but beyond that they were willing to pay an exorbitant fee for my services. I was a bit wary of working for an unseen employer, but since the dress's magic was benign enough I took the job and decided not to worry about it. I did, however, often look for the dress at parties, hoping to someday meet its wearer and thank them for their generosity.

Well, it seemed my wish had come true.

"That dress truly looks stupendous on you, Lady Fife," I said.

"Yes, well, it was finely made," said Lady Fife. "I'd always wished for a chance to wear it, but I felt like I owed it to my son to wear only his designs in public."

"I see." I knew that was true, but I wondered if there was more to it. "Or maybe you've never worn it before now because you didn't want to reveal your kind heart."

Lady Fife was much too refined to roll her eyes, but she ducked her chin as if to obscure a disbelieving smile. "Whatever do you mean, Mr Gallagher?"

"You commissioned this dress at a time when I was in quite dire straits, but since you didn't want it to look like an act of charity, you did it all under a cover of secrecy."

Lady Fife shook her head, a controlled movement that caused the gold teardrop earrings to sway only slightly.

"Andrew commissioned this dress, not me."

I didn't reply immediately. Instead I thought back to how Andrew had listened as I'd nattered on excitedly about the commission. He was always attentive when I was rambling, but I half remembered him having a knowing smile as I'd gone on about *this* dress. Or maybe I was just picturing it that way now thanks to Lady Fife's reveal.

"I didn't know that," I said.

"Of course. Andrew wished to keep it secret. I didn't think he'd succeed, but I guess he was able to keep quiet about it after all," Lady Fife said.

"I . . . your son was a good friend to me," I said. "I'm sorry for the way I treated him."

"Don't speak of him like he's dead." Lady Fife's voice was sharp, a hint of heat there behind her icy facade.

"Of course, Lady Fife. I'm merely saying that I recognize that, even if I hadn't done him such a bad turn, I'd still owe him a lot."

This seemed to placate Lady Fife. She leaned back against the couch and became quiet, lost in thought. I grew uneasy in the silence.

"I don't know if I can ever make it up to him," I said. "But I hope that, by getting rid of the Virtuis Party, I can start to undo some of the damage I've caused. I'll take on whatever price Eimer is asking."

Lady Fife shook her head. "No, Mr Gallagher, that won't be necessary."

"Truly, Lady Fife. If she's going to teach me the secrets of innate magic, then I should be the one—"

"No," Lady Fife said firmly, eyes still staring off into the corner of the room. "Eimer's taken enough from you already."

I couldn't help but feel moved by Lady Fife's words; it was the first time she'd ever sounded protective of me.

Yet despite the relief I felt, it was balanced by worry.

"Then does she want something from Kitty? In which case, really, I'd much rather it be me—"

"No. Not from Princess Katherine," Lady Fife said.

"Then who?" I said, getting a bit impatient. I ran through the list of people Eimer could possibly want leverage over: The queen? Sabina? Sabina's child? The last one made my stomach tighten into knots.

"Andrew," Lady Fife said, and for a moment I was confused, wondering why she'd said her son's name so randomly. Then I put it into context.

"She wants something from Andrew?" I said with an amount of disbelief that bordered on rude. "What does she want from *him*?"

Lady Fife rightfully glared at me.

"You need not worry about that," Lady Fife said. "They will ask for a favour from him at some future time. Luckily for you, I have contacted Andrew and he's agreed to their terms."

"Oh, Jesus," I said. "Tell him he doesn't have to do this."

"He knows," Lady Fife said lightly. "But there's more on offer than just Eimer sharing their trade secrets with you, Mr Gallagher."

"What do you mean?"

"If things go our way, the nation will have a new queen and a new Court Magician. But if you really want to change anything, down the line you will need to work with an amicable prime minister."

I sat up straight. "And you think Andrew could be that prime minister?"

"I always have."

I kept my reservations to myself.

"Eimer will not only help you but also Andrew," Lady Fife said. "After all, it is better in their interest to be owed a favour by a man in power than some lord in self-imposed exile."

"And Andrew wants this? To become prime minister?"

"He does," Lady Fife said. She hesitated. "Though his word alone is not enough. Eimer wishes him to undergo the promise spell."

"Why, yes, of course—wait, promise spell?" It was an old bit of lore—*Break a bone, make a promise, cast a spell that keeps you honest.* The idea was that back in the Dark Ages innate magicians had acted like solicitors, overseeing agreements between two parties. The people involved would make an oath to uphold their ends of the bargain, and the innate magicians would break a small bone in each of them, turning their oath into a spell. Anyone who failed to meet the terms of the deal would suffer terribly.

Eimer was going to perform that old bit of magic on Andrew, a binding contract that would result in Andrew either keeping his word or dying.

"Naturally. Eimer is a bone mage," Lady Fife said. "Did you think they'd be satisfied with a promissory note?"

"That's too much," I said.

"It's fine," Lady Fife said. "Andrew understands the stakes, not just for himself but the country."

"So you're just going to leave this all on Andrew's shoulders?" I said. "Because, look, your son is a kind soul, but he also once got stuck inside a phone box because he couldn't figure out how the door worked. Thank God he was at least able to call for help."

"Hmm," Lady Fife said. "And who did he call?"

"Me." I looked down at my hands, not willing to look up and meet Lady Fife's gaze. "It's just . . . Lady Fife, we don't have to do this. We could find someone else who will teach me these things, someone we can trust. And, well, what's the rush?"

"Gabriella von Melsungen can't create new mages," Lady Fife said, as if spelling out something obvious. "If we can show the British people that you can—"

"But why the need to make another mage maker?"

"A protomage, you mean?"

"That's a bit of an archaic term."

"I know, but I just find it so cumbersome saying 'make a mage maker' all the time," Lady Fife said.

"All right, fine, we'll go with that. Why is it so important that I make a 'protomage'?" The greatest power an innate magician had was the ability to make others like themselves. A Book Binder or cloth magician could make powerful magical items, but they didn't have the power to make other mages. Only a mage maker, or protomage, had that ability, and in Great Britain it was a power held only by the Court Magician. "Usually a Court Magician is on the job for a couple of decades before they have to make a successor." The process went something like this: when the current Court Magician was getting on in his years, candidates would be sought out to succeed him. Once the list was assembled, the Court Magician would perform the ritual to create his successor. In the process a dozen-plus upper-class lads would die, but in one of them the magic would take hold and give him the power to create other mages: Book Binders, cloth mages, and even other protomages. The lucky lad would study under the current Court Magician until the man died or retired, at which time he'd take on the mantle of Court Magician. "I mean, I'm only twenty-seven! Redfield didn't do the ritual until he was in his early fifties, and even that was seen as young."

Lady Fife looked out the window. "Back in 1953 I had a vision that Redfield was going to die in a few years' time. I advised him and the king that they should hold the ritual *then*, not wait. I knew if Redfield died without another protomage lined up to take his place, it would be disastrous. Russia might have seen it as an opportunity to make the

Cold War hot and attack a vulnerable American ally. But even during a stable, peaceful era, not having another protomage could throw the country into turmoil. This current civil war is proof of that."

"So that's why you want me to create another protomage now? So you have a replacement ready in case anything happens to *me*?"

"No one could replace you, Paul," Lady Fife said. "But if we are going to tell the public that we have a better way to create protomages, we will need to show them that. We don't have decades to wait. The battle for this country is happening now."

I sighed and rubbed my temples. I saw her point but that just made the pressure upon me even more weighty. "Can we truly trust Eimer? We're risking a lot here."

"We can try and anticipate their wants and act accordingly," Lady Fife said. "By seeing where our wants intersect with theirs, we can try and stay aligned."

"You seem to know Eimer quite well, Lady Fife. I don't mean to pry, but how far back do you two go?"

"Oh, quite a ways," Lady Fife said, pausing as if deciding how much detail to go into. "They killed my husband."

"What?" I sat up straight. "Lady Fife, are you serious?!"

"Do you think them not capable of it?"

"I just . . . I thought your husband drowned." That was the story Andrew had told me, the one I heard repeated as a common part of Lady Fife's biography. There had always been rumours about Lady Fife, but no one had ever suggested that her husband had been a victim of foul play. Even her enemies said theirs had been a strong, happy marriage, tragically cut short by a boating accident.

"Drowning was a convenient cover," Lady Fife said, all cryptic-like.

"But . . . but why didn't you go to the authorities?" I said.

"As if there were any authorities that could deal with that creature."

"Well, then why didn't *you* deal with her?"

Lady Fife gave me a wry smile. "I'm flattered you think me so omnipotent, Mr Gallagher. But the fact is that even if I could have had my revenge upon Eimer, at the time it wasn't advisable to do so."

"Why did Eimer kill the late Lord Fife anyway?"

"Oh, politics," Lady Fife said, as lightly as summer rain. "It was decades ago, so I won't bore you with the details now. Don't look at me like that."

"Like what?"

"Like I'm some reptile sitting under a heat lamp," Lady Fife said. "You may think me cold, Mr Gallagher, but I told you years ago that my greatest concern is this country, and beyond that, the continued existence of all life on Earth. Any other concerns are secondary."

"I . . . yes, of course, Lady Fife."

"Do you remember what you said to me the night you brought Godfrey back from the dead?" Lady Fife asked, a sincere inquiry to her words. "You said that I was all talk, that if someone truly dear to me was in danger, I would throw the whole world over—"

"Lady Fife, I was young and stupid and I didn't know your history—"

"You said that if Andrew were at stake, I'd betray all my lofty ideals in order to save him."

"I don't think I said that—"

"It was implied," Lady Fife said. "Well, I hope you are satisfied, Mr Gallagher. Satisfied in my devotion to saving this world, because I have now brokered a deal between my son and the creature who killed his father."

She tilted her head back and downed the drink that had been in her hand the whole time. She swallowed and closed her eyes.

"Forgive me," she said. "I had a few drinks before you arrived in order to steady my nerves."

It was oddly sweet to know that Lady Fife had been just as nervous as I was. "No need to apologize, Lady Fife."

She sighed, eyes still closed. "It will be a while before Andrew arrives. In the meantime, learn as much as you can from them."

"You mean Eimer, yeah?" I'd noticed that Lady Fife always used *they* or *them* when talking about Eimer and I wasn't quite sure what it meant, but I had no idea how to ask.

Lady Fife heard the question under my question.

"Yes. I've known them for decades now. Their name may change, or the gender they present as, but they are still the same." Lady Fife seemed very tired, the words sounding like they'd been dredged up from some distant part of her mind while she was focused on other things. I wanted to ask her more about Eimer, but the time didn't seem right. Instead, I offered to walk her back to her rooms and to my surprise she accepted.

CHAPTER 33

The first thing Eimer had me do was take up a running regime.

"I'm in fine enough shape," I told them.

"You're the type of city dweller who thinks taking the stairs down to the tube platform is getting their exercise for the day," they said. "That's not enough."

So I started doing predawn runs around the various courtyards, feeling quite ridiculous running in the snow, wearing an old jumper retrieved from the castle's lost and found box. Naveed joined me, not only keeping pace easily but chatting the whole time as we ran: "Knees up, Professor! Three more laps in this courtyard; then we'll move on to the next one! Keep breathing! What a spritely morning, eh?" Staying annoyingly chipper even as I turned phone box red.

After about a week of running Eimer showed me breathing techniques to use while on my runs. With practice, they said, I'd be able to slow my heart down at will.

"And why is that so important?" I asked.

"It makes the magic easier," Eimer said. "When you're performing innate magic on someone, it helps to get your heartbeat in sync with them, to breathe as they do. In your training as a mage you've already become attuned to sensing some things, like how a body changes when it's wearing magic clothes. But you must be even more in tune. You must be able to hear someone's heartbeat from the other side of the room, to feel the flow of blood through their body as easily as if you were dipping your fingers into a stream."

"All right, but when will I actually get to do some innate magic?" I said.

"Soon."

Lady Fife wanted me to do a live demonstration, to prove that my abilities were the real deal. Both Eimer and I were resistant to it: innate magic, at least the bone-breaking part, wasn't all that showy. A "demonstration" would just look like me breaking bones onstage.

"Still, it would be *something*," Lady Fife said.

"It's only January," I mused aloud, "but I imagine the second-year magic students around the country must be feeling antsy."

For most magic programmes, near the end of the second year was when students would get their arms broken in such a way to make them either Book Binders or cloth mages or a combination of both. But Gabs didn't have the power to make new mages.

"You were planning to offer your services?" Eimer asked.

"We shouldn't be making just any student a mage," Lady Fife said. "Not when they'll likely just go work for our enemies."

"Sure, I agree. But I do have three diligent students who are eager to become full-fledged mages," I said.

Lady Fife nodded thoughtfully. "Yes, that may do. You could break their bones live on TV, and once they've recovered, they could make magic outfits to prove that your innate magic skills do in fact work." She frowned. "But that still takes so much *time*."

Lady Fife's words startled me, or perhaps just her tone. She reminded me of Godfrey in many ways, and chief amongst them was their long view of things, their willingness to stay in the shadows so they could shape the arc of history. But now Lady Fife was fretting over weeks.

"Paul still has lots of training to do," Eimer said. "And he can't do it here anyway. Best bet is to break the kids' bones, and while they are healing Paul can go off to learn how to make another mage maker."

"I'd have to go away?" I said. "Why?"

"There's too many people here, too many contaminating elements," Eimer said. "You need a clear head for what we need to do. Certain supplies that can't be found here."

"But . . . but I'm needed here," I said. I looked to Lady Fife for guidance. She also looked unsure.

"If he goes away to study, how long will it take?" she asked Eimer, who grinned.

"As long as it takes."

There it was again, that worry on Lady Fife's face.

"If you want a demonstration of Paul's power in the meantime, you could show off the spell he did on Princess Katherine," Eimer suggested. They always spoke like that, using *you* instead of *we*, as if to highlight that they were just a freelance consultant, not someone truly tied to our fight. "It's a very interesting piece of magic—"

"No," I said. "It's a piece of magic that keeps the princess safe. If we advertise all the ins and outs of it, someone might be able to figure out a way to get past it and hurt Kitty."

Thomas, as a security measure, had been hard at work testing the limits of the protective spell I had cast on the princess. He'd spent days lobbing various objects at her, such as stones and eggs, and watching as they were flung haphazardly back by some invisible force. Thomas hadn't found any way to physically attack the princess, but he had discovered she was susceptible to poison. What if our enemies were able to figure this out as well?

"Look, I'll go off wherever, learn how to make myself a successor, and when I come back we'll make a big show of it, yeah?" I said. "In the meantime, at least I can make the Fraught Friends into mages."

Lady Fife frowned. "The who?"

~

Lady Fife got her wish: it was a live demonstration. We cleared out the banquet hall so the ritual could be done there. In the audience were three MPs from the Labour Party. Two of them were older white guys I'd never met before, but the third was Ralph Gunnerson. Despite the hall being full of people, we hugged, glad to see each other alive.

Eimer had walked me through it, but I still felt nervous when I broke first Naveed's humerus, followed by his radius and ulna. But I could feel the direction of the magic change within him, and by the time I did the same thing to Rosemary I felt a little more confident.

I only faltered when I got to Harriet. Having her sit in a chair, waiting for me to perform magic on her, it reminded me sharply of how her father had died.

"It's all right, Professor," she said, brushing her hair back so I could see her strong smile. "I'm not afraid."

But I was. I'd already caused Harriet so much pain in this life—what if something went wrong as I tried to turn her into a mage? I'd never be able to live with myself. Part of me wanted to tell Lady Fife that we should stop here for today, but everyone in the castle had gathered to watch, including the visiting MPs. If I didn't go through with this, we might lose their support.

I pushed away my fear and picked up the mallet.

CHAPTER 34

When it was announced that I'd be leaving temporarily in order to further study innate magic the Parkeesh family declared there would be a banquet to see me off. They had their servants take over the kitchen and bring out dish after dish of amazing Indian cuisine. It was delicious and by the end of the night it felt like I'd eaten more than I ever had in my life. Everyone seemed to be having a lovely time.

The only person who seemed upset was Thomas. After the banquet we found a quiet roof to sit on together, smoking a cigarette to keep us warm.

"It won't take me long to master whatever it is I need to do," I said, trying to inject my words with confidence. Thomas was sipping from a bottle of Newcastle IPA. He handed it to me and I took a sip. When I handed it back Thomas took a deep gulp. He was clearly glum, knees pulled up against his chest, eyes looking out at Slough as if he were counting the streetlamps.

"Are you sure I can't come with you?" he asked, sounding like a child. My heart broke. Most of my life, all I'd ever wanted was Thomas there with me. Even now, I wished he were coming on this journey with me.

"Eimer said—"

"Oh, fuck them!" Thomas said. "*You* are the Court Magician! If you insisted then—"

"And if I did, and the magic didn't work, then what?" I said, keeping my tone gentle. "I have to do this. And for this to work I have to do this alone."

Thomas huffed but didn't argue. He just downed the rest of the beer. For a moment I thought I had managed to calm him down, but then he chucked the bottle off the roof. It dropped out of sight and shattered with a harsh crash on the frozen stones below.

"Sorry," he muttered.

"I'll feel a lot better out there knowing you're here," I said. "You need to fill in for me as professor, teach those new mages about how to actually *do* cloth magic."

Thomas snorted. "No one can teach those kids anything. They act like they already know everything."

"We were the same when we were their age."

"You're still that way," Thomas said, but without any bite.

~

The day I was set to leave there was a minor hiccup: my brothers had gone on the BBC the evening before in order to denounce me. They said I had always been an ambitious schemer. That I hadn't even gone to my own father's funeral, since I couldn't fit in a trip to Liverpool around my plans for world domination.

"Good God, Professor!" Naveed said, bounding over with a copy of the paper as I sat down for breakfast. Rosemary was at his heels, watching me closely as I looked at the article. The picture of my brothers was above the fold, both of them still burly from their days working on the docks, the nice suits from when they'd moved into upper management. They were sitting on the set of a BBC news show, their faces serious.

"You know, I always said I wanted brothers, but if brothers are like this, then no thank you!" Naveed said. "Where do they get off, calling you 'an ungrateful parasite'?!"

"Want me to go to Liverpool and cut off their ears?" Rosemary offered.

"No, no! It's fine. It's all fine." I folded the paper so that I didn't have to look at my brothers' faces. "I'm glad they're doing this, really. By aligning with Buckingham Palace, it keeps them and their families safe. It's a relief, really."

Naveed was looking at me with admiration, Rosemary scepticism.

"Anyway, it's time for me to get gone," I said, standing up. I'd been eating breakfast alone. Thomas had some secret business to take care of—I was worried that *he'd* gone to Liverpool to maim my brothers.

Naveed and Rosemary accompanied me to Eimer's rooms. We'd set them up in one of the palace's many guest suites, and they'd been working away on some kind of outfit.

The heavy coat looked like something a Cossack would wear. It was a little much for the mild English winter, heavy and made from thick wool. It had a sunflower motif, which seemed like an odd choice for a winter coat. The sunflower faces had real sunflower seeds in the middle of them, though I noticed there were a few spots where the seeds had fallen loose, leaving bare patches.

Eimer helped me put it on and I wasn't surprised when it fit me perfectly.

"What exactly does it do?" I asked as they helped me tighten the coat's belt.

"It's a teleportation outfit," they replied. "It will only take you to specific spots though. Places where certain sunflowers were planted."

Eimer reached down and plucked a seed off the coat. They tossed it to Rosemary. "Plant this somewhere outside the castle gates so your professor can get home later, all right?" Eimer turned to me. "Paul, are you ready to go?"

I nodded. "What do I do?"

"Close your eyes and feel the sun on your face."

So I did.

CHAPTER 35

I pretended I was a flower, like the ones on the outfit I was wearing. My eyes were squeezed tightly shut, but I still noticed when things went just a smidge darker, as though the sun had gone behind a cloud. A winter's breeze rustled my hair.

"You can open your eyes now," Eimer said.

I was outdoors, standing atop a frozen, raised flower bed. A legion of pine trees surrounded the yard, their hulking mass unwelcoming. A grey sky hung low overhead.

"Come now," Eimer said, walking towards a tiny house. There was a latticework around the edge of the roof that made me think of childhood fairy tales. Would it turn out that this chocolate-brown house was actually made of candy? Or would it get up and walk around on chicken legs at night?

Inside looked like a regular, if rustic, living room and kitchen. Wooden stairs went to a loft bedroom. The place was neat but dusty, and in a few places some of the wooden frame of the windows had been worn away by the damp and changing of the seasons. There was a musty smell in the air. Eimer wrinkled their nose and opened up the windows.

"Ugh. This is what happens when you don't visit a place in almost a year." They looked to me. "Are you any good at home repair?"

"No."

They shook their head. "Classic mage. Great magical powers, no life skills."

"Where are we?"

"Bavaria."

That stunned me for a moment—I hadn't expected us to end up in *Germany*. "And *why* are we here?" I asked.

"There's a town nearby that owes me a favour," Eimer said. "I'm here to collect."

"Wait a second . . . how did *you* travel here?" It only just occurred to me to ask: Eimer was wearing clothes I'd seen them wear around the castle plenty of times before, a pair of black trousers and a silk blouse with a diamond pattern. It wasn't a magic outfit so how had they been able to teleport alongside me?

They gave me a half smile, as if to say, *Come on, you know how.*

"You . . . have innate magic within you that gives you unlimited teleportation?" That would be simply miraculous. Most mages could make teleportation outfits, but they always had to fit certain parameters or be tied to certain points. The idea that Eimer could just go where they wished was astounding. "Is that how you were able to sneak into the castle?! Eimer, please, you must teach me—"

"I agreed to teach you how to make mages and how to make a protomage," Eimer said. "But I can't teach you everything I know."

"Please, don't be stingy. I'll be a good student and—"

"I'm not being stingy; it's just that your life simply isn't long enough to learn all that I could teach you," Eimer said, with a smugness that felt a bit performative.

"Just how old are you?" I asked. Eimer pulled a chair out from a small round table that was in the kitchen. It creaked uneasily as they sat down in it.

"How old do you think I am?" they asked. I pulled out the other chair.

"My nan was from Kilkenny," I said. "When I was a babe, she would tell stories of the fair folk, how they came to Ireland from another land, like our own but not. They were not human—each and every one of them was a Superconductor, and some of them were neither man nor woman."

Eimer was still smiling, waiting to see what I'd say next with a glint in their eye.

"When we first met, I assumed you were a woman, because you were wearing women's clothes," I said. "And then as an adult, I held on to that belief because it was how I'd thought of you all my life. But you're something else, aren't you? Lady Fife always refers to you as 'they' when talking about you."

Eimer laughed at that. "Ah, Lady Fife, always so proper. She takes such great pains to pay respect even to her worst foes."

"Should I refer to you as 'they' as well?" I asked. "I want to get it right."

"Thank you, Paul. Truly. But you can keep calling me 'she.'" Eimer winked at me. "*You* always take pains to be nicer to girls."

I tried to think of what I'd said or done that would make them think that—I'd like to think that I was kind to everyone. Besides, perhaps in a bid to imitate Lady Fife, I already thought of Eimer as *they*.

"So what now?" I asked.

"Well, first I'll give you a tour," Eimer said, standing up. They showed me where the pots and pans were in the kitchen and how to light the woodstove so I could make tea and other meals. They showed me where extra blankets were up in the loft, as well as an empty wardrobe where I could hang my clothes.

"All I have is what I'm wearing," I said, gesturing to the outfit they had given me.

"Ah, yes. I'll need that back. I'll ask for some clothes for you when I go to the village."

They then showed me the grounds outside. Unlike the house, the area around it seemed well tended. In the underground cellar, there were jars of vegetables, fruit, and meat. The woodshed was stocked with fresh logs. Eimer nodded with satisfaction when they saw all this, like it was expected but still pleasing to see.

"You'll need to chop a lot of wood to cook your meals and keep yourself warm," they said. "It gets cold here at night." They had me chop a couple of logs, just to show them that I could in fact do it. My first couple of attempts were pitiful, off-centre swings, but by my third try I was almost able to split the log in two.

"Good," Eimer said. "It will get easier as time goes on. A skeleton mage needs good arm and upper-body strength."

"Do you have to call it that?" I said, wiping the sweat from my brow.

"What, skeleton mage?"

"Yes. It sounds so . . . morbid."

Eimer thought it over. "Some people call them marrowbone mages instead. We can go with that, I suppose." They had been sitting on a nearby tree stump as I chopped logs. They hopped to their feet and stretched. "Well, I need to go to the village and arrange everything else."

"Can I come?" I said, excited by the idea of meeting the local people.

Eimer shook their head. "The people here and I have a long history, and they would not feel kindly to a stranger like yourself showing up. I need to talk to them alone."

I thought Eimer's caution unwarranted. "Eimer, surely you realize that, as closed off as these people may be, *I* could win them over."

Eimer laughed. "Boyo, of course I know. But best there be some distance between them and you."

They went off shortly after that. There was a small river nearby, and I used a bucket to bring back some water. As I was washing my face I heard high-pitched giggling from the woods. I looked up and saw a couple of children peeking at me from behind a bush: two white kids, little girls with plaits and mischievous smiles. It made me miss Beatrix. I raised my hand to wave, but they just ducked out of sight and ran off.

~

I had found what looked like a jar of soup in the root cellar and had half of it for supper, leaving the rest on the stove for when Eimer returned. They didn't come until hours deep into the night. They sat down at the table without a word, looking more tired than I'd ever seen them.

"I was starting to worry that you weren't coming back," I said, a truthful joke. Eimer rubbed their temples.

"There was more admin to deal with in the village than I expected," Eimer said. "The old man who spoke the best English passed away, and his kids aren't nearly as fluent. Spent hours getting through simple terms and conditions."

Sometimes, with the way Eimer made deals and poisoned promises, it was hard not to see them as the literal devil.

"If communication is a problem, I could make an outfit of some kind to overcome the language barrier," I said.

"I know you could, Paul, but that's not needed here. In fact, it could hinder you."

"Why?" I said. "We need to be able to talk to the locals about keeping this place supplied, right?"

"Yes. But what we really need from the villagers are the villagers themselves."

The woodstove of the cabin had kept the place toasty but suddenly a chill crept over me. "What do you mean?"

"Surely you remember why we came here," Eimer said. "You need to learn how to make a protomage, and to do that you need live bodies to practise on."

I stood up and backed away.

"The people here . . . ?" My eyes darted around the cabin as if looking for something familiar to latch on to, but nothing here was mine. What did eventually catch my eye was a pile of clothes Eimer had brought back: simple men's shirts and trousers, borrowed from the locals so I could wear them. The sight of it just made me feel ill. "You'd have me practise on the unsuspecting people here?"

"They are far from 'unsuspecting,' Paul," Eimer said with a scoff. "Years ago, this village suffered a great calamity. A landslide buried the local school. I was nearby at the time and able to save the wee ones, but only after the adults agreed to my price."

"And what was your price? An eye for an eye and all that?" I said, unable to keep the scorn out of my voice. I couldn't imagine using such a tragedy to my own ends; of course distraught parents would agree to any deal put in front of them, if it saved their child from a slow, crushing death.

Eimer rolled their eyes. "Don't act so disdainful—you are the one benefiting from this. But you are correct: my price was a life for a life. Everyone here knew that eventually I'd be back to claim my due. So here we are."

Another chill went through me. I started pacing back and forth the length of the cabin, as if the tight turns and brisk movement might warm me up.

"But we only need one of them, right?" I said, as if Eimer and I were merely brainstorming possible solutions. Eimer held up their palms, empty hands to symbolize that they had nothing concrete to share.

"Perhaps."

"No, not 'perhaps,'" I said, my voice angled between angry and panicked. "You said you'd show me the true way to do innate magic, to make a mage maker on the first try."

"And you will," Eimer replied, "but it might take a bit of practice to get there."

"And by practice, you mean people." My Liverpool accent was coming on strong as we spoke—I don't know if it was from stress or just a side effect from speaking with Eimer and hearing their Irish accent.

Eimer sighed and tilted their chair back, gaze upwards as they looked at the ceiling beams of the cabin.

"Do you want to go back to Windsor Castle?" they asked. "If you don't want to do this, you can. Tell Kitty that you can't be the Court Magician after all. Tell Lady Fife that all her work was for naught. Tell your pal Thomas Dawes that he isn't needed here after all—"

Tell Laura you ruined her life and Beatrix's for nothing.

"Stop." I quit pacing and rubbed my temples. It was so dark, both inside and out, the light from the stove barely strong enough to even cast shadows. "I'll stay here. I'll do whatever is needed."

"Good." The chair came down with a crack as Eimer leaned forwards. They got to their feet and walked towards the door. "Well, good night, Paul. Sleep well. We have a lot of work to do in the morning."

"Wait, you're not sleeping here?" I said. I had just assumed that Eimer would be staying with me. They opened the door and looked over their shoulder with an incredulous expression.

"In this shit heap? Are you kidding me?" They stepped out, the door slamming shut behind them. I hurried forwards to open it, but Eimer was already gone, no sign of them in the yard or surrounding woods.

~

I slept fitfully that night, the musty mattress in the top part of the loft making me sneeze until I was finally too exhausted to stay awake. For breakfast I had a tart apple from the root cellar.

Eimer appeared suddenly midmorning and started bustling around the place as if making up for lost time.

"I suppose since the weather's nice we can do this outside," they said as they lugged the chairs, one at a time, from inside the cabin to the yard. I should have stepped forwards to help but I felt lost, afraid of doing the wrong thing. "It's such a mild day and it's so dark inside; better to have some light."

"Some light for what?"

"Well, mag—"

"Yes, I know, magic, but what exactly?"

"A man from town will be here after lunch," Eimer said. "You'll practise innate magic on him."

"Like, mage maker magic?"

Eimer shook their head. "No, we're going to start a little smaller than that."

"Oh." This was a bit of a relief to hear but still not a full answer.

"The mage maker spell can't take hold in someone who has never had innate magic practised upon them," Eimer said. "Don't ask me why; it just is. I think part of the reasoning goes back to the Mesopotamians: I once read a decree of theirs that said only mages can become mage makers, so I figure it started there."

"Eh?" The way Eimer was talking confused and intrigued me. Now that we were finally alone, I felt like I could ask them about things I'd been wondering my entire life. "So when I was a child and you broke my finger, is that why you did two breaks? The first one to cast some initial spell, the second one to make me a mage maker?"

"Ah, you have a good memory!" Eimer said, delighted—as if I could ever forget anything about that day. "You have it right—I did the first break to give you your wish, the enchantment that would help you get more friends. The second one, that was to make you able to practise innate magic."

"But . . . why?"

Eimer shrugged. "It's not so easy to make innate magicians in England, not amongst adults, anyway. The British ways of doing magic are too entrenched within them, and they aren't able to accept any other way. But you were different. You were still young and free thinking enough to conceive of other ways of being. Remember what you said to me, when I offered you a magical trinket in return for your help?"

"Yes." I remembered everything about that day. "I said thanks but no thanks, since a trinket could just be taken away from me."

"Right! True magic can't be taken on or off like a coat. And since you already knew the truth of that, I was inspired to give you the ability to practise it."

"But . . . why?" I said yet again, like a talking doll who had only so many phrases. "Why give a child that kind of power?"

"Well, like I said before, you weren't going to stay a child forever. If you didn't pursue magic, well, no harm done. But if you *did*, well, I thought it might throw a wrench in the workings of my enemies. And it turns out my shot in the dark paid off."

They grinned at me like we were coconspirators, which sat uneasily with me. I didn't want to think that most of my life had been dictated by someone who had done this monumental thing as merely a lark, that such a big part of me came from someone just trying to sow chaos.

Before I could sit with these feelings some more, Eimer was back to the matter at hand.

"Today you'll be doing more or less a spell you've done before. You were able to figure out how to practise innate magic on the princess, right? How did you come up with that?"

"Well, I just thought of what effect I wanted," I said. "I went with a rib since it's not easily removed, and being a bigger bone it would have a stronger effect, even if I was sacrificing some nuance by not using a smaller bone."

Eimer nodded at my textbook explanation. "Good. Then today we'll practise the opposite: a spell with a smaller effect but greater nuance. A finger bone."

My left hand twitched. Memories of the day Eimer had broken my bone came rushing back to me, how it felt like something had broken inside of me, but it had felt like something that had been *meant* to be broken, like undoing a seal or smashing the bars of a cage. Would I really be able to give someone else that sensation?

In the cabin Eimer lifted up a loose floorboard and brought up a small chest. Inside was a set of anatomical books. The chairs and table were already outside, so we sat on the floor and poured over the diagrams of the hand, the muscles, joints, cartilage, bone. Eimer had me feel my own hand as well as theirs so I could map the sensation of touch and feel onto those dry illustrations. Eimer went over the different finger-bone segments, explaining how each had a different level of power but also difficulty.

We were so engrossed that we didn't even notice the stranger standing in the open door. Then he cleared his throat and we looked up. He was an older man, in his early seventies, I'd guess, but hale and spry. His face had a lean, aristocratic mien at odds with his kind eyes and peasant's garb. He had his hat in his hands, fidgeting like a young boy.

Eimer got to their feet. "C'mon," they said to me, walking outside. I gathered up the books in case we might need them. The man nodded to us and said, "*Grüß Gott*," which Eimer ignored.

"Good afternoon," I said. He smiled.

Eimer's one acknowledgement of the man was to gesture towards one of the chairs on the lawn. He sat on it and put his hat down on the table.

"We're going to make this man a mage maker?" I said.

"That is the plan," Eimer replied dryly. "But first you need to do some smaller form of magic. Something to get the blood flowing, so to speak. You have your tools?"

No, I did not. What I had was an armful of books. I put them down on the table, the tower of tomes sliding off each other. One flopped open to a picture of a woman's skull being cut open by surgeons; the old man sitting at the table winced. I had no time to comfort him or even shut the book. My nerves were humming with excitement, my feet barely touching the ground as I ran back into the cabin. I got the small marrowbone mage tool set that Eimer had pulled up from under the floorboards. They had shown it to me back at the castle: two mallets, one large and one small; various metal clamps; wooden awls.

"Usually when someone breaks their finger in a natural way, it is one of the segments coming out of the joint, the most common break being the one at the base of the finger." Eimer touched the base of the man's left pointer finger. He looked down at where Eimer was pressing into his skin, confused as if a strange bug had landed on his hand. "But with innate magic, the bone itself needs to break, not just become loose. For small bones, what we are aiming for is something like a stress fracture. It requires precision." Eimer took the tools from me and unrolled them atop a textbook. They took the small mallet and an awl in one hand. With their other hand, they guided the man to lay his left hand flat against the table. Once that was done they held the awl over the segment on the man's left pointer finger. When they brought the mallet down he screamed, a scream that cut through the woods and seemed to make the trees shake. Birds flew off and the bushes rustled, as if every prey animal in the area had heard the warning and was now fleeing on instinct.

Once the initial scream was over the man kept keening but gritted his teeth, trying to keep the pained sounds from escaping. He tried to hold his injured left hand, but Eimer wouldn't let him—they grabbed hold of it.

"See? See how the index finger is askew thanks to that break, but only from the point of the break on? See how I didn't pierce the skin, and how the bone didn't puncture it either?"

"Yes, yes, I see," I said quickly, as if my quick agreement might help ease the man's pain. "But what about the magical component? What kind of spell did you do?"

Eimer shook their head. "Spell? That was just to show you how the break itself needs to be done."

A rush of anger went through me at that. It felt like we'd made this old man suffer for nothing.

"Jesus Christ!" I said. "This is just torture!"

"It's to *teach* you," Eimer said. "We can stop at any time."

I stood there, feeling like my anger would melt the snow. Some of that anger was for Eimer, but most of it was for me. The fingernails on my right hand had begun to grow back, but they were stubby things. I could still remember how it had felt when Van Holt had removed them, how I'd prayed to God for help. And now I stood by the side of a man going through similar torment, and I did nothing.

I told myself that I'd make it up to the man, that the whole nation of Great Britain would owe him a great debt once this was done.

"Now, for the magical component, as you say, we need to think of a small effect," Eimer said. "Like . . . 'everyone you meet will like you.' It can be a kind of charm spell like that or even heal some physical ailment. It could also alter a quirk of someone's personality."

"But . . . but intent and will are a big part of magic," I said. "For this to work, it has to be something this bloke actually *wants*."

Eimer gave a half nod, a gesture of theirs I had come to recognize as *you're right but you're also wrong*. "Consent is the key more than want, though want helps. When I returned to this town I laid out what would happen out here, and the people agreed to it."

The old man in the chair was sweating bullets and breathing short, pained bursts from between clenched teeth, but he was still sitting in the chair, a determined cast on his face. Maybe Eimer was right. Maybe the townspeople knew what they were getting into better than even I did.

"All right, so the spell we'll be practising is a simple little physiological one. A good thing for you to practise. The break we'll be doing is so that this fella never suffers a hangover again in his life."

The mundaneness of it left me speechless for a moment. "*That's* the spell we're doing?"

"That's right. I used to have a cracking practice doling out this spell, back in the days when innate magic was legal." Innate magic had been illegal in Britain since the 1600s, soon after that in Ireland, but I didn't have time to ask Eimer about it before they spoke again. "This is old hat for me, but I want to know how *you* would do it."

"Well, I guess there are several ways to go about it. You could monkey paw it, make it so the person can't get drunk, let alone hungover."

"If I had done it like that, I would have been run out of town. C'mon, think of a more genuine way to go about it."

"We'll make him immune to poison," I said. "That's pretty much what being drunk is, right?" If I could devise a spell like that, I could use it on Kitty to further protect her.

Eimer scrunched up their face. "That could work. What I would usually do is give them slightly better regenerative abilities, but we can try your way. You'll need to break a small bone for that, a middle phalanx at least. On the pinkie finger."

It was nerve racking for both the old man and me, but I managed to bring my hammer down in such a way that the finger was broken correctly. I had to be careful handling his broken pinkie but eventually I felt like I was able to shift something inside him and allow a new magic to take root.

The old man had stopped crying out, but he was pretty damn pale.

"Let's stop here for today," Eimer said. "If he survives the night, tomorrow we'll make him a mage maker."

~

In the morning the old man was pale and trembling—not from fear but from the effects of the previous day. Eimer brewed some kind of concoction and had him drink it. The act of doing so brought him back to his senses, and he met our gaze with a grim smile.

It was a cold, grey day but Eimer still insisted we do the work outside.

"I suppose it would be best if I showed you how it's done." Eimer smiled. "Though I did show you once already."

"Yes, quite a long time ago."

"True. Best we do a refresher." Eimer picked up my mallet and awl. "With this break it's a small but specific intent. For this you need to break the second segment to get the result. Like so." They brought the mallet down on the awl. The man merely made a whimper when the bone broke, as though he were screamed out after everything he'd gone through yesterday.

"Did . . . it work?" I asked. I suppose I'd been expecting some grand sight, a flash of light or a halo shining above the man's head. But he seemed the same as before; the magical aura around him hadn't changed.

"Well, I broke the bone, if that's what you mean," Eimer said. "But I didn't do the spell."

"What?" I had thought Eimer was going to demonstrate it for me. "Why not?"

"So that you can take a crack at it, to pardon the pun." They handed me the mallet and awl. Gingerly I took them.

"But to get the magical effect . . ."

"Keep in mind the effect you want: for him to be able to make other mages," Eimer said. "You know how with cloth magic it helps to try and weave in attributes from nature? Try and hold an image in your mind that conceptualizes what you're doing here."

I thought it over. What came to me was the idea of a spring of water, unending. We usually thought of magic as a circuit, but I wanted this old man to be able to share what he had, to be no longer a closed loop but overflowing.

The man seemed barely conscious but his eyes followed the hammer as I lifted it up.

I brought it down and heard the faintest crack. The old man let out a huff, as though he'd just stubbed his toe. My hands were shaking because I could feel the deeper change within him, a new hum of magical energy. The man must have felt it too. His eyes widened and his face flushed. He leaned over the side of the chair and threw up his breakfast. I stepped back just in time before any of it could land on my shoes.

"It . . . worked?" I said, looking to Eimer. "I mean, I remember feeling sick after you did it to me—"

Before I could finish speaking something changed within the old man. He started shaking as though he were experiencing a very localized earthquake. He clutched the side of his chair and started vomiting again, a deep-purple sludge coming out of him.

"Jesus Christ!" I didn't know whether to go to him or to run away, so instead I just stood there, watching as more came out of him. It seemed like I recognized the things coming out of him, at least in abstract: lungs, as flat as a sail on a windless day; chunks of bone; veins whipping around like live wires. "Eimer! Help him! Please, stop this somehow!"

They did. They stepped forwards, knife in hand, and cut the man's neck. The deluge stopped as he slumped forwards, blood still letting out of him like a thin curtain. He had been a pretty strong man for his age but his frame was depleted, the skin sunken in on itself.

In the stillness the smell suddenly hit me. My head swam and I stumbled back, blanking out just long enough to fall backwards onto the snow. It felt like my own insides were liquefying, like any moment now I'd throw up my organs in a pile next to the man's. Oh God, what had I done?

Eimer glanced over at me.

"Don't take it too hard," they said. "The first time never goes right."

~

That night I watched with a mix of amazement and disdain as Eimer gnawed charred meat off a boar's leg. The old man had brought it with him when he'd arrived the day before and Eimer had cooked it over a spit in the yard.

"How can you eat after seeing that?" I said. They shrugged.

"Can't lose heart now," they replied and gestured to my plate. "Eat up. Tomorrow morning another villager will come."

"Is that the plan, then? Just have these poor people show up one after another till the magic takes?" I asked. "Jesus Christ, that is literally no different from the mage making ritual in Britain! You were supposed to show me a different way!"

"I will. I am," Eimer said tersely. "But it's not so simple."

"Maybe you're just a bad teacher," I said with almost childish spite.

"Maybe, but I'm the only one you've got," Eimer said. They put down the boar leg. "The thing about magic is that it's largely guided by intent, but part of that depends on what you already believe. We all grow up hearing about magic and what it's capable of, but we grow up hearing different things. That is what allows some people to do things, others not. Magic is a mindset. The mages of Britain are raised believing that the only way to create a new protomage is to kill a dozen people or so before the magic takes hold. So for them, that's the way it is."

"Then am I doomed?" I asked. "I'm a British mage."

"But from a young age you *knew* there was another way, didn't you?"

They paused, watching me curiously, a slight smile on their face.

"Yes," I said, "because I met you."

"Exactly, child!" Eimer said. "You didn't know the hows and whys of it, but you knew there were other mage makers out there than the ones sanctioned by the British Crown. So no matter what happens, hold on to that."

"All right, so even if I know that there's more than one way . . . I still don't know *a* way. When are you going to show me that?"

Eimer shook their head. "That's where it gets a mite tricky. For this to work, it needs to be *your* way. You will find the key you need to make protomages. Maybe it's something you have to do for it to work, or maybe it only works when you do it on a specific type of person. As we try it again, we'll take note of all the different variables, see what overlaps."

It amused me to hear Eimer, usually so mystical, talking in the language of science. Then the deeper meaning of their words got to me.

"You talk like we're going to do this multiple times," I said. I thought of how in the twilight I'd dug the old man's grave right on the border of the yard and the forest, shoulders straining to break up the near-frozen ground. I had wanted to send the body back to town so his family could pay their respects and bury him in a proper cemetery, but Eimer had said no: "The people know what's going on out here, but seeing it would just cause trouble for everyone." How many more graves did Eimer expect me to dig?

"Who knows? Maybe you'll get it right with the very next one," Eimer said with a shrug.

The next day an old woman came to the cabin and I broke her bones. First, a small finger break to give her the same healing spell I'd given the old man. After that Eimer said to make the mage maker break immediately. I did so, waiting anxiously to see if she would liquefy. She did not. Instead she screamed as her skin crisped up: it crackled as though she were in an oven, heat radiating off her even as it started snowing.

"Well, that's it," I said. "I'm done."

Eimer actually rolled their eyes at me, as if I were throwing a fit over spilled milk rather than murder.

"It takes time," they said. "You just need to figure out a way that works for you—"

"No." I left the still-smoking body in the yard and went back into the cabin. Eimer followed me in. The old lady had brought a dark bottle of rather yeasty beer. I took a swig from it, the carbonation sending prickles down my throat. Eimer stood in the open doorway, arms crossed as they stared at me.

"Why can't you just tell me how you do it?" I said. "You said the magic works because mages believe in it, because they're taught a certain way and take those teachings to be truth. If you explained that, it would take hold then, right? I'd be like, *Oh, well, Eimer does it this way, and they not only made me a mage maker but taught me how to go about it—*"

"You don't want to do it the way I do it," Eimer said.

"Why not? Surely it's better than killing a bunch of old people!"

"You don't want to do it the way I do it," Eimer repeated. "Remember how I said that for some mages, they can only make new mage makers out of certain types of people. So you are right: if I told you it would probably take. But you don't want to."

"How could it be so bad?" But even as I spoke I was thinking it over: Eimer could only make certain people mage makers, but they had made *me* a mage maker. So what type was it then? Brunets? Scousers? Men?

No—I hadn't been a man when we'd met. I'd been a boy. A child.

Eimer didn't answer my question—they could see from my face that I had come to my own conclusion.

"Don't say it, and don't think any more on it," Eimer said. "I mean it. Putting it into words will only give it power and only hinder you further."

But how could I *not* think about it? Both of the people I'd tried to transform so far had been elderly, people with grey hair and gnarled hands. What if it hadn't worked because I could only transform children? And what if it didn't even take, but because of how I'd grown up hearing about the UK mage making ritual, I had to kill a dozen kids before getting a new mage maker? Not only was that monstrous, but it wasn't even a better alternative to what the country already had. Why even keep trying if it was all fucked?

Eimer sighed. "I should leave."

That caught my attention.

"Leave? To get supplies? Or talk to the villagers?" I asked. "How long will it take you? When will you be back?" Eimer often flitted away, off doing who knew what. It wasn't odd for them to leave, but it was odd for them to announce that they were leaving.

"I'm not coming back," they said. "I've taught you what you need to know—"

"Apparently not!" I said, gesturing out to the front yard, where the woman's corpse still sat.

"—and my presence here might be detrimental to you."

"Well, you're not exactly a barrel of laughs, but I wouldn't go that far." Eimer always made me uneasy even if I was desperately curious about them. They fed into both those feelings by constantly making cryptic comments or dropping little bon mots about history or magic. There were times when we got along swimmingly, such as when we were poring over textbooks, and times when we were practically at each other's throats, like when we fought over whose turn it was to use the good spoon. But as infuriating as they were, I still would rather have their presence there than nothing at all.

They went up to the loft and retrieved the folk costume I'd worn the day I'd come to the cabin, the one used for teleportation. They undressed and I turned away to give them some privacy, not that I could see much from my spot on the lower level of the cabin.

"Why exactly are you leaving?" I said, anger making my voice clipped.

"Maybe I'm the reason you haven't succeeded yet," Eimer speculated. "Maybe by going it alone, you'll have a breakthrough."

"But you'll come back to check on me?" I said, now more worried than angry. I imagined a hundred awful fates: *I catch botulism from fruit in the cellar that's gone off. I fall from the ladder that leads to the loft and break my neck. I'm torn apart by the villagers who have had enough of this mad wizard in the woods.*

Eimer didn't answer. When I finally turned around to look at them the loft was empty. Eimer was already gone.

~

Several weeks went by, turning into months. Every few days a different villager would arrive and I'd turn them away. As I ushered them down the path away from the cabin they seemed a mix of confused, afraid, and relieved. I also had mixed feelings—I didn't want any more blood on my hands, so I was sure of my call to send the villagers away. But a sense of urgency was growing in my breast, making my heart beat fast at random times. Back at Windsor Castle, everyone was counting on me to have some kind of breakthrough, to come back and be able to give others the same power I had. But I couldn't do it if it meant murdering the whole local population. I felt stuck, unable to do anything but unwilling to go back to Windsor.

The cabin didn't have any alcohol in it beyond the one beer the old lady had brought, which was probably a good thing since I might have disappeared into the bottle. I didn't want to stray too far from the property—wolves howled at night and I was afraid of getting lost in the woods. So instead I escaped into physical activity, chopping down trees like a beaver trying to build a palace. There was no radio to listen to, no books to read save for the anatomical textbooks. I talked aloud to myself, and when that wasn't enough to entertain me I partitioned off a part of my mind and pretended it was a telly, one that I had no control over. It would show me memories and little made-up stories, silly stuff that would make me laugh and delight me. "That was a good memory," I'd say. "I wonder what's on next."

In one of my few moments of self-awareness and reflection I thought about how I had never truly spent any significant period of time alone. Growing up I'd had my family: my mother, my father, my brothers, Thomas included. And then as young men Thomas and I had lived cheek to jowl in those tiny rented rooms and apartments. When Thomas had left I'd been quick to move in with Tonya—at the time I would have said it was because we were in love, but the reality was that I couldn't function without someone to bolster me. And then when Tonya had finally left me, I'd jumped at Laura Spratt's offer to be her tenant, because even though I'd be living alone in the cottage, I'd liked the idea of people nearby in the main house. Now that I was truly alone, save for the dead, I was terrified.

I was walking around the yard, muttering to myself about how pathetic I was, when Harriet arrived.

CHAPTER 36

"Professor Gallagher!" she said, seemingly more surprised than even I was. I guess I was a pretty sorry sight. My coat was stained with blood and other fluids—no matter how much I tried to clean it the stains remained, but I didn't have a huge wardrobe and couldn't afford to be picky. Often in the evenings I would just strip down and do my chores in the cabin in nothing more than my pants and undershirt—once I had accepted that Eimer wasn't coming back it felt like I could get away with such slovenliness. Even the cold didn't bother me anymore.

Luckily, Harriet hadn't caught me in my skivvies, but I was wearing a badly stained shirt under a ragged jacket. My hair was in need of a trim and for the first time in my life a beard had taken hold on my face. The cabin didn't even have a mirror, so I had no idea how it looked.

"Oh, Professor!" She'd been standing on top of the frozen flower bed, but now she rushed over. Harriet looked wonderfully put together; the coat was a close enough fit, and the embroidered flowers on it gave her a healthy glow. Her wavy brown hair was pulled to the side by a blue ribbon. There was a faint smell of a perfume that was popular amongst the ladies at Windsor Castle. I saw that her left arm was no longer in a cast. Right. It had been two months since I'd broken her arm in the mage making ritual.

"Did it work?" I asked, then realized she needed more context. "The ritual to make you a cloth mage, I mean?"

"Oh, yes! I'm wearing the first dress I made!" She took off her coat to show me the linen dress she was wearing underneath. It was a simple shirtdress with odd black lines crisscrossing it. "I made the pattern using the old radiators around the castle! It keeps me warm even when it gets drafty!"

It obviously wasn't enough to keep her warm outside though, and she shrugged the heavy jacket back on.

She stepped forwards to touch my cheek, either to comfort me or to see what my whiskers felt like. "Please. Tell me you are all right."

I blinked at her, not used to talking to another person. "Of course I am, now that you're here." I meant for it to sound charming, but when you're used to talking to yourself the meter gets thrown off: you speed up and slur words, coherence a low priority since *you* always know what you're trying to say. So what I actually said to Harriet sounded more like: *OF COURSE Iamnow thatyYERhere.*

Harriet gave me a half-hearted smile that couldn't cover up the worry in her eyes. Gently she took my hand.

"Can we talk in there?" she said with a nod towards the cabin. "It's rather bright outside."

I wanted to make a joke about how in England we weren't used to such sun so of course Harriet wanted to escape it as soon as she could, but I couldn't quite make it come together. Instead, I returned her nod and we walked hand in hand into the cabin.

Harriet sat down before peering around, as if using the lower vantage point to get a good look at the rafters.

"This place is charmingly rustic," she said.

"Yeah," I replied. I was just glad the graves were on the other side of the cabin, opposite to the gardens and front yard.

"Have you been here alone this whole time?"

"No. Eimer was here now and then. But they left when I wasn't able to make it work." I sat down and started telling Harriet about how the villagers had come here one after another, like lambs to the slaughter, and described how the first two had died. Oddly enough, even though the subject matter was upsetting, the act of talking felt good, and as the words came out I felt like I could finally remember how to speak to another human being, when to pause and when to emphasize certain words. Harriet listened intently, even though she looked pained when I spoke of the deaths.

"And now you're here," I said. "So you're pretty much all caught up on my failures."

"Professor, you mustn't be so hard on yourself—"

"For fuck's sake, Harriet, people are dead!" I'd never yelled at her before. She shrank in her chair, the big coat she was still wearing puffing up around her like a protective buffer. I felt a flush of shame. She'd only been trying to help me, but her sympathetic platitudes had set me off.

"I'm sorry," I said. "I didn't mean to shout like that. It's been a tough time."

"Professor, forget all this," Harriet said, still drawing back in her chair, as if afraid I'd lash out. "You don't need this magic, but we need you back at Windsor Castle. Everyone is always fighting and no one can agree on a thing. I know if you were there, you could make sure everyone got along."

"Well, that's very sweet of you to say, but if I'm to be Court Magician, I *do* need this kind of magic. The British public isn't just going to take my word that I'm good for it." I flexed my fingers and sighed as I looked down at my hands. "Jesus, I just hope it's all worth it."

We sat in silence for a while.

"Do you know what your father did during the war, Harriet?"

"Of course! In the Great War he was a young man in the trenches, and in the second war he was in France—"

"Until he was sent back home to help with the Department of Magic Regulation," I said. "Do you know that part of the story?"

Harriet was silent.

"He worked with a politician named James Godfrey and Dr Myers, Oberon's dad, to try and find a new magical weapon, something like the artificial Superconductors Russia had. They experimented on little children, thinking their purity was the key. But it never took. They killed at least three kids that I know of, but probably many more. When I first learned about it, I felt so sick. Sick to be living in the same world as those men, as if I were complicit just from sharing the same air as them. I couldn't conceive of such evil. But now . . . I hate that I can see where they were coming from. I've tried so hard not to become them. I stopped after the second villager died. But I don't know what to do now."

Harriet still had no words, but she sat up a little straighter in her chair, no longer shrinking away from me. The silence lingered, broken by the sound of a bird chirping in the woods.

"Harriet, I killed your dad," I said.

"I know, Professor."

"Ah." Of course she knew. "How long have you known?"

"Since before I met you," Harriet said. "James Godfrey told me."

That made me look up sharply. "You've *met* James Godfrey?"

She nodded. "Shortly after I left the asylum, Peter brought me to meet him. Mr Godfrey told me stories about my father. He also told me how you'd killed him, as part of a ritual to bring Godfrey back to life. That you and my father were friends. I decided to study cloth magic because I thought it might help me get close to you—Fairweather and Godfrey encouraged it. And then Fairweather had the plan where I'd stay at Mrs Spratt's so I could spy on you. And I also wanted to get closer to you for my own reasons."

"Like what, exactly? Revenge?"

"Well, no." Harriet fidgeted with her hair. "More like to satisfy my own curiosity, I suppose. My father, he was always so distant. I never really felt like he loved me or my brother or even my mother. Godfrey had implied that . . . that my father might have loved you. So I wanted to meet someone my father had actually loved and see what made them special."

My heart broke for her. "Oh, Harriet, he never loved me. All that made me special in his eyes was that he had a use for me . . ." And he'd had no use for his family, aside from the cover they'd given him, the image of a perfect domestic life. Perhaps he had loved Godfrey, but rather than face the fact that he'd loved another man so deeply, he had dressed it up as admiration and obscured his goal of resurrecting the man as an act of patriotism. But when he was young, before Godfrey's death, maybe he had truly believed in their cause. Really believed that they were doing right by killing those children. They were in the middle of a war against Nazi Germany. It would have been so easy to justify those deaths. And I'd fallen into the same mindset.

"Men can do the evilest things if they think they are in the right," I said aloud.

"You're talking about my father," Harriet said.

"I'm talking about myself."

We were quiet for a few minutes.

"I don't think I can go back to England," I said. "There's something wrong with me, with the magic within me. I'm just as bad as Godfrey, doing horrible things with nothing worthwhile to balance the scales. The lot of you back in Windsor are better off without me."

"Please, Professor! Don't talk like that." Tears shone in Harriet's eyes. She leaned forwards to cover my hands with her right one. "There were plenty of times in my life when I felt that way. When I was in the asylum, it was awful, but the worst part was knowing that I couldn't protect my brother, that I failed him and was useless. But eventually I got out of there and . . ." Her voice trailed off, perhaps because the story didn't quite have a triumphant ending: Sure, Harriet was out of the asylum, but now she was a rebel against king and country. It was unlikely she'd be reunited with her brother anytime soon. She brightened. "But I haven't given up hope, Professor, and you mustn't either. There was a time when the pain of my failure just seemed like too much, how I hadn't been strong enough when my family needed me. But I told myself that I couldn't make amends if I were dead, that as long as I was alive I would someday see Troy again. I still believe that we will win this war and I'll be with my brother again. But to do that, we need you, Professor. Not because of what you can do but *because* you're you. Please, come home."

She was quiet, as if giving me space to stand up and say that she was right. Instead the silence lingered. Harriet drew back and grew thoughtful.

"The people you tried to transform," she said gingerly, "you never told me their names."

"What?" I said, as startled by her question as I was by the sudden shift in topic. "No, I never got their names." Early on Eimer had stressed that we should keep our distance from the villagers.

"Oh. Well, it just seems to me that's so unlike you," Harriet said. "You usually try to be so accommodating with people, really try to see them for themselves. It seems odd that you wouldn't do that here, even with people who don't speak the same language as you. Maybe if you had . . ." She thought better of her words and bit her tongue. But it was enough. Maybe if I hadn't followed Eimer's lead and had actually gotten to know the people who came here, things would have been different. Wasn't that the basis for my own innate magic? That it made people like me and made me want to please them? The trigger for it was the act of introducing myself, and I hadn't done that with a single one of those poor souls who'd come out here.

Eimer had spoken of how I needed to find my type. What if it wasn't strangers but friends? Hope started to spark within me, turning into excitement.

"Harriet," I said. She looked at me, sensing the gravity in my tone. "I have no right to ask this, and you have every right to say no. But if you allow it, I believe I can make you a protomage."

"*Me*, Professor?" she said in an excited—or perhaps nervous—squeak.

"Yes. You know the risks—I can show you the graves if you need to see them for yourself—but, well, with you showing up like this and the way I know my own magic works, I really believe it's fate."

Do you know where the word happy *comes from?* Hollister's voice echoed through my head. A shiver ran through me. Was I about to visit the same crime upon a new generation? Would she die under my hands like Hollister had? A small, dark part of me felt a sick relish at the thought—if Harriet died I would feel truly anguished, a punishment due me for the deaths I'd already caused and felt numb over. But I shook that feeling off. Harriet deserved more in this world than to serve to teach me a lesson.

Also, I knew in my bones that this time it would work. I'd finally hit upon the type of person I could transform into a mage maker—not strangers, not candidates on a state-approved list, but people I cared about. I couldn't just turn anyone into a mage maker; it had to be someone dear to me. I remembered the feeling I'd felt when I'd first laid eyes upon Harriet, that she'd been sent by God to aid me. I felt that now again, even surer and stronger.

Harriet's face was pale but her gaze was steady as her eyes met mine. She nodded.

"Yes, Professor. If you really will give me this gift, then I will accept it."

I didn't take the chairs outside. This time I would do it inside the cabin—there would be no mess to clean up this time. I didn't do the first finger break that I'd done with the others. Harriet was already a mage, so she'd had a bone magically broken before. We traded a glance and a smile before I brought the hammer down.

~

Harriet felt unwell that night, a fever burning lightly before breaking at noon the next day. She looked at me with clear eyes, amazed.

"Just like that, I'm a mage maker?" she said.

"Well, you have the capabilities," I said, speaking like a true expert now that I'd successfully done it. "But I still have to teach you *how* to do it."

Harriet nodded eagerly, eyes bright even though her face was still worryingly pale. "Can you teach me now?"

"I will, someday," I told Harriet. I'd been away from Windsor Castle for so long; I didn't want to delay getting back. Plus, I barely had a handle on my power—I didn't think I knew enough yet to teach Harriet how to use it. "But in the meantime I will teach you other things about magic. I know you're already making magic clothes, but there's still so much to learn!"

Harriet nodded, still too drunk on her new power to be truly disappointed. We had a large supper that night, clearing out what was left in the cellar. Harriet slept in the bed in the loft, while I rolled out the extra mattress on the ground floor. It was the same one the old man had slept in that night he'd stayed with us. Even though it looked clean I swore I could smell the man's lingering sweat, a scent of fear. Sleep came fitfully, but I felt the need to do it, to feel close to my first victim, to remind myself of the human life lost. I'd find out his name and the name of the woman who'd come after him. I fell asleep making promises about how I'd make things right someday.

The next morning Harriet and I followed the path to a main road and saw a bus trundle down it. Seeing such a modern vehicle after weeks of being in the woods was a shock. Like a curious animal, it slowed to a stop in front of us, its doors opening with a huff as if it were sniffing us. The driver, a young man with a friendly but curious look, asked us something in German. Harriet and I looked at each other, embodying the worst British stereotype: we didn't know a single language other than English. The man sighed.

"Are you heading for Munich?" he asked in English.

I wasn't sure if riding the bus was the right call or not—surely the village had to be close by, since the elderly had always arrived on foot. But as I didn't truly know where to go or even where we were, I figured our best bet was to climb on. We found a couple of empty seats near the back. I heard people speaking English. They spoke of beer halls and the skiing in the Alps. They all had American accents, and it seemed to be either groups of young men or older men with their wives. Realization snapped into place when I noticed one older gent frowning at my messy hair—he had a military buzz cut, as did many of the young men. They were all American soldiers and their wives who'd been stationed in West Germany, doing a little spring sightseeing.

We drove for hours. Eventually the dark woods and hills gave way to flat farmland, which was beautiful in its own right: dusk had fallen and in the red sunset the light spring snow glistened like a rainbow. Tiny towns broke up the flat horizon.

The bus pulled into one of the little villages, stopping near the main square. It was dark now, but the town was cheery, illuminated up by soft light coming from the small bars and restaurants surrounding the town square. I took it all in while Harriet gave the bus driver some money to retroactively buy us bus tickets. Thank God she had brought some cash with her.

We found an abandoned farmhouse on the edge of town and slept the night there. It was cold and Harriet and I had to huddle for warmth. The conditions were miserable but one thought gave me comfort—soon, I'd be going home.

CHAPTER 37

The next day Harriet and I went into town and bought some sewing supplies and yellow fabric—it was clearly dyed hospital linen. The sight and feel of it made me flash back to my childhood during the worst point of wartime rationing. The German town we'd found ourselves in was charming but faded, still clearly reeling from the war even ten years on. The old granny we bought the fabric from eagerly snatched the money from us and hid it in the pocket of her apron, as if someone might take it from her.

I had Harriet hold the fabric and think of me. I would have liked a larger sample size, but as she was the only person in town who knew me, it would have to do. Eventually I felt a kind of hum from the fabric, a sense that something had taken hold in the cloth. The effect I'd been going for was a teleportation cloak that would allow me to go to wherever people were thinking of me, so I tried to hold everyone's faces in mind as I worked on it in the farmhouse. When it was done I had a lightweight yellow coat, its top jacket shape taking a few cues from the jacket Naveed often wore, the lower half hemmed with some lace that I'd found that had reminded me of Rosemary. I hoped these little touches would help further connect me to them.

Harriet and I tested out the distance: She'd stand in the woods. She'd stand in an alleyway. She'd stand in the middle of a nearby field. Each time she'd think of me, and I'd feel it from where I was. To go to her I merely had to focus on the feeling. It was a thin but firm connection, like a silk thread, and by mentally tugging on it I'd find myself teleported to wherever Harriet was.

"Oh, Professor, it truly works!" she said when I'd appeared in the otherwise empty parking lot.

"Of course it does." I wanted to sound assured but my giddy smile betrayed my delight. "Now we can go back to England."

Harriet looked worried. "Will it really work across such a great distance? What if something goes wrong . . ."

"It will work," I said, taking her hands in mine. "This magic is based on the bonds between us, on the space I take up in your heart. As long as you hold me in your thoughts, Harriet, I'll make my way to you."

Harriet's face glowed up at me, all doubts obliterated. To someone on the outside looking in, it might have looked like a love confession, but it wasn't like that. Harriet had come through for me when I was at my lowest, and even though she'd seen me at my worst, her admiration hadn't diminished.

But she was still pragmatic.

"If something does go wrong," she said, "let's meet back at the cabin, all right?"

I nodded. It was a good backup plan: Harriet could use the folk-art jacket to get back there, while I could walk or take a bus. But I knew we wouldn't need to reconvene there: when I wore the jacket I felt Harriet's pull on me for sure, but not only her: faintly I could feel tugs from farther away, all the way, I suspected, in England. I did not feel anything from Windsor Castle, but that made sense since the castle was shielded from magic by our guards.

Harriet took a few steps away and closed her eyes. Then she was gone, just her footprints in the snow to show that she'd ever been there.

I took a deep breath, looked around, farming fields on my left, the town on my right. It felt odd to be leaving this country after being there for over two months but I was ready to go home.

Not only that, I could feel that the others back in England *wanted* me home. That tug pulling on me was growing stronger, and all I had to do was lean into it. The farmland around me melted away, replaced by the slate-grey and brick-red buildings of Slough. Cars zoomed around me—I was standing with Harriet in the middle of a roundabout.

"Professor!" she said, bounding over from where she'd been standing in a flower bed. We were on a round patch of grass the city had put in the middle of the roundabout in an attempt to freshen up the place. It hadn't worked—the grass hadn't had a chance to fully grow in yet so it just looked muddy. There was a flower bed where I guess Rosemary had planted the sunflower seed Eimer had given her.

When I opened my mouth to reply to Harriet I breathed in a lungful of petrol exhaust. After weeks of clean living the scent burned my throat and tickled my nose. I hacked for a few seconds before I could speak.

"Harriet," I said, straightening up. "Let's go back to the castle."

~

The guards at the castle entrance were surprised to see us, so much so they had us wait outside the gates while one of them got Thomas. I appreciated their caution: for all they knew we were two intruders wearing magic clothes to disguise themselves as Paul Gallagher and Harriet Hollister. Thomas emerged less than five minutes later, wearing a null cloak that would have let him see through any artifice. His eyes widened when he saw me. He speed-walked over to us and, to my surprise, embraced me. It was probably one of a handful of times in my life when Thomas had been the one to initiate a hug.

"Took you bloody long enough," he said, words muffled by my shoulder. Eventually he stepped back, gave a nod to Harriet. "Where have you been? What are you wearing? And what's with the beard?"

"Do you like it?"

Thomas tilted his head to the side. "You look different," he said with a frown but didn't give me any more guff about my facial hair. He led us into the castle courtyard.

As we walked briskly Thomas caught us up on the events of the last few months: As the war had gone on, more servants had left the castle. The Parkeesh family had brought more of their own servants in, which had further alienated the stalwart Windsor staff, who saw the castle as their turf.

"This is all fascinating as a workplace drama," I said. "But do such tiffs really have any effect on the fate of the whole country?"

They sure fucking did, Thomas told me hotly. Lady Fife was rarely at Windsor Castle these days as she was travelling the country trying to shore up support for our cause. In her absence, the Parkeesh matriarch, Naveed's formidable grandmother Elspeth, had taken charge of things. This had led to rumours that the Parkeesh family was trying to get Kitty on the throne so they could rule the country through her.

"Wait, who's been saying this?"

Oberon. And Oberon was so convinced that the Parkeesh family was up to no good that he'd contacted his cousin Sabina and told her they were trying to wrest control of the crown away from her unborn child. In a panic, Sabina had left her hiding place and hoofed it to Windsor Castle. She was now here with her American cousin.

"Her American cousin? You don't mean . . ."

Yes. Tonya was here at Windsor Castle.

~

I came upon Sabina and Tonya together in the castle library. Sabina was looking well, wearing a floor-length, wine-coloured maternity dress. Last time I'd seen her she'd been barely showing, but now she looked like she could give birth any day (not that I really knew much about pregnancy or babies). The sight of her round stomach gave me a rush of worry—we hadn't told the public about Arthur's secret marriage or his unborn child. Having such a visual reminder of that fact stressed me out.

Sabina scowled at the panicked expression on my face.

"*There* you are, Mr Gallagher! I was quite shocked when I arrived here and you were nowhere to be found."

"Well, I was quite shocked to come back and find you here," I said. "Sabina, why did you come out of hiding? It was best for you to stay where it's safe—"

"So you can continue to give away my child's birthright?" Sabina said, hands on her stomach. "Oberon told us that you already gave away Ireland. What are you planning to trade away next?"

"I didn't give away Ireland—"

"Obie says that you made a promise with some Irish terrorist, that you'd give them anything in return for greater magic."

"Look, it's a little more complicated than that—"

"Well, I'm here to make sure that you don't give away any more of my son's kingdom."

That gave me pause. "How do you know it's a boy?"

Sabina smiled, looking down as if the babe were already in her arms. "I just know."

"She's going by old wives' tales," Tonya said. She was wearing a lavender V-neck sweater, a pleated skirt, and black tights. She'd cut her hair—it was now in a stylish bob. She had a navy-blue beret askew on her head, and when she turned I saw she was fiddling with an extremely long necklace—the whole look seemed both modern and classic, a New York spin on the flappers of old. "Say, Sabina, could you give me and Paul a moment? We have a lot to catch up on."

Sabina looked like she wanted to lecture me some more, but eventually she let out a huff and left the library. I waited until the sound of her footsteps had faded away to speak.

"Tonya, what are you doing here?"

"That's quite the harsh hello, chum," she said, her voice relatively amicable considering the way we'd ended things. She sat down in a plush chair.

"Why are you here, Tonya?" I said. "I can get why Sabina came back, but why are you here in England?"

"I don't need to account for myself to you, Paul. I can go where I want." Now some heat was coming into her voice.

"Oh, so you decided to come to a country you hate that's in the middle of a civil war?"

"A civil war that has my cousin at the centre of it."

"Since when do you give a damn about her?" I asked. "All the time you lived here, you never sought your cousins out, never tried to have some big family reunion. Heck, Sabina was a bitch to you whenever you were in the same room! I remember that! So why are you with her now?"

Tonya traced a pattern on her arm. "She came to me," she said. "A few months ago she showed up at my apartment, pregnant and without a friend in the world. So I took her in."

Right, Sabina had said that she had a place to go, but it just wasn't somewhere she *wanted* to go. New York City was actually a brilliant place to hide—a port city full of millions of people, including Sabina's secret cousin. "I hope she appreciated you taking her in."

Tonya gave me a half smile. "She did. She's not the easiest person to get along with, but she's just trying to protect herself and her child. I will admit, though, I *was* relieved when she decided it was time to go back to England. She's an awful houseguest. Towels on the floor, food left out, you name it." She tilted her head. "I came back here to support Sabina, but it's not my only reason for being here. There is something I want from you."

"Oh?" I said, intrigued but a little scared.

"Yes. I want you to make me a Book Binder."

I certainly hadn't been expecting that. "You what?"

"I got so used to using magic Books while I was here in Britain, and when I went back to America, not having them around . . . well, it was a pain in the ass. So I want to learn how to make magic Books, and when I go back to the States I'll more or less have a monopoly on them."

"You want to be a mage," I said, just to state it clearly. Tonya glared at me, as if looking to see if I was doubting her. "I can do it," I said, and her posture relaxed somewhat, "but you'll have a broken arm for weeks. And I'm not a Book Binder myself, so I can't show you the ropes."

"That's all right; there are plenty of other mages who can teach me."

We were silent for a moment before Tonya looked away.

"I'm sorry about your father," she said softly. "He was a gem of a man. I know it must have cost you a lot, losing him."

Being reminded of my father's death made me think of Laura, of the many days we'd spent in the wake of his passing, her listening to me when the grief was at its worst or us going out for picnics and outings on the days when I just wanted to push all dark thoughts away.

I felt like such a bad son in that moment, because as much as I missed my father, I missed Laura more.

"Yes, thank you," I got out, my voice rough.

Her hand dropped. "When I went back to New York, I saw my mother for the first time in years."

I searched her face for clues, but she was looking away from me. "Saw your mother? You mean, you went and visited her grave?"

"No. I went and saw the woman herself," Tonya said.

I was still confused. "But your mother's dead . . ." Both of them—the woman who'd given birth to her had died the day Tonya had been born, while the woman who'd raised her had died shortly before Tonya had left New York the first time.

"No, she's very much alive," Tonya said, quickly and lightly, as if trying to breeze past an uncomfortable truth. "Not Abigail Myers. Shelly. The maid that David Myers gave me to, Oberon's birth mother. I know I might have made it out otherwise—"

"Made it out?! You outright said she had drunk herself to death!"

"And when I left New York the first time, she was well on her way to doing so," Tonya replied. "There were times growing up when she was awful to me, Paul. Just awful. And even when she was at her best, she could barely look after herself, let alone me. So when I left America to come here, as far as I was concerned she was dead to me. I'd tell everyone she was dead and have nothing to do with her again."

"I . . . see." I didn't see. I thought of all the years Tonya and I had spent together and how she'd always referred to her mother in the past tense.

Tonya saw the disbelief on my face.

"There was another reason why I acted like my mom was dead, but if I tell you I just know you'll put me on a pedestal and completely warp everything I just said." Tonya twisted her hands in her lap. "So just to be clear, I said my mom was dead because as far as I was concerned, she was. That would have been the case regardless of if I had stayed in New York or gone to Timbuktu rather than London, got it, chum?"

"Yeah, got it."

"But . . . well, there was also a practical consideration for telling everyone that Mom had kicked the bucket," Tonya said. "I didn't know what type of man David Myers was, only that he was a ruthless murderer. I worried that if he knew that Mom was still alive in New York City, he'd send someone after her."

"Oh!" Now *that* made sense to me. Tonya had treated her mother as dead all these years because it was the only way to keep her alive. She'd orphaned herself to protect her mother, a flawed woman who had barely been able to protect the child in her care. What a sacrifice Tonya had made, using her callousness to cover up how much she actually cared.

"Hey! You're doing it!" she said, jabbing a finger in my face. "I can see it in your eyes. You're performing some kind of mental canonization even when I *told you* not to. I'm not a saint, Paul. Neither is my mother. But . . ." She took a deep breath. "When I arrived in New York, I sought her out. Wanted to see a familiar face, I guess." Tonya said the last part flatly, a dullness to her eyes, and I knew she was remembering those days following our breakup, when the heartbreak had been fresh. I knew I was the cause of that pain, but it wasn't the time to apologize. Tonya continued. "When I found her, she'd been sober for three years. Found religion." Her mouth quivered into a smile. "She apologized for failing as a mother . . . and I decided to let her back into my life."

"A resurrection of the dead," I said. "You performed a miracle. Maybe you are a saint after all."

Tonya gave me a wan smile before looking away once more.

"I heard that Oberon Myers is here," she said. "That's another reason I felt like I needed to come here in person. I needed to speak to him."

"Oberon?" Why would Tonya need to see Oberon? Then it came to me. "Ah."

"The night of the gala, I also told him that my mother—*his* mother—was dead. It was a little bit out of spite, some petty revenge aimed at my mom. But a little bit of it was done out of kindness for Oberon. I figured he was better off without her in his life." She gripped her hands tightly. "But that was the wrong call. So now I'm here to make things right."

"Have you told him yet?" I asked.

She nodded and a small smile graced her face.

I felt sick. Seeing Tonya again had brought back a whole ocean's worth of emotions: shame, lust, fondness. And now, from listening to her talk, a new current of jealousy. Both my parents were dead, but now, as though through magic, Tonya's mother had been restored to her. And not just Tonya's mother but Oberon Myers's mother! Why did other people get to have living parents while mine were in the ground?

"So what exactly is the endgame here, Paul?" she asked. "Even if you managed to get the Virtuis Party out, what next?"

"Well, I'm sure Sabina's told you. When her child is born, we'll announce them as Kitty's heir. When the child is eighteen, Kitty will abdicate, and—"

"And all of Britain will accept a mixed-race child as their ruler?" Tonya said with an incredulous twist to her mouth. "No way."

"Tonya, the British people—"

"Will never go for it." Tonya gave a laugh. "Oh, I know what you'll say, that I'm a jaded American, that things are *so* much better here."

"Well, I mean . . ." Tonya's glare cut me off.

"You know, once I was in an art gallery in London," she said. "I wasn't watching where I was going, and I bumped into a white guy. He immediately told me that I should 'go back to whatever island I came from.' When I told him off, saying that I wasn't from some island, I was American, his whole tune changed. His whole face lit up. 'Oh, you're American? No wonder you came here! They treat their Blacks so horribly over there.'" Tonya's shoulders slumped as if exhausted. "White Brits love to go on about how much better they are than the 'Yanks,' but they don't seem to realize that they're still pretty awful."

"Tonya, I know it won't be an easy road, but this was the best plan that Kitty, Lady Fife, and I could come up with—"

"Wow, three white people deciding to put all this on a Black child who isn't even here yet to defend themselves." She got to her feet. "I know Sabina's all gung-ho, but let the record state that I think this is a bad idea on just about every level."

~

Tonya's reappearance in my life dragged up some complicated feelings, but it wasn't like I had time to really deal with them: we were at war after all. As the former gossip columnist "Verity Turnboldt," Tonya was actually a great help, using her old contacts in the world of UK journalism to get us into a broadcasting studio.

"You need to sell the British public on you," she said. "You can't just be 'not the king' or 'not the Virtuis Party.' You have to offer something better."

So I went on television for the first time—an odd sensation, talking to a camera. I pretended I was speaking to a long-lost imaginary friend, one I hadn't seen since childhood. I introduced the nation to Harriet Hollister and explained that she was my apprentice and already had the ability to make more mages. Harriet stood next to me, shoulders back and chin high—becoming a protomage had done wonders for her self-confidence. Still, she looked young. It had caused a quiet uproar in the castle when everyone had found out that I'd given this power to Harriet, and there'd been debate over whether we should keep her abilities secret or not. In the end, I felt it was important to have the nation meet her. I wanted the world to know that I was the country's Court Magician, the only hope of magic continuing in the country.

After that, I moved on to the other arrow in our salvo. I talked about how our magic wouldn't rely on gaols or arrest quotas but instead one person.

At this point Princess Katherine stepped up onto the stage.

"I used innate magic on the princess in order to protect her, but she will put this power towards protecting the entire nation," I explained. Thomas stepped up onto the other side of the stage, a throwing knife in hand. We'd debated beforehand how best to demonstrate the princess's invincibility—we wanted to make sure we chose something that looked impressive but not cheap.

Thomas flipped the knife in his hand, then threw it at Kitty. She gave a gulp of fright but stood her ground even as the blade flew towards her. As it approached her it began to slow down, and then with a flick of her head it sailed off and embedded itself in a wall.

"This spell protects not only Princess Katherine but any country she stands upon," I explained to the viewers at home. This was a bit of a bluff on our part. In theory it could work, if Kitty practised. Thomas had been working with her to try and enlarge the field around her, in the hopes that someday she could in fact protect the country. I believed it would happen, but in the meantime I prayed that Godfrey didn't call our bluff by dropping bombs on us. "And I will teach others how to do this spell as well so that future rulers will likewise be able to act as guardians of the United Kingdom. We don't need to turn on each other or to treat ordinary citizens as criminals just so that the so-called law-abiding citizens can sleep in bed at night. I'm sure not one amongst you doesn't have a loved one in gaol right now, or you've seen the state they are in once they've been released. They are used-up shells of themselves. The current system is a machine that is always hungry. You can comfort yourself that you're safe, but once they need *you* in those prisons, nothing will stop the Virtuis Party. It doesn't have to be that way. There is a better way forwards—hell, for once it's even the easier way forwards. Doing the right thing doesn't always come at such a huge cost, aside from being brave enough to do it."

I realized I was starting to ramble, so I took a deep breath.

"Please, we need you in the streets, demanding that Parliament call a fair and free election. This may be our only chance to set things right."

After the camera stopped running Tonya came up to me. She took my hands in hers with a big smile.

"You were perfect."

~

Thomas had no such praise for me. He slipped away from us after the broadcast, but I didn't want to go back to the castle without him. I found him in a bar in Slough, a squadron of soldiers hanging back to act as bodyguards, trying pointedly to pretend that they didn't see Thomas absolutely sloshed.

"How did you drink so much so quickly?" I asked. Thomas shrugged.

"I knew I wouldn't have much time before you found me."

I knew that, if Thomas had wanted to stay hidden, he very well could have. He wanted me to find him, to talk.

"What's gotten into you?" I said. "The broadcast went well, right?"

Thomas swished his beer around in the glass. "You know, before this all went down, I'd left Lady Fife's service," he said. "It's not that I was tired of being a spy or that I'd fallen in love. It's because it seemed like all I was doing was keeping things level. I knew my work kept things from falling to shit, I knew that, but it never seemed to actually make things *better*."

I took the drink from his hand so I could have a swig.

"You really think it doesn't matter what we do here?" I said. "You'd rather the Virtuis Party and King Harold—"

"Of course not!" Thomas said. "Of course we should kick the fascists out! But for what? So we can return to the banal, subpar system we had before?" He sighed. "We may be a rebellion, but there's only so far we can push the envelope. At the end of the day, even when we win, all we'll have done is maintain order, not made anything better. There will still be a royal upon the throne, the same useless bickering in Parliament, and everyone will be happy to have it that way."

I watched him for a while. I'd known Thomas nearly my whole life, and even as a child I would have characterized him as a pessimistic misanthrope (maybe not in those exact words but the general idea would have been there). I never would have pegged him as an idealist, someone who could be disappointed by the world, so much that he had to take a step back from it. I wondered if this was something new he'd developed or if it had always been a part of him and I'd just been blind to it.

"Well, we'll have power soon enough," I said. "What kind of changes would you like to see?"

Thomas snorted, but because his nose was stuffed up the action lacked its usual disdain.

"Like I said, I don't expect anything—"

"Come on. Tell me."

"Well, honestly, I say we do away with the Crown," Thomas said, eyebrows raised. He had me there: The scant army support we had was from monarchists (monarchists rebelling against the current king, sure, but monarchists all the same). They wanted the traditions of old to continue, for there to be a reigning figurehead they could swear allegiance to, rather than some nebulous concept of a republic. And a lot of citizens of the country felt the same way.

"Is there something else?" I asked.

Thomas looked down, seeming to consider it thoughtfully. "When we're in power, we'll do away with the cloth magic prisons."

"Yes, of course, of course." That had always been the plan.

Thomas nodded. "That's good. But I'd like to go a step further. I want to get rid of prisons completely."

"What?" I couldn't even picture what Thomas was asking. "Wait, so you'd have us bring back corporal punishment? Whippings in the town square, putting offenders in stocks?"

"No! That's not what I'm suggesting either," Thomas said, gaze shooting up. "God, no. But I don't think taking people and sticking them in a hole for a couple years does any good for them or for the rest of the world. I've known many criminals—heck, according to most people, I am one—and I've known lots of blokes who went to crime not because of some inherent evil but because of desperation. They hurt other people because that's the only thing they've ever known. They steal because there's no other way for them to keep above water, and when they get out of prison they're just worse. And the people they hurt? They're left at a total loss. Rather than sending people to prison and digging a deeper hole, we should try and find ways to help people before they hurt others, and if they do cross the line, find a way for them to make amends to their victims."

This appealed to my Christian sense of morality: you couldn't in good conscience ask for God's forgiveness until you had sorted things out on the earthly plane. But I felt the need to play devil's advocate.

"But what about punishment? Making amends is one thing, but what if it's not enough to stop people from killing and looting?"

Thomas shrugged. "We have harsh enough deterrents right now, and it's not stopping people from committing crimes. And there could still be some kind of penalty built into it, like something the family and state decide on that will act as a consequence."

"This sounds fine and good for something like, I don't know, a stolen bicycle," I said, "but what of worse crimes? Rape, murder, severe injury. Acts that can't be undone or repaired."

"I'm not claiming it would be easy," Thomas said. "And maybe in extreme cases, we use, I dunno, the Isle of Man as a place to put those who have proven themselves to be a danger to society—"

"That sounds like a prison to me."

"It would be, but not like the ones we have now," Thomas said. "A place where offenders could have their own space and learn skills. Unlike the crowded shitholes we have now."

I nodded. "All right. Let's do it."

Thomas's eyebrows shot up in surprise. "Really?"

"Yeah, why not? What's the point in usurping the king if you're not going to bring about some changes, right?" I smiled at my little brother. "It won't be easy, but we can do it."

Instead of happiness, a scowl grew on his face.

"It will never happen." He stalked off, pushing aside the soldiers as he went past them.

CHAPTER 38

"We figured any additional fastenings like zippers or buttons would interfere with the simplicity of the design's purpose," Harriet said excitedly. "I drew up the pattern but Mr Myers helped with the creation."

"The blue material came from a doctor's surgical uniform, the green from a patient's outfit," Oberon explained.

"It's reversible!" said Harriet.

I tried it on. The fit was good, the cuffs of the sleeves resting at my wrists. Despite its simplicity, it felt oddly ostentatious as I put the hood up. Harriet looked at me with shining eyes.

"My goodness, Professor! You look like a wizard of old!"

"Thank you, Harriet," I said, taking her compliment in the spirit it was intended. But the problem was, she was right. This cloak made me look like some stodgy medieval mage. We were trying to sell the public on the image of a new world, a country led by young people such as Kitty and me. I wanted to look hip and with it, not old and mystical.

"Harriet, I left my sewing kit in my rooms. Would you run back and get it? I see a place where the hem is loose," said Oberon.

"Really? Where?" Harriet asked, peering at the edges of my cloak.

"It's a small one, but it's going to bother me if we don't fix it now."

Harriet nodded. "All right. I shall be as fast as I can."

She rushed out the door, leaving Oberon and me alone.

I wasn't crazy about being alone in a room with the man. I knew he was on my side—his quick actions the night of Prince Arthur's death proved that. But when I looked at his face, I felt like his hands were once more cutting off the air in my body. Even if I knew that Oberon was an ally now, some part of me was still terrified of him, unable to move past the night he'd almost killed me. And so I tried as best as I could to avoid him, something that he'd surely noticed.

"You don't like it," Oberon said, gesturing to my outfit.

"No, no, it's grand," I said but I couldn't work up much enthusiasm. "It's just . . . I asked you to make a kind of healing cloak I could wear in public. I'm going to stand out wearing this, aren't I?" I'd asked them to make it because I was worried about Sabina. Kitty had her own innate magic to protect her, but Sabina (and the heir she carried) was still vulnerable to attack. I had considered seeing if Sabina wanted protective innate magic cast upon her, but in the end I worried it might interfere with her pregnancy. So I'd asked Oberon to show Harriet how to make a recoup cloak, an outfit designed with healing magic in mind.

Oberon shrugged. "I thought you liked to stand out. Look, I'm sorry if you don't like the style, but it *works*. Here." He took out a small Swiss Army knife and pulled a blade out. I took a step back but Oberon merely used the blade to nick his thumb. A bead of blood welled up.

"Just touch me," Oberon said, holding out his hand, a thin line of blood running down his thumb. "It doesn't have to be where the wound is; it just has to be skin to skin."

I thought of Oberon's hands wrapped around my throat.

"Just touch you?" I said.

"Yes. Just by touching a person, you'll take on their wounds. So while wearing it, do not touch anyone unless you want to take on their injuries."

"Would I be taking on their sickness as well?" Just how deep did the magic penetrate?

"No. It only deals with flesh wounds. Fresh ones." He said the last bit pointedly. I took a deep breath, steeled my nerves, and bit my tongue so hard I tasted blood. Teeth still clenched, I took hold of Oberon's hand.

At once I felt a little cut on my finger, my flesh stinging as blood met air. I pulled away. Now there was a tiny bit of red running down my hand.

Oberon, meanwhile, was also wincing. "Did you . . . did you bite your tongue?"

I realized that my mouth felt fine—there was still the residual taste of blood, but no pain lingered in my mouth. "Yeah, I did."

"Interesting. I'd made this cloak assuming that the wearer would be in perfect health when they were swapping states with the target, but obviously that was an oversight on my part," Oberon said. "Well, before you use it to save anyone, make sure you're not injured yourself, hmm? If you're in a bad way, you'll just be conferring those wounds onto them."

"Noted," I said.

I was eager to take the thing off—it was too powerful, more of a threat to me than a way to help someone. Before I could, Oberon spoke again.

"Thomas has been in a funk lately, hmm? I figured he'd snap out of it once you returned, but he's just gotten worse." Oberon grew thoughtful. "Maybe he's just missing Samira."

"Who?"

Oberon's eyes grew wide like a startled owl's.

"He hasn't told you about him? I mean, her?"

"Oberon, what exactly are you talking about?"

Oberon scratched his neck, looking very much like he regretted raising the subject.

"Well, I've had some run-ins with Thomas over the last few years," he said. "Sometimes he'd pop up wherever I was practising medicine.

We even worked together a few times." Oberon had a nostalgic little smile at that. I'd never thought that I'd be jealous of Oberon Myers over anything, but now that I knew that over the last couple of years he'd been having adventures with *my* best friend, I felt quite green indeed. "Thomas was doing work for Lady Fife, trying to spoil the Virtuis Party's attempts at starting World War Three. It was tough, nasty work." Oberon's smile faltered. "There are tales I could tell . . . but I don't think it's my place to tell you."

"Right," I said.

"Anyway, after a couple of years Thomas was pretty much done with it. He told me he was getting out of the cloak-and-dagger business. There was this other spy, Samira, that he'd grown close to—"

"Wait, Thomas had a girlfriend?" I'd known Thomas since he was six years old, and in that time I'd seen him have a crush on a girl every couple of years, but never had he acted on it. I'd tease him about it, but only a little. I figured that he just wasn't all that interested in dating or sex.

"Uh, well, not exactly," Oberon stuttered.

"Oh my God, were they married? Did Thomas have a *wife*?"

"No! Well, I don't know!" Oberon said, still tripping over his words. "I met Samira a couple of times, and each time I never knew how they'd appear. They used cloth magic to be a master of disguise. Sometimes they were a young woman, other times a young man. I don't know why; I just chalked it up as some kind of spy thing."

As Oberon babbled on, I tried to take in his words. It was one thing to picture Thomas with a woman—unexpected, sure, but Thomas had expressed at least a passing interest in girls. But picturing Thomas in some kind of queer relationship was a whole new thing to figure out. I had always thought that maybe Thomas was scared of physical contact—he was all right with me, but with anyone else he'd duck away if they tried to put an arm around him or the like. Maybe his relationship with Samira was platonic while still being romantic. Or maybe being with them had helped Thomas work through the fears and worries he'd been holding since he was a small child.

Again, a pang of jealousy, this time aimed at someone I didn't even know. It wasn't that I'd ever been attracted to Thomas like that, but I still felt guilty and envious that someone else could be closer to him than I could be.

"Anyway, whoever Samira was . . . Thomas was probably the only one who really knew them," Oberon said. "About a year ago they decided to get out of the spy game altogether. Thomas said they were going to set up a pub somewhere on the coast of the Adriatic Sea. And they did. They opened up a little place off the coast of Montenegro. I never got a chance to go visit, but from what I heard it was pretty popular." He sipped his tea. "So that's why I was surprised to see Thomas wrapped up in all this. He'd told me he was done with this life."

He'd told me that too once years ago, or at least a more personal variation of that: *I'm done cleaning up your messes, Paul.* And yet here he was, doing exactly that.

Harriet came in, holding Oberon's sewing kit.

"Oh, Professor Gallagher! Your hand!" She practically chucked Oberon's sewing kit at him before running over to me. I held up a hand to stop her.

"No, Harriet! Don't touch me! You'll—"

"I know," she said while taking hold of my hand with both of hers. At once the pain in my thumb was gone. Harriet smiled at me even as her thumb bled.

~

I found Thomas in the castle gymnasium, practising what looked like judo moves with Naveed.

"Oh, Professor!" Naveed said when he saw me. His grin was as big as ever but I noticed he had quite the shiner.

"Say, Naveed, how'd you get that black eye?"

"Oh, this beaut? Don't worry about it, Professor. You should see the other fellow!" His grin had somehow grown, but I didn't feel reassured. "Well, I'm meeting up with my sisters for tea, so I better go take a shower. Ta!"

I watched Naveed go. It wasn't like him to scurry off—usually he tried to talk my ear off about this or that. He'd been rather scarce since I'd come back from Germany, as if he was avoiding *me*.

"I worry about that boy," I said, his bruised face still fresh in my eye.

Thomas snorted as he did some stretches. "You have enough to worry about without adding that lollygagger to the list."

"It's just, that was a nasty bruise, and he's usually so careful about his looks." I'd seen Naveed flirting with the soldiers stationed around the castle. What if he had fallen in with a violent lover? He was still so young, and if he had found a dangerous yet attractive military man to tumble with . . . he'd get hurt, even more than he already had been. "Maybe I should ask him about it, make sure he's not being mistreated. I know you're going to tell me to mind my own business, but I can't just stand by and—"

"He got the black eye boxing last night," Thomas said.

"What? Boxing?"

"At night we come down here and set up a makeshift boxing ring," Thomas said. "Naveed had a match with some private. Oberon worked as the ringside physician, though he also took on a few challengers."

This was news to me. To think that while I slept, there was a whole other world going on in the castle.

"And you too?" I asked.

"Yup."

"What brought all this about?"

"Everyone needed to blow off some steam," Thomas said. "The soldier boys were getting antsy without someone to fight. It's also just a good way for settling petty grudges that pop up."

"I . . . see." I didn't really. Maybe, because I'd never really had the option of hitting someone, I couldn't conceive of it as being therapeutic. Wouldn't hurting someone just make you feel worse? Wouldn't getting hurt yourself just . . . hurt? When I'd been caught up in brawls, I'd never felt anything but fear. When lovers had asked if we could try doing rough stuff, I'd always demurred. Was I really so different from most men? If this seemingly common desire was so alien to me, would the army men who'd sided with us ever respect me? If they saw me as weak would they abandon our cause?

"Do the men . . . do they hold it against me that I don't box?" I said and felt silly to be voicing such things, like I was a child worried that the other tykes didn't like me.

Thomas's eyes widened and he shook his head.

"No, no! Nobody expects you to throw punches with the common rabble. You're the Court Magician. The premier mage in Great Britain. You're above all that."

"Right." While I was glad they didn't see me as weak, it was also odd being seen as an authority figure. I decided to change the subject.

"Oberon told me . . . well, he told me that a year ago you quit working for Lady Fife," I said, choosing my words carefully. "That you'd met someone and had decided to start a new life together."

Thomas let out a long sigh, like a kettle brought to boil.

"Did he now?" he said.

"I'd like to know more about them," I said. "Your partner, I mean."

"They don't matter now," Thomas said, voice still sharp.

"Really?" I said. "Thomas, I've known you pretty much all your life, and this is the first time I'd ever heard of you falling for someone hard enough to actually make a go of it with them."

"Yeah, sure, it's true," Thomas said. "For three years I wandered the earth, dealing with the worst kinds of people so that the fuckers back here in London didn't start World War Three. And there came a point where . . . where I guess I got tired and decided to get out. Samira—did

Oberon tell you their name?—we opened a little bar. We had a good thing going for a little bit."

"And then?"

"And then Lady Fife came and showed me some pics of Godfrey getting all chummy with people in power. So I came back here." He sounded bitter and looked away from me.

"And Samira?" I asked. "Are they still running the bar the two of you opened?" *Are they waiting for you to come back?*

"Fuck if I know," Thomas said with (I felt) performative callousness. He looked at me and seemed to read the unspoken question on my mind. "Don't worry. I made it clear to them I wasn't ever coming back, so don't worry about that."

"Ah." I didn't know what to say to that; should I thank him? Apologize? Maybe I should tell him that I'd also left someone behind and how I worried that, even if we won this war, I'd never see Laura again. But it felt so childish to compare my feelings for Laura with Thomas's feelings for Samira; mine were just a one-sided crush while the two of them had actually made a life together. In the end I said nothing, just left.

CHAPTER 39

"Lady Fife, you don't have to go through with this. Eimer didn't hold up their end of the bargain," I said. "In the end, they just stranded me in Germany!"

"Yes, we could certainly make a good case for ourselves, but to what court, Paul?" Lady Fife was finishing a letter in her office, her coat already on as if she were that eager to go. "As far as Eimer's concerned, you had a breakthrough *because* they left you stranded in Germany."

Eimer had sent a letter earlier in the week demanding that we pay up. They said they were going to Andrew to perform the old promise-making ritual, and they asked that somebody from Windsor Castle be present as a witness. A witness seemed unnecessary to me—it was a magically binding spell, after all. That was the whole point. But I suspected Eimer's true goal was to needle Lady Fife.

And to my amazement, it had worked. Lady Fife had declared that she was leaving ASAP to be by Andrew's side. That she'd be back once the whole matter was dealt with.

"Lady Fife, please, reconsider. We need you here," I said. "I know you worry about Andrew and about Eimer harming him, but . . ."

Lady Fife finished writing her letter.

"If I don't go, I worry things might go awry," she said. "I can't leave Andrew to deal with Eimer on his own."

"Lady Fife . . ." I knew what I was about to say was dangerous, but it had to be said. "Look, I love Andrew as well. And of course he's your son, and I know you love him more than anyone else in the world . . ."

"But at the end of the day he's only one person, whereas we are fighting for the fate of the nation?" Lady Fife said, not even looking up as she sealed the letter. "That I once said I wouldn't put my own son ahead of the world?"

"I didn't say that," I replied, hands in my pockets, eyes not meeting her gaze.

"No, you didn't. But just in case you were *thinking* it, let me assure you of my priorities," Lady Fife said. "I believe this deal with Eimer *is* the best way forwards. Better to have them as an ally than an enemy, and if I'm not there to see this through . . ."

She stood.

"But Lady Fife, we're supposed to meet with the generals in an hour," I said, and I hated how I sounded like a scared child. "Brennan dislikes me for no good reason. And Kent, he's your man."

Brennan and the soldiers loyal to him were relatively new to the castle, having arrived shortly after Sabina had returned to the UK. Kent and his men, meanwhile, had been with us since the beginning and seemed more loyal to Lady Fife than to Kitty.

"Then it's time they start listening to you," Lady Fife said, as if it were that simple.

I met with the generals in the room that I had commandeered for my office: the King's Drawing Room. Between the size of the space and the over-the-top portraits on each of the four walls, I felt like I was in a public art gallery rather than a private meeting room. I did like the olive-green colour scheme, though.

Thomas and the two generals were there. Once I explained that Lady Fife had been called away on other business, we set to figuring out our next step.

"Our lads are getting anxious," General Kent said. "Guarding this castle means they are constantly on high alert while bored out of their bloody minds."

"Isn't that the soldier's life?" Thomas said.

"What we all want to know is, When are you going to make your move, Gallagher?" General Brennan asked.

"Well, gents, you tell me: Is it militarily advantageous for us to ride on London tonight?"

"Of course it's bloody not, and you know it," Brennan said. "We have enough troops to defend this city, not enough to take on the rest of the British Army! But we can't just hole up in bloody Slough until the world tilts off its axis! We figured that *you* had some ace up your sleeve, some new Superconductor or the like. Something that would make this less of a lost cause."

"We could look to more practical means of support," Thomas said. "The other day we were talking about joining forces with the British republicans."

Brennan snorted. "*You* were speaking of it, Dawes. It's a preposterous idea. They are terrorists, mere anarchists blowing up mailboxes and the like."

"They are following in a proud tradition of British civil disobedience," Thomas countered. "They hate King Harold and the Virtuis Party as much as we do. We should reach out to them. The enemy of my enemy—"

"Reach out to them?! You've already reached out and then some! You've been diverting funds to them since the start!" Brennan said.

This was news to me. I looked to Thomas, waiting to hear an explanation. He squared his shoulders.

"I was paying informants—"

"Oh, you don't have to explain all your spy crap to me," Brennan said. "Lady Fife plays the same games. Difference is, she knows what she's doing. But do you?"

He directed the question to me. The generals clearly wanted to see if I had the wherewithal to lead, to hold this crumbling house together without Lady Fife's near-omnipotent hand guiding me. Maybe Lady Fife wanted to see too.

I wasn't sure if I did. But I'd come too far to let everything fall to pieces now.

"We won't be siding publicly with the republicans," I said. Thomas looked as though he wanted to interrupt but I turned to him and kept talking. "You say they want the same thing, but that's not true. They want to do away with the Crown altogether and build a republic. We want to see the monarchy continue, with Princess Katherine as queen. They'll never accept any compromise. But please keep an ear to the ground as to what they're up to."

The two generals seemed satisfied with my words. They left.

There was a sudden silence in the office, broken when Thomas let out a sigh. He dropped down onto the nearest couch, hugging his arms in tight.

"I'm sorry," I said to him. "I need the generals, and—"

"No, I get it. You need to keep them on your side," Thomas said. "The one you need to watch out for is Cobalt. He's gotten cosy with the princess. It's pretty clear he's angling for your job. With Lady Fife gone he might feel bold enough to make a move. But I think he's too smart for that. More likely he'll bide his time and, once Katherine is on the throne, try something then. We should deal with him now before it's too late."

"'Deal with him'? Do we talk like American mobsters now?" I said. "Cobalt is a protégé of mine and a friend. Sure, he made a bad call when he ratted me out to the king, but he had good intentions and we all make mistakes. I'm not going to listen to you talk so casually about . . . about . . . 'bumping him off' or whatever."

"I'm serious, Paul," Thomas said, worry clear in his face. "We should do something while I'm still around to help you."

A tense silence descended between us.

"Thomas, are you dying?" I said slowly.

Thomas looked away, and in those few seconds my heart beat double time.

"No," he finally said. "But we have to assume I'm not going to see the end of this war. That's why we should think about the future now. I can help you win this, but I won't be able to help you afterwards."

"What? What in Jesus's name are you talking about?"

"The generals were right about us needing some grand bit of magic to win," Thomas said, "but what they don't know is that we *have* it already. You can do a type of magic that no one else in the world can do."

"What?" I said again, but this time with more horror.

"Your deep magic," Thomas said, as if my question had been genuine. "What you did to Hollister. You were able to bring a man back to life! And that was just scratching the surface! If we wanted, we could wipe out all our enemies in one go or raise a new capital city from the ground. You said it yourself—this power is on biblical levels. We have a trump card, a surefire win if we can just figure out how to use it."

"But that power, it's a disgrace. It's a crime against God," I said. "Plus, for it to work, I need to skin someone, someone willing who . . ."

Thomas gave me a level look. "Why do you think I came back?"

Coldness washed over me like an ocean wave.

"You can't be serious."

"Of course I am. I am one of the few people on this planet who know what you're capable of," Thomas said. "The spell needs that, right? Belief that it will work? Well, I've got it. I've seen it work firsthand. And I've got a strong will, one that wants Godfrey gone. So whenever we need to deploy that spell, I'm ready. Hell, we can do it right now if you want."

"But . . . you'd die," I said in a small voice.

Thomas shrugged. "I always knew that was on the table. I'd rather go out in a way that ensures our win, rather than being taken out by some random enemy. Don't worry, Paul. When the time comes, I'll be ready. I want this."

"But I don't!" I said. "Jesus, you expect me to carve up my best friend?! No, no. I swear on all the angels and saints, it's not going to happen."

Thomas kept his face neutral.

"Well, I'm just saying, it's something we have in our back pocket."

Thomas's words were supposed to make me feel better, but the actual effect was far from it. If the present was bad, the future looked even worse, like staring into a deep hole.

~

"I'm sorry we haven't had a chance to talk alone before now," I began. "I—"

"I know you've been busy, Court Magician," Cobalt said. "If anything, *I'm* sorry for not being more help to you. I often miss the simple days back when I was your assistant."

The two of us were eating lunch together in Cobalt's quarters. It was a small room next to Kitty's, where her own personal maid used to stay. Though it wasn't grand, one nice thing it had was a door to a little rooftop terrace. Small plants grew in ceramic pots, flowers pushing their way up through the soil. The sight of the small buds on the plants made me briefly think of Sabina—she was seven months pregnant now.

I'd sought out Cobalt to see if what Thomas said was true. I figured that by talking to the man, I'd be able to get the measure of him.

"Well, you assist the princess now," I said to Cobalt. "She needs you. It's really a big relief to me, knowing that you're by her side. So we're all square."

Cobalt started to nod, but it turned into a shake of his head, the movement reminding me that he had nearly the same haircut as Tonya.

"Is it really, though?" he said, looking at his steepled fingers like an architect looking over a building for flaws. "I betrayed you, that night you and Kitty got caught up in the raid. I can't help but feel like everything that followed came from that one action of mine."

"Cobalt, this schism in the country was a long time coming. Something would have happened, no matter what you or I did."

"Still, you trusted me," Cobalt said, looking up through his fringe to meet my eyes. "And you trust me even now, even though you hardly know me."

"Is that so," I said. "I like to think I know you quite well."

"No one does," Cobalt said, matter-of-factly, "but I'd like it if you did."

"I'd like that too."

Cobalt took a deep breath. "I more or less grew up in the Tower of London. My grandfather was a beefeater, my mother was head of the servants. I was usually the only child on the grounds, but I loved it. I felt like the king of the castle growing up. When the war came, I was so sad that we had to leave. Did you know there's a myth about the ravens in the tower?"

"Of course," I said. "If the ravens ever leave, then London will fall."

"Well, during the war, we actually took the ravens from the tower. Moved them into the countryside for their safety. It made me so distraught as a child. I was sure we were going to lose the war solely because the prophecy had come true at our own hands." He chuckled. "All in all though, it was a pretty happy childhood. I was really lucky, in a sense. I was an odd child, but everyone was very kind to me. I didn't realize it at the time, but I actually had a lot of freedom." Cobalt paused, head tilted, staring out into space like someone looking at a cluster of stars and straining to see a constellation. "The one thing I lacked growing up was a father. When I turned seventeen, my mother finally told me my father's name. He was a French diplomat. He'd met my mother when he visited the country. My mother says he was charming, kind. She fell for him hard. He took an interest in her right away, and he was so different from all the other men she knew, so cultured and interesting. He swept her off her feet."

Cobalt listed off his father's good points with an increasingly stony face. He blinked and looked at me. "She was sixteen. Of course he seemed impressive. He was a forty-five-year-old man. She was dazzled by him, but he knew exactly what he was doing." Cobalt let out a hiss and steepled his fingers. "I went to France to confront him, to take him to task for what he'd done. He was an old man by then but still an important figure. My plan was to go to Paris and reveal my existence, besmirching his so-called good name. He still had a big family, lots of children—legitimate children—who were themselves now figures of note. I wanted revenge on them all.

"But before I went public with my story, I wanted to meet him. That was my mistake. He *was* charming, greeting me like I was a beloved child he'd known all his life. He seemed truly delighted to finally meet me. He said that he'd heard that Edith—my mother—had had a child but had never heard anything about it being his. He talked of how he wished to make up for lost time, to do right by both myself and my mother. He was—is—rich, his family nobles who somehow managed to keep their heads through the revolution."

"I always thought you had an aristocratic air to you."

Cobalt smiled. "Thank you." His smile dropped. "My father asked me what I wanted to do in life, and I told him how I wished to be a cloth mage. It had always been my dream, but just that: a dream. I couldn't afford the tuition at the UCL. My father offered to pay the cost. He also said he'd give me a stipend to live on, since he knew that cloth mages often needed additional funds for materials."

"That's handy," I said, thinking of Thomas's and my school days and how we'd had to scrimp and save just to buy the most basic linen.

"He said it was the least he could do for me, since he couldn't publicly acknowledge me as a son. This way at least, he could support me. The unspoken exchange, of course, being that I'd keep his secret in return." Cobalt stopped steepling his fingers in order to ball his hands into fists. "Well, I suppose you can guess what happened next. I took his money, kept my silence. I hated myself for it. Still do. I'd gone to him intending to have him pay for his crimes, and instead I let the bastard buy me off."

"Cobalt, mate, you're being too hard on yourself," I said. "I would have done the same."

Cobalt stared at me, wide eyed. "You would have?"

"Yes. Exposing him would have felt good, but eventually you'd come back home to England and nothing here would have changed. You'd be in no better a position to help your mum; you'd have no way to learn magic and become a mage. You were in a tough spot and you had to make a call. Sometimes there are no good choices, but like I said, I would have made the same choice as you."

"Really?" Cobalt said, sounding younger than usual. "Th-thank you. That means a lot to me." He ducked his head. "I was really nervous about telling this to you. Lamb was always talking about how hard you struggled financially as a student, so I worried you might judge me for having such a dubious source of income."

"Lamb said that?" I wasn't surprised; it would be just like Lamb to notice how guilty Cobalt felt over having an easy ride and to needle him about it. "Did he tell you the full story? To fund our education Thomas and I took out a whale of a loan from an East End crime boss. The only reason we never had to pay it back was because the man died in a pub brawl." That wasn't a fair epitaph for McCormick: the man had been so much more than that, and he'd died saving my and Thomas's lives. But that glib summary would have to do for now. "It was hell, and if I had some rich benefactor offering me a bunch of money, of course I would have taken it."

"Even if there were such odious strings attached—"

"There always are. Money's always tainted by something. You needed it to survive. I'm not going to judge you about that. I've been there. We all have."

Cobalt seemed relieved. "Thank you. Like I said, I've been so nervous about telling you. Even now I feel like quite the heel. I should have told you all this long ago. Even now I'm telling you this under duress."

"What do you mean?"

"Mr Dawes has been using his contacts abroad in Europe to ask about me," Cobalt said, some tension creeping back up into his shoulders. "I understand his reasons—I've always been very secretive about my past—but as you now know I have multiple reasons for doing so. I fear Mr Dawes believes me to be some sort of French spy. I swear to you, Mr Gallagher, that is not the case. I am loyal to you, to the princess—" His hand came up to touch his eye patch, but at the last moment he dropped the gesture.

"I know," I said quickly. "Everyone here knows it."

"Well, then perhaps you could convince Mr Dawes of it as well?" Cobalt said. "Word has already gotten back to my father that people are looking into me. If the truth of my parentage comes out . . . well, my line of credit will be cut off, but I don't care about that. I've spoken to my mother about it, and she does not wish to become part of a public scandal. She's been through so much already and has only ever been the most loving parent to me. I've caused her so much trouble just by existing; if I were to bring any more pain to her, I . . ."

"Of course, Cobalt," I said. "I'll explain all this to Thomas and he'll back off."

Cobalt let out a shuddering breath.

"Thank you. I'm glad in a sense that I was forced to bare all to you. I know I have betrayed your trust in the past, Mr Gallagher, but I wish to start anew. I believe you are the Court Magician this nation needs, and I hope that in some way, I can support you."

"Of course, Cobalt," I said. "Jesus, out of everyone here, I should know what a sharp mage you are!"

"Thank you," Cobalt said. He'd been saying it a lot over the course of the conversation—it had been gratifying at first but now I was starting to get uneasy. "I must admit, I've greatly missed you. Obviously, you have many duties to attend to, but I admit that I'm a wee bit jealous of the young ones, the three new mages. I wish I had gotten to have you as my professor."

"Well, those three need a lot of professoring. Like you, they are the future of magic in this country."

"I suppose Harriet Hollister needs special guidance," Cobalt said, "if she is to be a mage maker alongside you."

"I don't see Harriet making any mages for a while yet," I said. "She still has a lot to learn, and it is a heavy burden to carry."

Cobalt nodded. "Indeed. And I think you have hit upon a good idea, of having multiple mage makers at once. Look at what happened to this country when it was seemingly left in limbo without one? It fell into war. In the Britain we are making, there could be one Court Magician and multiple mage makers. It would be a far more stable system, both for the country and the people involved directly."

"Yes, perhaps." Having multiple mage makers was also riddled with its own set of pitfalls: What if one went rogue and made their own little army of mages? What if there was something off with their magic and they created a line of tainted mages? But I had no one to blame but myself for this can of opened worms: I had made Harriet a mage maker, and now everyone wanted to know how she fit into the big picture.

"Well, if there's any way I can help shoulder your burden—or hers, for that matter—I am ever your obedient servant," Cobalt said.

CHAPTER 40

I bumped into Naveed as he was leaving the kitchen. He didn't greet me, just scowled my way before heading down the hallway. My stomach was growling something fierce by that time, but instead of grabbing some grub I felt compelled to hurry after him.

"All right, so why are *you* avoiding me?" I asked with more heat than necessary. Naveed let out a bitter laugh, slowing him down enough for me to catch up.

"You're really asking me that? Maybe you're not as smart as I thought you were, Professor."

"Maybe not," I said, walking double time to keep up with his long stride, "so clue an old man in, eh?"

It seemed that I had caught Naveed in a rare bad mood because instead of denying it his scowl deepened.

"Of course, you'd *have* to be stupid to make Harriet your successor," Naveed said. "The girl should have never left the asylum, and now someday, what? She'll be one of the most powerful mages in the world? What the hell?"

"Don't talk about her like that. Harriet's worked just as hard as you—"

"Exactly!" Naveed stopped to face me. "We've all worked hard, yet she's the one who gets to be your heir apparent or whatever?! *I'm* the one who sought you out, who asked you to be my mentor, my teacher. She just attached herself like a barnacle."

"She came to me in Germany," I said. "She was there when I needed her—"

"Only because Rosemary and I helped her! We had to distract Eimer so Harriet could steal her teleportation cloak! She didn't do any of this on her own, but she's the only one who benefits!"

"It's not that simple—"

A sound came from down the hall: Obie's booming voice carrying around the corner to us. Naveed and I shared a mutual look of distaste: no matter what lay between us, neither of us really liked Oberon. We were right by the entrance to the library, and with no other place to hide we ducked in there just as Oberon and his companion turned the corner. But even that wasn't enough—as Oberon came closer his footfalls slowed down and it seemed like they were coming to the library. In silent agreement Naveed and I took the stairs up to the second floor. It was still risky that we might be spotted, as the second floor was really a wraparound balcony where more books were shelved. From where we were we could still look down and see the first floor, and likewise someone on the first floor might look up and see us. We held our breaths as the library door swung open.

"—so you can see, there have been many times when Book Binding saved my arse when it comes to keeping medical records," Oberon was saying. He held the door open and Tonya stepped through after him. It wasn't uncommon to see the two of them making the rounds about the castle together. Because he'd dabbled in Book Binding a bit during school, Oberon had become Tonya's private tutor when it came to learning Book Binding, as well as something of her personal valet, carrying items for her and doing errands that were impossible for her to carry out with one arm—I'd broken her arm about a week ago and Oberon had been by her side almost as soon as the ritual was done. Tonya seemed both amused and bemused by his attention. I was certainly a bit taken aback—didn't Tonya remember how this man had been ready to kill me? To kill her? Was Tonya just a better person than me, able to truly forgive without reservations?

Aside from that, I was just a bit jealous. I would have loved to have been the one to bring Tonya her meals and the like, but I just had too much to fucking do.

Tonya's arm was still in a sling but she was looking as wonderfully put together as always. She was wearing a black peasant's blouse and a wide skirt. That outfit, combined with a handkerchief keeping her hair back, made her look like a fortune-teller. She was listening to Oberon with an indulgent—perhaps even fond—expression.

"Well, I don't see myself doing that kind of magic right off the bat, but I do want to try the different spells for sorting data," Tonya said.

"Ah, great," Naveed whispered to me, sarcasm coming through despite the quietness of his words. "We get to eavesdrop on such scintillating Book magic talk."

Tonya and Oberon stepped towards a shelf directly under where Naveed and I were hiding. I let out a quiet sigh of relief that we hadn't been spotted but cut it short when Oberon started speaking again.

"Ah, here is what you need!" he said as he pulled a hefty tome off the shelf.

Tonya sighed. "Michael, I'll break my other arm trying to carry that."

Michael. The name made me pause. During Gabs's wedding reception Oberon had introduced himself as Michael while he was in disguise, said it was the name his mother had given him.

"Don't worry, I've got brawn as well as brains," Obie said. "Now, Tatianna, do you want to look over this here, or in my rooms perhaps?"

"Oh God. If they read it here we'll never be able to leave," Naveed whispered. I barely heard him. Oberon had called Tonya Tatianna. How did he know that name? Why did he use it? I'd thought Tonya didn't even like it, that it was just a mark of a person she never had been and never would be. What were they doing acting all cute in an empty library and calling each other Michael and Tatianna?

"Let's go to my room," Tonya said. "I stole some grapes from the kitchen earlier. We can snack on them as we read."

"Oh, goody!" Oberon said, more cheerful than I'd ever seen him in my life. The two of them left, chatting idly.

"By Jove, that was close!" Naveed said with a grin, the close call clearing up his bad mood. His smile dropped when he looked at me. "Professor? What's wrong?"

I was shaking, hands gripping my knees. Oberon and Tonya had been in the library for all of one minute, but I kept replaying it in my head, stretching out individual words and moments like taffy. All this time, she and Oberon had been growing close and I hadn't noticed. I'd just taken it for granted that I was the person Tonya was closest to in the castle. I'd even thought that maybe we'd become lovers again. But now I saw that I had been deluding myself. I was alone.

"Hey! Professor! Snap out of it!" Naveed said, hands on my shoulders.

But it wasn't that simple. I felt tears welling up.

"They called each other by their birth names," I said.

"They . . . what? What do you mean?"

"The names their parents gave them." Of course. I was such an idiot. Tonya and Oberon shared a unique life experience that only the other could even begin to understand. They weren't brother and sister but they had parents in common. In a different world, they would have lived each other's lives. By talking to each other, they could get to know and understand an aspect of themselves that would otherwise remain untouchable. Of course Tonya would be drawn to Oberon. I could never compete with that kind of bond.

"Hey, hey, Professor," Naveed said. "Don't cry here, all right? If someone sees you, it could be bad. My room's close. Hold your tears till then, all right?"

Naveed helped me up and we then hurried to his room, mercifully not running into anyone along the way.

Naveed's family was living in a wing of the castle that was usually reserved as quarters for high-level guests. His room was ostentatious with heavy lace on not only the curtains but the drapery that swept around the bed. Aside from the bed there was also part of the room with two couches and a coffee table between them. It seemed like Naveed spent more time in this half of the room: shirts of his were hanging over furniture, and a radio had been left on and was softly playing classical music. On the table were various magazines splayed out. Most of them were sports mags or old issues of the *Radio Times*, but one thin pamphlet had a pencil illustration of a muscular young man. I picked it up: inside were more drawings of brawny blokes, many of them doing the kinds of stuff that could make the pope blush.

"Oh!" Naveed grabbed it out of my hands, a slight blush on *his* face. "Don't know where that came from. Let me tidy up here."

Naveed tried to clean up his room, but he did so like a man figuring it out as he went along: he'd pick up a shirt and stare at it as if he'd never seen it before. Eventually he just took all the dirty clothes and old mags and shoved them under his bed.

"There! That's better!" he said, sitting down on the couch next to me. "Now, tell me, Professor, what's got you so distraught, hmm?"

"Oh, it's nothing." I had calmed down enough that I felt silly for going to pieces. "It's just . . . I hadn't realized that Tonya and Oberon had grown so close. I had always assumed that I was her closest confidant in the palace."

Naveed looked at me sceptically, his thoughts obvious: *You thought she was closest to you, the ex who cheated on her?* But he did not say so aloud. He smoothed his expression into a more sympathetic cast.

"Do you want a drink?"

"Honestly, I'd much rather have something to eat," I said.

Naveed nodded. He went to a chest of drawers and took out a bag of walnuts and a bottle of rum.

"These aren't great, I'll admit. Kind of stale. I think the cook was saving them to use in baking? Sorry, I know they're not grapes."

I took the bag from him and popped a couple of walnuts in my mouth. They *were* stale and left a sawdust-like texture on my tongue. It hardly made a dent in my hunger—in fact, all it had done was make me thirsty on top of it. A piece got caught up in my throat, making me choke.

"Ah! Professor!" Naveed started hitting me on the back. I managed to cough up the offending walnut chunk, but the act brought tears to my eyes and once the tears came I couldn't stop them.

"Um, here, have some of this—maybe it will help," Naveed said, handing me the bottle of rum. He got up to grab a glass but I was already unscrewing the top and downing it.

"Whoa! Hey, chap! You're supposed to let it rest on the tongue, not pour it down your gullet!" Naveed grabbed the bottle from me, causing rum to spill on my shirt. Having gulped down hard liquor had somehow made me feel physically better but mentally worse.

I thought of Tonya and how she and Oberon were probably feeding each other grapes at that very moment while I sat in another part of the castle, crying on Naveed's wank-off couch. Then an even more unwelcome image came to me: Laura, at home with her husband. It was late—were the two of them in bed right now, sleeping side by side? Or were they awake, acting as man and wife once again?

It had been months now since Laura had gone back to him and each second felt like it was not its own unit of time but a small weight being added one after another to an ever-growing pile. I'd never considered myself the jealous type before: I fell in and out of love freely, so I never begrudged others for doing likewise. If the person I was with wanted to be with someone else, I was generally fine with it as long as we talked about it first. But with Laura my feelings were different.

Thinking about her having sex with that man made my stomach roil. And sure, part of it was out of guilt—she had tried so hard to get away from him and ended up back in his arms thanks to me—but a bigger part of it was plain old possessiveness. I had no grounds to feel that way; I knew that. Laura had promised me nothing. But the feeling was still there.

And there was nothing I could do. No entreaty I could make, no gesture to win her over from him. She'd always be with him and I'd always be apart from her.

I threw up, but since I had next to nothing in my stomach it was just bile and bits of walnut chunks. I tried to cover my mouth to keep it from getting on the floor but it seeped through my hands.

Naveed swore, letting loose a string of colourful phrases that sounded as though they'd been workshopped by a whole dorm's worth of teenage boys.

"A-are you sick, Professor Gallagher?" I knew he was actually concerned because he sounded sincere when he said "Professor." His room had an en suite bathroom—Naveed took my arm and gently led me to it. I washed my hands, gargled some mouthwash, and then rejoined a worried Naveed on the couch.

"I'm having a rough time," I said.

"Well, um, what exactly can I do?" Naveed asked.

"I need food. Real food."

"Righto!" Naveed said, invigorated by having a goal. "I'll be back with a whole feast! Don't die on me before then, all right?"

"Okay," I said. Naveed raced out of the room. Upon his return he knelt down by the couch and held up a ham sandwich on a plate like a knight offering up a sword to their liege. "Please, eat this."

Grudgingly I sat up straight and took the plate from him. Naveed sat next to me, watching anxiously.

"Is it good?" he asked. "I made it myself."

"It's good," I said between mustardy bites. Naveed didn't relax till I had eaten every last crumb.

"Now, what's all this about you were saying in the library about being alone?" he asked.

I groaned, embarrassed—back in the library I hadn't realized I'd said that aloud. "Oh, just an old man's ramblings," I replied. "Sorry to get so soppy all of a sudden. Thanks for looking after me."

Naveed nodded but looked troubled.

"Right," he said. "But you know that you're *not* alone, right?"

"Oh, yes. I know everyone in the castle—" I started to answer, but Naveed's question had been a rhetorical one, a prelude to going in for a kiss. He was smooth but my reflexes were quicker, bringing up a hand to stop him before he made contact.

He pulled back, blinking in surprise. "What's wrong?"

"I can't do this with you," I said, suddenly feeling very clearheaded. Naveed tried not to pout and failed.

"Why not?" he said. "I'm an adult, you know."

"Yes, I know."

"Don't you think I'm fit?"

"Very fit," I said. "But you're also my student. And I made a promise to myself years ago that I would never sleep with my students." I would never turn into Lamb.

Naveed's face fell. He leaned back into the couch, hands behind his head.

"Well, bloody hell," he said. "I've liked you for a long time, you know? You stopped by the cloth magic department once while I was in first year. We didn't get a chance to meet but you talked to my class. And ever since that day I schemed about how to set us up together. I thought I was being so clever asking you to be my tutor. If I'd known that was the one thing that would make me off limits, I would have just asked you out for a drink."

I smiled at that. "Well, they say man plans, God laughs."

"Yeah. I bet that old fucker in the sky's having a right laugh right now." Naveed leaned back and stretched. "Well, you can't blame a fella for shooting his shot, right?"

"No, of course not." The fact Naveed had taken his rejection so lightly put me in a slightly better mood. It was never fun rejecting someone, and Naveed was right: a lot of my malaise would have been cured by fucking someone. Sleeping with Naveed would have probably helped my overall mood, but it would also be a guilt that I'd carry for years to come.

I stood.

"Thanks for this, really. I do feel better." Well, not better, but there was a grim certainty settling in—I had to shoulder my burdens alone.

Naveed was sad to see me go, even offered to sleep on the couch if I wanted to take his bed, just so I wouldn't be by myself, but I turned that offer down too. Eventually I was in the hall, and after I closed the door to Naveed's room I let myself have a minute of quiet, just to capture my breath. But as soon as I exhaled, I sensed that I wasn't alone. Down the hall at the door to her room stood Rosemary. She was watching me. She was never the most expressive of people but in that moment her face was unnervingly blank, her gaze all the more intense for how inscrutable it was.

I raised a hand and half smiled, unsure what to say—she was a few yards away, too far to chat quietly. But I wanted to say something, to explain that this wasn't what it looked like, that I wasn't leaving Naveed's room all dishevelled-like for any tawdry reasons. Before I could fumble out the words Rosemary was gone, closing the door to her room with a quiet yet definitive *klak*.

~

Two nights later Van Holt called me.

It was a rainy April night. Thomas ran to get me and ushered me down to the north-gate guardhouse. Thomas and I were the only two people in the little space, Thomas having kicked out the soldiers.

Not sure what to expect, I picked up the receiver.

"Hello?" I said.

"I thought of just telling you after the fact that it wasn't me," Van Holt said, voice pitching all over the place. "But then I told myself that wasn't really in the spirit of our agreement. We fought about it for a while, myself and I, but obviously I won out in the end."

"Van Holt?" I said. Thomas was next to me, making a motion for me to hurry up and get something out of the man. "Peter, what are you talking about?"

"Tonight the arrests happen," Van Holt said. "MPs, anarchists, republicans, anyone you've ever talked to. They will be rounded up and put in magic cloth that will keep this great nation safe."

Thomas heard this and hurried outside to talk to the generals.

"Peter, don't get me wrong, I'm glad you told me this, but why?"

"Why do you think? We made an agreement, didn't we?"

"Yes, that we'd make sure no harm came to the women or children in our life . . ." My words trailed off. I gripped the phone tight. "Is Laura on the list?"

"I didn't tell them about her," Van Holt said. "I don't know how they knew, but Godfrey was talking about how she was key to getting to you. I swear, I never breathed a word—"

I dropped the phone and raced out to the courtyard.

Thomas was already barking orders at the soldiers. "There's a crackdown happening tonight. We'll need volunteers to go into the city and pick up the targets before the cops reach them—"

"Thomas!" I wanted to grab him by his shoulders and shake him, my worry was so great, but the innate magic upon me didn't allow it. Thomas seemed to hear the stress in my voice however, because he spun around to face me.

"Paul? What's wrong?"

"They're going after *Laura*," I said. "You need to get her out of there before they arrest her."

"General, I'll let you take it from here," Thomas said, then put his hand on my shoulder and guided me aside. His eyebrows were scrunched together with concern at the fear in my voice. "Laura who exactly? Laura Spratt, your old landlady? Why would they go after her?"

"Yes, Laura Spratt. While I was staying in the cottage next to her house, I fell hard for her," I said. Thomas's eyebrows went up in surprise. "Godfrey somehow knows she's important to me. That's why Van Holt called. You and I, we have to go and—"

"*You're* not going anywhere," Thomas said. "This has all the markings of a trap."

"I'm sure Van Holt's telling the truth—"

"Sure. But it could still be a trap," Thomas said. "I'll go to Laura's house and get her out of there, but I can't do that if I'm trying to keep you safe as well."

"Still . . ."

"Don't worry. I'll bring the Parkeesh kid."

I followed Thomas's gaze over my shoulder to see Naveed striding towards us.

"What's going on, chaps?" Naveed asked, coming to join us.

"Hey, Parkeesh, the Virtuis Party is making a move tonight. We're going to go pick up Laura Spratt before they can scoop her up."

"Finally some action!" Naveed said, hopping on his feet. "Yes, let's! Time to bash some fash!"

"It's going to be a lot more covert than that," Thomas growled. "We're going to be in and out. If you can't handle that, stay here."

Naveed stopped hopping but couldn't keep the smile off his face. "Right, right. You're the boss, Dawes."

Thomas rolled his eyes. He turned to me. "We'll leave right now. Call Laura and tell her what's going on."

"R-right," I said, head spinning at how fast everything was moving. Already the soldiers were climbing into jeeps and rolling out. Thomas and Naveed got into Naveed's Mercedes and were off.

I used the phone in the guardhouse and tried to call Laura. There was no answer.

Holding the phone made me think back on Van Holt's words. He said he hadn't told anyone about Laura, and I believed him. But then, how had they figured out our connection? It was public knowledge that I'd been renting a cottage from her, but that wasn't much to go on. It seemed like a leap to assume that we were anything more than landlady and tenant.

Unless someone had told them that I loved her.

If anyone in the world knew, it would be the Fraught Friends. They'd spent countless hours at Hillcrest, had seen how I looked at Laura. If Naveed was a traitor, I'd just sent him off with Thomas. Had I just set up my best friend?

If it wasn't Naveed, then it was Harriet or Rosemary. The two of them were still in the castle.

I put the phone down and walked stiffly into the castle itself, moving without thought, like a windup toy. My suspicion was awful, but it made sense. I didn't want to believe there was a traitor amongst my students. I'd been so suspicious of Harriet early on—had I been right all this time? And Rosemary, always so quiet and watchful. Was she just gathering intel for the Virtuis Party? But why would she join an anti-immigrant group like that lot?

In the hallway I bumped into Tonya.

"Paul! You're white as a sheet! Are you okay?"

"I'm fine," I said, my voice tinny. "Say, have you seen Harriet lately? Or Rosemary?"

"They're both in the library. Are you sure you're okay?"

"Yes. But the Virtuis Party is doing a crackdown tonight. You should get on the horn to any journalist you've been in touch with. Warn them that they need to go to ground."

Tonya's eyes widened and she hurried off.

I walked towards the library with a heavy tread, trying to figure out if this was even the right call to go see the girls—maybe I should wait for Thomas to come back, or grab a couple of soldiers to come with me. But I felt like if I spoke to them myself first, I'd be able to discern where their loyalties lay.

I pushed the door open to the library.

Harriet was in the middle of the room. She pivoted in place to smile at me. "Professor!"

In that moment, I knew in my gut that Harriet wasn't the traitor.

Rosemary and Oberon were on the far side of the room, looking at a book together. They likewise turned to see me. I stood there in the doorway, tongue tied as I stared at Rosemary.

"Ah," she said, before clapping the book shut. She put the book back on the shelf, then stepped forwards and made a motion as if she were pulling on something on either side of her.

In the moment it was hard to say what happened, but the result was clear: Harriet was cut into several pieces, clean cuts that went right through her at various angles. Oberon was also cut though he wasn't bisected like Harriet was: His face was bloody on the left side. The hand he held up to his jaw was also bleeding and missing a pinkie. He was screaming. Harriet was just a pile on the floor.

I tried to step forwards to . . . I didn't know what exactly. I had some vision that if I could just push all the pieces of Harriet back together she'd be all right. But a sharp sting stopped me. I stepped back and felt my cheek—there was blood on my fingertips. I reached out through the doorway into the library and felt the same sting again, like there was something invisible and sharp in the room.

"Do you like it, Professor? I made a suit that lets me lay invisible wires around a room, and then when I need them I just give a little tug and . . ." Rosemary gestured to the bloody scene before her. Oberon had slid down to the ground, both hands on his face now as if trying to hold it together. He was still screaming but somehow I could hear Rosemary over the noise, as if my brain had isolated his screams and turned down the volume. There was also a strange ringing in my ears.

Rosemary tilted her head to look at me. "You heard about Mrs Spratt, yes? I was hoping you wouldn't guess it was me, but that was a foolish wish." She closed her eyes and started walking over to the doorway, taking a curved path to avoid Harriet's body. "I hope you also realize that I didn't do this out of any ill will for you or her. It is not like that at all! I like both of you very much, and it was so hard watching you mope over her. Sitting in the castle will never win her back. I thought that by doing this, it might spur you to play the hero, that by rescuing her you two could finally be together. Oh well."

She walked through the doorway and I took a step back into the hall. She finally opened her eyes again. She smiled.

"Well, I've known for a while that there is no place for me here," she said. "It makes me sad. I wish there was. But since there's not, I shall go."

She waited as if giving me a chance to say something, but my mind was full with the image of Harriet's remains, the sense that her blood would keep flowing until it filled the castle.

Rosemary shrugged and left.

I couldn't even turn my head to watch her go. My head was locked in place, staring at the horrible scene in the library.

What broke me out of this trance was the fact that Oberon wasn't screaming anymore. He was still breathing but he'd passed out, his hands falling to his sides, the blood on his face flowing freely.

I was starting to realize that Harriet was beyond help, but Oberon was still alive. I needed to go in there and get him out of that room.

I stepped forwards and reached out slowly. Again, my hand felt something thin and sharp, one of the many invisible wires Rosemary had put in place. But Rosemary herself had been able to walk through them unharmed. Was the weaver immune to them? No, there was a trick to it. Rosemary had closed her eyes as she'd walked through the room.

I tried it myself. With my eyes closed I reached back into the room. Nothing. I took a step in and was still fine.

I walked into the library, remembering only at the last second that in the very middle of the room sat Harriet's remains. I curved around, but not far enough—my left foot slipped out from under me when I stepped in some blood. I hit the floor hard but immediately scrambled away from where Harriet lay in a heap. When I stopped I realized I was lost—I could open my eyes but what if a wire ran me through?

"Oberon! Oberon!" I yelled. I heard a faint grunt in reply. I steeled my nerves and crawled towards the sound, soldiering on even when I once more passed through blood.

I hit the far shelf and then felt my way to where Oberon was slumped over.

"Okay, Obie, time to get out of here," I said, trying to sound casual even as my teeth were chattering. I kept my eyes screwed shut tight as I put Oberon's arm over my shoulder. In my panic I had forgotten just how much bigger than me Oberon was: I couldn't lift him. But he seemed to come back to some consciousness, enough to stagger to his feet.

"Keep your eyes closed, all right?" I said. He didn't reply but stayed in step with me as we staggered our way towards the other side of the room. I felt the way to the doorway.

"Help!" I started yelling as soon as my fingers found the doorframe. I would have called out sooner, but I was terrified at the idea of some poor soldier running into the library and getting sliced to ribbons. "Help! We need a doctor!"

We stepped through the doorway and I nearly shoved Oberon to the ground, I was so eager to be out of that room. I sank down to my knees next to him. I tried to open my eyes but found I couldn't. Even though I told myself that it was safe now, my mind refused to believe me.

I heard the sound of feet coming down the hall and then Tonya screaming.

~

As more people gathered round I was able to open my eyes again. Tonya and a couple of soldiers bandaged Oberon's face and bundled him into a car to take him to hospital. Tonya hopped into the car to go with him ("Somebody has to, and I'm all he's got"). The soldiers swept the palace looking for Rosemary, but a couple of guards as well as an on-duty mage said they had spotted her leaving the castle.

I went to sit with Sabina, keeping watch in case anything else should happen. I must have looked to be in rough shape because after her initial barrage of questions Sabina let me be.

Around dawn Thomas returned.

"Paul," he said, "I have some bad news."

CHAPTER 41

We went to Lady Fife's office. I so badly wished that Lady Fife were there to hear the bad news instead of me.

Thomas's bad news came down to the fact that Laura had been arrested, and so had Naveed. I nodded, looked down at my hands.

"I'm sure you heard about Rosemary," I said. "And how Oberon's been maimed and Harriet's dead."

"Yes, I did hear."

I felt a coldness spreading through my limbs. "Harriet has a little brother." It was important to me that I get this out before the coldness reached my vocal cords and I was unable to speak. "Troy Hollister. He's only fourteen. He's the world to her. We need to get word to him that his sister's dead."

"There will be time for that later," Thomas said gently.

"The time for that is *now*!" My hands clenched into fists and it felt like ice was cracking around my bones. "Jesus Christ, her body's still in the library—"

"No, some soldiers have collected her remains," Thomas said. That made me pause.

"And they weren't cut apart?" Maybe Rosemary's wires only worked for a limited time, or maybe they disappeared after she took the coat off. The question of how exactly the magic worked distracted me for all of two seconds, and then everything came crashing down. I sank deep into the couch. I tried to wipe away the tears but the motion made me think of Oberon in the library, trying to hold his face together.

Thomas put his arms around me and held me close as I let it all out. It meant a lot to me since Thom was usually one to shy away from physical contact. I don't know how long we stayed like that but after a while I calmed down enough to remember to breathe.

~

If there was something good that came out of the night of arrests, it was that suddenly the Tories were willing to meet with us for the first time.

"MP Wilcox was supposed to be arrested last night but managed to give them the slip," Thomas said as we sat in my office. I had taken a couple of pills to help me sleep and now was drinking coffee to help keep me awake. "MP Collins was not on the arrest list but is still laying low. Both of them are key figures in the Conservative Party, leaders of opposing factions. The fact they made a joint appeal to us I think bodes well."

"Great," I said dimly. Thomas paused.

"It's important that we meet with them as soon as possible," he said. "The Virtuis Party has tightened their hold on the country but further eroded their legitimacy. Now is our chance to overthrow them."

"Right, right." After arresting nearly two dozen MPs from both the Labour and Conservatives, the Virtuis Party had put "temporary representatives" or "appointed members of Parliament" in their place. These "AMPs" were all Virtuis Party members or allies of them.

Thomas ran a hand through his hair.

"Also at the meeting will be Jack Spratt."

That woke me up. "Laura's husband? Why is he coming? He's not an elected official."

"Well, his dad is a sitting lord, and I imagine that now that his wife is in the clink, he has a vested interest in getting her out," Thomas said. "Just a guess. And I don't know, maybe he's curious about you."

I was likewise curious about him.

"When is the meeting?"

~

The meeting was in St Albans at dusk. During peacetime, I loved visiting St Albans. Small enough that one could see it all in a day but with a deep history that rewarded return trips. I loved the towering cathedral in the field, the Roman ruins on the outskirts of town, the medieval market that still had the trading bell from hundreds of years ago. But it seemed that for this trip all I'd get to see of the place was a tiny pub.

Thomas and I both wore magical disguises. Some of our soldiers also went with us in plain clothes, guns and knives hidden under their jackets. They infiltrated the pub first and, when it was safe, made a sign so Thomas and I could enter.

The publican showed us to a back room where the three men were waiting for us.

Wilcox had bushy white hair and a ruddy if friendly face. Collins had dark hair and, though his face wasn't as lined as Wilcox's was, seemed older. Maybe it was from the scowl as he stared out the window, keeping watch.

But of course I only had eyes for the youngest man amongst them, Jonathan "Jack" Spratt. I'd seen his picture before, both in the news and from a few stray photos left up around Laura's house. But now, seeing him in person, I had to admit something I'd always tried to deny: he was a handsome man. Attractive in a kind of odd way, a skinny-white-boy way, with a vulpine face and curly russet hair. If we'd met in another life, I might have offered to buy him a drink.

He seemed somewhat startled by my gaze as he stood and held out his hand to me.

I shook his hand. I felt my magic working on Spratt, making him like me, though more than anything it seemed to just leave him confused. He let go of my hand with a puzzled frown.

"Jack Spratt," he said. "Though I assume you already know that, Mr Gallagher."

"That's Court Magician Gallagher to you," Thomas said.

Collins snorted. "Getting a bit ahead of yourselves, aren't you?"

"Hardly," I said. "The king is upholding an illegal government. His current Court Magician can't even make mages. The people are being represented by appointed stooges rather than the people they voted in." Collins scowled; that very day in the Houses of Parliament an AMP had taken Collins's place and made votes on various laws. "I am as much the country's Court Magician as you are the MP for Gloucester."

Collins was still scowling but my words had moved him from windowsill to table. Thomas and I likewise sat down. We started talking of the future: If we were to dispose of King Harold and the Virtuis Party, would the Tories recognize Katherine as head of state? There was some hemming and hawing but the general read I got from Wilcox was that he would support an uprising against Harold and all that came after it. Spratt nodded in seeming assent. But Collins stayed silent, a grey cloud over his head.

"And what do you think there, Gloomy Gus?" I asked Collins when his silence had gotten too much for me. "If you have something to say, now's your chance. Maybe you don't want me as Court Magician?"

"Oh, no! Better a Liverpool lad like you than the woman or the Afrikaner. What concerns me, 'Court Magician,' is just how vital you plan to make the monarchy to Britain."

I straightened up a little, surprised by Collins's words. "This is England. The Crown's always had power here."

"Yes, as a *symbol.* And once upon a time, actual power too. But for the last couple of hundred years, we as a populace have moved away from the ideas of divine rule of kings, of prima nocta, of one all-powerful ruler anointed at birth. Little by little we have shifted control of this Commonwealth from something inherited by one to something representational of all. And you would undo that. By giving a monarch the ability to protect the nation, themselves alone, you'd be investing in them a power that no king or queen has ever held before."

I could see why Collins was so persuasive when arguing his case in front of the other MPs.

"You are exaggerating, MP Collins," I said. "Queen Katherine will not have any more power than any other modern royal. The royal family will once again live to serve the British people."

"So you'd bind them with this spell and then leave them powerless? Just pampered sacrifices?" Collins said. "I find that hard to believe."

"Well, even so, you must admit it's better than what we have *now.*"

"I don't know about that," Collins said. "Right now the people who protect Britain are prisoners repaying a debt to society. Rather than leveraging their position for power, they are working to get back to the level of a respectable citizen. It's a far better system."

"For *you*, maybe," Thomas said hotly.

"For everyone," Collins said. "If you manage to overthrow King Harold and get the Virtuis Party out of power, myself and my contingent of the Conservative Party will recognize Katherine as queen. But I will not vote for any measure that puts more power in the hands of the Crown and out of the hands of the people."

"Yet you're happy to lock up those same people and use them as magical batteries," Thomas said.

Collins shrugged. "I represent the good, law-abiding people of my riding."

"Well, not right now, you don't," I said.

He nodded. “We may disagree on some policy, but I want those appointed MPs out of Parliament as much as you do.”

“Yes,” Wilcox said, butting in, “and you will give us your word that once Katherine is in power, she will call an open and general election?”

“Of course. It’s the only way for the country to move forwards from this takeover,” I said. Wilcox and Collins traded a glance and the smallest of nods.

“Then I think we are all in accord,” Wilcox said. With the sense that the meeting was over, we stood. For the first time since we had introduced ourselves, Spratt spoke up.

“Say, Gallagher, I was hoping I could speak to you alone for a moment,” he said, so casually it came off as inappropriate. Everyone froze, then looked to see my response. It suddenly felt less like a clandestine meeting with powerful men and more like a community potluck where everyone was just looking for fresh gossip.

“Yeah, sure,” I said. I let Spratt go out the back door first. As I followed him out I felt Thomas use the magic of his suit to slip into my shadow and disappear from sight.

Spratt and I stood outside. It was a nice night, a muddy, spring scent in the air. Next to the pub a thin stretch of the river Ver slowly flowed. There were lots of trees and bushes framing the river, and if it weren’t for the looming cathedral and other buildings around us, I might have thought we were in the woods.

Spratt had been very nonchalant in the pub, but now he seemed to have trouble finding his words.

He had stopped fidgeting and put his hands into the pockets of his overcoat. He squinted at me, as though trying to make me out in the moonlight. “She asks about you all the time, you know.”

“Laura does?” I said, heart beating double time.

“No. Beatrix,” Spratt said.

“Oh.” That made me smile, but I tried not to let it linger. I was able to sober up when I thought of how, because of me, Laura had been torn from her daughter, the one person on Earth she wanted to protect. "I'm really sorry about what happened with Laura. The Virtuis Party bigwigs, they got it into their heads that there was something more between us, but nothing ever happened."

"I know," Spratt said haughtily. "Laura told me."

That made me pause. I'd been telling the truth in that there had been nothing physical between us; Laura and I had never kissed, never even walked hand in hand. But the thought of Laura explaining this to Spratt . . . it felt ironically like something intimate between us had been exposed.

Because I was also lying: there had been *something* there, a frisson that had never been acknowledged until it was too late.

"But, well, regardless of whether it is true or not, here we are." Spratt had the kind of posh accent that made all his *r*'s *w*'s. It was so distracting that it took me a second to notice when he pulled a gun out of his pocket.

Thomas sprang from my shadow so quickly that Spratt barely had time to react. Thomas grabbed the hand with the gun and twisted it away. There was a scream from Spratt as Thomas yanked the gun away: in the struggle Thomas had broken Spratt's trigger finger.

Wilcox and Collins rushed out.

"What kind of joke is this?" Thomas asked, gesturing towards Spratt with his own gun. "You asked us here as an ambush?"

"Good God, no!" Wilcox said. "What happened?"

"We were just talking and he pulled a gun on me," I said.

Collins stepped forwards and slapped Spratt upside the head. "You idiot! You'd endanger the nation to settle some personal score?"

"I wasn't going to kill him!" Spratt whined. "The deputy minister called me earlier and said if I delivered Paul Gallagher to them, they'd let Laura go."

Collins slapped him again.

"Really? And you believed them?" I asked, curious. At Spratt's words, I felt a flutter of hope.

"Well, yes. Why would they keep Laura if they have you? And my family still wields some power—they'd want to stay on our good side."

"Oh God," Collins said. "If Spratt here has turned traitor, the military might already have this place surrounded."

"I didn't tell them about where tonight's meeting was," Spratt said. He looked at me. "Gallagher, if you truly felt sorry for what happened to my wife, you'd turn yourself in. I'd offer myself up for her, but they don't want me; they want *you*."

"How convenient for you, eh?" Thomas said, levelling a light kick at his side. "Go home and be a family man, then."

Thomas pulled me away, leaving Wilcox and Collins to tend to the crying Spratt.

~

My first meeting with Jack Spratt had been eventful, to say the least. It was probably the only time in my life when my opinion of a person had gone up after they had pulled a gun on me. I'd believed him when he'd said he was just trying to save Laura. And when he'd said that I should just turn myself in, that had rung true too. In fact, on the car ride home, the sense of his words became more and more apparent, until I grew nearly deliriously happy as I realized that it would solve all my worries. If I handed myself in, they would release Laura. If I handed myself in, I could talk to Rosemary and keep her from killing anyone else. If I handed myself in, I'd never have to cut up and kill Thomas, because I'd be dead.

Of course, while handing myself over would solve a lot of problems, I also knew it would be a huge blow for the princess's cause. But even that proved a flaw in our side: the fact that everything rested so heavily on *me*. Sure, it was flattering some of the time, but oftentimes it was crushing, not just in the moment but when I considered the future; if something were to happen to me, we'd be a lost cause. Everyone we'd lost along the way—Harriet, the soldiers, the villagers—we'd join them in the grave with nothing to show for it.

The morning after our meeting with Spratt and the Tories I found Cobalt muttering under his breath while on washing-up duty.

"Good morning, Cobalt," I said, rolling up my sleeves to pitch in. He startled when he saw me.

"Oh, good morning, Paul," he said. "What are you doing here?"

"I'm on the roster for morning dish duty, aren't I?"

"Yes, but after everything that happened, Thomas took you off for the week." Cobalt stood and dried his hands. "I'm sorry about Harriet Hollister. She was a very nice girl."

I didn't even think that Cobalt had ever talked to her.

"Yes." She was, but she was so much more than that. Resilient and strong but at times obnoxiously naive. Driven and loyal but not to the point that she couldn't make a break when her conscience got the better of her.

"Honestly, I'm surprised you are up and about," Cobalt said.

I tried not to bristle at that—every time people had commiserated with me, there had been an edge of judgement to their words and expressions, surprise that I wasn't falling to pieces after watching my protégé be slaughtered. But I was the Court Magician. My duty was to protect Kitty, her mother, Sabina, and everyone else in the castle. Of course I had to hold it together. I would have been judged even more harshly by everyone if I'd curled up into myself. Even in my grief I always put too much weight on what other people thought.

Only Thomas had seen me really lose it over Harriet's death. That night, after I was done crying, I had asked him if he would perform deep magic on me: I could then use the power to restore Harriet to life, just like how her father had resurrected Godfrey.

Thomas hadn't said no outright, perhaps worried that if he did I'd just seek out Cobalt and get him to do it.

"That's always an option," Thomas had said. "But before you go about carving yourself up to bring back the dead, maybe ask yourself if there's living people who still need your help."

"It has been difficult," I said to Cobalt. "But unfortunately, times being what they are, we can't fully give the dead their due. Someday we'll be able to mourn them properly, when Kitty's in power and we've set things right in this country."

Cobalt nodded and handed me a plate to dry. We worked in silence for a couple of minutes before I spoke again.

"I've been thinking about what you said," I said. "If I had died the other night, it would be a major blow. I'm not trying to puff myself up here. It's just as you said: having only one mage maker at any time is a liability."

Cobalt nodded, his hands shaking slightly as if he was afraid to speak.

"I want to make you a mage maker," I said.

Cobalt turned to me, splashing some water on the floor. "Truly?!"

"Yes, truly," I said. "Let's do it tonight."

Cobalt nearly dropped a plate but swiftly caught it with his other hand. "T-tonight? Why not tomorrow? I need some time . . ."

"To what? Put your affairs in order?" I asked. I was smiling but my voice was sharp. "Do you think it's not going to work?"

Cobalt straightened up. "No. I know it will work. Let's do it tonight."

"Good." I went back to drying dishes. "I need you to keep it secret, and I mean it. Don't mention it to Thomas."

Cobalt glanced at me, then nodded.

And so that night, with Kitty as a witness, I broke the small segment on Cobalt's finger. He cried out but smiled just as quickly as the change came over him.

~

I thought of leaving Thomas a letter explaining my actions, but I worried he might discover it before I had a chance to leave and then he'd stop me. It felt wrong going without saying goodbye, but if I really did want to slip away I couldn't let anyone catch on to my plan.

As far as getting in touch with Rosemary, I simply called the boardinghouse she lived at. I left a message with her landlady, telling her I would deliver myself into Rosemary's hands but only if she came alone. I wanted to talk to her, and I figured this was my best chance. Actually leaving the castle was easy enough: I just stepped out through the gate. The guards were nervous about me going out on my own, but at the end of the day I wasn't a prisoner. They had to let me go. They probably rushed word to Thomas as soon as I was through the castle gate, so I double-timed it to put distance between myself and Windsor.

The plan was to meet Rosemary near the train station. I waited in an alley for her, watching the soldiers checking over the passengers who had arrived on the train—by the look of it, commuters from Slough to London who were now caught in the middle of this civil war. They seemed somewhat resigned to having to prove their residency to the soldiers, and the soldiers, used to the routine, joked with the people as they checked their names off the list. Thomas would have scowled to see it; he would say that the train station guards had become complacent and needed to be rotated out.

Hands snaked up around me from behind, loose but intimate like a lover's caress. I spun around to see Rosemary.

"Hello, Professor," she said. "What are you wearing?"

"It's the outfit that Oberon and Harriet made for me," I said, my voice catching slightly on Harriet's name. "It's a recoup cloak."

"A recoup cloak? An odd choice."

"I wanted to wear something nonthreatening." I took in her outfit—the black sheer lace overlaid on brown satin. "Oh, Rosemary. You didn't have to wear your hypnotism dress. I'm here willingly."

"I believe you, Professor," Rosemary said. "But this just makes it easier for everyone."

"I wanted the chance to talk with you. Alone."

"There will be time for that later," Rosemary said. "But for now I wanted to tell you of a cathedral in Estonia. It is a wondrous building, constructed in such a way that its earthen walls create the most compounding echoes. They say that a single step in the church nave will echo fourteen times. Imagine that. A single step and fourteen echoes. One, two, three, four, five . . ."

Rosemary's words were low and soothing and seemed to seep into the crevices of my brain. Everything grew hazy and I was only dimly aware of Rosemary taking my hand in hers. Everything felt nice, like I was drifting in a hot bath.

Then I felt something tighten on my wrist and I snapped back to awareness.

Fairweather's face was in front of me, his eyes wide in surprise.

"Oh, he's awake!"

I recognized where I was: the wine cellar at Buckingham Palace. The walls were made of taupe and beige blocks of stone. On the other side of the room were racks of wine. The dim bulbs overhead almost gave the place a romantic lighting. The soft atmosphere was undercut by the fact that I was tied to a chair and surrounded by enemies.

Aside from Fairweather, Gabs and Van Holt were also there. Near the wall I saw Godfrey and Rosemary, talking quietly. All of them looked to me. Gabs and Van Holt nearly bowled over Fairweather as they hurried over. All three started talking at once.

"Oh, dear heart, why did you come here?!"

"Young man, you are going to pay for what happened to my dear little Harriet!"

"I hope you are ready to die, Gallagher!"

Their tones were a mix of angry, worried, and astounded. I had never felt so popular.

Godfrey strode over and their haranguing fell silent.

"Why did you come here, Jim?" he asked. He said it kindly, like a friendly but distant uncle asking how your studies were going. But the name Jim was always like a knife in the gut.

"I heard from Spratt that you'd release Laura if he brought me to you," I said, trying to match Godfrey's casual tone. "I figured I'd cut out the middleman."

"Ah. You called it correctly, Miss Panyi." Godfrey looked back to me. "She's a classic Judas, that one. Sold you out for a bit of silver. A mercenary with no ties."

"Aren't you afraid she might betray you in turn?" I asked.

Godfrey shook his head. "You couldn't outbid us. She said that if we had Laura Spratt in hand, we could draw you in."

Van Holt was looking at me imploringly, as if wishing to say, *See? See? I didn't tell them about Laura.* But I had bigger things on my mind than reassuring Van Holt.

"Did you let her go?"

"Of course. Her father-in-law is a pretty big wheeler and dealer in the House of Lords—it pays to have him in our debt or at least afraid of us. So we'll throw the old dog a bone this time. Laura Spratt is back where she belongs, with her husband and child."

That last bit was definitely meant to hurt. I closed my eyes and breathed deeply—now wasn't the time to get upset about Laura living with another man. The important thing was that she'd live. "Good. That's good."

Godfrey patted me reassuringly on the shoulder.

"You must pay for your crimes, Gallagher!" Fairweather said, heat in his voice. "You tore this country apart in your bid for power and used your sexual sway to bring not one but two vulnerable young girls under your power! None of this would have happened if Princess Katherine had married me!"

"I mean, sure, that's probably true."

"And also, *Harriet would still be alive*!" Fairweather was looking apoplectic now, more colour in his face than seemed healthy. "She died because *you* tricked her into becoming a mage maker, because *you* used her as a pawn!"

"No," I said, throat tight. It seemed odd that Fairweather was having a go at me when Harriet's *actual murderer* was in the room, but I could unfortunately see where he was coming from. I'd put a target on her back when I'd given her such powerful magic.

"Which limb do you want to lose first?" Van Holt was staring down at me like I was a bug he was going to enjoy crushing.

Before I could answer there was a knock on the door. Godfrey went up the cellar stairs and answered it. He quietly conferred with a young man in the hall. Both Van Holt and Fairweather were practically buzzing with a need to hurt me. Gabs gave me a pitying look. Rosemary just looked bored. Eventually Godfrey shut the door and returned to us.

"Thomas Dawes has broken into the palace. He's already killed a dozen men all on his lonesome."

"Gallagher's best friend is here?!" Van Holt said, voice shaking with excitement. "*Yes!* This is better than killing Gallagher!" He turned to me. "I'm going to go find Dawes, kill him, then I'm going to come back here and toss his head in your lap."

"Oh, Peter, no. Don't go seek out Thomas," I said. "He'll kill you."

Van Holt was stunned into silence, as if my concern for his safety was a bigger blow than any insult could have been. Stiffly, he turned to Godfrey. "Don't kill him before I get back."

Godfrey shrugged. "Well, you best hurry then."

Van Holt didn't need any further encouragement. He bounded up the cellar stairs two at a time.

Gabs sighed. "I suppose that someone should *actually* go and stop Dawes, hmmm?"

"If you would be so kind, Interim Court Magician," Godfrey said.

Gabs looked at me.

"Aren't you going to try and stop me?" she asked. "Tell me not to throw my life away?"

Gabs was wearing a silvery gown that seemed to fold over itself in artful ways. I wondered what kind of effect it had and whether Thomas would be up to the challenge of defeating her. Especially here, effectively on her home turf, surrounded by our enemies.

Why did that stupid guy have to break in here? He was about to undo the whole point of my sacrifice. Maybe I should have left him a note after all.

"Don't go, Gabs," I said. "I'll miss your company."

Gabs smiled and leaned down to kiss my cheek.

"I'm sorry, pet," she said. "Call me a coward but I just can't stand to watch you die a horrible death."

"Ah, so you'll help me get out of here then?"

She chuckled and drew back. She was standing in front of me, a fond if bittersweet smile on her face; then a second later she had teleported to the top of the cellar stairs and was out the door.

"Well, I'm sure our esteemed interim Court Magician has things under control; things are getting rather hot here at the palace," Godfrey said. "I'll be coordinating the next phase from my office. Rosemary, I need you to ask your professor here about how he manages to do the magic he does. Get it out of him by hook or by crook."

"Or by pliers and knives?" I asked, watching as Fairweather opened a suitcase full of sharp, nasty-looking devices.

"Well, eventually, I suppose, yes," Godfrey said. "Just pretend you're teaching a class. Rosemary here wants to learn *everything*."

"I'll do it," Fairweather said, voice steely. "I'll get it all out of him."

I'd never heard Fairweather sound so sure before, so intense. Gone was his usual vapid grin; instead his mouth was a flat line, his hands shaking as he took out some chains. I felt not only fear but also guilt. Whenever Harriet and Kitty had confessed to me how uneasy Fairweather had made them, I had always been sympathetic and understanding, but later on in private I'd chuckle. I could understand disliking Fairweather and being annoyed by him, but being *scared* of him? I wrote it off as them being teenage girls with nervous dispositions.

Now, seeing how dead set he was on torturing me, I saw that I'd never had the right read on them or on Fairweather.

"Well, I'll be off then," Godfrey said, barely glancing my way before leaving the cellar. I almost felt insulted—I'd brought the man back from the dead after all. He could have stayed to chat a little bit longer before leaving me to die.

Fairweather didn't even look up as Godfrey left, too intent on examining a torture device that looked like a mini guillotine.

Rosemary stepped in front of me, blocking my view of Fairweather.

"See, Professor? I told you we'd get a chance to talk," she said.

"This . . . isn't exactly what I had in mind." I tested the bonds. I was sitting in a chair that was ornate but also common; there were probably two thousand chairs just like it in Buckingham Palace, with curved rosewood arms and backing and a pink, floral upholstered seat. It was an awful chair to torture someone in—my blood would just seep into the seat cushion.

"Well?" Rosemary said. "I do want to hear what you have to say."

Before it gets ripped out of me, I thought.

"Jesus. I can't believe those idiots think you're doing this for *money*," I said.

Rosemary tilted her head to the side to look at me.

"Why am I doing this, then?" she asked.

"You got bored," I said. "It's like you said—I was sitting in the castle when I should have been taking the fight to the enemy. Well, I'm here now."

"So this was all part of some larger plan?" Rosemary asked, a light in her eyes. "You were just a Trojan horse of some kind?"

"Well, not exactly. I really did come here all by my lonesome. I wanted to talk to you, Rosemary. Come back to me."

"Really? You'd take me back even after what I did to Harriet?"

What I did to Harriet. As if she'd said an unkind word to her rather than sliced her into a dozen pieces.

"Why, Rosemary? Why would you do something so awful?"

"Godfrey told me that if I was discovered, to kill her. But it was quick at least, wasn't it?" She spoke earnestly, searching my face for reassurance.

I sighed. I'd long noticed that there was something off about Rosemary but I'd never thought too deeply on what it was. If I'd been a better teacher, if I'd spent more time with her, maybe I would have seen her for what she was: a psychopath. Things didn't have to be this way. If I'd known she was capable of this remorseless cruelty, I would have taken her under my wing, tried to guide her along a less violent path.

But it was too late for that now. I didn't bother asking Rosemary again how she could do such a gruesome thing to someone who was her friend. That line of talk would just confuse Rosemary and time was of the essence as Fairweather narrowed down which torture tool he wanted to start with.

"It's not enough to make it quick. You can't just kill people like that. You could have left the castle without killing anyone; I know you could have."

Rosemary considered this, then shrugged and nodded.

"Yes, Professor, I could have, but I didn't want to," she said. "It wasn't just boredom that made me turn traitor. I was a bit jealous. I was so happy when I was your student, studying alongside Harriet and

Naveed. You were the first person I've ever met that I actually wanted to impress." Her mouth twisted in distaste, as if she hated admitting this. "I wanted to be special to you. But then you took Harriet as your protégé and Naveed as your lover, and it felt like there was nothing left for me but to become your most hated enemy."

"I don't hate you." It was true. I felt conflicted on that, since I knew that I should have hated her for Harriet's sake. But I knew Rosemary wasn't like most people. It wasn't fair to judge her by the same norms.

Rosemary smiled sadly. "So I have failed even there."

I shook my head. "No, Rosemary, you are special to me. You and I, we see things clearly in a way the rest of the world doesn't. We'd be very lonely without the other."

"Do you mean that, Professor? You have so many friends, so many people who love you. Do you really hold a special love for me, apart from all of them?"

"Rosemary," I said, "look how far I've come just to talk to you."

That got to her—a softness coloured her face and the doubt in her eyes melted away. The moment was ruined when Fairweather, while playing with some clamp-like contraption, set it off with a clatter. He yelped and let the device fall to the floor.

"Do we have any plasters?" he called over to Rosemary. She glared at him and he flinched. The exchange made me chuckle—finally, a teenage girl who scared Fairweather rather than the other way around.

"Ah, found them," Fairweather muttered, then went about treating the small cut on his hand.

Rosemary turned back to me.

"Professor, as much as I wish to help you, I don't know if it would be the right call in the long run."

"In the long run, the Virtuis Party will ruin this country."

"Exactly," Rosemary said, eyes bright as though backlit by a fire burning in her skull. "This country, the people here live in such ignorance of the evils committed on their behalf. They eat food that has been stolen from other countries. They colonize other lands and then treat those indigenous people like shit, doubly so if they come to Britain to make a life for themselves. I think it would be funny to see the very people who champion these beliefs die by them. To watch the people of Britain drink the poisoned tea that they themselves have brewed."

"Rosemary, I know in your childhood you had to make your way alone across Europe, and you must have seen some horrific things and maybe you even blame Britain for some of it. But—"

"Professor, I am not here for justice," Rosemary said, aghast. "I don't care about that. I just thought seeing this country run into the ground by fascists would be *funny*."

Fairweather had finished treating his cut. He picked up some kind of clamp and looked at it inquisitively. I was running out of time.

"Do you really, Rosemary? Has it been any more exciting running with this lot than with the crowd at Windsor? A few minutes ago, when Godfrey told you to torture me to death, you looked fucking *bored*. I'd be insulted if I weren't so frightened."

Rosemary smiled at that, so I pressed on.

"Look, I know there are great injustices that need to be addressed, and under Katherine's reign, we as a nation are going to do our best to try and make things right—"

"Professor, I already told you, I don't care—"

"I know," I said, cutting back in. "I know. What I'm saying is, those of us in the country who oppose the Virtuis Party, that's about all we have in common. The various groups want different things: to do away with the cloth magic prisons or keep them, to keep the Crown or abolish it. That's just the tip of the iceberg. You've lived in Windsor Castle. You saw how we were barely able to agree on a dish-washing rota. Now we'll have to hash out matters on a global scale! And everyone's so well intentioned but petty and prideful and convinced they are right. It's going to be a fucking mess. At the end of the day, wouldn't it be a lot more interesting for you to watch us try, rather than watch these creeps win?"

Rosemary said nothing, just stared at me.

"Aha!" Fairweather came over with some unpleasant-looking instrument that looked like something a dentist might use. "I think we'll start with this!"

"I thought you didn't like such brutality," I said, thinking of the last time I was tied to a chair.

Rosemary left us to go over to the box of devices and I tried not to lose all hope as she sorted through it.

"Usually I abhor violence but you have been such a cancer on this country it seems necessary," Fairweather said, opening and closing the device a few times.

Rosemary returned, holding a large mallet and something else, something so small I could only see what looked like a few loops of wire. As she came to stand next to Fairweather she dropped the mallet onto the floor. It landed by Fairweather's feet.

"Oops," Rosemary said flatly. Fairweather gave her a side-eye glance but knelt down to pick it up.

Rosemary took out the tiny item in her hand: it was a length of piano wire attached to two little knobs of wood. She looped it over Fairweather's head, then drew it tight.

Fairweather's eyes widened as the wire squeezed his throat. At first he tried to claw at it, but when his fingers found no purchase, he tried to stand. Before he could Rosemary stomped her foot hard into the back of his knee, bringing him down to all fours. Fairweather's face was vermilion now as he gasped for air. His fingers were scratching his skin in an attempt to get under the wire, but it was no use. He locked eyes with me and I couldn't look away, watching his long, pale face become bloated and red. Then it was over. His hands fell to the side and his whole body became deadweight.

Rosemary waited, grip still tight on the wire, holding up Fairweather's corpse. After a minute she unlooped the wire and let Fairweather's body hit the floor.

"Sorry, Professor, I thought it would be quicker," she said, winding the wire up. "I wish I could have seen his eyes. Such a revelation he must have had in the moment, knowing he was about to die."

The chair I was sitting in had one leg shorter than the other three—it clattered against the cobblestone floor as I shook.

"Oh, Professor! What's wrong?" Rosemary knelt down and placed a hand on each of my knees. The weight of her palms was light and warm and would have been comforting if not for the body lying next to her. "You're shaking!"

"Y-y-y-you just always have such a profound effect on me, Rosemary," I managed to get out.

Rosemary smiled. "Always the charmer, hmm, Professor?" She was obviously amused that I was able to flirt even while traumatized, but I knew I couldn't keep up such banter forever. I was worried that when I faltered, Rosemary might just kill me as well.

"Rosemary, i-if you stay kneeling on the floor like that you'll get your dress dirty."

"Oh!" She stood. "Thank you, Professor. Let us go."

She undid the bonds on my arms and legs. When I got to my feet I felt an extreme head rush and wobbled. Rosemary grabbed hold, steadying me. Making use of our closeness, she reached into my trouser pocket and left something there.

"It's a present for you," she whispered into my ear. "Don't you want to take it out and see what it is?"

I knew that whatever it was, it would be upsetting.

"I think I'd rather save it for later, if that's all right with you," I said.

She frowned and I could see the calculations going through her head: if I took it out right now she'd get the pleasure of seeing my reaction, but if I put it off that would build suspense and make it all the better once I finally took the thing out of my pocket.

"All right." She drew back, arms snaking over me as she pulled away.

"We should go find Thomas," I said, glad my panicked stammer was gone.

Rosemary nodded. "Yes, but let us free Naveed first."

~

Naveed was being kept in a room in the guest-quarters wing of the palace. Rosemary had me stay out of sight while she hypnotized the guards: from around the corner I heard as she ordered them into the room. Soon she signalled for me to come in.

As soon as I stepped over the threshold Naveed had his arms around me.

"Professor! I knew you'd come! Bloody well done, chap!" He was only wearing a white undershirt and navy-blue-striped boxer shorts. He did not seem to be injured, which was a relief.

Rosemary had handcuffed the two guards to a radiator in the corner, their faces dazed, their minds still clouded.

"Nice place," I said. Naveed's "cell" was even nicer than his room at Windsor Castle. Naveed rolled his eyes.

"They were trying to kill me with kindness. They thought that if they just asked nicely and often, eventually I'd join their side. Each time I just told them to jog on."

"You've been very brave," I said. Naveed rolled his eyes again but this time he grinned and blushed.

"Well, Professor, I am ready to repay their hospitality with a little bit of home reno. Let's tear this place apart! Who else is here? Dawes?"

"Yes. We're going to go find him."

"All right. And who else is here in fighting form? Doc Oberon? Harriet?" Naveed had been bouncing on his feet, but when he saw my face he stopped. "What's wrong?"

"Harriet and Oberon are dead," Rosemary said. "I killed them."

Naveed looked back and forth between us. "What?"

"Why are you upset? You didn't even like them," Rosemary asked, curious and callous.

"Were . . . were they traitors?" Naveed asked.

"No, silly. I'm the traitor," Rosemary replied.

Naveed took a step away from both of us, face going ashen.

"Oberon lived," I said to Rosemary, who shrugged. I looked to Naveed. "Rosemary was a spy for Godfrey and under his orders she killed Harriet. But I've talked with Rosemary, and she's agreed to help us. Right, Rosemary?"

"That's right," she said brightly.

"This . . . this is a lot to take in," Naveed said.

"I know," I said. "At the moment, my main concern is you two getting out of here alive. Can the two of you promise me you'll look out for each other?"

"Yes, I can do that," Rosemary replied with a chipper tone.

"Naveed?"

He was quiet but eventually nodded.

I headed out the door.

"Now, to find Thomas, I figure we just have to find a trail of bodies and see where they lead—"

I stopped so suddenly that Naveed and Rosemary bumped into me. Down at the end of the wide hall was Gabs.

I whirled around to face Naveed and Rosemary.

"Get out of here. I'll hold her off."

"Fat chance of that, Professor! We'll stick by you. The three of us can take her on!"

"Naveed, you don't even have magic clothes. You don't even have *clothes*."

"No, but I still have a good left jab and a mean right hook." He started bouncing on the balls of his feet.

"I've always wanted to fight her," Rosemary said, eyes past me and on Gabs.

"No. I need you two to go find Thomas and help him. *Please.*" The three of us might have been able to take out Gabs, but we'd all probably die in the process. If I could get these two kids out of here, maybe I'd be able to give Gabs the slip on my own.

The desperation in my voice seemed to reach them. Naveed and Rosemary traded uncertain looks, their bravado leaching away. Then they flinched, eyes wide as they both looked at something just behind me.

"Pet, you should have escaped while you had the chance," Gabs said from right behind me.

I turned around slowly. Gabs stood there, having seemingly teleported from one end of the hall to where we were. She stood there, back straight and bare handed and as intimidating as ever.

I smiled. "Without saying goodbye to you?"

She returned the smile but it was frosty. "Now you've put me in an awkward position. I *said* I didn't want to watch you die horribly, but I can't exactly let you and these two rapscallions go."

Behind me Naveed shifted his feet as he got in a fighting stance. I took a deep breath.

"Gabs, let the kids walk away," I said. "I'm the only one you want."

She started to shake her head, so I spoke again, forcing a smile.

"C'mon, babe. Am I your number one guy or not?"

Her smile at that was genuine, if sad.

"Always," she said.

"Then let's go and talk. Just you and me."

It felt like Naveed and Rosemary had stopped breathing. Eventually Gabs acknowledged them with a curt nod.

"Get lost, tots."

Both Naveed and Rosemary stayed where they were. I turned to face them.

"You heard her. Go."

They didn't look happy about it but they turned and ran down the hall and around the corner.

I smiled back at Gabs. "Finally, alone together."

"Always the charmer," she murmured, and I thought it was funny that she was the second person to say that to me in one night.

~

Gabs led me to a nearby room—not just any room but *her* room. It hit me when I saw the various half-finished projects littering the space, the opulent moulded furniture consumed completely by fabric swatches and sketches covering them. There was a table near a bay window with perhaps the only clear chair in the whole spot. I could imagine Gabs sitting there with a cup of tea, looking out at the London skyline. There was another chair at the table, but sitting in it was a mannequin. Gabs moved it onto the ground.

"Wow, is that thing fully articulated? I'm still using the most basic dress forms," I said.

"Usually I do too, but sometimes I want to see how my clothes would look on people while they're sitting down," Gabs said as she adjusted the mannequin into a comfortable sitting position, moving it lovingly like it was a friend. It felt odd to be talking shop with Gabs, like nothing had changed.

She stood. "Would you like a drink?"

"Yes, please." The liquor cabinet was right next to me and I turned to look over my options, but suddenly my view was blocked by Gabs. Not only had she teleported to be right in front of me, but she was also midpour.

"Aha!" I said. "It's not a teleportation outfit at all! It freezes time!"

She gave me a wry smile and I realized I should have kept my mouth shut, not shown my hand so blatantly.

"Here. Hope you don't mind your rum neat—I don't have any ice or mixers handy."

"Ah, right. I forgot you were a rum drinker." Gabs had once told me her proclivity for rum was a family trait, a legacy left over from when her family had been pirates, robbing ships passing through the Atlantic triangle before returning home to Cornwall.

We downed our drinks and Gabs poured us another.

"Since you know how my magic works, I think it's only fair that I hear about yours," Gabs said, eyeing my coat.

"It's a bit of healing magic. It allows me to take on other people's injuries," I said.

Gabs rolled her eyes. "Out of all the things you could wear, why that?"

"Because I came here to help people," I said.

"It's funny. Back at school you were crap at recoup cloaks and the like."

"I didn't make this one. Oberon and Harriet did," I said, my voice growing quiet.

Gabs softened, but only a little. "I'm sorry. I heard about what happened. Their deaths must have been quite a blow."

"Oberon's still alive," I said.

Gabs's eyes lit up. "Oh, I'm so glad to hear that!"

"Mmm." Earlier that day I had talked to Tonya on the phone—ostensibly to get an update on Obie's condition, but I'd been more invested in hearing her voice one last time before I died. Tonya had said that Oberon's condition was stable and he wasn't in mortal danger. As for his face, they had a surgeon coming in who was an expert in facial reconstruction.

"He helped pioneer the field! He did a lot of groundbreaking work helping World War One soldiers who were maimed during the war," Tonya had said with strained optimism. I'd seen some of those soldiers during my childhood and knew just how rough those fixes had been.

Gabs saw how distraught I looked and didn't ask for more details about Obie, even though I could tell she wanted to.

"Let's sit down," she said. We took a seat at the table, her in her usual seat, me where the articulated dummy had been minutes earlier. We sipped our rum until I broke the silence.

"Gabs, why are you working with these people?"

Gabs tilted her head to smile at me quizzically.

"What other options do I have?"

"Come work with us! Jesus, with an ace mage like you on our side, this whole thing would be over!"

"And do you think 'your' side would forgive me?" she asked. "Cobalt? Katherine? Do you think they'd ever trust me after I plucked out Cobalt's eye? How about Thomas or Obie?" She took in a shuddering breath. "Do you think Andrew would ever forgive me? Or Lady Fife?"

"They would understand. This is war, and we need all the strength we can get."

"Hmm. Still seems rather optimistic." Gabs traced the edge of her drink with her finger. "But there's more to it than that. When we talked at Lady Fife's house, you accused me of selling my soul for worldly power. But it's not like that, Paul. I haven't gone against my morals. I *agree* with Godfrey."

"What?! You agree with the mass arrests, the—"

"No, I don't agree with all of it," Gabs cut in. "But the cloth magic prisons not only keep the country safe, they provide jobs for thousands of cloth mages. For the first time in our lifetime, cloth magic is a sought-after profession! And the need for workers has opened up the field to women. The only people who suffer for it are criminals."

"No one should have to suffer for it! Under Katherine's rule—"

"That scared, stuttering, sun-shy little girl?" Gabs said. "Even if she were just to be a figurehead of this country, she would still not be up to the job. And you want to give her actual responsibilities? I can't get behind that."

"You aren't giving her enough credit. She's always been strong, even before all this went down."

Gabs shook her head. "I think you flatter the child."

"Gabs, Godfrey and his lot are only using you as long as they need you," I said. "As soon as they get their hands on a mage maker, they will shove you out the door or kill you outright."

"And you say there's a future with you and Princess Katherine?" Gabs asked, looking at me with a half smile, as if I'd made a bad joke and she was humouring me. "If I joined you, would you give me mage maker powers?"

In my head, I heard Thomas's voice yelling about what a bad idea that would be. If Gabs had the ability to make mages on her own, I could never relax. I'd always worry that Gabs was building up a power base to supplant me—she'd already made it clear she didn't want Katherine on the throne. And time and time again she'd shown that she had no qualms about using me to get what she wanted, whether it was marital harmony or political power.

"It's something we could discuss," I said. As soon as the words were out of my mouth I knew I hadn't successfully carried off the lie. Gabs knew me too well.

She looked away and nodded, her face downcast, tears beading in her eyes. Before I could try once more to win her over things changed in a blink. Gabs was sitting up straight, a stiletto knife in her hand. The knife's edge had a thin line of blood on it. There was a sharp, stinging pain in my neck, warmth as blood ran down onto my chest.

"I'm sorry, dear heart," Gabs said, and yes, there were tears in her eyes. "Oh, Paul. I wish this could have ended some other way."

Me too. I put one hand to my neck—it was a deep but clean cut. I could feel life bleeding out of me.

“Gabs.” The cut wasn’t deep enough to sever my vocal cords but it still clearly sounded like I was dying. I reached out to her. She was quick to grab my hand, the connection causing the tears to fall freely down her face.

Immediately the pain in my neck was gone. I felt totally fine except for a slight stress headache. Gabs gave a silent scream of surprise as the side of her neck opened up. For a whole horrible second I watched blood gush out of the wound. Then her upper body tilted forwards, forehead hitting the tabletop. She didn’t react.

The room was silent save for my ragged breathing. Her blood dripped off the table and the droplets were swallowed up by the plush carpet.

CHAPTER 42

For a moment I just sat there, breathing deeply, telling myself that I was all right. My left hand was still clutching Gabs's, so with my right hand I kept feeling my neck, making sure the skin was in fact intact.

From some other part of the palace came a loud bang, an explosion that rocked the room. It was enough to remind me that I was in fact still in danger. I had to find the others and get out of there.

Gabs's hand was growing cold in mine. Her grip was still loose but it took great effort on my part to free my hand from hers. Her last real act in life had been to take hold of my hand, to offer me comfort. To let go of that was to face that she was dead, that I'd killed her. I set her hand down gently before I pulled my own away.

I checked myself over one last time to make *sure* that I wasn't hurt. My shirt was still wet with blood and I felt a little woozy as I tried to pull the wet fabric away from the skin. Maybe Gabs had a clean men's shirt I could wear—

No. I knew I was stalling. Afraid to leave that room and confront whatever new horrors were out there. But if I stayed here in Gabs's room, eventually her allies would come looking for her and I'd be found, still sitting across from her corpse, shivering as the blood dried.

I got up and had to take a deep breath with each step, the carpet cushioning my shaky footfalls. Eventually I reached the door and took in a lungful of air, like I was about to dive into the Mariana Trench. I opened the door and ducked my head out into the hall.

A figure flew in and pushed me back into the room, a hand covering my mouth to muffle my scream of surprise. It was Thomas.

"There you are! Thank fuck! I've been looking all over for you—" He looked past me to see Gabs slumped over on the bloody table. "What the fuck? What happened here?" He looked at me, eyes full of disbelief and even a little respect. "Did *you* kill her?"

"Yes."

"But . . . *how*?"

"I couldn't convince her of a better future."

Thomas furrowed his brow, clearly wanting a less abstract answer. But he dropped it, stepping away to look me over with a scowl.

"Are you hurt?" he said, eyeing my bloody shirt.

"No. It's my blood but I'm fine, really. The wound's gone." Now that I was over my surprise at Thomas's appearance, anger was starting to bubble up. "What the hell are you doing here, mate? Attacking Buckingham Palace on your lonesome?!"

"What the hell are *you* doing here?!" Thomas replied. "Why would you just hand yourself over to the enemy?!"

"I did it to save Laura—"

"There were a million other ways we could have gone about that—"

"And to save *you*!" I said. "If I'd stuck around, eventually things would have gotten bad and we'd convince ourselves that the only way to win was to skin you alive. Well, I don't want to do that. I'd rather die."

"You think I *want* to be skinned alive?! Surprise, surprise, I *don't*, actually! But it's not just about what I want or what you want! It's about saving this country and the world!"

"If saving the world means using you like that, then fuck it," I said, anger coalescing into solid certainty. "I mean it. You're too important to me. You're a human being, not some handy tool. My best friend, not just some block of skin and muscle to be carved up."

Thomas swallowed, his own anger giving way to some other emotion. "Paul, it's all right," he said, blinking rapidly. "Everyone dies. If we do this, I get to die in a way that actually matters."

"Your life is worth more than your death," I said. "I know you don't always believe that, but I do. Lots of people do. So no matter what happens, I'm not going to trade your death in for anything."

Thomas nodded and ducked his head, but not before I saw a fleet of expressions flit by: relief, joy, surprise. It was strange to see such a mix of positive emotions on Thomas's face and his mouth and eyes twitched, as if unsure how to express them.

When he looked back at me, he was serious once more.

"I may have come here alone, but the others back at Windsor Castle are still helping me."

He had a messenger satchel with him, and from it he took out my yellow teleportation jacket, the one I'd used to get from Germany back to England. "Everyone there is thinking about you. The Parkeesh family, Kitty, Cobalt, the queen, the servants. Put this on and you'll be back with them."

I took the cloak from Thomas's hands.

"But what about you?"

"I can fight my way out," Thomas said.

"And what about Naveed and Rosemary? They're still here."

"I know. I ran into them earlier—they gave me the tip that you were in this part of the castle," Thomas said. "I will look for them and try and get us all out. I have some things I need to do here first anyway."

"But—"

"Paul, *please*!" Thomas actually stamped his foot. "I can't do what needs to be done if I'm worried about you! Please, just put on the cloak and go back to the others."

"All right." But still I hesitated. "Just . . . be careful, yeah?" What if this was the last time I talked to Thomas? What if he was killed by Godfrey or Van Holt or some random palace guard? Thomas seemed to be thinking the same thing, but like me he was suddenly tongue tied. He merely responded with a curt nod.

I took off my blue healing coat and stained shirt. Thomas found a spare man's dress shirt—it wasn't quite finished but Thomas quickly sewed on the missing buttons so I could wear it. I put it on and then the yellow cloak.

Immediately I felt the pull from Windsor Castle, the draw of several minds all thinking about me in concert. But there was another pull on the other side of me, one mind but with stronger, sharper focus. I opened my mouth to tell Thomas that something was wrong, but then I was somewhere else.

It was a dark, large room. There was the scent of fresh-cut flowers and the sound of wind rushing through the trees outside. The smell and shape of the place was familiar, and as my eyes adjusted to the darkness, I realized that I was in the front sitting room of Hillcrest.

In the darkness, I heard muffled sobs.

"Laura?" I asked, voice thick with confusion. "Why are you crying?"

Laura got up from the couch, her silhouette barely an outline in the dark. But then she threw herself at me, arms around my neck.

"Paul!" she said, more of a gasp than a word. "Paul, is it really you? Are you a ghost? Am I dreaming?"

"Do I feel like a ghost?" I asked, putting an arm around her waist. We'd never been so close before, never embraced like this, but in the moment it felt like we'd always been in each other's arms.

"No. And it doesn't feel like a dream either." She smiled before bursting into tears. "Jack told me you were dead."

"I'm not," I said, my other hand coming up to gently wipe her tears away. "I turned myself in so they could let you go. They only ever arrested you because they heard that I cared about you."

"So you handed yourself over? For me?" Laura said, eyes wide.

"It wasn't right for me to be free and you to be away from your husband and child, so I had to do it. Now the three of you can live in peace." I said this with what I hoped was a brave smile. It would do no good to make yet another declaration of love to Laura, not when we'd never be together. No need to put that on her. She'd been through enough already.

She stared at me in disbelief. "That's why you did it? So I could be reunited with my husband?"

"Well . . . yes." I could feel my resolve from just a few seconds ago starting to slip away. "I mean, it was my fault you were arrested, since the Virtuis Party got an idea in their collective head that there was something between us."

"Are you saying they had the wrong idea?" Laura said, her voice growing smaller. "Are you saying you don't love me anymore?"

I had no idea what to say to the woman I was still holding in my arms. It was almost a relief when I felt the jacket pulling me away. Someone was obviously thinking about me very hard, so hard it was activating the magic in my coat. My arms lost their grip on Laura as I teleported away.

I was in a bright room. It took my eyes a second to adjust, and my first thought was that I had made it back to Windsor Castle: I was in a room decorated in the usual baroque style with yellow striped wallpaper and ornate mouldings on the ceiling. But the room was a mess, tables and chairs knocked over, clothes ripped up and flung over the overturned furniture. There was no sign of the Parkeesh family or Kitty or Cobalt, but sitting by the window, revolver in hand, was Van Holt.

I wasn't in Windsor Castle. I was back in Buckingham Palace.

Van Holt looked up. Tear marks were clear on his surprised face. He looked like he'd been through the wars: his white hair was mussed up and his skin bruised.

He raised his gun and fired. I hit the floor a second too late, but luckily the shot was wide anyway.

"Wow! What luck!" Van Holt said. "I was just about to kill myself, but then I got thinking about how I'd much rather kill Paul Gallagher! Speak of the devil and he shall appear!"

He tried to take another shot but the gun clicked, the hammer hitting empty chamber after empty chamber. With a snarl, Van Holt slammed the gun down on the table and opened the cartridge box. Reloading a gun one handed turned out to be a lot harder than either of us thought. Van Holt spit and growled as he put the revolver into his lap, using his one hand to load several bullets.

I got to my feet, ready to run to the door. I started running just as Van Holt fired off the second shot, the bullet cutting through the space where I'd been standing seconds before. I was moving towards the door but it felt like I was running through water, practically in place even as I pushed my limbs to their limits.

Then I felt a familiar pull. I was no longer in Van Holt's bright quarters but in Laura's dark living room. She was right in front of me but I couldn't stop running. I hit her and we crashed to the floor.

"Paul!" she said, grabbing my shoulders and looking up at me. "My husband's sleeping upstairs! We have to keep it down!"

Laura's husband was the least of my worries in that moment. Already, I could feel Van Holt's anger drawing me back.

"Laura, I don't have much time and I'll probably die in the next few moments, but before I do you must know that I love you, have loved you for some time, with a deep abiding devotion that guides my every thought and action. You are the core of me. Okay, bye."

And with that I was lying on my stomach in Van Holt's room. Instinctively I rolled to my left just as a bullet buried itself in the floor.

The gun clicked once more and Van Holt swore loudly in Afrikaans. He was standing in the middle of the room, but instead of going back to the cartridge box on the table he strode towards me, raising the revolver like a club. The gun was one of those heavy World War II models, a two-pound piece of metal. Just as I got to my knees, Van Holt brought the gun down in an arc to land between my shoulder blades. I collapsed back onto my stomach.

Van Holt tried to bring the gun down on my head next, but I rolled onto my back and was able to bring up my arm in time to block him, my forearm holding strong against Van Holt's wrist.

"You don't have to do this," I said to him.

"But I *want* to," Van Holt said.

"And once you do, then what?" I asked, stalling for time.

"Isn't it obvious? I'll kill myself."

"Wow," I said. "You really are a changed man."

I said this thinking of the coldly calculating Van Holt of old, the man so ambitious he'd taken every xenophobic snipe in stride, who'd always found a way to turn a bad situation to his advantage. My words seemed to crack something in Van Holt. His eyes widened and he stopped pressing down on my forearm so forcefully.

Then I felt the pull—Laura. I picked up that mental thread and followed it. Within a second I was gone from the palace. I was lying on my back in Laura's living room.

I bolted upright.

"I have to get this jacket off." With shaking fingers I tried to free the buttons from their eye hooks, cursing myself for making this jacket so hard to get in and out of.

Laura knelt down next to me and put one of her soft hands over my jittery ones, stilling them.

"No," she said. "All you have to do is just stay here with me."

I was about to irritably explain that it wasn't so simple as all that when she kissed me. It was a deep kiss, like she was trying to share months of loneliness and need with me.

After I got over my initial surprise, my hands dropped from my coat buttons. I brought one hand up to feel her hair, confirming that it was as soft as I'd always imagined it to be. My other hand pressed against her back, pulling her in closer. Laura was happy to oblige, throwing a leg over me to straddle my lap.

We stayed like that for a while, our greed for each other all-consuming after months apart.

"I didn't know you felt this way," I said as we gasped for breath. Laura pulled away to look at me incredulously.

"Are you having a laugh? Of course I feel this way about you! Didn't I say so the night you left?"

"Well, you said you'd come with me if it were just you . . ."

"But that I had Beatrix to think of, yes. I thought it was pretty clear."

"*I* thought you were just trying to let me down gently."

Laura rolled her eyes. "I'd never go so far to spare some man's feelings. I meant what I said. That night was one of the worst nights of my life, not only because it meant going back to Jack but because I had to leave you. Those months where we lived alongside each other were the happiest months of my life."

"Mine too," I said. "Laura, I know the world's a disaster and our own lives terribly complicated, but if you'll have me, I'll give you a lifetime of happy months."

"Oh, Paul, you don't know how much I want to say yes to that," Laura said. "But you have to understand, my first priority is always going to be Beatrix—"

"I know, I know, I understand," I said. "And I know you could go it alone, just the two of you. When all this is over, if that's what you want to do, I'll help you do that. I'll do whatever I can as a friend to help you get on your own two feet. But if you feel the way I do, if you love me, then I think we owe it to ourselves to give it a try."

I was holding her hand tightly in mine. Though our conversation was charged, we were both speaking in whispers, lest we wake up the rest of the house.

She put a hand on my cheek.

"I've done so few things for myself in my life," Laura said. "It's a bit scary, but I want to do it."

"Me too," I said. We started kissing again. I felt a ping, a slight echo of a feeling—Van Holt, sitting alone in his room, wishing I were there. My heart twisted. I told myself I didn't owe Van Holt anything, that it would be stupid to go to him in some vain attempt to save him from himself. I hadn't even been able to save Gabs, and we shared a deep bond and history. What did Van Holt and I share?

Just a promise that we'd look out for each other's loved ones. And now here I was, finally reunited with Laura, while Van Holt was about to blow his brains out.

"Laura," I said. "Are you sure Beatrix is all right? I thought I heard her cry out just now."

It was a dirty trick, but it worked; Laura's attention shifted off me and was wholly on her daughter's welfare. While she was distracted, I grabbed hold of the thin thread connecting Van Holt and me. He was hardly thinking about me at this point, so I really had to lean into it.

It worked. I was sitting upright in Van Holt's ramshackle room.

He was back to his chair. I was somewhat surprised that some guards hadn't come to check up on him after he'd fired off a couple of shots, but then again the whole castle was in disarray, to the point that no one was too bothered by the sound of gunfire.

Van Holt looked at me with red-rimmed eyes.

"You shouldn't have come back here, Gallagher," he said. "I have one bullet left. If I have to choose whether to shoot you or myself, you might not like what I pick."

"Yeah, I probably won't." I got to my feet—if Van Holt was going to kill me, I wanted to die standing at least. I also started the laborious process of taking off my coat. "It's a lose-lose situation for me. If you kill me, that's bad. If you kill yourself, then I'll feel like a heel for not keeping our promise."

"Our promise?" Van Holt said, some light coming into his eyes.

"Yeah. I promised you I'd keep Olena and Gayle from harm," I said. "And, well, losing you would hurt them a whole lot."

Van Holt squeezed his eyes shut, his hand clenching the gun tightly. "They are better off without me."

"C'mon, man, do you really believe that?"

"I do!" Van Holt said, eyes snapping open. "I lost my standing in society, my dominant arm, my ability to do magic! I am no good to them now, just a burden for them to carry!"

"Your wife and kid don't care about that. They love *you*—"

"They loved a man I pretended to be," Van Holt said, his voice cracking.

"No, they loved *you*," I repeated. "Do you really think Olena didn't know? She knew, and she was still with you. Even Gayle probably knew something was up. She's a smart kid."

That got a half smile out of Van Holt. "It's true. Can't get anything past her."

"I know it's been tough for you, and I'm sorry for my part in it," I said. "But now, after going through hell, on the other side of it all is a chance to be with your family fully and for real, in a way you never were able to before when you were trying to live two lives. You need to grab that chance and take it."

Van Holt looked doubtful. "It's not that I don't *want* to," he said, which gave me hope, "it's just . . . I don't even know what I'd do with the rest of my life."

"You'd have the rest of your life to figure it out," I said.

"But . . . my arm, my magic . . ."

"As for your arm, there's cloth magic that can help with that." It was true. After the wars, a couple of cloth mages had focused on making special clothes for amputees, outfits that helped with mobility or by recreating limbs. It wasn't a huge field, as the high cost of magical outfits and their personalized nature kept it from helping the masses, but surely there was something there that could help Van Holt. I'd look into it myself if I had to. "And as for your magic . . . if you want I can make you a mage again."

Van Holt looked at me sharply. "You *can* do that? You would do that?"

"Sure." I'd never actually heard of a case of someone becoming a mage twice over—I'd have to look into it to make sure I didn't kill Van Holt in the process. "I'll do some research, see if it's possible. I figure all I have to do is break the bones on your remaining arm."

Van Holt dropped his chin to his chest, a thoughtful look on his face.

"I don't even know if I want that anymore."

"Well, whatever it is you do want, you'll have lots of people willing to help you out," I said. "Including me, if you give me the chance. So can you please put the gun away?"

He looked at the gun as if he had forgotten it was there. I worried I had made a mistake, calling attention to it.

The door slammed open and a palace guard was standing there.

"Van Holt, what the hell are you still doing here—" His words died in his throat when he caught sight of me.

One more shot rang out. The palace guard slumped over to the floor.

Van Holt stood.

"All right then, Gallagher," he said, putting the now-empty gun on the table. "Let's get out of here."

CHAPTER 43

"Actually, I have my own way out," I said, picking up my yellow cloak.

"Ah, yes. A teleportation cloak, hmm?" Van Holt said, coming over to take a closer look.

"Yes. I'm going to use it to get back to Windsor." I felt like I owed it to Thomas to do that, after he had begged me to not put myself in danger anymore.

Van Holt cackled at that. "Oh, that's the last place you want to go."

"What? Why?"

"The whole town is being firebombed right now," Van Holt said with unnerving glee. "Godfrey was just waiting for an excuse to attack. He had Rosemary bring you here because he knew that Dawes would attack the place in retaliation, giving the Virtuis Party a cover story for finally moving on Windsor Castle."

"Firebombing? A British city?" I said, fingers clutching my coat tight.

"That's right."

I thought of not only Kitty and the others but the various citizens trying to live out their lives in Slough. A paralyzing fear gripped me—what if everyone died but me? What would be the point of all this then?

"I need to find Thomas and figure out a plan," I said, sounding much calmer than I felt.

Van Holt nodded. "You'll never find him on your own." He picked up the gun from the table, which made my heart speed up until I remembered that it was empty. I still couldn't help but flinch when he pointed it at me.

"Well? Ready?"

~

Van Holt's plan, which he explained only *after* he pointed a gun at me, was that I was to act like his prisoner and he would make it look like he was taking me back down to the cellar. I walked in front of him, no longer wearing any magic cloth at all, while Van Holt walked behind me, gun levelled at my back. We ran into only a few ragged-looking palace guards, who luckily bought Van Holt's cover story—he delivered it in such a laconic, bored way it was hard to believe it was anything but the truth. He'd also ask them if they'd seen Thomas Dawes around. The soldiers usually went pale before answering. From what we were able to gather, Thomas was somewhere near the main receiving room.

We knew we were getting close when we passed a quartet of fleeing soldiers—well, it was more accurate to say that they passed us, barely even giving us a glance before rushing to some other part of the palace.

A second later Thomas appeared around the corner.

"Thomas!" I called.

Surprise lit up his face. Then he saw Van Holt behind me, still pointing the gun at my back. In a blink, Thomas had a knife in hand.

"No!" I waved my arms to get Thomas's attention. "Thomas, it's all right! He's helping us!"

Thomas warily lowered his hand but didn't put the knife away. He came over to us, eyes on Van Holt. Van Holt took a shaky step back, dropping the gun on the floor as if it were burning him.

"It's empty, Dawes!" Van Holt said. "See for yourself if you don't believe me!"

Thomas evidently didn't believe him, because he checked the chamber. He tucked the gun into the band of his trousers.

"What the hell are you two doing here?"

"It's a long story," I said. "What you need to know is that the army is attacking Slough. Van Holt says they're firebombing the place."

"It's true," Van Holt said. "It was always part of the plan."

Thomas nodded, taking the news in stride. "All right. I know what we need to do. But first, Paul, you need to get to a safe place and—"

"Oh, shut it," I said. "The whole country's on the brink of annihilation; nowhere is safe. You need me, so just tell me what we need to do." Thomas still looked hesitant, so I pressed on. "I don't know what it is, but I know you can't do it without me. We need to do this together."

I must have been right because Thomas nodded.

"We need to find Godfrey. The king is just the figurehead; we need to go after the *actual* head. Make him call off the attack."

Van Holt laughed. "Godfrey's long left the palace! Do you even know where to look for him?"

"No, I don't. But I bet you do, don't you, Van Holt?" Thomas said, advancing towards him. "So just how many times tonight am I going to have to beat you up?"

"Godfrey's in St Stephen's clock tower," I said. Thomas and Van Holt just stared at me.

"How do you know?" Van Holt said, amazed. "Did he tell you?"

"No. David Myers did." All the comments he had made in his office about Godfrey hiding in plain sight. Plus, I knew that when he was a living MP, Godfrey used to work out of there.

"Well, you're right," Van Holt said. "But don't think I'm going to help you get in! I'm done with all this fighting. All I want is to go home to my wife and child."

"I know. I want that for you too," I said. "I get it, Peter. You can go."

Van Holt suddenly looked uncertain.

"If you want to go, you better go now, Van Holt," Thomas growled. Van Holt stumbled backwards, then turned and quickly speed-walked away.

When he was gone Thomas turned to me. To my surprise he had a grin on his blood-smeared face. "You just couldn't stay out of the fire, eh, you stupid bastard?"

"I could say the same to you." I couldn't help but grin back. Even in a building filled with death, I felt like now that Thomas and I were together again, everything was going to be all right.

~

We had to travel on foot from the palace grounds to the clock tower. We stopped at a phone box since Thomas said he needed to call a contact. The stretch of road we were on was by St James's Park. Behind us was the palace, the occasional muffled explosion or gunfire still echoing out. I took such sounds as a good sign—it meant Rosemary and Naveed were still alive. Meanwhile, ahead of us lay Central London. Even in the dark I could see smoke rising over the city skyline. Had rioters started those fires, or had the army? In the end, I suppose it didn't matter. What did matter was getting control of the country so we could put the fires out.

Thomas left the phone box, the door clattering shut after him. "Let's go."

"So how exactly are we going to get into the tower?" I asked. It wouldn't be as heavily guarded as Buckingham Palace. At night the Houses of Parliament were near deserted save for a few late-night cleaning staff. And, of course, guards. Not only would there be armed patrols, but they'd be wearing cloth magic outfits specifically designed to keep people from using magic to sneak in.

"One of the guards is on our payroll," Thomas explained. "He'll let us in."

"Oh. Well, three cheers for the spy network, then."

And it really was that easy, slipping into Parliament through a side door as a guard talked my ear off about how he knew the country was better than this and how he believed in us and the cause. I was touched by his words, then noticed Thomas discreetly slip him money before we parted ways. We left the guard to continue on his patrols to keep up the appearance of normalcy. Following his directions, we travelled through the dim halls of Parliament towards the base of the clock tower.

"I feel like Guy Fawkes," I somewhat giddily whispered to Thomas, stress channelling itself into excitement.

"Let's hope we're more successful than he was."

"And that we meet a better end," I said, now regretting the comparison.

The door to the clock tower was unlocked, which made Thomas and I share an uneasy look. Everything had been going too well, too smoothly. Was this just a long con of Godfrey's? Were we walking into yet another setup?

Well, even if that was the case, we had no other option but to press forwards, going up the rickety stairs that lined the inside of the tower. In the middle the pendulum of the clock swung languidly and gears as big as me rotated and clicked into place. The size and sound made me think of giants playing chequers—*klak klak klak*.

"You know, a lot of people call this tower Big Ben, but that's wrong," I said, chattering away nervously in a low voice as Thomas and I tried to quickly but quietly walk up the stairs. "Big Ben's just the name of the bell. Back when it was cast—"

"Paul, shut the fuck up," Thomas said, sounding nervous in his own way.

When we walked up what would have been something like seven storeys of stairs there was a roof above us, but as we emerged on the other side, we saw it wasn't so much a roof as a kind of way station: in the middle the guts of the clock continued to turn, but along the perimeter was a wooden floor. On the other side of the tower the stairs continued upwards for another few floors before they hit yet another wood partition. Beyond that, I imagined, was Big Ben himself and the actual clock faces.

On our level was Godfrey's office. There was a desk and a telephone, as well as a radio. Thomas strode over and turned it on. It cackled to life with human voices, military men barking out orders crisply. It took a second for my ear to adjust to their military speak, but once it did my blood ran cold.

"Did he just say the bombers will arrive in twenty minutes?" I asked Thomas. Thomas didn't reply, just balled his hands into fists, as if he could punch those planes out of the air. He strode over to the phone.

"Hello. It's Dawes," he said. "They are going to firebomb the city. You need to evacuate everyone in the castle and the city—well, then fight your way out! If you stay there—" Thomas took a deep breath, closing his eyes as the general on the line spoke. "God damn it. Yes, yes, of course run the air raid sirens. We will . . . we will see what we can do from our end." Thomas hung up the phone with a violent clatter. He ran his hands through his hair, something he always did when he was at the end of his rope.

"The Virtuis Army has encircled Slough," Thomas said. "Anyone trying to leave has been killed. The generals are getting everyone in the palace into the bomb shelters—"

"What about the thousands of people outside the castle?!"

"There are still some civilian bomb shelters throughout the city left over from the war. When they hear the sirens, hopefully they will remember their training and go there."

"But it's not going to be enough, is it?" I looked around the office, as if making sure one more time that Godfrey wasn't there. If only he had been, we could have made him call off the attack. That was our only plan, our only hope of saving everyone.

Well. Not our only plan.

"Thomas," I said, my voice cracking from the get-go. "Thomas, I'm so sorry. I'm so, so sorry, but . . ."

Thomas caught on immediately. He looked sad, but what really got me was the look of resignation on his face, like he'd known it was coming. One more broken promise, one more case of Thomas coming last behind everyone else.

"It's all right," he said, taking off his jacket, the jacket that let him slip into shadows and attack unseen in the darkness. The fact he had removed it so readily showed how serious it was. "It's what needs to be done."

"B-but what will you even do?" I said.

"It will give me the power of God, right?" Thomas said. "Surely swatting a couple of planes out of the sky should be child's play."

I nodded, tears already running down my face. I felt even worse for crying—it wasn't me who was about to die. No, just my best mate, by my hand, a mere hour after I'd told him it would never come to this.

Thomas handed me a knife of his—it had a couple of wicked-looking teeth near the curved tip, but the side was sleek and sharp. It would be good for peeling the skin off him.

"I . . . I don't know if I can do this," I said, using my sleeve to wipe the snot out of my nose.

"We don't have a lot of time," Thomas said gently, a hand on my shoulder. Right. The planes were already in the air.

Thomas took off his shirt and held his arm out. We were both crouched down on the floor for some reason.

"For Hollister, I had to tie him down," I said.

"I'm made of sterner stuff than Hollister," Thomas said.

"Yeah." I made the first cut. Thomas hissed and flinched slightly but did not pull away. I made several more cuts, moving quickly because time was of the essence and I didn't want to dwell on what I was doing. But that didn't work—eventually my hand stilled, the magic within me keeping me from hurting Thomas further.

"Paul?" Thomas asked as I held the knife in midair.

"It's fine." I concentrated on the fact that I was doing a spell—I was going to turn my little brother into an avenging angel. He would save us all with his sacrifice. And as I began cutting again, magic began to become visible in the air around us. When I moved on to Thomas's other arm, his eyes started to glow gold. Dark wings highlighted with embers began to form from his back. As I kept cutting they grew more and more solid, and Thomas seemed less and less human.

I was almost out of skin on his right arm. I didn't want to cut his face and the belly seemed too risky, so I opened my mouth to ask Thomas to please remove his trousers so I could skin his legs.

Before I could a shot rang out. The magic was gone. The forms and patterns that had been building in the air disappeared. Thomas's wings vanished, and the gold glow in his eyes was gone. All that was left was a look of very human surprise on his face, before he slumped forwards into my arms. I screamed when I saw the blood coming out of the back of his head, blood oozing out of a neat bullet hole.

Standing at the top of the stairs, still holding the gun he'd just shot Thomas with, was Jim Godfrey.

CHAPTER 44

My screams felt torn out of me, not sound but something physical, a thick ectoplasm that was expelled into the air and ground between the cogs of the clock. I kept screaming and clutching Thomas's body until Godfrey came over and kicked him out of my arms.

"Been waiting years for a chance to do that," Godfrey said, gesturing with his gun to the back of Thomas's head. "One good shot deserves another, right?" He crouched down and, with a naked finger, poked at the wound. I flinched. "Did you lads come here looking for me? Sorry to keep you waiting."

The radio crackled again, a pilot reporting in. Ten minutes until they reached Slough.

"C-call the planes off," I said, as if I had any means to make Godfrey do so. I was sitting on my ass, still dazed and with my best mate's blood on me. Godfrey, meanwhile, looked fit as a fiddle, gun in hand.

Godfrey shook his head. "You know, you did better than I thought you'd do," he said. "Almost destroyed everything I'd been working for. I knew there'd be resistance—there are always soft hearts like you unwilling to change, too afraid of the sacrifice needed to make this country strong."

I only dimly heard Godfrey's drivel. My gaze was still fixed on Thomas's body. My closest friend in the world was dead, and he had died thinking that I didn't care about him, or that I only cared about him as far as I could use him to save everyone else. I should have never broken my promise to him. It had all been for nothing anyway. If I had stayed strong, told Thomas that we weren't going to do deep magic, well, we'd still be buggered but at least he would have died knowing I loved him.

I wished Godfrey would stop talking and just shoot me. I didn't want to be alive to hear the reports from the pilots after they dropped the bombs. It was bad enough I'd just watched Thomas die. I didn't want to outlive all my friends.

"Of course, you had some help. The people I had working under me were weak. Von Melsungen, Fairweather, Van Holt . . . each of them undone by their own innate flaws: pride, lust, covetousness. It was a mistake to rely on them, but I was impatient and they were the tools I had at hand."

I'd never really understood suicides before, never really could fathom why anyone would take their own life—why give up on the hope of a new day? But now I felt like I understood. The pain I was in, the guilt over my betrayal of Thomas, it was too much. Even if hell awaited me, at least the pain would be from another source rather than one of my own making.

"Next time I'll be more circumspect about it," Godfrey said. "I tried to take over this country using what was already in place rather than cultivating something myself. I'll start with a younger generation, shape them into the adults I need. I have nothing but time—if it takes decades, so be it. I can start with Troy Hollister—"

That name snapped me out of my spiral. I reacted using an instinct I hadn't even known I had: I punched Godfrey. He stared at me, eyes wide. I was shocked too. I hadn't hit anyone since I was six, back before Eimer had put the spell on me that prohibited me from physical violence.

But Godfrey wasn't a person. He was a reanimated corpse, a soulless thing that managed to walk and talk and kill but had no magic within him.

I leaped on him. It wasn't much of a chance, but by Jesus, I'd take it. I bit and scratched as I tried to wrestle the gun out of his hands. I didn't have much experience grappling, but my desperation gave me an edge. Like a rabid dog I wrestled Godfrey to the edge of the platform. I almost had the gun from him, but before I could take it he let it fall from his hand. It clattered down the seven storeys below us, the echo of metal on metal reverberating as it hit the gears and scaffolding.

I let out an angry growl and bit Godfrey on the face, a lifetime of suppressed violence coming out. But Godfrey had gotten over his initial surprise and punched me. It was a cannon of a punch and managed to get me off him. He didn't even flinch when I took a bit of his cheek with me.

I landed on my back, dazed from the punch. I barely had time to spit out the bite of Godfrey's flesh in my mouth before he was on me, straddling my torso to put his hands around my neck. Panic set in—I'd almost died once this way, and this time Tonya wasn't around to save me. I tried to buck Godfrey off, but dead man or not, he was strong and stocky, heavier than me.

Calm down, a part of me thought. I remembered I still had Rosemary's "present" in my trouser pocket. I stopped scratching and clawing at Godfrey to reach into my pocket. As I closed my fingers around it, I felt the wire and knobs of wood—it was the piano wire garrotte she'd used to kill Fairweather.

It was the best option I had in the moment. I pulled the thing out and wrapped it around Godfrey's neck. His eyes widened in surprise as the wire tightened around his neck but he kept his hands clutched around my throat. There was more strength in his arms than there was in mine, and he had a better position. Even as I pulled the wire tight, he didn't seem worried. Horror crept up on me as it dawned on me that this motherfucker didn't actually *need* to breathe.

But I did. Even as my lungs burned and darkness started to bleed in on the edges of my vision, I kept my grip tight on the garrotte.

Suddenly Godfrey's body slammed down into mine. He lost his grip on my throat and I was able to get in a few painful gasps of air.

Thomas was standing behind Godfrey, foot planted firmly between the man's shoulder blades. He looked the same as he always did, stern and ticked off, ready to fight God himself if the Creator looked at him the wrong way. He leaned down and took one of the handles of the garrotte from me. I put both my hands on the other one. We pulled.

The wire sank into Godfrey's flesh, hitting bone with a sharp reverb that carried through the wire and up through my arms. But Godfrey was still alive: his eyes looking back and forth between us as if searching for weakness. He sat up, jerking both Thomas and me forwards with him.

At this point it was two against one. In theory we had the advantage, but Godfrey seemed nearly impervious to damage. If this went on too long, I couldn't help but feel like Godfrey would get the win. We needed to defeat him *now*.

Between the edge of the platform and tower of twisting gears was a space of about three feet. I looked over the edge and tried not to think about how far down the floor was.

"Thomas, hold tight!" I said, my words carrying despite how scratchy my throat was. Clutching the handle of the garrotte, I stepped over the side of the platform.

My heart lurched as I dropped down. The wire yanked tight on Godfrey's neck and brought him down to the floor with a thud, followed immediately by a snap as the wire cut through bone. Godfrey's head popped off and fell into the machinery below—there was no clank this time, just a dull squelch sound.

My shoulders hurt from supporting my hanging body.

"Hey, Thom? Can you pull me up?"

Thomas was a beat slow, maybe in shock from the sequence of events that had just played out, but he pulled hard on his end of the garrotte. Once I was able to grab the edge of the platform he took hold under my armpits to lift me up the rest of the way. For a moment we sat there, catching our breath next to Godfrey's headless corpse.

"You're alive?!" I managed to get out between gasps.

Thomas nodded but then self-consciously touched the back of his head, as if making sure.

"Yeah," he said. "When Godfrey shot me, it didn't kill me right away. I mean, I think I was more or less dead—like, brain dead at least. But there was still a part of me that was aware of what was going on. So I used that—and your deep magic—to heal myself and bring myself back from the edge."

"Jesus! Did you do it because you saw how Godfrey was about to kill me?" I asked.

Thomas opened his mouth to answer but cut himself off with a scowl. "No. I should tell you the truth. I didn't do it for you. It was just . . . in that moment, I knew I was dying, and I was scared. All my big talk about using your magic to save everyone was just talk. In the end, I wanted to live."

I grabbed his hands, ecstatic. "Thomas, that's all I've ever wanted for you." But his words triggered a wave of anxiety through me. "Oh, Jesus, everyone else!" I scrambled over to the radio and cranked the dial up. By now the planes had surely dropped their bombs on Slough and the castle.

There was confused chatter on the radio, compounded ironically by other voices asking for people to keep the channel clear. Thomas got on the telephone while I strained to sort out the different voices on the radio—the line got even more frantic, a barrage of yelling and explosions, the pilots' voices going out midscreams. After the last one went quiet there was no chatter from the soldiers on the ground, just a stunned silence.

Thomas turned to me, the phone still to his ear. "Kitty saved them," he said, wonder in his voice. "She stood on the castle ramparts and used her innate magic to fling the bombs and the planes into the sea." He went back to having a hushed conversation with the general on the phone. I picked up the radio transmitter. Before I could speak, Naveed's voice cut across the channel.

"Hello, this is Prince Naveed Parkeesh, a supporter of Princess Katherine," he said, a worried edge to his voice. "We have taken Buckingham Palace. The remaining guards here support the princess. King Harold will be on the air in a second to announce his abdication. Princess Katherine is now the head of the nation. Attacking her and the others is treason. Stop your attack on Slough now."

I breathed a sigh of relief that Naveed was still alive. I wished I could tell him that his family was safe, but so much was still unknown. I opened the channel to speak.

"This is Court Magician Paul Gallagher," I said. "The interim Court Magician is dead. Godfrey is dead." It felt almost taboo saying Godfrey's name out loud—most of the bastards fighting for him had never even known who he was or that he was the one pulling the strings. But the bigwigs who *did* know, they needed to know he was gone for good. "To the army surrounding Slough, surrender immediately to the forces at Windsor Castle."

There was another long silence on the radio. Then one battalion reported in, saying they would surrender. A slew of other voices joined in, resigned but calm, as they recognized Katherine as their new sovereign.

CHAPTER 45

The day of Katherine's coronation was a bright day, blades of light cutting through every window of Westminster Abbey. The city was in a celebratory mood. It had been weeks since the Battle for Slough. We hadn't been the only ones fighting that night: riots had broken out across the country in all major cities, citizens rising up against the police and soldiers who were ready to round them up and send them to cloth magic prisons. Things had only calmed down once word had gotten out that the army had surrendered.

It still blew my mind at times that we had somehow come through it all. We had Katherine to thank for that. When Slough was under attack, instead of going down to the bomb shelter she had gone up on the castle ramparts—the pilots themselves radioed in that they could see her as they did a flyby. When those same pilots released their bombs, Kitty used her innate magic to divert the attack, sending bombs and planes miles away to land in the sea. One of the pilots even survived.

After that we had to move fast—not just for our own sakes but for the sake of the nation. It needed a monarch, and it needed a functional government. Prime Minister Hywell was arrested for his part in the illegal takeover of the country, as were many higher-ranking Virtuis Party members. We appointed the leader of the opposition as temporary prime minister. Once Kitty was crowned, one of her first acts would be to call an open election.

"It's too soon," Thomas said while helping me with my tux. "Calling an election now while the country is in shambles is just a nightmare. Who knows what opportunistic jackals might claw their way in?"

"We did all this so there could *be* a free election," I said. "If we dawdled on that, we'd be barely better than the Virtuis Party."

"And what if the Tories get in?" Thomas said, scowling. "Who knows how many of them are just Virtuis Party wolves in sheep's clothing?"

"Well, that's always the risk," I said.

One of the other changes was King Harold agreeing to step down and live out his life confined to an island. Thomas had wanted to kill him, but Kitty had overruled him. Now Kitty herself was to be crowned queen. In the whirlwind following our ascension, we had to fit in a couple of hours going over the pageantry of the ceremony, how Kitty should enter, where I should stand, how she should accept the sceptre, crown, and weird little jewelled ball thingy. The old folks coaching us through it acted with great reverence, not towards us but towards the process—it felt like they didn't care so much who was wearing the crown as long as they wore it right.

Something new, however, was the fact that this would be the first coronation in Britain's history to be televised. We all hoped that broadcasting the moment would make all Britons feel a part of it.

I was in a daze as all the pomp and glamour rolled out, everything happening so seemingly grand but in slow motion. Naveed was there with his family, all of them dressed to the nines. The queen mother was there, of course, looking on proudly as her daughter was crowned. Sabina was not there, as the baby was due any day now and the doctor had advised that she rest. That would be our nation's next test: seeing whether they accepted Arthur's child as Kitty's heir.

Rosemary wasn't there. After helping Naveed take control of Buckingham Palace, she had slipped away into the night. Probably for the best—Naveed had been willing to fight alongside her when there was no other choice, but she had still betrayed everyone at Windsor Castle and nearly destroyed us all.

Van Holt was absent, gone off to Amsterdam to start a new life with his wife and child. Lady Fife was still in France with Andrew. Oberon was still in hospital, Tonya still by his side.

Afterwards we had a small celebration at Buckingham Palace, a gathering of just the Windsor crew. Much of the palace still lay in shambles—while trying to fight off a plethora of palace guards Naveed and Rosemary had lobbed various explosives they had made out of cleaning supplies. Some rooms were scorched, others oddly bleached, and many still had blood staining the floors and walls. But despite all that hanging over us, the dozen of us found an untouched sitting room where we could celebrate. We popped open a couple of bottles of champagne. Our laughter had an edge of disbelief to it—not only that we were here, in power, but that any of us had survived at all. There was an edge of delirium to our celebration, and people acted drunk before they'd even taken their first sip of champagne. Even Thomas cracked a smile.

At one point Cobalt shook my hand vigorously.

"Oh, Paul, it's happening, it's actually happening," he said. "Everything's going to be all right now."

"God willing," I said, feeling like a party pooper for being anything less than euphoric. Cobalt clapped me on the back, a rare casual gesture from him.

"Of course it is! Kitty's on the throne, you're Court Magician, and I . . . well, I'm here for both of you! What do we have to worry about?"

He didn't give me a chance to answer that question, just moved off to go stand next to Kitty. Kitty looked both radiant and a little overwhelmed as she chatted with her mother and Naveed's grandmother. She relaxed when Cobalt came over, and even laughed as he told her a joke. Cobalt, for his part, seemed utterly at ease, perfectly at home next to Queen Katherine. I sipped my champagne, trying to dispel the chill I suddenly felt.

~

It was a few more days before I could get away from London and go down to the seaside, to the hospital where Oberon was staying. A nurse showed me to his room.

Obie was out of bed, standing by the window so he could look at the Channel. He wore what looked like blue cotton pyjamas, his hair neatly combed, posture straight.

"Hello, Oberon," I said after the nurse had left.

He turned towards me. His beard was gone—I imagined they'd had to shave it for surgery (well, the part that hadn't already been cut off by Rosemary's wires, at least). The left side of his face was paler than the right and slightly puffy. A line of demarcation was clear; the graft started an inch below his left eye and ended around his jawline, affecting most of his left cheek but not his nose. It honestly was not as bad as I'd been imagining. But the sense of relief came from something even bigger than that; the surgery had changed Oberon's face to the point that, when I looked at him, I no longer saw my would-be murderer. Seeing him no longer made me flash back to that night. For the first time in a long time, I didn't feel worried and scared and angry in his presence. I was even able to smile, happy at the unexpected change.

Oberon's face had a stoniness to it.

"You're the first person to see me and not flinch," he said flatly.

I felt a little bad about that—my reasons for not flinching were purely self-centred.

"They treating you well here?" I asked, one of the lines I'd prepared in case things were awkward. Considering the odd vibe in the air, I had been right to do so.

Oberon nodded. "Everyone here is very professional. And Tonya is often here to advocate for me, so I'm not lacking for anything." He paused and thought it over. "Just a pinkie."

He said it so dryly that I worried he was serious. Even so I couldn't help but let out a bark of laughter. Oberon smiled, which was a relief. He still didn't move from the window. It was a grey day outside, the roiling waves overlapping with Oberon's reflection in the glass.

"I heard from Tonya that they are going to let you out of here soon," I said, trying for chipper.

"Hmm. I'm not in a hurry," Oberon said.

"What? C'mon, mate, why would you want to stick around here? Surely you have places to go."

Oberon was quiet. It dawned on me that he wasn't looking out at the waves—he was looking at the faint reflection in the window. There was no mirror in the room. Perhaps this was the only way he could look at himself and take stock of what had changed.

"Before, Tonya and I talked about going to New York City together," Oberon said, and I felt a little twist in my heart even though I knew I had no part in this story. "The plan was she'd show me around town and . . . and I'd meet my mother. Before this happened, I imagined all the different ways our first meeting might go. I . . . I had hoped that she might recognize me on sight."

He fell quiet at that. Raindrops splattered against the window, obnoxiously loud.

"You should go to her," I said. "She will know you."

"But . . ."

"If I had a chance like this, I'd go."

Oberon didn't reply to that.

"Look, I'm having a little get-together in a few days at Hillcrest," I said. "You need to get discharged so you can come. There's something really important we need to do and I need you there."

That got Oberon's attention. "Mrs Spratt's house? So the rumours are true? Laura Spratt has tossed her husband out once more in favour of the new Court Magician?"

I blushed a little, unaware that my personal life was so widely discussed.

"I'm renting the cottage on her estate once more," I said, a thin bit of plausible deniability. Oberon chuckled.

"Whatever you say."

A nurse knocked on the door and popped her head in.

"Mr Black, it's almost lunchtime. Would you like an extra pudding again?"

Now it's Oberon's turn to blush. "No, one pudding will suffice."

The young nurse nodded, gave me a shy smile, and then left. Oberon let out a huff.

"Wow, an extra pudding for Mr Black. They do treat you well here," I said. "I forgot you were checked in under a pseudonym."

"Well, since Kitty was crowned, it's more of an open secret. But everyone here has been discreet." Obie sat down on the edge of his hospital cot. "I don't mean to be rude, but I feel a bit self-conscious with other people watching me eat."

"Oh, right. Sure, I'll go, but . . ."

Oberon looked at me, hands on his knees and a strained smile on his face.

"When we talked at Gabs's wedding, I didn't know it was you, and I told you that next time we met, it should be as friends, not as strangers."

Oberon's shoulders went back, a tenseness to his whole frame.

"And you said that I probably wouldn't feel that way if I'd known who you really were," I continued. "And, well, you were right. Even though I talked big about forgiveness, I wasn't there yet. So when I did see you again, I was pretty rotten the whole time, even when you were just doing your damnedest to help."

"Paul—"

"No, please, let me finish. This time I mean it."

I held out a hand. Oberon looked at it sceptically, then searched my face, looking for something. When he finally saw that I wasn't offering my hand out of pity he relaxed and shook it.

"All right. Thank you," he said, blinking as he looked away. "And I shall try to make it to your event at Mrs Spratt's."

~

Tonya and I went for a walk along the seaside. It felt odd having the hospital at our backs—I kept imagining Oberon watching us from his hospital room—so I suggested we take the wooden steps down the cliffs to the beach itself.

"The coronation looked beautiful. A big crowd of us watched it on a TV in the hospital common room. A few people even cried when Katherine was crowned—happy tears, at that." Tonya said, a shocked hand over her heart. "People I've talked to actually seem pretty on board with this whole coup thing."

"That's well and good, but we need to talk about something important," I said. "Which is: Did I look good on telly?"

Tonya laughed. "Yes. You looked stately but young, which is what people are expecting from this new court."

"I'm glad I have you to get a read on the public for me."

Tonya looked away. We were sitting on the beach. She'd slipped off her flats and was now drawing circles in the sand with her big toe.

"I'll be going back to New York soon."

"Right, and Obie's going with you, yeah?"

"He's dragging his feet, but probably." Tonya took a deep breath. "What's between Obie and me—"

"Is none of my business," I quickly interjected. Tonya rolled her eyes, clearly not appreciating my magnanimity.

"What I was going to say is that it's complicated. And I know that he hurt you in the past, but he's not that guy anymore."

"I know," I said, quickly. "I'm glad you two have each other . . . however it is you have each other." I felt like a fool, fumbling over my words. "What I want to talk to you about isn't Oberon. It's . . . look, Tonya, when you go back to New York, are you planning to stay there?"

Tonya searched my face, looking for the question I was actually trying to ask.

"Well, yes," she said. "I mean, I might visit here from time to time, but otherwise I plan to stay in America. I told you my whole plan, about becoming a Book Binder in America."

"Good, that's good." She looked confused by my words, so I continued. "Things seem like they are all right now, but the future is shaky. When Sabina's child is born, you're right—it will be tough to get the British public to accept him or her, and it will be a couple of decades before the kid is able to sit on the throne. I'm not so naive as to think that no one's gonna try and make a move in that time, and if they do, there's a good chance they might come after me."

Tonya's eyes went wide but she said nothing.

"I made Cobalt a mage maker," I said. "I did it in secret. No one but Kitty and Thomas know." That had been a fun conversation. Thomas had been right angry with me, and I'd had to talk him out of just straight up killing Cobalt. I didn't want to agree with Thomas, but I was a little wary. I wanted a backup plan, just in case. "But if Cobalt is indisposed . . . or if he's one of the conspirators . . . I want there to be another mage maker out there. Someone who'd be staunchly on Sabina's child's side—"

"She wants to name him Gregory," Tonya said, voice distant.

"I see." Gregory was a good name. "I want there to be a mage out there who is staunchly on Gregory's side but who people wouldn't automatically think of in connection to him." Oberon was, as far as the public was concerned, Gregory's mother's cousin. Thomas was my shadow and therefore would also be a target. But Tonya, an American mage with no public ties to the royal family—people would not see her coming. "I want to make you a mage maker."

She looked away, her eyes still wide.

"That's a big ask, chum."

"It will only be in case the worst should happen," I said. "Please. You're the only one I can trust with this."

She took a deep breath and looked out at the sea. Idly, her right hand traced the cast still on her left arm.

"All right, chum. But you better do your damnedest to make sure the fate of this island never comes to rest on me."

"Of course. Thank you so much, Tonya."

"Don't sound so relieved. If you actually get yourself killed, I'll never forgive you, got it?"

I laughed. "Got it. I'll try and stay alive, if only so that I stay on your good side."

~

A few days later Laura and I were out, walking around the woods near the estate. Beatrix had run ahead, hitting each tree with a stick as she passed them. Laura and I took our time, walking arm in arm. We walked slowly, trying hard to stay in the moment.

"I . . . I'm scared to say this, because I don't want to scare you off," Laura said with some trepidation. "But I think you should have some idea of what you're getting into with me."

"Laura, your honesty is one of the things I most admire about you," I said. "Please, say whatever you gotta say."

"It won't be easy, if you truly wish to marry me," Laura said. "I'm going ahead with my divorce from Jack, and I think it will be smoother this time around. He seems to have accepted that things are over between us, so he won't fight it. But the rest of his family . . . they might not be so quick to give up. If they can't have me, they will go after Beatrix."

"Well, she'll have both you and me as her protectors."

"There's something else," Laura said, a worried look on her pretty face. "It's about me. I wasn't a very good wife to Jack. No, no need to defend me, it's true. I wasn't. Now that I've had a chance to live apart from him, I greatly value my independence. Don't expect me to wait on you hand and foot. I'll never be the sweet thing who's good at cooking or sewing or really anything domestic."

I laughed at that. "Laura, I'm the Court Magician. That comes with its own set of baggage. I promise I won't be in your hair all the time. If anything, the issue will be me not being home enough!"

She hugged my arm. "Well, yes, that certainly would be a problem if I never saw you at all."

"We'll figure it out," I said. "I should be getting back to the garage with the others. Do you want to join us?"

Laura blinked in surprise. "Aren't you all up to something rather gruesome and secretive?"

"Yes, but seeing as it's happening in your garage, I figure it's all right for you to see," I said. "Besides, it's a chance for you to meet some of my friends."

"I'd like that," Laura said. She turned to Beatrix. "Dear, Mummy and Mr Gallagher are going to the garage to chat with his friends. Don't bother us for a bit, all right? Just play out here."

Beatrix waved in confirmation and ran off. Laura and I headed to the garage, slipping away from each other as we got closer. Even amongst friends, it was important to keep up the cover story that we were merely landlady and lodger. I didn't care so much, but it was important to Laura.

We used the side door to enter. In the middle of the room, on two sawhorses set up to be a table, were the bloody remains of James

Godfrey. Oberon stood over the body, a medical mask covering the lower half of his face. He was directing Thomas where to cut in order to divvy up the corpse into smaller pieces. Tonya and Naveed were taking the bloody limbs and binding them with twine, chatting and laughing, flirting in the over-the-top way people do when they click but immediately know that it will never go anywhere. The radio was on, a big band song filling the space with bombastic notes. The cheery atmosphere was at odds with the abattoir smell.

The four of them were so industrious that they didn't immediately notice that we had entered. Only when the door shut behind us did they look up.

"Oh, Paul!" Tonya said. She was wearing what looked like an airman's jumpsuit—she wiped her bloody hands on it without a second thought. Everyone, even Naveed, was wearing stained rags.

"Laura, you've met Naveed before," I said. For a moment the words caught in my throat—Naveed, the only Fraught Friend still around. I mentally pictured Harriet in the room, whistling along with the radio as she helped dismember Godfrey. I swallowed and continued. "This here is Verity Turnboldt—"

"Please, call me Tonya."

"Tonya?" Naveed said, surprised.

"Yeah. You didn't think Verity Turnboldt was my real name, did you?"

"Over here is Oberon Myers," I said. Oberon pulled down his mask to nod hello. Laura returned the nod, eye flicking over the skin graft but not dwelling on it. "And Thomas, who you met earlier."

"Hello. It's nice to meet you all, or to see you again in some cases," she said, directing a smile to Naveed. "So what exactly are you doing?"

"This body has regenerating powers." Thomas had stopped sawing long enough to nod hello to Laura, but now he was at it again, hacking at the muscle around the right shoulder. "We never found Godfrey's head, but there was enough blood to assume that it was ground up by the gears of the clock. Just to be safe though, we're going to divide up the body and deposit the pieces across the world."

"Why not just burn the body?" Laura asked. Thomas shook his head.

"Tried that. The ash is just drawn back together, like it's magnetized. I figure if the parts of the body are separate, they won't be able to join back up."

"So where will you take the pieces then?" Laura asked.

"India!" Naveed said brightly. "My parents and I are going as part of a goodwill tour, trying to establish a relationship with the new Indian state. While we're there, I'll find some place to squirrel away my portion."

"I'll take mine with me back to America," Tonya said. "I'm not going to leave right away—Sabina wants me to stick around since she's about to become a new mother. But once I do go home, I'll find somewhere safe stateside to hide a body. Well, part of it, at least."

"I'll take mine down to Italy," Oberon said. "Apparently my father . . . my biological father . . . was a Sicilian man. I want to go and see if I can find any trace of him."

I hoped he found his father quickly or at least found whatever answers he was looking for. It seemed folly to me to chase after his father when his mother was waiting for him in New York, but I kept my opinion to myself.

"And how about you, Thomas?" Laura asked. "Where will you hide your portion?"

"I haven't decided yet," he said, with so little inflection it was clear he was lying. I pictured Thomas at the North Pole wearing heavy furs, tromping through the snow in order to bury one of Godfrey's arms right at the top of the world.

"Wow," I said. "What a series of adventures! I'm kind of jealous." I was stuck firmly in London for the time being as we sorted everything out. Eventually, when Thomas got back from wherever he planned to go with his corpse packet, we'd accompany Kitty on a tour of Great Britain. I was looking forwards to it, to seeing parts of the country I'd never even set foot in before. But that grand tour seemed ages away—in the meantime it was all politics and paperwork. "I can't believe you're leaving me all alone here."

"Oh, I hardly think you're all alone," Tonya said with false innocence, looking everywhere but at Laura. Naveed smiled.

"Yeah, and we all won't be gone long, Professor," he said. "Plus, we'd all come back PDQ if we had a reason to."

"Yes, some happy event to celebrate," Oberon said.

"Oh, yes, certainly," Tonya said.

"I have no idea what you are talking about." I sneaked a glance at Laura. There was a slight blush on her cheeks but she was smiling, which made me smile too.

"They are speaking of your wedding to Mrs Spratt, Professor," Rosemary said.

I whirled around to see her standing in the doorway. She was holding hands with Beatrix, who was looking at the bloody scene in the garage with a wide stare.

"Bea!" Laura rushed forwards to scoop her daughter up, clutching her close while also covering her eyes. She backed away, warily.

Rosemary took in our aghast faces with bemusement.

"Well, hello," she said. "You all look like you are having so much fun without me."

Oberon was the first to recover. "What the hell are you doing here?"

"You should shut your mouth while you still have half a face," Rosemary said. "No need for that kind of language. Why are you not all happy to see me?" She looked to Naveed. "Did I not help you take over a whole palace?" She held up her hands in amazement. "I expected a happier welcome from you all."

"Is it true you killed Harriet?" Laura asked.

Rosemary blinked. "Oh, yes. But so much has happened since then, yes? Why dwell on such things?"

I still hadn't gone to talk to Troy Hollister about his sister. It was so easy to put it off, to get swept along in all my official duties. I made a mental note to talk to Thomas afterwards, to see what we could do to help the kid.

Rosemary's smile fell as she took in the stony faces looking at her.

"I see. So that's how it is. You're not grateful for my help at all. Maybe I made a mistake helping you all."

Thomas had a saw blade in his hand but I could see him set it down, going for a large knife on the table.

"Don't be silly, Rosemary. Of course we're all grateful to you. You saved my life and were key to us taking down Godfrey," I said, voice firm. I went over and picked up one of the bundles that Naveed and Tonya had put together, an arm wrapped up in a bit of tarp and tied up with twine. "It's only right that you take this. Please, hide it somewhere secure."

Rosemary looked horribly flattered, like I was holding out a bouquet of roses. She took it from me reverently.

"Oh, why, of course, Professor."

"Fantastic," I said. "Well, I'll see you out."

"What? Oh." It seemed to dawn on her that this was as good as things would get. But the gift of the limb had quelled any anger or hostility on her part. Now she just seemed somewhat sad. "All right."

Thomas made a move to follow me but I waved him off. Everyone was silent as Rosemary and I left the garage.

Rosemary hefted the parcel under one arm, then threaded her other arm through mine.

"They were all so mad at me," she said, eyes ahead as she pouted.

"Yeah, well, you did maim Oberon and kill Harriet. Surely you can see why people might not be willing to welcome you with open arms."

"Yes, I did those things, but on a bigger scale, didn't I help you all? In the end, didn't I do more good than bad?" Rosemary pressed. "And I did the good things more recently! Doesn't it count for something?"

"It counts for a lot, Rosemary, but it's not so simple," I said. She sighed and leaned her head against my shoulder.

"People are exhausting," she said. "You try and do the things that will please them, and they call you a monster."

"I know. It can be tough, but you should still try and do better," I said. "Will you try, Rosemary? Will you promise me that?"

Rosemary thought it over, then smiled. "All right. I will make that promise, but I will only keep it so long as you keep your promise to me, Professor."

"Which promise is that?" I asked, with some trepidation.

"You promised me that it would be more exciting watching you try and build this country back up than it would be to watch Godfrey tear it down," she said. "So as long as that's the case, I'll be good. But if things go too well and I start getting bored . . ." She shrugged and pulled away from me. She cradled the tied-up package. "Thank you for this." She then turned and walked down the road. She wasn't even out of sight before Thomas popped out of my shadow.

"I know you care for her, but it would probably be best if I just killed her," he said.

"Thomas, we can't just kill anyone who might be a threat. If we did, we'd be—"

"No better than the people we just deposed, yes, yes, I know," he said, like a child who'd heard the same lecture one too many times.

"Yes, that's right." The sun was shining and it promised to be a beautiful spring day. I didn't know what the future held, but there were some things I was sure of. No, not things, people: Thomas, Laura, Oberon, Tonya, Naveed. I'd be all right as long as they were all right.

"Let's go back to the house," I said. "There's cake."

-END-

ACKNOWLEDGMENTS

First off, thank you, person reading this. It means the world to me to be able to share my words and silly stories with you.

This book (and the book preceding it) would not have been possible without the tireless efforts and unsinkable faith of my agent, Rebecca Strauss. To Adrienne Procaccini and the rest of the team at 47North, thank you so much for giving me the chance to continue Paul's misadventures. The scenes and characters in these books have lived large in my mind for years now, and getting the chance to let them loose has been a dream come true.

I want to thank my Clarion West 2014 classmates for their continued support and the wider Clarion West community for helping promote the first book and celebrating its release. A special shout-out to Micah Huw Evans for organizing all those early-morning write-ins—I did a lot of editing during those Zoom sessions!

I have many talented, smart friends who were kind enough to give me feedback on the book. I'd like to thank Stewart Delo, Tanya James, Jennifer Giesbracht, and Yang-Yang Wang for their patience and insight.

A lot of this book draws on my time in London working at the National Portrait Gallery (shout-out to my fellow VSAs!). Rehana Gittens, an old coworker of mine, once gave a talk there about Sara Forbes Bonetta Davies, a woman with a fascinating life story (Sara is loosely the inspiration for the character of Sabina). I learned so much about British history from my kind, passionate colleagues at the NPG and wish all of you the best. I hope someday we can grab a pint together again.

My family has been a pillar for me my whole life—I was able to become a writer because my parents were always supportive of the idea. Thank you, Mom and Dad. I'm also lucky enough to have not one, not two, but four awesome younger siblings who always have my back. Thank you, Rourke, Genny, James, and Zach, for being there for me.

This book started out with a dedication to Chris, and I'll end with one too: Thank you, Chris, for your support and love. Even when I was in the middle of a whirlwind, you kept me grounded. I can't wait to see what adventure lies in store for us next.

ABOUT THE AUTHOR

Photo © 2020 Rourke Fay

Shannon Fay is the author of *Innate Magic* in the Marrowbone Spells series. A writer living in K'jipuktuk/Halifax, Canada, she attended the Clarion West Writers Workshop in 2014 and has a day job editing manga. She lives with her biggest critic (a very vocal, very fluffy white cat) and her biggest supporter (a very kind human). When not writing novels and short stories, she likes to go ice-skating (in the winter) and play board games (year-round). For more information visit www.ayearonsaturn.com.